KITCHEN TALK

KITCHEN TALK

CONTEMPORARY WOMEN'S PROSE AND POETRY

EDITED BY
EDNA ALFORD &
CLAIRE HARRIS

Red Deer College Press

THE PUBLISHERS
Red Deer College Press
56 Avenue & 32 Street Box 5005
Red Deer Alberta Canada T4N 5H5

CREDITS
Design by Alex Haas, Hodgson + Hass Design Associates
Cover Photo by Chick Rice, Vancouver
Edna Alford's Photo by Charles Lamb
Claire Harris's Photo by Lennox K. Harris
Printed & Bound in Canada by Best Gagné Printing Ltée
for Red Deer College Press

ACKNOWLEDGEMENTS
The publishers gratefully acknowledge the financial contribution of the Alberta Foundation for the Arts, Alberta Culture and Multiculturalism, The Canada Council, and Red Deer College.

The editors would like to thank Adele Wiseman and Janice Williamson for their encouragement and support, Dennis Johnson and Red Deer College Press for taking on the project, and Carolyn Dearden for her invaluable editorial assistance.

CANADIAN CATALOGUING IN PUBLICATION DATA
Main entry under title:
Kitchen talk
ISBN 0-88995-091-1
1. Canadian literature (English)—Women authors. 2. Canadian literature (English)—20th century. 3. Women—Literary collections.
I. Harris, Claire, 1937– II. Alford, Edna, 1947–
PS8235.W7K58 1992 C810.8'09287 C92-091328-8
PR9194.5.W6K58 1992

ACKNOWLEDGEMENTS

"His Kitchen" from *Being on the Moon* by Annharte. Used by permission from the publisher, Polestar Book Publishers, Vancouver. Excerpt From *The Edible Woman* by Margaret Atwood. Used by permission of the Canadian Publishers, McClelland & Stewart, Toronto. Excerpt from *Dancing in the Dark* by Joan Barfoot © 1982. Reprinted by permission of Macmillan Canada. "Spring Cleaning" by Sandra Birdsell from *Agassiz Stories* (Turnstone Press, 1987) © Sandra Birdsell. Reprinted by permission. "Married Woman's Complaint" from *The Killing Room* by Marilyn Bowering © 1991. Reprinted by permission of Beach Holme Publishing. "Recipe for a Sidewalk" from *Covering Rough Ground* by Kate Braid © 1991. Reprinted by permission of Polestar Book Publishers, Vancouver. Excerpt from *Luna* was first published by Fifth House © 1988 by Sharon Butala and is used here by permission of the author. Excerpt from *Halfbreed* by Maria Campbell. Used by permission of the Canadian Publishers, McClelland & Stewart, Toronto. Excerpt from *The Book of Small* by Emily Carr. Reprinted by permission of Stoddart Publishing Co. Limited, Don Mills, Ont. "Italian Spaghetti" from *From A High Thin Wire*, 1982, by Joan Clark. Reprinted by permission of NeWest Publishers Ltd. "Dreaming Domestic" and "Domestic Scene I" from *Angels of Flesh* by Lorna Crozier. Used by permission of the Canadian Publishers, McClelland & Stewart, Toronto. Excerpt from *In Search of April Raintree* by Beatrice Culleton. First published by Pemmican Publications, Winnipeg, April, 1982; now reprinted by Peguis Publishers, Winnipeg, 1992. "The

Disgrace" and "Pieta '78" by Mary di Michele are reprinted from *Bread and Chocolate* by permission of Oberon Press. "Teeth" (Parts 1, 2, 3) by Cathy Ford from *The Desiring Heart* (Caitlin Press, 1985). © Cathy Ford. Reprinted by permission. "Living Alone" from *Complicity* and "Chocolate: A Love Poem" from *The Power to Move* by Susan Glickman, Signal Editions, Véhicule Press. "Aprons" from *Private Properties* by Leona Gom, © 1986 by Sono Nis Press, Victoria, B.C. "Mother with Child" and "Waiting" from *The Collected Poems* by Leona Gom, © 1991 by Sono Nis Press, Victoria, B.C. "Mornings Like This" by Pat Jasper is reprinted from *The Outlines of Our Warm Bodies* with the permission of Goose Lane Editions. © Pat Jasper, 1990. Excerpt from *All of Baba's Children*, 1987, by Myrna Kostash. Reprinted by permission of NeWest Publishers Ltd. Excerpt from *The Fire-Dwellers* by Margaret Laurence. Used by permission of the Canadian publishers, McClelland & Stewart, Toronto. "The Unquiet Bed" and "The Taming" from *The Woman I Am* by Dorothy Livesay. Used by permission of Guernica Editions, Montreal. Pat Lowther. "Kitchen Murder" from *A Stone Diary*, © Oxford University Press Canada, 1977. Reprinted by permission of the publisher. "A Breakfast for Barbarians" from *A Breakfast for Barbarians* by Gwendolyn MacEwen. © 1966. Reprinted with permission from the author's family. "Reliquary" reprinted from *The Litmus Body*, © Nadine McInnis, by permission of Quarry Press, Inc. "Rising, Batoche" is reprinted from *Batoche* by Kim Morrissey (Coteau Books 1989) with the permission of the publisher. "Polonaise" from *West South West* by Erin Mouré © 1989. Reprinted by permission of Véhicule Press. "How I Met My Husband" from *Something I've Been Meaning to Tell You* by Alice Munro. © 1974 by Alice Munro. "Conversation During the Omelette aux Herbes" from *Cocktails at the Mausoleum* by Susan Musgrave. Used by permission of the Canadian Publishers, McClelland & Stewart, Toronto. Reprinted by arrangement with Virginia Barber Literary Agency, Inc. All rights reserved. "September" by Sharon H. Nelson is reprinted from *The Work of Our Hands* (The Muses Co., 1992). © Sharon H. Nelson. Reprinted by permission from the author. "Brazilian House" from *Poems Selected and New* by P.K. Page © 1974. Reprinted by permission of Stoddart Publishing Co. Limited, Don Mills, Ont. Excerpt from *The Tin Flute* by Gabrielle Roy. Used by permission of the Canadian Publishers, McClelland & Stewart, Toronto. Excerpt from *Memory Board* by Jane Rule © 1987. Reprinted by permission of Jane Rule. "Eating Avocados" from *South Hill Girls* by Barbara Sapergia © 1992. Reprinted by permission of Fifth House Publishers. Excerpt from *Honour the Sun* by Ruby Slipperjack. Pemmican Publications Inc., Winnipeg. Reprinted with permission. Excerpt from *Rapture of the Deep* by Anne Szumigalski © 1992 reprinted by permission of Coteau Books. Excerpt from *Goodbye Harold, Good Luck* by Audrey Thomas. © Audrey Thomas, 1986. Reprinted by permission of Penguin Books Canada Limited. "Borrowed Beauty" from *Borrowed Beauty* by Maxine Tynes. © Maxine Tynes, 1988. Reprinted by permission from the author. Excerpt from *The Tent Peg* by Aritha van Herk. Used by permission of the Canadian Publishers, McClelland & Stewart, Toronto. "The House on Hazelton" by Miriam Waddington, from *Apartment Seven: Essays Selected and New*, © 1989 Miriam Waddington and "Profile of an Unliberated Woman" from *Collected Poems* © 1986 Miriam Waddington. Reprinted by permission of Oxford University Press Canada. "Food" from *The Stubborn Particulars of Grace* by Bronwen Wallace. Used by permission of the Canadian Publishers, McClelland & Stewart, Toronto. "Calligraphy of a Maritime Kitchen" by Liliane Welch from *Syntax of Ferment* (Goose Lane Editions, 1979). © Liliane Welch. Reprinted with permission from the author. Excerpt from *The Sacrifice* by Adele Wiseman © 1956. Reprinted by permission of the author's family.

CONTENTS

COFFEE ON MARY HILL

THE LADY OF THE HOUSE

MIXED MESSAGES

In memory of Adele Wiseman

"My women friends and I still gather there, as women have gathered around the cooking fires since the beginnings of time ... "
–Jennifer Blend "Dream Kitchen"

FOREWORD
Edna Alford

One Sunday morning at Turtle Lake, my sister counted 37 people who had stopped by our mother's kitchen before 11:00 a.m. for coffee, counsel or company—some for a pail of water. We remember this as a record, though the kitchen of our childhood was frequently filled with aunts, uncles, friends, cousins, conversation, innumerable and incomparable loaves of bread and cinnamon buns hot out of the oven, and pots and pots of strong coffee, freshly brewed Norwegian style. The cinnamon buns were famous among our friends, could and did fetch as high as $1.25 each on the black market at lunchtime or after school throughout the 60s for certain siblings who shall remain nameless. The table was often laden with enormous turkeys, hams, roasts of beef or pork and all the trimmings—colourful salads, homemade pickles and garden vegetables; for desert, there were pies, cakes, cookies, fruits and puddings of all kinds—pumpkin pie with whipped cream, butter tarts and deep chocolate cake with brown sugar icing come to mind as personal favourites, and thin pancakes and Krumaker made with my grandmother's cast iron pan brought over from the old country, still stamping out heart-patterned confections which we shaped into cones for Christmas.

Often, the whole house would be empty except for the kitchen, where those who were lucky enough to get chairs gathered around the table while others stood against walls, leaned against cupboards, crouched with their backs resting against the refrigerator door or another person's chair leg. After meals, people lingered at the table indefinitely, discussing every conceivable topical issue, sometimes quietly, sometimes "hot and heavy," as we used to say. Everyone was entitled to participate and everyone did. They still do on long weekends, Christmas, Easter and summer holidays. In quieter times, we shared confidences, disappointments and grief in pairs or small groups at the same table.

Ours was not a wealthy family; my parents worked very hard, but there were many mouths to feed. They shopped carefully, preserved much of their own food and wasted nothing. Cooking was a necessity. It was a key component in the survival of the family. Both boys and girls participated in the preparation and cleanup after meals. (I am still inclined to peel a Dutch oven full of potatoes when company comes just to make sure there will be "enough for everyone.")

Our mother's kitchen was and is regarded with respect. The utensils and equipment for her work there were of the highest quality we could afford; their acquisition and maintenance were given the same priority as the quality and safe-keeping of our father's carpentry and cabinet-making tools with which he made our living. Perhaps because of this balance of power in the home, my experience in the kitchen was, in the main, positive, not oppressive. I was, however, well aware at a very early age that not all kitchens were like ours, nor were all women who worked in kitchens held in such high esteem as our mother. All too often, the case was quite the opposite.

When Claire Harris invited me to join her in the exploration and collection of writing by Canadian women about the kitchen, I was simultaneously excited and depressed, a personal reaction which had become familiar to me over the years of my own work specific to the imagination and experience of women. I recognized the ambivalence at once.

I was excited because here was an opportunity to study the kitchen as a significant site, to gather a wide range of work which would reflect the complexity of imagery, both positive and negative, surrounding nurturing and survival, creativity and captivity common to so many women in this particular room.

I was depressed because of the nearly intransigent pall cast by the historical devaluation of nurturing and the trivialization of "women's work" which included their communication with each other while they did this work—"kitchen talk." I was depressed by the fact that many of us had internalized this external evaluation. Where on earth had the assessment originated? Who on earth designated the "field of battle" as a significant site and the "field of nurturing" as an insignificant site? (Questions addressed eloquently, by the way, by Nicole Brossard at the World Congress of PEN International in the fall of 1989 in Montreal.) Finally, I was depressed by the alternative celebratory lip service given to women in the kitchen and their female progeny, "mother's little helpers."

As the anthology evolved, however, I realized that Canadian women writers had seriously addressed these issues and images as well as their wider implications as far back as Susanna Moodie. Instead of encountering difficulty finding appropriate work for the collection, I was faced with an embarrassment of riches. It was rather like coming upon an extraordinary patch of ripe berries in the sun. There were back kitchens, summer kitchens, camp kitchens, open-air kitchens; the kitchens of the wealthy, the middle class, the impoverished; the kitchens of those in bondage and those who were free; there were restaurant kitchens, communal kitchens, tropical kitchens, Arctic kitchens, Russian, Chinese, French, German, Ukrainian, Lithuanian, Japanese, Dene, and British kitchens—an astonishing array of kitchens, private and public, pioneer and professional. All of them sites of significant human experience—celebration, damnation and everything between, including, on more than one occasion, the infamous "kitchen sink." All of them alive with the heat of the words of women.

We have a tradition on the prairie of calling the women out of the kitchen after banquets to thank them personally for the meal with our applause. Tonight I imagine calling each woman who contributed to the anthology from her desk, one by one, and thanking her, the women who helped other women tell their stories, the women who sent new work, the women whose contributions were made in the past through their distinguished literary legacy. The applause is not imaginary. *Tak fer matin.*

1992

FOREWORD
Claire Harris

I arrived from Trinidad knowing the kitchen only as a place where meals were prepared; where one's mother on carefully selected occasions initiated one into the mysteries of family recipes, of spices, of bush teas, of garlic syrups, of orange peel teas; where occasionally the women of the family gathered to prepare the delicate dishes, the breads and cakes of celebration. Most important, I was taught how to give an illusion of grace to survival foods: barefoot rice, bakes, how to make coconut oil, how to preserve meats, make rice-water milk. Though the ability to cook was highly regarded, the kitchen was hot and often stuffy. No one lingered there. Even the maid retired as soon as possible to the cool back veranda, or her own room.

In my personal experience cooking was an art, a place to illustrate a refined sensibility. Or it was a job. In any case it was a woman's place and one escaped as quickly as possible from it to the "real" world. In Canada, it quickly became obvious to me that the kitchen was a very different idea. This is the territory that Edna Alford and I decided to explore. Because we wished the book to be truly representative, we have included oral testimony from as many ethnic groups as possible; life writing from women who have never considered publication; as well as work of writers from most spectra of women's thought. Traditionally the work of women has been devalued in the "canon." No one can read this anthology without being startled by the relish and ease with which we use the images of our captivity, or our nurturing to discover our deepest thought about what it means/has meant to be female in the twentieth century.

Finally, we should like to thank all the women who contributed, and waited with such patience while we stumbled to Bethlehem.

1992

INTRODUCTION

Phyllis Webb

Divine smells—cloves, cinnamon, ginger, dill, and on the counter gleaming in their glass jars peaches, crabapples, plums; pasta curling out of the pasta machine, pickles pickling on the stove, bitter-sweet taste of burnt sugar; a salmon is stuffed with watercress and wild rice, carrots grated, lettuce tossed, click of knives and forks, kettle hissing as through the room the women come and go—and kids, and men, cats and dogs. A sewing machine speeds and zings through memory. Little Emily gets a rough scrub in a Saturday night tub. And is that a piano? A baby being born? The corpse of a beloved young mother on the kitchen table? Screams, blood, a knife coming at her throat, a plate hurled, a gin bottle, radio blaring out the weather report from Beijing, the world crashing through a Prairie window on a sunny day. If you can't stand the heat, as the saying goes, stay out of the kitchen!

The kitchen is a power-site where all the senses are called into action and that primary appetite hunger compels us into the communal, the feast, the drama of familial and sexual politics. It's also a place of transformations and creativity where work, like art, sometimes looks like play.

This remarkable anthology takes a handful of this, a handful of that, mixing fiction, poetry, interviews, essays into a satisfying blend that's peculiarly Canadian. We're given a glimpse into the wonderfully noisy and busy kitchen of Muriel Betsina, a Dene Indian, who tells us how to dry meat in just two days, and much else besides. We hear about the moral and religious dimensions of food preparation in a Hindu family; reminiscences of life in a Chinese village, of Ukrainian Easters in Manitoba. I'll never forget the huge pots of mashed potatoes in Sharon Butala's powerful evocation of a communal supper being prepared by farm women, the subversion of this passage from *Luna:*

> Selena thought of all the times since she was a girl, since she was Phoebe's age, she had come into this kitchen carrying a salad, or three dozen buns, or two pies, or some combination of these, and then had worked here for hours getting a meal ready for the community. Aware of the ache in her legs now, she thought, I wonder what would happen if we all quit.

When I was asked to contribute a poem to this anthology, I refused. I thought the enterprise would only reinforce the stereotype of the little woman in the kitchen. Does it? There are few men in this book *doing the work* (Annharte's poem "His Kitchen" and Lorna Crozier's "Domestic Scene I" are among the exceptions), though men are powerful presences throughout the collection. We smile when we encounter Mrs. V's testimony (she came from Russia in 1947) that things really have changed:

> Son married now. Has nice house, good kitchen. Is terrible! *He* cook! *He* wash dishes. Everything ... Daughter married too. Big house. Big kitchen. Is happy. Good husband. He *cook.* He *wash dishes.* Everything!

Well, they don't seem too unhappy, and it strikes me that the intensity of pain and conflict in so many of the stories and poems comes not so much from changing gender roles as unchanging gender roles—and from class, racial, and intergenerational strife. Yet the rebellion and vitality here are inspirational. Details of these often anguished revelations are charged with potentiality and meaning: bread dough rising—always save a part of your culture for tomorrow—a caribou thigh thawing, a cake becoming an edible woman, a meat fork a weapon. "Everything here's a weapon," Pat Lowther writes in "Kitchen Murder." The raw and the cooked. Nature and culture. Secrets shared or not shared, lessons taught or otherwise: KEEP OUT. STAND BACK. DON'T TOUCH.

I can just hear the mother in Marlene Nourbese Philip's story "Burn Sugar" saying at this point, "Cake is for eating not thinking about—eat it and enjoy it—stop looking for meaning in everything." And her daughter responding, "You wrong, Mammy, you wrong—there have to—there have to be a meaning." I think the readers of this book will also be searching for reasons, meaning, significance as they savour the many pleasures of the text.

MAL DE CUISINE

A BREAKFAST FOR BARBARIANS
Gwendolyn MacEwen

my friends, my sweet barbarians,
there is that hunger which is not for food—
but an eye at the navel turns the appetite
round
with visions of some fabulous sandwich,
the brain's golden breakfast
                                        eaten with beasts
                                        with books on plates

let us make an anthology of recipes,
let us edit for breakfast
our most unspeakable appetites—
let us pool spoons, knives
and all cutlery in a cosmic cuisine,
let us answer hunger
with boiled chimera
and apocalyptic tea,
an arcane salad of spiced bibles,
tossed dictionaries—
                                        (O my barbarians
                                        we will consume our mysteries)

and can we, can we slake the gaping eye of our desires?
we will sit around our hewn wood table
until our hair is long and our eyes are feeble,
eating, my people, O my insatiates,
eating until we are no more able
to jack up the jaws any longer—

to no more complain of the soul's vulgar cavities,
to gaze at each other over the rust-heap of cutlery,
drinking a coffee that takes an eternity—
till, bursting, bleary,
we laugh, barbarians, and rock the universe—
and exclaim to each other over the table
over the table of bones and scrap metal
over the gigantic junk-heaped table:

by God that was a meal

DOMESTIC SCENE I
Lorna Crozier

I mop the floors, admire again the grain,
the beautiful simplicity of wood.
The cat we named Nowlan after the poet
who just died, cries for his tin of beef.
You stuff the salmon with wild rice
and watercress, its flesh pink
as Nowlan's mouth, his perfect tongue.
How lucky we are to have found each other,
our fine grey cat, a fresh Atlantic salmon.
Tomorrow we may get drunk and fight
or buy two tickets to Madrid.
But tonight the light in our kitchen
is as good as you'll find anywhere.
The plates glow with possibilities
and the cat licks himself completely clean.

FROM *THE BOOK OF SMALL*
Emily Carr

All our Sundays were exactly alike. They began on Saturday night after Bong the Chinaboy had washed up and gone away, after our toys, dolls and books, all but *The Peep of Day* and Bunyan's *Pilgrim's Progress,* had been stored away in drawers and boxes till Monday, and every Bible and prayer-book in the house was puffing itself out, looking more important every minute.

The clothes-horse came galloping into the kitchen and straddled round the stove inviting our clean clothes to mount and be aired. The enormous wooden tub that looked half coffin and half baby-bath was set in the middle of the kitchen floor with a rag mat for dripping on laid close beside it. The great iron soup pot, the copper wash-boiler and several kettles covered the top of the stove, and big sister Dede filled them by working the kitchen pump-handle furiously. It was a sad old pump and always groaned several times before it was poured. Dede got the brown windsor soap, heated the towels and put on a thick white apron with a bib. Mother unbuttoned us and by that time the pots and kettles were steaming.

Dede scrubbed hard. If you wriggled, the flat of the long-handled tin dipper came down spankety on your skin.

As soon as each child was bathed Dede took it pick-a-back and rushed it upstairs through the cold house. We were allowed to say our prayers kneeling in bed on Saturday night, steamy, brown-windsory prayers—then we cuddled down and tumbled very comfortably into Sunday.

MAL DE CUISINE
M. Travis Lane

An office would be worse: the desuetudes
of desk and dust and carbon, idiocies
which must be done.

This is a private freedom, here—
the freedom of the sink,
abandoned island, no right way
to peel the carrots, the rich stink
of old necessities returned
three times a day.

Oh counters of conformed desire
and polyester holidays! Flights out
to quickfood, frenchfries, and motels!

The housewife labours for herself.
Who else? A cupboard clean, a spare
and solitary worship of the thing—

An egg, perfection—but the shell,
the dish, the burned toast crumbs—
A bird weeps out the window as it does
each spring.

To fly from here, to wallow in the wild
and find a clean world after me
to come back home to!
Everything

continues, more or less, the same.
It may be luck.
The day moves as you push it,
only just.

MRS. S. (BRITAIN) BORN 1925 (CAME TO CANADA IN 1957)
Inge Israel

When I lived with my parents, the kitchen was our living room and dining room. Every Friday my mother baked and every Saturday, the brasses had to be polished and the stove blackened with blacklead—dreadful stuff! When an electric stove replaced the old iron one, a fireplace was put in its place and my mother's and father's armchairs were put on either side of it. Everybody else sat around it on other chairs. Every second Saturday night, my mother and father had their friends in and they played bridge until past midnight. At the end of it, they always had tongue sandwiches. The next morning, in the kitchen, the previous night's game was gone over and over by my mother and father with great recriminations of: why did you do this? ... Or: why did you play so and so? ... And I made up my mind I would never play bridge as long as I lived.

In these old tenements, the kitchens were all-purpose places which also had beds in them, set back in an alcove behind a curtain which would be drawn by day. The "front room," a sort of glorified parlour, wasn't much used at all, except that it, too, served as a bedroom at night with a bed set in a curtained-off alcove that used to be a cupboard. This was the usual thing, and people brought up two, three and four kids in these two rooms. It was worse for those who only had one room.

We were on the top floor, which meant that the rain often came in. Above the kitchen was the water-tank. When it froze in the winter, my father would climb up on the rafters with one of the neighbours and set paraffin lamps up there to thaw the water. Of course, sometimes the pipes burst anyway.

There was a treadle sewing machine in a corner—my mother sewed quite a bit. And she did the washing right there and hung it across the kitchen on a pulley where it steamed away nicely because of the fire.

The kitchen I had after I got married in the early 50s in England was dreadful—just a little outhouse stuck on at the back of the house, with a stone floor and a stone sink. All of it dirty and sooty from the coke used for the fire, which heated all the water. Canada was a welcome change when we came in 1957. It all seemed so much cleaner and fresher, and the appliances made work so easy. But it did seem very impermanent somehow ... When my mother came to visit us here the first time, she looked around my kitchen and said, "It's like Hollywood!"

I used a dual system in my baking—scales for the English recipes and measuring cups for the Canadian ones. We'd still had rationing in Britain in the 50s, so the Canadian recipes seemed far too rich and sweet and we found them hard to digest.

I never resented being in the kitchen. What I resented far more was being in a classroom as a teacher where I was bound by a strict timetable and had to teach 30-40 children, whether they wanted to be taught or not. Of course, there were moments of great satisfaction in teaching, but I was much happier at home in my kitchen where I could do as and when I pleased. When I was growing up, we were trained, or indoctrinated, to feel that there was a certain worth in what we were doing at home and that we could be proud of it. We were much less inclined to think of ourselves as being denied freedom to do this, that or the other, the way the younger ones feel nowadays. Perhaps it was partly lack of imagination. But in the kitchen, you were yourself and you didn't have to conform to anybody else's standards or regulations. You could stop when you wanted to and read a book or sew or do a little gardening. When the children were growing up in the 70s, I did go outside the home again for a while—perhaps because getting paid for your work is a sort of recognition.

APRONS
Leona Gom

are uniforms, we use them
the way soldiers would, identity,
excuses, maybe mostly as camouflage,
to blend us like wallpaper into
our kitchens. when we work,
tools, weapons (sometimes we forget
the difference) fit our hands
like fingers. we are patriots,
will see the last child evacuated
safely to adolescence.
we have the patience of light
stored in stone.

some of us wait too long,
will say we feel undressed without
aprons, soldiers who wear
uniforms on the streets,
never want to go back to civvies.
but there are those of us who take off
our aprons. we move among men
like ordinary people.
we are not innocents, we know
what happens when someone gives us
a recipe with ingredients missing, how
to get stains out before they set

into our personalities. and
our hands are full of memories.
sometimes they twist on our laps,
it is dangerous to ignore such need.
they will close around
whatever is put into them.
be careful what you give us.

FROM *ALL OF BABA'S CHILDREN*
Myrna Kostash

> Mother taught us girls how to decorate Easter eggs. She didn't make them too fancy, just very simple. As long as there was a line around and some leaf. You see, they believed very much in all that from the old country. The line that encircles the egg has no beginning or end so it symbolizes eternity. And a pine tree, she always made a pine tree to signify eternal youth and health. She made roosters, eternity and fulfillment of wishes, and always a fish for Christianity. Mother never made reindeer, but other people did. They must have come from a different village. The dyes were all from the old country, beautiful dyes.

Of course, there were always a few farm women whose artist's pride was expressed in very refined and painstaking decorating and embroidery (especially for ornamentation in the church). But the majority, bent exhausted under a kerosene lamp with eyes half closed and hands cracked and calloused, could produce only the crudest arts.

Nothing, however, could cramp the celebration of Christmas and Easter. Traditionally, these were the occasions when the need to gather together and have a good time superceded the demands of the land and when the church's authority became more impressive than the state's. It was the same in Canada. The family's wealth was invested in food, its time in ritual observances and its emotional vulnerability in the mass. Even the sceptics, the anti-clerics, the apostates would repeat the ancient gestures: cooking enormous amounts of food, bundling up for the sled-ride to church, inviting carollers into the house for a drink. They did it because they were Ukrainian and knew no other way—until, that is, the kids came home from school prattling about Santa Claus and Easter bunnies. Foolishness, if not blasphemy! Let Miss Jameson at the school celebrate Christmas and Easter as the joyless and overly sensible Anglo-Saxons saw fit. In this house, the holiday mood would be an orgy of food and prayer. Two weeks before Christmas mother would start the baking—the braided breads, the buns, the honey cake—and the kids would set to with a mortar and pestle, pounding poppy seed into mush. The day before Christmas, a spruce tree or simply poplar branches would be strung with home-made decorations, nuts wrapped in foil from cigarette packages, paper chains and berries strung together—a Canadian custom—and the traditional sheaf of wheat propped in a corner. Hay, to symbolize the manger, was spread on the floor under the table and under the tablecloth. Then, finally, jubilantly, at the sighting of the first evening star, the family would eat, all twelve customary dishes if they could afford it, cabbage rolls, borsch, cooked wheat with poppy seed, two or three varieties of fish, bread, lentils, thin, sweet pancakes, cakes, till the candle in the *kolach* flared and went out and the neighbours came around to visit. Christmas Day mass was a five-hour affair. One could miss church all year except for this service. Feast and mass were repeated for Epiphany and the kids would make little crosses out of straw and stick them to the window. They stuck to the inch of ice on the inside of the pane. Throughout the season, carollers went from farm to farm, frozen from the sleigh-ride, thawed from whiskey, refrozen on the ice-bound sled. "January 6 would be our Christmas. We never knew there was one on December 25."

The Easter celebration was intensely religious although there was, like Christmas, the bellyful of food. Easter Thursday's mass. Easter Friday's procession around the church at midnight, men carrying an icon of Christ, girls carrying that of the Virgin Mary: three times around the little church with a band of boys playing noise-makers because the church bells could not be rung at Christ's death. Inside, a crown of thorns and a spear are "buried" in a table in front of the altar, on the altar the icon of Christ, kissed by the devout, crawling on their knees. On Sunday morning, this icon would be carried by the priest to the altar—the Resurrection—and the three huge bells in the wooden belfry in the churchyard would ring out and mass would be celebrated until two o'clock in the afternoon—"in those days nobody was in a hurry"—usually without benefit of pews or chairs. After mass, the priest would bless the food baskets of the families: a little *babka* (fruit bread) and *paska* (sweet bread), a piece of pork, raw onion, horseradish, pickled beets and, in a little bowl, cream cheese impressed with a cross of cloves. Finally, at home, the feast. Easter Monday's mass and the afternoon's "fertility rituals" when young men visited young women to throw water at them, a modification of the old country custom of actually throwing the girls into creeks and ponds.

Depending on the degree of one's devotion, one could also celebrate Epiphany and Epiphany Eve, Whitsunday, Feast of Jordan, Saints Peter and Paul Day, not to mention secular holidays commemorating various events important to old country patriots and the birthdays of the most honoured Ukrainian writers. Anything, really, to get out from behind the plough and stove and socialize like a civilized human being.

There was nothing quite so sociable as a wedding and to the extent it was exuberant and bawdy, it was more pagan than Christian. The guests laughed and got drunk and the bride cried; it was a reminder that the community's renewal through marriage was paid for by the sorrows of married women.

> My oldest sister's wedding: Saturday night the bride is getting ready. Her bridesmaids came over to visit. (She was married in '26 at sixteen and he was nineteen.) Mother was getting food ready. Sunday morning they went to church and got married. The bride and groom came home for dinner. Then he went home by himself, the bride remained in her father's house—that was the custom—until the following Sunday when we had the wedding feast, at his home and at ours at the same time. Dancing, dinner and supper. About four in the afternoon the groom comes with his attendants to get the bride who is usually in the house behind the table. She's in her wedding dress again. They take her dowry—quilts, pillows, trunk—and drive over to the groom's place where he was living with his parents. Everybody's waiting for them there and they have a supper and dance. I know that Mom and Dad met them at the gate after the church service with kolachi. The dinner: borsch, holubtsi, nachyna, roast chicken, jellied salads, cakes, cider. Kolachi but no wedding cake like now. Very elaborate with little birds and beautiful big braids.
>
> By the time I got married it was different already. Went to the church in the morning, came back home for a dinner and had a small reception. A band played, a violin, a drum, tsimbaly, they played good dance music—not Ukrainian dancing though—but at my sister's wedding the men danced the arkan and some ladies would sing such sad, meaningful songs about the girl leaving home and not knowing what her life was going to be like. It would make you cry.

FROM *LUNA*
Sharon Butala

"They're starting to come in," Helen called over her shoulder from the doorway between the kitchen and the hall. She had to raise her voice to be heard over the hissing of the big pots on the two stoves, the clatter of dishes being washed in the sink, and the voices of the other women hurrying around the kitchen. Selena leaned past her to look down the hall. It was filled with rows of long tables covered with white paper tablecloths and set with cutlery, salt and pepper shakers and cream and sugar sets. Rena was moving among the tables, setting small vases, each holding a pink and a blue artificial daisy and a sprig of artificial fern, two to a table. She was moving quickly, straightening the chairs and benches arranged on each side of the tables, while her daughter Tracey followed, carefully carrying the tray of vases, her expression serious, both of them intent on their work.

At the far end of the hall, by the main entrance, Selena saw Phoebe and Melissa sitting at the reception table. As she watched, Phoebe stood up, accepted a shining, silver-wrapped parcel from the couple who were bending to sign the guest book, and carried it to the table behind them, which was beginning to be piled with gifts. Selena smiled without meaning to, because Phoebe looked so pretty in her white cotton dress with the pink belt, her shoulder-length, light brown hair carefully brushed and shining. Then she scoffed at herself—an ordinary teenager, like all the rest of them here, she thought. Yes, but my own little girl. She threw the tea towel she was holding over her shoulder, then hastily took it off again: don't put your tea towel over your shoulder, your hair will touch it, it's a messy habit, her mother's voice still echoing in her ears after all these years. Sometimes she thought she would never shake her mother's teachings. It both angered her and pleased her to think that she was what her mother had made her.

Phoebe was seated again, laughing with Melissa about something, and more people were coming in, smiling and calling to each other. And Phoebe? she wondered, watching her, what have I made her? Phoebe was standing again, moving quickly, several parcels piled up in her arms. She tried to think of what she had taught her: don't let the boys touch you, was the first admonition that sprang into her mind, seeing her now, so womanly and pretty. But no, earlier than that. She frowned, trying to remember. Wash your hands often, it's important to be clean. Be neat, comb your hair whenever you think of it during the day. Don't make a lot of noise, nobody likes a roughneck girl. Be polite ... more admonitions came crowding into her mind.

No, she thought, as Phoebe returned to her chair. Surely those weren't the things that would make a woman of Phoebe. It wasn't that they weren't important, it was just that something seemed to be missing. What was it that was missing? It seemed to her that there was some core to what it meant to be a woman that she had never had the words to talk about. Was it God? Phoebe had asked her about God more than once over the years. Yes, there is a God, Selena had told her; ask the minister, ask your Sunday school teacher. Maybe she should have tried harder to answer Phoebe herself. But what answers do I have? she wondered.

"Excuse me," Joanne sang in her ear. She had to turn sideways to squeeze through the door past Selena. She was carrying a dish of pickles in each hand and her cheeks were flushed with the heat in the kitchen, her eyes too bright. The ties of her apron barely met at the back.

"Let me take those," Selena said, reaching for the thick glass dishes without waiting for Joanne to answer her. She took one in each hand, and nodded toward the only chair in the kitchen, pushed back into a corner in front of the cupboards. "You better go sit down."

"I'm fine," Joanne protested, not smiling.

"Do what she tells you," Ruth called from behind them. "You'll work hard enough once the baby comes." Ruth was a cousin of Joanne's so she could boss her around. Joanne went slowly to the chair and sat down, then began to fan herself with a paper napkin.

"If it weren't so hot, it wouldn't be so bad," Enid remarked to Selena. "I'll take those." Before Selena could move, she had taken the two dishes of pickles from her and had hurried out into the hall with them. Selena made a little face at her back.

"Those potatoes are ready," Ruth said. Selena hurried to the stove. Together they lifted the steaming pot and drained the boiling water off into one of the sinks. Phyllis and Lola had begun cutting the pies onto rows of dessert plates. Phoebe came into the kitchen, asked Helen something, then went out again. Ruth and Selena set the big pot of potatoes onto a backless chair and began to take turns mashing them with a long-handled potato masher.

"It's so hot," Ruth said, "but you can't open the blamed door for the flies and grasshoppers. Did Phoebe make her dress?"

"In Home Ec." Ruth mashed vigorously for a moment, then lifted her head and straightened, panting, her face red, her temples glossy with sweat.

"Let 'em have pretty dresses while they can," she said. "Lord knows it don't last." Selena thought of Ruth's husband, Buck, and shuddered inwardly, thinking of Phoebe. At least Brian was a decent kid, drank only a little, if Phoebe could be believed, had no reputation for being hard on vehicles or mouthy with the older men. Didn't touch drugs, Phoebe swore. Still, you never knew. Marry a man, then find out what you've gotten yourself into.

She took the masher from Ruth and bent, raising and lowering it, thrusting hard, holding it with both hands. It took all her strength to push it through the mound of potatoes.

"Okay, no more lumps," she said. At the table in the centre of the kitchen Enid and Ella were mashing another big pot of potatoes. The milk and butter sat on the table beside them and Selena reached for them, poured in a quantity of milk, then cut off a piece of butter which she broke into smaller pieces and added to the potatoes which Ruth had already begun to whip, using the masher. Selena grasped the pot and held it steady for her.

"Look out everybody!" Lola had opened one of the oven doors and was pulling out a roaster, which she set on the oven door. She lifted off the lid and a cloud of steam and the smell of roasting beef swept through the sweltering room. Ruth's husband, Buck, detached himself from a group of men he'd been standing with near the doorway and put his head into the kitchen.

"Give me a hand in here," Lola called to him and he hurried in, took the oven mitts from her and lifted the roaster onto the table. Ruth lifted her head from the potatoes, and Selena saw her send a sharp glance toward her husband's back, her lips tightening. Lola, after two children, still had her figure; she was still young and attractive. And there was Buck, grey-haired, gnarled, with a lined, reddish face from hard work and drink, being jovial and overly helpful.

"Does he do that at home, too?" Selena muttered to Ruth, half grinning, and laughed at Ruth's sarcastic "hah!" Selena took the masher from her and began to whip while Ruth held the pot.

"Where's Diane tonight?" Ruth asked. Her head bent, working hard to move the masher swiftly through the potatoes so they would cream and whip up, Selena hardly had the breath to answer. She hadn't even noticed that Diane wasn't there to help. Diane had never been as faithful as many of the members. Some women were like that. Sally Macklin was another one, although sometimes Selena suspected she didn't come too often because the women didn't really accept her. She had always been a little bit different anyway, but when she started writing poetry and getting it published, it was worse, nobody knew how to talk to her. But Diane—maybe Kent was right, maybe Diane was just a little bit lazy.

"I think that's enough," she said, standing back, panting. "Diane must have gone to get Rhea." She turned toward the second pot to help, but Ella was already working at it, talking to Enid as she mashed.

"For a pot this size, it takes about a pint, sometimes more, depends on the potatoes, what kind you use and how old they are and so on."

"I've never cooked such a big potful," Enid said, apologetically. She came from a town seventy-five miles down the road. They must do things differently there, Selena thought.

"You young ones'll have to take over when us older ones give up," Ella said, puffing as she whipped.

"I'll do that," Enid offered, and Selena had to smile at how the young ones always think they're stronger than the ones who've been at it for years. Enid would play out long before Ella would, she thought.

Rhoda had begun to fill two big serving bowls with creamy potatoes. Lola and Ruth were slicing the big roasts of beef and Phyllis was standing at the stove, sweating, and stirring the gravy. Selena stood back out of the way and looked around the busy, crowded kitchen in search of another job that needed doing. The commotion out in the hall was growing louder by the minute and people kept spilling into the kitchen, looking for a drink of water or a damp cloth to wipe a child's face, or to gossip, or to offer help.

Selena thought of all the times since she was a girl, since she was Phoebe's age, she had come into this kitchen carrying a salad, or three dozen buns, or two pies, or some combination of these, and then had worked here for hours getting a meal ready for the community. Aware of the ache in her legs now, she thought, I wonder what would happen if we all quit. She saw the hall, deserted, weeds growing up through the steps, the windows broken or boarded up. Why, the community would fall apart. Nobody but us women would do this. There'd be no more community if we quit celebrating people's anniversaries and weddings, births and deaths, departures and arrivals.

"Imagine," she said to Ruth, who had come to lean against the counter beside her, things were coming together now, the buffet tables were ready, the people were lining up and beginning to fill their plates, "if we all quit the club, if we all stopped working like this." Ruth turned her head quickly to look at Selena, a surprised expression on her face. She laughed, a short, stout, older woman in a cheap, neat dress, looking up at Selena with wide amused eyes.

"I wouldn't have varicose veins, maybe," she said. "My God, the hours I've put in here on my feet. I've baked enough buns over the years to stretch from here to Swift Current and back again." They relaxed, and watched their neighbours file by, filling their plates with the food they had prepared. "That'd be the end of the community," Ruth said.

"Some of the towns are getting men's service clubs," Selena remarked.

"They think they can take our place?" Ruth asked. "Let them try. Did you ever know a man who could even remember his own anniversary, never mind anybody else's? And who'd do the cooking?"

"They sure know how to make money," Selena said. "Not like us, working our feet off just to break even."

"Well, we don't do it for money," Ruth pointed out.

"There's not many young ones coming up to take over," said Margaret, who had been listening to their conversation. "What with the kids getting away to the cities to school nowadays, and all them farms going down, people moving away." She shook her head reflectively. "Heaven knows where it'll all end."

You could always depend on Margaret for doom and gloom, Selena thought. There'll always be farms. Or will there? She risked a quick glance at Margaret, who after all had been here a lot longer than she had, and therefore ought to know more. But Margaret was smiling serenely at the people filing by, as if she herself hadn't heard what she had just said.

FROM *RAPTURE OF THE DEEP*

Anne Szumigalski

We women sitting in the downtown bus on our way to buy new duds for an event which should have been foreseen but however long you wait for a day it always surprises you with its sudden coming the calendar speeding up when you're not looking and none of us wants to find herself in last year's finery at a whitwalk or picnic where we are to be admired our coiffes neat as helmets of dried-out curls thin on top which we try to hide with the help of various Mandys and Terris for why should we do it ourselves at our age haven't we earned with our years something a little special at least once or twice in a grey moon shading to foxy red or brassy with a tint of dust about it.

Later in the church hall kitchen catching up on the gossip behind a wedding just now being celebrated with thump of feet and sweat and jello in plastic dishes with a dab of ice cream on top melting milkly into the raspberry like the world upside down and the white sea melting into the red sun which of course it has long ago done for us ladies whose only good now is the proof of our hard work on such occasions as this our not believing we have worth in anything but the number of steps taken or juicy glasses and plates stacked or if we make the best mashed potatoes in the bunch which is hard to do as with all this practice we are every one so very good at it for we believe in the salvation of food given and taken and floors scrubbed and beds turned down at the edge for infrequent visitors from out of town yet still we grumble happily over tea on the days we allow ourselves the indulgence of a bus ride to go shopping and not to one of those goodworks meetings which are so many but varied of course to give everybody a change from the church there are societies for visiting the sick those other more decrepit women lying sourly in their beds in nursing homes all with the names of the bishops who laid the foundation stones places which far from subtly let it be known that they'd rather not accept those of another religion but will do it at a pinch to prove goodwill among christians and jews and other stranger faiths which wouldn't happen here if only they had kept to the immigration laws of long ago which we all agree were much kinder to all concerned in the end for there was far less tension in those days and now everybody is so violent you have to be careful going out at night no matter what part of town you live in.

And so back to the bus where we sit side by side knitting tiny sweaters and bonnets even occasionally something for ourselves so as not to waste time there is so little of it left but what there is wearying and long not many miles to go but the foolish fellow at the wheel he drives so careful and slow.

MRS. R. (NEAR LACOMBE, ALBERTA) BORN IN 1912

Inge Israel

Out on the farm we had real bread, made from scratch. All of us children had to help. We'd sit in the kitchen to clean the wheat and separate out the chaff. That bread tasted really special. Not like what you'd buy in the store now. And when my mother made pickles, there was a lovely smell of spices and vinegar.

Every time Dad killed a pig, my mother would make a box full of soap. She used lye, and rinds and fat from the pig. That was the only soap we had. We used it to clean everything, even to scrub the eight-inch boards of the kitchen floor. When I was 12 that was what I had to do. I can still smell it, a good clean smell.

The kitchen was the main part of the house. That's where we did everything. My mother's sewing machine was there. She used to make shirts out of old horse blankets. When the shirts had to be washed, whoever had been wearing them had to go to bed until they were dry again. There weren't any to change into. She did all the washing in the kitchen. We'd carry in the pails of water and she'd boil it, and then use a board to scrub the clothes clean.

We had our baths right there in the kitchen too, one after the other. Several of us had to use the same water. If someone came into the kitchen, my mother made us duck down into the water. She was very particular about that. Our bodies were very special to us.

One year the coyotes came and snapped off the turkeys' heads. We had no money for groceries. So my Dad would make a bunch of firewood and take it into Lacombe to sell it for two dollars. Then he'd buy groceries for that and bring them home. My happiest moments were listening for the jingle of the bells on Dad's horses.

For a special treat, Dad would hook up the two-seater democrat and we'd go for a ride in the country and we'd all sing. We sang a lot. And in winter, there were always the bells. They had a special meaning, keeping time with the horses' trotting.

I wouldn't want my children to have such a hard life. But I wouldn't trade mine for my children's easy one.

RISING, BATOCHE

Kim Morrissey

the best bread the best pain
is made when your heart
seems ready to burst
with the asking

bread or pain, it is always the same:
you start with water and flour
and a culture
passed from mother to child
start your culture, rub in salt
and be ready
to wait

pain is not hard:
but you must be ready
to set it aside
and to wait

after awhile
what has happened before
begins again—it is always the same

when the timing is right
fold it over itself
over and over until the flour
stops sticking, stops creasing
folds as soft and as full
as the nape of your new baby's neck

oil it and lay it down gently
cover with a cloth
or a towel
or a flag
and ignore

this is called resting

when your pain swells so great
you can't speak start again
and leave it aside even longer

let it work let it
double its bulk
fold it into yourself
not out—like you cut with a knife
and push hard till it hurts
kneading they call it, but don't
punch hard—hard
for the good of the bread

the more risings the better, but
two risings will do

the first is always too small
heavy and tight as a pony's laid ears
punch it down   set aside
form into loaves and be patient
when the pain grows again
it grows shaped for the job
it bakes hard and high
dusky brown with the heat of the flame

always remember:
save a part of your culture
for tomorrow

BURN SUGAR
Marlene Nourbese Philip

It don't come, never arrive, had not—for the first time since she leave, had left home; is the first, for the first time in forty years the Mother not standing, had not stood over the aluminum bucket with her heavy belly whipping up the yellow eggs them and the green green lime-skin. "People does buy cake in New York," she say, the Mother had said, "not make them."

Every year it arrived, use to in time for Christmas or sometimes—a few time well—not till January; once it even come as late as in March. Wherever she is, happen to be, it come wrap up and tie up in two or three layers of brown wrapping paper, and tape up in a Peak Freans tin—from last Christmas—oven-blacked black black from the oven. And it address on both sides—"just to make sure it get there," she could hear the Mother saying—in the Mother funny printing (she could never write cursive she used to say). Air mail or sea mail, she could figure out the Mother's finances—whether she have money or not. When she cut the string she use to, would tear off the Scotch tape—impatient she would rip, rip off, rip the brown paper, prise off the lid, pause ... sit back on she haunches and laugh—laugh she head off—the lid never match, never matched the tin, but it there all the same—black and moist. The cake.

The weeks them used to, would pass, passed—she eating the cake, would eat it—sometimes alone by sheself; sometimes she sharing, does share a slice with a friend. And then again—sometimes when she alone, is alone, she would, does cry as she eating—each black mouthful bringing up all kind of memory—then she would, does choke—the lump of food and memory blocking up, stick up in she throat—big and hard like a rock stone.

She don't know—when she begin to notice it she doesn't know, but once she has it always, was always there when she open the tin—faint—but it there, undeniable—musty and old it rise up, an odour of mouldiness and something else from the open tin making she nose, her nostrils twitch. Is like it cast a pall over she pleasure, shadowing her delight; it spoil, clouded the rich fruity black-cake smell, and every time she take a bite it there—in she mouth—hanging about it hung about her every mouthful. The Mother's advice was to pour some more make-sure-is-good-Trinidad rum on it. Nothing help, it didn't—the smell just there lingering.

And then she know, she knew that something on its annual journey to wherever she happened to be, something inside the cake does change, changed within the cake, and whether is the change that cause the funny smell, or the journey, the travel that cause the change that cause the funny smell ... she don't know ...

It never use to, it didn't taste like this back home is what the first bite tell she—back back home where she hanging round, anxiously hanging about the kitchen getting in the Mother's way—underfoot—waiting for the baking to start—

"Wash the butter!" The Mother want to get her out of the way, and is like she feeling the feel of the earthenware bowl—cool, round, beige—the Mother push at her. Wash the butter, wash the butter, sit and wash the butter at the kitchen table, cover with a new piece of oilcloth for Christmas; wash the butter, and the sun coming through the breeze blocks, jumping all over the place dappling spots on she hand—it and the butter running competition for yellow. Wash the butter! Round and round ... she pushing the lumps of butter round with a wooden spoon.

Every year she ask the same question—"Is why you have to do this?" and every year the Mother tell she is to get the salt out of the butter, and every year she washing the butter. The water don't look any different, it don't taste any different—if she could only see the salt leaving the butter. The Mother does catch she like this every year, and every year she washing the butter for hours, hours on end until is time to make the burn sugar.

Now! She stop. The Mother don't tell she this but she know, and the Mother know—it was understood between them. The coal-pot it waiting with it red coals—the Mother never let she light it—and the iron pot waiting on the coal-pot, and the Mother waiting for the right time. She push her hand in the sugar bag—suddenly—one handful, two handful—and the white sugar rise up gentle gentle in the middle of the pot, two handfuls of white sugar rise gently ... She had never, the Mother had never let she do it sheself, but to the last grain of sugar, the very last grain, she know how much does go into the pot.

She standing close close to the Mother, watching the white sugar; she know exactly when it going change—after she counted to a hundred, she decide one year; another year she know for sure it wasn't going change while she holding her breath; and last year she close she eyes and know that when she open them, the sugar going change. It never once work. Every time she lose, was disappointed—the sugar never change when she expect it to, not once in all the years she watching, observing the Mother's rituals. Too quick, too slow, too late—it always catch she—by surprise—first the sugar turn sticky and brown at the edges, then a darker brown—by surprise—smoke stinging, stings her eyes, tears run running down she face, the smell sharp and strong of burning sugar—by surprise—she don't budge, she stand still watching, watches what happening in the pot—by surprise—the white sugar completely gone leaving behind a thick, black, sticky mass like molasses—by surprise. If the pot stay on long enough, she wonder, would the sugar change back, right back to cane juice, runny and white ... catching she—by surprise.

The Mother grab up a kitchen towel, grabs the pot and put it in the sink—all one gesture clean and complete—and it sitting there hissing and sizzling in the sink. The Mother open the tap and steam for so rise up and *brip brap*—just so it all over—smoke gone, steam gone, smoke and steam gone leaving behind this thick thick, black liquid.

She look down at the liquid—she use to call it she magic liquid; is like it have a life of it own—its own life—and the cake need it to make it taste different. She glance over at the Mother—maybe like she need the Mother to taste different. She wonder if the Mother need her like she need the Mother—which of them was essential to the other—which of them was the burn sugar?

She stick a finger in the pot and touch the burn sugar; turning she finger this way and that, she looking at it in the sunlight turning this way and that, making sure, she make sure she don't drop any of the burn sugar on the floor; closing she eyes she closes them, and touching she touch she tongue with her finger ... gently, and she taste the taste of the burn sugar strong and black in its bitterness—it bitter—and she skin-up she face then smile—it taste like it should—strong, black and bitter it going to make the cake taste like no other cake.

She hanging around again, watching and waiting and watching the Mother crack the eggs into the bucket—the aluminum bucket—and she dying to crack some in sheself—if she begged she got to crack a few but most of the time she just hanging, hung around watching and waiting and watching the Mother beat the eggs. Is like the Mother thick brown arm grow an appendage—the silver egg whisk—and she hypnotizing sheself watching the big arm go up and down scraping the sides of the bucket—a blur of brown and silver lifting up, lifts the deep yellow eggs—their pale yellow frothy Sunday-best tulle skirts—higher and higher in the bucket. The Mother stop and sigh, wipe she brow—a pause a sigh, she wipes her brow—and she throw in a piece of curly, green lime-skin, add a dash of rum—"to cut the freshness"—a curl of green lime-skin and a dash of rum. She don't know if the Mother know she was going to ask why, to ask her why the lime-skin—anticipating her question—or if she was just answering she own question, she don't know, but the arm continued, keep on beating as if it have a life of it own with a life of its own, grounded by the Mother's bulk which harness the sound of she own beat—the scrape, swish and thump of her own beat.

She watching the Mother, watches her beat those eggs—how they rise up in the bucket, their heavy, yellow beauty driven by the beating arm; she remember the burn sugar and she wonder, wonders if change ever come gently ... so much force or heat driving change before it. Her own change had come upon her gently ... by surprise ... in the night of blood ... by surprise ... over the months them as she watch her changes steal up on her ... by surprise ... the days of bloodcloth, the months that swell up her chest ... by surprise ... as she watched watching the swelling, budding breasts, fearful and frighten of what they mean, and don't mean. There wasn't no force there, or was there? too old and ancient and gradual for she or her to notice as she watch the Mother and wait, waiting to grow up and change into, but not like—not like she, not like her, not like ... she watching ... the Mother face shiny with sweat shines, she lips tie up tight tight with the effort of the beating arm, lips held in tight and she wondering, wonders whether she, the Mother, have any answers ... or questions. Did she have any—what were they?

Nobody tell she but she hand over the bowl, the bowl of washed butter she pass to the Mother who pour off the water and put in the white sugar—granulated and white she add it to the lumpy yellow mass, and without a word the Mother pass it back to her. She hand too little to do it for long—cream the butter and sugar—her arm always grows too tired too soon, and then she does have to pass it back to the Mother. But once more, one more time—just before the Mother add the eggs, she does pass it back to her again for she to witness the change—surprise sudden and sharp all the way from she fingers right up she arm along she shoulder to she eyes that open wide wide, and she suck in her breath—indrawn—how smooth the texture—all the roughness smooth right out and cream up into a pale, yellow swirl. When she taste it not a single grain of sugar leave behind, is left to mar the smooth sweetness.

She want it to be all over now—quick quick, all this mixing and beating and mixing, but she notice the sound change now that the eggs meet the butter—it heavier and thicker, reminding her it reminds her of the Mother—she and the Mother together sharing in the Mother's sound.

She leans leaning over the bucket watching how the eggs and butter never want to mix, each resisting the other and bucking up against the Mother force. Little specks and flecks of butter, pale yellow in defiance, stand up to fight the darker yellow of the eggs, and little by little they disappear until the butter give up and give in, yields—or maybe is the other way around—the eggs them give in to the butter. Is the Mother hand that win, the Mother's arm the victor in this battle of the two yellows.

The Mother add the dry fruit that soaking in rum and cherry brandy for months now, then the white flour; the batter getting thick thickens, stiffens its resistance to the Mother's hand, the beating arm, and all the time the Mother's voice encouraging and urging—"Have/to keep/beating/all the/time"—the words them heavy and rhythmical, keeping time with the strokes. The batter heavy and lumpy now, and it letting itself be pushed round and round the bucket—the Mother can only stir and turn now in spite of she own encouragement—but she refuse to let it alone, not giving it a minute's rest.

The Mother nod she head, and at last she know that *now* is the time—time for the burn sugar. She pick up the jar, holding it very carefully, and when the Mother nod again she begin to pour—she pouring the Mother stirring. The batter remain true to itself in how it willing to change—at first it turn from grey to brown—just like me she think, then it turn a dark brown like she sister, then an even darker brown—almost black—the colour of her brother, and all the time the Mother stirring. She empty the jar of burn sugar—her magic liquid—and the batter colour up now like she old grandmother—a seasoned black that still betray sometimes by whitish flecks of butter, egg and sugar, and the Mother arm don't stop beating and the batter turning in and on and over itself.

"How you know when it ready?"

"When the spoon can stand in it," and to show what she mean, the Mother stick the spoon in the batter and it stand up stiff stiff.

Her spoon like the Mother's now stood at attention—stiff and alone in its turgid sea of black. It announced the cake's readiness for the final change of the oven. Was she ready? and was it the Mother's cake she now made? Or her own? Just an old family recipe—the cake had no other meaning—its preparation year after year only a part of painting the house, oiling the furniture, and making new curtains on the Singer machine that all together went to make up Christmas. She had never spoken to the Mother about it—about what, if anything, the cake and the burn sugar might mean ...

It was its failure to arrive—the absence of the cake—even with its 'funny' smell that drove her to this understanding, this moment of epiphany as she now stood over her cheap, plastic bowl and watched the spoon. She looked down at her belly, flat and trim where the Mother's easily helped balance the aluminum bucket—not like, not like, not like her—she hadn't wanted to be like her, but she *was* trying to make the Mother's black cake, and all those buckets of batter she had witnessed being driven through their changes were now here before her—challenging her. And she *was* different—from the Mother—as different perhaps as the burn sugar was from the granulated sugar, but of the same source. Here, over this bucket—it was a plastic bowl—she met—they met and came together to share in this old old ritual of transformation and metamorphosis.

The Mother would surely laugh at all this—all this fancy talk with words like "transformation and metamorphosis"—she who had warned of change, yet was both change and constancy. "Is only black cake child, is what you carrying on so for?" she could hear the voice. They didn't speak the same language—except in the cake, but now the Mother was sitting looking at her make the cake.

"Look Mammy—look, see how you do it—first, the most important thing is the burn sugar—the sweetness of the cake need that bitterness—you can't have black cake without it." Mammy was smiling now.

"You was always a strange one."

"Shut up Mammy and listen," (gently of course) "just listen—the burn sugar is something like we past, we history, and you know that smell I always tell you about?" Mammy nod her head, "I now know what it is—is the smell of loneliness and separation—exile from family and home and tribe—even from the land, and you know what else Mammy—is the same smell of—"

"Is only a cake child—"

"The first ones—the first ones who came here rancid and rank with the smell of fear and death. And you know what else Mammy? is just like that funny smell of the cake when I get it—the smell never leave—it always there with us—"

"Is what foolishness you talking child—fear and death? Just make the cake and eat it."

"But Mammy that is why I remember you making the cake—that is what the memory mean—it have to mean something—everything have to have a meaning—"

"Let me tell you something girl," Mammy voice was rough, her face tight tight—"some things don't have no meaning—no meaning at all, and if you don't know that you in for a lot of trouble. Is what you trying to tell me, child—that it have a meaning for we to be here—in this part of the world—the way we was brought here? That have a meaning? No child"—the voice was gentler now—"no child, you wrong and don't go looking for no meaning—it just going break you—"

"Mammy—"

But Mammy wasn't there, at least not to talk to. She looked down at the batter. The burn sugar she used was some she the Mother had made earlier that year, accompanied by the high-pitched whine of the smoke alarm. She had made the batter by hand, as much of it as she could, even adding the green green corkscrew of lime-skin, although according to Mammy "these modern eggs never smell fresh like they suppose to—like those back home."

When they were done she almost threw the cakes out. She had left them too long in the oven and a thick crust had formed around them; the insides were moist and tasted like they should—the bitter, sweet taste perfectly balanced by the deep, rich, black colour. But the crust had ruined them. Obviously she wasn't ready, and only the expense of the ingredients had prevented her from throwing them out immediately.

It was the Mother's advice that saved them. Following her instructions by phone she cut all the crusts off the cakes, then poured rum over them to keep them moist. She had smaller cakes now—not particularly attractive ones either, but they tasted like black cake should, and without that funny smell.

Was that hard crust a sign of something more significant than her newness at making the cake? Was there indeed no meaning to the memory, or the cake, or the funny smell? She wanted to ask the Mother—she almost did—but she knew the Mother would only laugh and tell her— "Cake is for eating not thinking about—eat it and enjoy it—stop looking for meaning in everything."

She thanked the Mother, lowered the receiver slowly and said to herself—"You wrong Mammy, you wrong—there have to—there have to be a meaning."

CALLIGRAPHY OF A MARITIME KITCHEN

Liliane Welch

In their winter kitchen
a fiddle plays,
on the radio.

Smell of nutmeg, smell
of thyme.
Sunlight,
where her fingers strike
the dough.

Smell of exile, smell
of sage.
In mid-room,
suspended,
the man with
the gleaming face.

FROM *THEY SHOULDN'T MAKE YOU PROMISE THAT*

Lois Simmie

What ever happened to Saturday night? The kind of Saturday night you looked forward to all week because you knew you were going to spend it with someone you liked a lot, maybe even loved, someone who was looking forward to spending it with you, too. That kind of Saturday night.

The kids still have them. We're eating early so they can get on with the interesting part of living that goes on outside the house.

They have a Saturday-night look about them. Kate, fresh from the shower, a secret, inward look in her eyes as she drinks her milk, as if she is anticipating the moment when she will walk out the door and become the person she becomes out here, the warm, loving Kate I keep hoping to know again. Philip is starting to make the transition from his bloodhound-worried, will-the-axe-fall-this-week med student look to one of mere anxiety with moments of looking almost happy. And Michael is Michael; he can look happy even on Monday morning.

Next to Michael, across the table from me, is a tense person with the permanent look of a man with gravel in his shorts. Their father, my husband. Hugh. With him, in moments of passion or mechanical love-making, I conceived the other three; three times I have divided, like a cell, and there they sit. And we sit, Hugh and I, with a space much larger than a table between us.

I stealthily slide my chair back from the table and light a cigarette, holding it at an awkward angle and blowing the smoke over my shoulder in the faint hope that no one will notice.

"Eleanor, must you smoke while we're still eating?"

He didn't even look up; smelled the smoke, clever fellow. I push my chair away from the table. On my left, Philip drops a piece of macaroni from his fork as he peers myopically at a thick anatomy text beside his plate. Philip crams at all kinds of odd moments, a habit which annoys his father.

"Philip, must you read at the table?" Hugh asks, buttering a bun with quick, efficient movements. Must you smoke, must you read, must you say must you? Yes, the January blahs have struck again, and last year they lasted until June.

"Sorry, Dad," Philip answers mechanically, and nudges his glasses up, the better to see the page. Hugh returns to his supper with a martyred who-listens-to-me look, and Philip shoots a guilty glance at me. I smile brightly. I've been doing that a lot lately and am getting quite good at it.

"Pass the milk, Dad, please," Kate says. She has been aggressively silent all during the meal, and her expression tells us that she may have to eat with cretins but she doesn't have to like it. It is similar to her political-prisoner expression, in which she clamps her lips together and you know that come hell or high water she will not talk. This look is reserved for those occasions when we ask her where she is going or where she has been. There have been moments lately when I have felt a frightening, unmaternal urge to punch her out and make her talk: *All right my dear, hand over that microfilm that's hidden in your navel. We know it's there and we have ways of dealing with people like you, ha ha ...*

"What's the matter with her?" Michael interrupts this pleasing fantasy. He is peering at Kate through a mess of auburn hair. He views this particular mood of Kate's as a challenge.

"I don't know," I say. (What's the matter with all of us?) "We aren't exactly the Walton's, are we?"

"Now Maw," Michael grins, "you know Philip Boy is studying hard to be a big city doctor. And Paw is just tired from ploughing the back quarter because Grandpa got ornery and wouldn't pull the plough."

Thank God for Michael; at fifteen he isn't subject to the moodiness that Kate wields like a weapon. But then, Philip wasn't either, maybe only girls ...

Kate has washed her hair before supper, and it is drying the colour of dark honey with sparks of gold under the light. Long eyelashes shadow her good cheekbones, still padded with the baby fat she tries hard to get rid of. She'll be grateful for that bone structure someday, because no one is pretty forever. I never was, not the way she is; Kate will be beautiful someday. Beneath her soft blue sweater her unrestricted breasts are firm and full. We didn't have breasts when I was her age, we had bustlines with stiff, seamed bras that pulled our sweaters into a taut ridge.

"Did you make dessert, Eleanor?" Hugh asks. He runs a finger under the collar of his blue shirt, a Christmas gift from his mother; the colour isn't good, it drains his face, but his mother insists on buying him everything in blue. Mrs. Smith—Mildred, as she would have me call her—never got over having a blue-eyed boy.

"Collar too tight?" I ask.

"Naw." Michael drains half a glass of milk at a single swallow. "Paw's collar's not too tight. He was in a hurry to start ploughing and got his head through the buttonhole by mistake."

Philip and I laugh, and I get up to add Dream Whip to the dishes of congealed chocolate pudding on the counter.

"What are you talking about?" Hugh asks Michael. He always does that. Sometimes I talk to him for minutes before I realize that he isn't listening. Then he wants a rerun.

As I clear the plates, Philip smiles up at me, picking an oily leaf of lettuce from his book and dropping it on his plate. Kate hands over her plate without looking at me.

"Some of the customers are in a bad mood tonight," I say. "I bet I don't even get a tip from the one in the blue sweater." Kate sighs and raises her long-suffering eyes to the ceiling. "Oh God, Mother."

"I'm not your godmother," I say. I wish I was. Michael laughs, he loves any kind of play on words. But why did I say that? Why can't I just ignore it when she's like this, no wonder she tunes me out. Kate sighs again.

"You shouldn't sigh so much," Philip looks at her with clinical interest. "You're going to start hyperventilating."

"Oh, sit on it."

It's just a stage, I tell myself for the thousandth time, but if it's a stage, I sure wish somebody would pull the curtain.

Hugh looks distastefully at the chocolate pudding. Sorry, sir, we're fresh out of cherries jubilee but I could try to set fire to it for you; Varsol ought to do it.

"Tea?" I ask, and three cups shoot forward. I sit down and light another cigarette, remembering a black lung in Philip's anatomy text that I wish I'd never seen. Hugh has sent Michael to the living room for the paper and now disappears behind it; the daily newspaper is just one of the things Hugh hides behind. Must you read at the table, Michael mouths to the back of the newspaper.

"Are you still buying camomile tea?" Hugh must be talking to me; I am the one who charges up and down the aisles at Safeway's, firing things into the cart in a frenzy to get it done and get out of the place.

"Yes. Why? Shouldn't I be?"

"It contains a highly toxic substance and has caused several deaths." Good God, we've been swilling it down for years, especially the kids. I started buying it at the health food store. Hugh takes a special delight, or so it seems to me, in reading the tidbits of this nature aloud, and I'm never sure if he's doing it to keep us one jump behind disaster or if he just likes scaring the hell out of me. I decide to ignore it.

"Would you like to go to a movie tonight?" I address the question to a picture of Charles Bronson on the back page of the paper. *Deep dark voice rising from a diaphragm of heroic proportions: "I would go anywhere with you, Eleanor. You are a beautiful woman and I should know, I am surrounded by them. Raquel Welch is a frump compared to you. Just let me put my arms around you and hold you ...* Fade. Damn. Saw too many movies in my formative years where they faded after the clinch.

Hugh has not answered my question and I try again with the same result. His arm reaches around the paper, his hand closes unerringly on the handle of his cup, and he carries it to the other side without spilling a drop, as far as I can see. That's very good, it takes practice to master a trick like that. Michael gets the can of Dream Whip and smothers his remaining spoonful with an artistic swirl of lumpy cream. How can he eat like he does and stay so thin? Hugh's disembodied arm returns the cup to the saucer, and I wonder if anyone would notice if I got up and dunked a camomile tea bag in it. Still no answer from Hugh, might as well talk to the wall. I turn my chair a half turn and address the wall.

"How are you tonight?" I say. "Bored? Oh, that's too bad, I'd take you to a movie but I don't think we could reserve a whole row. You're what? Tired of wearing that yellow flowered paper? Well, I suppose we could get you some new paper, sort of a belated Christmas present. No, not stripes, not with your figure. You what? Had a rotten Christmas? Gosh, I'm sorry to hear that but mine wasn't so—"

"Eleanor!"

Hugh is staring at me. Philip and Kate, too. I have their undivided attention.

"What was that in aid of?" Hugh says, biting off each word as if he is giving a lesson in diction.

"I was talking to the wall," I say, and reach across the table for the entertainment section of the newspaper. Let him make what he wants of it, I always overexplain, it's one of the things about me that gets Kate where she lives. Like the other day at Safeway's when I wanted ten chops and they were only packaged in eights and I explained to the butcher that eight was not enough and sixteen too many and if I took two packages I'd have to freeze six and his eyes glazed over in the middle of it. Kate was mortified and has given me notice that she will never go shopping with me again.

I look at the theatre page. *Snow White and the Seven Dwarfs* has been held over from the holidays, sandwiched in among the usual fare of blasting guns, knifed bodies, exploding buildings and bare behinds. I look again; yes, it says Walt Disney—with a title like that you never know, it could be a new porno. It looks lost on the page, overwhelmed by the other ads, a faint little cry from the age of innocence. I would like to go but know that I won't. I scan the other movies and settle on *Earthquake* as the one possibility Hugh might consider if he gets around to considering any. Hugh and Philip are talking, which means that Hugh's vocal cords are working again and I would probably get an answer if I asked about the show, but suddenly I don't want to go. Not with him, anyway. *An Unmarried Woman* is on again. If my friend Gena were here I would ask her to go with me, but Gena is in Spain living it. I wonder what time it is there and what Gena is doing.

I pour a cup of tea and read Ann Landers to the accompaniment of cutlery scraping on stoneware. A woman is being driven crazy by her practical-joker husband who puts whoopee cushions in her chair when they have company and fills the toes of her slippers with strawberry jam. I hand the paper to Kate, who also likes to read Ann Landers. It is one small thing we have in common.

"Stop licking my ankle!" Kate yells, and I jump and drop the paper. "Mother, can't you make that dog stay away from the table. It's gross."

Gross. Still her favourite word. You'd think they'd have come up with another one by now. I look down at Jude, our ten-year-old Lab, who is eyeing Kate's ankle again. Michael swipes some whipped cream on Kate's ankle and Jude licks it, prompting a scream from Kate and a fiendish laugh from Michael.

"Dad! Do something about him."

Hugh frowns. He doesn't know what is going on, but it wouldn't make any difference; a frown is his first reaction to any outside stimulus, and has been for some time. I think I'd even trade him for old Jam-in-the-Slipper. I try to remember the last time I heard Hugh laugh. Was it a month ago? Two?

"Good supper Mom, thanks." Philip picks up his book and leaves the table and then I hear him talking on the phone in the hall. Saturday night, so he'll have to take Patti someplace he can't really afford. It's none of my business, he earns it, but the truth is I don't like the girl. I hope I'm not one of those nobody-good-enough-for-my-boy mothers. I could be, with Philip.

Kate has left the table without offering to help with the dishes. Her glare at Michael should have zapped him into oblivion, but he is absorbed in one of his favourite pastimes, reading the Classifieds. Hugh excuses himself and the television in the den goes on to the frenzied sound of "Hockey Night in Canada."

"Listen to this, Mom." Michael glances up to make sure I am listening. He is looking for a part-time job and this after-supper reading of the want ads has become something of a ritual. "Sensible secretary wanted for Doctor's office," he reads.

"You going to apply?"

"I'm not a secretary."

"Or sensible," I agree. "I wonder what the last secretary was like."

"Silly, obviously," Michael says. He scans the rest of the ads, his green eyes narrowed in a businesslike way, but he apparently finds nothing that requires no experience and pays ten dollars an hours. He drops the paper and stands up.

"I gotta go, Mom. Swimming practice. You know I'd love to help you with the dishes but the coach will kill me if I'm late."

"Ha!"

"Anyway, that's women's work," he says, ruffling my hair as he goes past my chair. He is trying to get a rise out of me but I am not up to it.

I pour the dribble of cold tea that is left and pick out a cat hair floating in it. The kitchen is a mess; cluttered table and counter top, cat and dog food drying in bowls on the floor, newspaper under the table—I should call Michael back to pick it up but it's nearly bus time. The house is quiet except for the muted roar of the television in the den and water running upstairs; Kate bathing again, when she just had a shower before supper? If I bought her a snorkel she'd never have to come out. She's got a date with Lenny, no doubt. Hugh will have a fit if he comes roaring up on his motorcycle again, and he will because it hasn't snowed since the last time he was here and it's just like spring. Kate is the one person Hugh worries about.

Hugh comes into the kitchen and plugs in the kettle for Sanka. He gives me a fishy stare and I know I'm going to hear about the talking-to-the-wall business. We never fight in front of the kids.

"That little scene at the dinner table was charming, Eleanor," he says, his back to me, searching in the cupboard for a clean cup.

"Thank you," I say politely and resist the urge to remove my feet from the chair. Stay cool; he hates it when I yell but hates it even more when I don't. He has found a cup. Why he couldn't use his teacup, which is still on the table, is beyond me; they're all the same, afraid of getting their own germs. He measures out the Sanka, still not looking at me, and I think of J. Alfred Prufrock measuring out his life in coffee spoons. I'm tired of watching Hugh measure out Sanka. I wish he'd get reckless and perk a pot of coffee for a change, or better still, get roaring drunk.

"It's getting damned tiresome, Eleanor. You've always got a bee in your bonnet about something."

Crash. Down come the feet from the chair. I wasn't born cool, like Hugh.

"Tiresome, is it? Well I'm sorry, I'm ever so bloody sorry. All I wanted was a simple answer to a simple question."

"What question?" He looks genuinely puzzled; maybe he didn't hear it after all.

"I asked you if you wanted to go to a show tonight."

"Oh, that." He drops the spoon to the sink. So he did hear.

"Yes, that. I realize it's not an earth-shaking question but—"

"You know I don't like going to late shows," Hugh cuts in.

"Well, it is Saturday night, you know. Remember Saturday night? It's the night when people throw discretion to the winds and stay up until eleven-thirty ... maybe even midnight."

"What's the matter with this plant?" Hugh is frowning at the ivy, drooping on the windowsill. It looks even worse than the last time I looked.

"I don't know what's the matter with it. What has that ivy got to do with this conversation?" A lot, I suppose, if you want to look at it symbolically, which I am overinclined to do.

"Have you been forgetting to water it?" He leans over it solicitously.

"No I have not been forgetting to water it. I water it, feed it, take it out for walks, I am even thinking of buying another ivy to keep it company. Will you stop changing the subject, damn it?"

"Mother said it was impossible to kill an ivy." He looks at me accusingly.

"Did she? Oh thank God, maybe there's hope. Do you think she could fly in to take a look at it?" I seem to recall that Hugh's father was the one who looked after the plants; if you ask me, Hugh's mother could kill an ivy just by looking at it.

"I should have known better than to try to have a sensible conversation with you." Hugh picks up his coffee, walks out of the kitchen without looking at me and goes back into the den, closing the door. I had to resist the urge to trip him as he went past my chair. Shit. If that was his attempt to have a sensible conversation, I'd hate to hear him try to have a foolish one. And as far as the damned ivy goes, he's the horticulturalist in the family, I'm not.

My stomach hurts; this man is going to give me an ulcer if I don't do something about it. But what? That's the burning question. Hugh was wrong about one thing; I do not have a bee in my bonnet, I have wasps. Lots and lots of wasps, a whole crawling, buzzing swarm of them. And I'm afraid of wasps.

Philip comes in to say good night, looking very nice in tan cords and a brown sweater, his black hair still damp from the shower. He shrugs into his suede jacket and searches the pocket for his car keys.

"What are you and Dad doing tonight?" he asks, filling a glass of water at the sink.

"Oh, I don't know. Maybe smoke a little pot."

Philip laughs. "Do you good, probably."

He downs the water and zips up his jacket. "You should go to a movie. *Midnight Express* is on."

A movie about prisons I don't need, but I don't say so. "We'll think about it. Have fun," I tell him, and he's gone. One by one they go, leaving Hugh and me to our Saturday night revels. And what will I do while Hugh watches the hockey game and whatever comes after that? Read? Knit? Look out the window? Slash my wrists?

I remember when it was different. When we would hire a babysitter, get all dressed up and go to a party, see each other as people saw us—our best-looking, most charming selves. I'd find myself seeing again the beauty of a well-shaped hand below a snowy shirt cuff; the attentive bend of his head as he listened to someone talk; the lovely, smooth plane of cheekbone and jaw. We'd have a few drinks, enough to get relaxed and horny, and he couldn't pay the babysitter and get her home fast enough to suit me. Sometimes we didn't even make it upstairs to bed.

And damn, it was good. Hugh went to work and I stayed home with the kids and our friends were doing the same; we were all busy, and tired a lot of the time, but it was a good life. I think about those two people sometimes, and I swear to God I don't know how they turned into us. You close your eyes to a lot of things when you're young and in love, or think you are. Of course it wasn't all his fault. It wasn't his fault that he was so damned beautiful I couldn't keep my hands off him. I wasn't the first to get married for that reason and I won't be the last. Of course there were other reasons too and if I sit here long enough I may think of one.

The two cats wander into the kitchen, check the dishes, turn accusing eyes to me, and begin yowling in unison for their supper. One of them is a cross-eyed Siamese called Mildred. She belongs to Gena, who says Mildred becomes neurotic when left at a kennel. Hugh is not amused that this creature shares his mother's name, and does not go out of his way to make Mildred feel welcome. He can't stand her mournful howling, and says she gives him the creeps staring her cross-eyed stare at him. Actually, it is impossible to tell what Mildred is staring at.

I begin slowly scraping bits of macaroni and burnt cheese from the inside of the casserole dish. I'll give the pieces of leftover tuna to the cats. When I started making this dish, I thought it was God and Mr. Kraft's gift to the weary weekend housewife; and now I am sick to death of it.

I scrape the greasy mess into the garbage, already full to the top with other greasy messes. Nothing tonight to go into Hugh's compost pail—his roses are picky eaters. Hugh grows roses and I sort the garbage, where's the justice in that, I ask. I have spent half my life bent over a garbage can, scraping, chipping and slopping. I have a recurring nightmare in which I am drowning in garbage. As I open my mouth to scream, it fills with coffee grounds, crushed egg shells, soggy cigarette butts and something soft and mouldy.

"CONVERSATION DURING THE OMELETTE AUX FINES HERBES"
Susan Musgrave

I met a dead man walking in the woods today,
myself a healthy woman, barely twenty-seven.
His breath smelled of white wine and wild
strawberries—the finest white wine and the
ripest fruit.

It was intoxicating.
Our dogs gambolled together,
one black and the other white.
I told him the story of my whole life,
as far back, that is, as I chose to remember.
He wanted to know if I would be his wife—
I said under the circumstances
that would be impossible.

We reached the road that led to my house—
he kissed me, very gently.
He wanted to take me all the way,
after another kiss I agreed and invited him in
for a small meal and some light music.

One kiss more and I was on the floor
when who should walk in but my husband,
a horticulturist.
He had a cauliflower from the garden
he wanted to show me but when he saw us lying there
he said your dog is in the garbage
fighting with another dog

I just thought I'd mention it.

My dead man revived quite quickly,
aroused by being caught in such a compromising position.
I assured him my husband abhorred all forms of violence
and poured us each a stiff drink in the drawing room.

"Your wife tells me you enjoy gardening,"

our guest says, as I slip off into the kitchen to make
a good cheese sauce for my husband's cauliflower.
Small talk has never interested me
particularly.

MRS. A. (FRANCE) BORN IN 1940 (CAME TO CANADA IN 1970)
Inge Israel

My grandmother was in the kitchen from from early morning till late at night. A First World War widow, she was confined to her wheelchair during the last 20 years of her life, but ruled undaunted with an iron hand. Her widowed daughter-in-law, my aunt, did the cooking.

I can still see them in my mind's eye: they were so alike, two tiny, strong-willed women and, all around them, those huge saucepans. They had to be big; there were 16 of us round the table at mealtimes, including the bakers and two seamstresses. The seamstresses worked right there in the kitchen—doing the household mending. The kitchen led straight into the bakery and then, into the shop beyond. The connecting door was always kept open, so we could see the customers come in. My grandmother missed nothing of what went on and everything worked like clockwork.

The shop was a general store that carried anything and everything—even cartridges for guns. They were made right there. I used to watch all the parts being pressed together: the lead, the wad, the powder, the charge and the fuse. It was fascinating. I didn't give any thought to the product.

I didn't help in the kitchen until we moved to the island of M. From then on, my mother was away for several months at a time and, during her absences, my father expected me to feed the family. I was 11 then and somehow managed. Preparing the dog's food was one of the most time-consuming things I had to do. My father prized his dog highly and was very fussy about what he was given. Meat, rice and other ingredients had to be cooked especially for him and blended in just the right proportions. Once, I forgot to buy the meat. By the time I noticed, the shops were closed. Very nervous, I looked in the cupboards to see what I could concoct for the dog's supper that would satisfy my father. I found a tin of corned beef and mixed it with rice and vegetables. It looked all right to me and he ate it with his usual relish—but it turned out to have been spoilt! The dog became very ill with botulin poisoning and it was touch and go whether he would live. My father's anger haunted me, not just for days or even weeks. It stayed with me for years and years. Strangely enough, it wasn't my almost having killed his favourite dog, that made him angry. It was the fact that I hadn't done my shopping properly, that I'd been so forgetful! Whereas in my mind, the kitchen became the place where life was at stake.

MRS. P. (GERMANY) BORN IN 1928 (CAME TO CANADA IN 1958)

Inge Israel

Every Friday there was the smell of the carp that my mother cooked. As soon as I smelled it, I ran out of the house because I was allergic to it and it made my lips and tongue burn and swell. But on other days I loved being in the kitchen. In a recess, in one corner, there was plush sofa which figured very large in my life. It was while sitting there that I learned how to tie bows and interweave strands of hair into braids. It was there that I petted the cat and listened to gossip, or discussions about food and linen.

One day I came into the kitchen from the street where I'd been playing and was overcome by what I saw. Some of my aunts and uncles and my parents were there, all in a highly emotional state. I didn't really understand what was going on, but everyone kissed and hugged me, as if for the last time. The words "going away" kept recurring. It seemed everyone was going away. I didn't know how or where—they all seemed to be very vague about it themselves. Until then, "going away" had always been a happy thing—it had meant going on holiday or on visits to relatives in other places. But this time they made it sound sinister. All the women, including my mother, were crying. I didn't know why, but I cried too.

The kitchen table was laden with the week's grocery shopping. Vegetables and fruit were spilling out of bags. I wondered why my mother had bought so much if we were going away. We soon left, and I was puzzled by the fact that no one was carrying any suitcases, as we always did when we went on holidays.

Only later did my mother explain that she had deliberately piled groceries on the table, to make it look as if we would be back shortly. Then, when the Nazis came to the house, they would not realize that we were leaving Germany and it might give us time to cross the border into other countries. It did.

WAITING

Leona Gom

after the meeting the women go to lunch.
the waitress watches, awkward on her high heels
like some odd hoofed animal, while we decide.
a smile is stapled on her face like part

of the menu.   small puckers of burns
are splattered part-way up one arm.   she is
all of us, our first lurch into the working
world, learning to sell service, it is
where we begin, before we become
the women who go to meetings, the ones
who are never satisfied, we are pains
in the management ass, we're as tired of it
as they are, but we still keep asking,
saying, 64% is not enough, the waitress
is still who we are, coins rattle
their judgements in her pocket.
when she brings us our bill she asks
is there anything more that we want.

FROM *MEMORY BOARD*
Jane Rule

David picked up the menu and was looking at it. "Your mother always said she had to choose what we ate all the time; so it was my job when we went out. How do you feel about it?"

"Not the same way at all," Laura answered. "At home I eat what Jack and the boys like. I want that extravagant crab salad."

"Good for you," David said.

He ordered a hot meal for himself so that he wouldn't have to be bothered with anything more than a snack in the evening.

"You know," Laura began, "after we talked about Aunt Diana that night, I was shocked, but when I talked it over with Jack, I realized I was partly shocked because you weren't. And he told me I might be shocked by a lot of things you think because there was so much in our family that was never talked about. Do you think that's true?"

"Jack thinks you girls were very sheltered, and I suppose, insofar as we could, we did shelter you."

"But even from what you privately think is right and wrong?"

"Not so much that as not admitting I didn't put as many things in those categories as your mother did. If it had been my job to teach you to brush your teeth, I probably would have talked more about cavities and less about moral obligations."

"You used to say, sometimes even to Mother, 'Don't be so quick to judge'."

"Well, your mother thought she could spot an embezzler by the color of his tie and a lecher by the shine of his shoes. I'd hate to admit to you how often she was right."

"How do you really feel about Aunt Diana, Daddie?"

"Much as you feel about your sister, I suppose," David answered, "loyal, critical, protective, puzzled. But, if you mean how do I feel about her relationship with Constance, it awes me a little. It always has."

"You don't feel there's anything wrong with it?"

"No," David said, "but I've known quite a number of gay people. You do in my line of work. It's my experience that the only people shocked by homosexuals are the people who don't realize they know any."

"That would certainly include me," Laura said.

"Yet you have," David said. "Do you remember Peter Harkness, for instance?"

"Peter who used to work with you when we were kids?"

"That's right."

"But Mother loved Peter. We all did."

"He transferred to Toronto. He thought it might be easier in a bigger city," David said. "One thing I've always regretted is that those of us who cared about Peter didn't make it easier for him here. He never brought his lover with him when he came to see us, and Casper was a delightful man. You would have liked him, too."

"Mother would have known then?"

"Knowing how she felt ... "

"Couldn't you talk to her ... just the way you're talking to me?"

"I should have tried," David said. "I keep knowing that these are the conversations I should have had with her."

"Weren't you ever shocked?"

"No, not in the way you mean. I wasn't a very worldly young man. If I thought anything about homosexuality, I thought only extraordinary people were, like Shakespeare and Michelangelo."

"Shakespeare!"

"Some of the sonnets are written to a young man," David said. "When Diana came home with Constance, I was shocked to know they were in love, physically shocked. And maybe even a little jealous—of Diana or of Constance, I don't know. But D. was so extraordinarily happy and clear about going into medicine that it would have been stupid to question her choices. I found it hard to be around them, and not just because they made your mother uneasy. I envied them, I think, and I felt shut out. Before Diana left, I was the most important person in her life. We didn't have any gradual time to get used to the changes."

"So you never really had any doubt they were lovers, even at the beginning?"

"I didn't put it to myself in those terms," David said and then added, "until your mother did."

"Maybe she never knew how you really felt," Laura said. "How many years have I been married to Jack? And I didn't know until just the other night what an ignorant bigot he thought I was. Oh, he put it much more tactfully than that, but that's what he meant."

David shook his head.

"But I am," Laura insisted. "Except when anything touches me, I don't think for myself. I just soak up attitudes like a sponge."

"We all do that."

"You know," Laura said, "I don't even know how you vote."

David laughed. "I haven't voted for years."

"Mother always did."

"I know. That's why I didn't. I don't have strong political views. She did, and it seemed silly for me to cancel them. Anyway, closet socialists haven't a hope in our riding."

"That's exactly what Jack said you were!"

On the way home, David made a mental note to buy Laura some fresh crab for Christmas. It would be too smelly under the tree, but he could wrap it in Christmas paper and put it in the fridge. Men must almost forget what they don't like to eat, not having been served it all their married lives.

"What extraordinary creatures you women are," he said.

Laura glanced over at him quizzically, but he simply shook his head, not knowing quite how to put what he meant. Had Constance and Diana ever actually said they liked fish?

David grew nervous as Wednesday approached. He decided to make a halibut and cheese casserole ahead of time and then realized it would be too awkward to carry on the bus. Never mind, he'd take a cab. He didn't want in this first attempt to do anything complicated at the last minute nor anything that would make a great mess of his sister's kitchen. Broccoli and boiling potatoes would be good with the cheese sauce. He could take one of the bottles of plum wine Jack had given him, which would provide a natural opening for him to talk about that family. Dessert? He couldn't use frosted grapes because of the boycott. Would that surprise Laura, too? Patricia didn't believe in boycotts or picket lines, either.

David should explain to Laura that it wasn't that he didn't take Patricia's views seriously enough to disagree with her. It was his own views he usually didn't take seriously enough. But what about dessert? What had they served him? A strudel, he remembered, one of the sort you could get frozen at the store. Ice cream. That might melt. A melon. There were still melons in the store.

On Wednesday afternoon, when David had finished the casserole, he rummaged around in the storeroom and found an old picnic hamper they used to take down to the beach for supper when the girls were small. When everything was assembled, he folded his own chef's apron in on top, a bit of costume to give him comic courage for his part.

From the moment David walked through the door, he felt a different sort of space open up to him. Diana kissed him, as if casually, on the cheek, and there was a look of real recognition on Constance's lovely face. The living room seemed in warmer light, or perhaps the Mozart just finishing colored it, ordering even the fire to dance. Above the mantle a painting by Gordon Smith, which on past evenings David had tried to avoid looking at because of the weight of its images restrained by straight lines as taut as moorings, tonight seemed full of an energy to break free. He knew the room now and no longer had to sense his way around it to avoid those areas which belonged by custom to either Constance or Diana. At first the chair he now thought of as his own had also warned him away from occupancy, but by now whatever ghost of prior claim had been routed.

On his way by cab, he'd stopped at a liquor store; so he carried not only the heavy basket but a paper bag which contained a bottle of gin, a bottle of scotch, and a bottle of Frangelico, a liqueur the flavor of hazel nuts, and of lighter sweetness than most.

Diana went with him to the kitchen, a room he had not been in until now. He felt privileged to be introduced to the ample twenty-year-old appliances and relieved to see that the stove was old enough to speak English, "left front, right front," rather than the dots and squares of international sign language. And there was a dishwasher, freshly emptied and ready.

"Tell me what cooking things to get out," Diana said.

"Just two pots for the potatoes and broccoli."

"Do you want a steamer for the broccoli?"

"Excellent," David said, already fiddling with the oven control.

"It bakes hot," Diana warned him.

"The casserole isn't temperamental," David said as he placed it on top of the stove, ready when the oven was heated.

The bottles and glasses and ice bucket were already on the kitchen table, but David added his own contributions.

"All that wasn't necessary," Diana protested, but there was no rebuke in her tone, rather pleasure at his excesses.

"Why don't you make the drinks while I set this up?" David suggested.

The vegetables were already prepared for cooking. He only needed to ask for a dish for the raw vegetables he'd added at the last minute, thin carrot sticks, cherry tomatoes, small bursts of cauliflower, each in a separate plastic bag to make arranging quicker. The casserole was in the oven, and David had twenty minutes to enjoy his drink by the fire.

"I must say you're a very relaxed cook," Constance commented.

"Have you always cooked?" Diana asked.

"No," David said. "Patricia kept the kitchen pretty much to herself. I learned when she was ill. I wanted to keep her home from hospital as much as I could. And anytime she was up to it, we had friends over for dinner. I discovered I liked cooking. You have to keep enough of your mind on it to make it a real distraction, and it's such a nice, straightforward thing to do for people, to feed them."

"I don't mind it," Diana said, "but I have no flair for it "

"Oh, I don't either," David said. "Patricia said a man should only be allowed to cook if he was brilliant at it. That was before she got sick. Then I demanded the right to be ordinarily good at it."

"I think I begin to see what you mean by 'ordinary'." Diana said, smiling at him.

She hadn't flinched at the mention of Patricia, and now she conceded him a point before he was really aware of having made it. It was as if an emotional minesweeper had been through the room and left it free of all the dangers he'd worked so hard to avoid on other evenings when nearly everything he said had the potential for irritating Diana and confusing Constance.

They even *looked* festive, and David realized they had, in their own fashion, dressed up for the occasion, Constance in a bright red silk blouse which reflected in her intently lively face, trimly cut grey trousers with soft grey leather shoes to match. Diana wore over brown slacks a densely and darkly patterned long tunic which must have been made for her because it hung so becomingly over her ample body, giving her handsome authority. And even her brown shoes were not obviously orthopedic.

"You both look wonderful tonight," David said. "You should always wear red, Constance, and D., you look as if you might burst into song."

"Well, we decided we ought to clean up our act a bit for the occasion," Diana admitted.

"I've even got on earrings," Constance said in a tone of surprise, one hand at her ear.

"Shall I fix you another before I go into my act?" David asked, holding up his own glass.

He returned in his apron, and both women laughed as easily as he had hoped they would. There had been too little silliness in their relations so far.

"I'd think you were a professional if it weren't so clean," Diana said.

"Oh, traces of blood and old soup would be overdoing it," David said.

His last act after he brought the food to the table and lighted the candles was to take off his apron and throw it over the back of a kitchen chair.

"This wine," David said, as he poured it first into Constance's and then into his sister's glass, "is made of plums by my son-in-law, Jack."

"Why, it's very good," Constance said, "not sweet at all, and it doesn't really taste of plums until after you've swallowed it."

"He's very proud of his wine," David said, as he began to dish up the food. "Actually, the whole family is because Laura and the boys all help. They pick the fruit, bash it up, and, when it comes time to rack it off and bottle it, they're on hand, too. Jack handles the chemicals and timing."

"It is good," Diana concurred. "You know, that's always been something I wanted to learn to do. Is it difficult?"

"I don't really know," David said. "I've often been down in the wine room to admire one stage or another; so I have some idea of how it's done, but I don't know how hard it is to make it good."

"Ask him," Diana said.

"This fish is marvelous," Constance said. "Who is this fine fellow? Did we hire him?"

"I'm David, Diana's brother," David said with the mock formality which he hoped conveyed his pleasure in introducing himself to Constance, as he did sometimes half a dozen times during an evening.

"Of course you are," Constance said, smiling at him in a way to make him wonder if it had been a joke at herself.

"I wonder," David said, not wanting to lose his opportunity, "if I could bring Jack and Laura over one evening for a drink. Then you could ask Jack yourself about wine making."

"I'm ready if you think they are," Diana answered much more directly than David had expected she would.

"I'm never ready for anything," Constance said. "Diana uses me as an excuse, you know, because I'm so unpredictable, but I'm not a bad bluff when I need to be, am I?"

Diana smiled at her. "You're very good at it if no one calls you on it."

"Let me remember something for you," David said. "When you had your gardening business, you did spring and fall cleanup for Jack and Laura. They have a house on Thirty-sixth Avenue near the bush. They already know you. Laura even remembers the board of seed packets you had in your truck to help you remember the names of the flowers."

"I remember that. You made it for me," Constance said, turning to Diana. "I remember things so much better than people."

"What does Jack do?" Diana asked.

"He's a chemist," David said, "attached to the university, but he doesn't teach very often. He seems mostly to be on loan to industry or government. At least part of what he does has to do with toxic wastes."

"Then perhaps he'll be able to tell me whether the Tory feds' taking thirty-five million out of the cleanup program is revenge for Ontario's returning a Liberal government," Diana said with some relish.

"Perhaps he can," David agreed. "He doesn't talk much about such things with me since I retired from the news."

"Do you really not even read a newspaper?"

"No," David said. "My excuse is my eyes, but I wouldn't if I could."

"Have they got that bad?"

"My doctor doesn't seem to think so, but I can't keep reading. What I miss is not being able to hole up on a winter day and waste it with a good novel."

"Have you tried talking books?" Constance suggested.

"Not yet, but it's time I started thinking about constructive solutions. It's so much easier to complain."

Diana asked for a second helping of fish, perhaps simply to please David, but it occurred to him that it must have been a long time since she'd tasted anything but her own cooking. They never went out to dinner. What they might have had sent in could be nothing but standard junk food. David had been so clearly directed by Diana's first letter not to think about the confinement of their life but of their contentment that he tried to turn his mind away from such speculations, but they came to him more and more regularly.

David found himself plotting as he loaded the dishwasher. If Jack and Laura were a success, Constance might grow accustomed enough to them ... but he mustn't push ahead farther than he was. If Diana got the faintest whiff of anything afoot that smelled to her of liberation, they would all be banished. Whatever enriching of her life came to her through David must be seen as as much of a gift to Constance as to herself. And so it should be.

David could see for himself what real contentment they shared, and unlike David, Diana did read, evidence of that everywhere, not only on the bookshelves. There was always a book by her chair, and there was a book on top of the flour canister here in the kitchen. They were not novels. She read history and biography, and she also had a taste for those scientists like Loren Eisley who could make their fields intelligible to the general reader. Obviously Diana was used to turning to books rather than people for sustained thought. On the whole, books would be more satisfying, but it was too narrow a human world they had retreated into. As far as David could find out, they had very few friends.

He had to go on being careful and patient. Though he knew tonight marked a new acceptance of his place here, the reassurance must not make him reckless.

"Will you try Frangelico with coffee?" David asked when he'd finished cleaning up.

"Why not?" Constance said.

"But you mustn't get us into bad habits," Diana said.

"I don't think we'd make riproaring drunks," Constance said. "We'd be more inclined to stupor."

"By the way," David said as they sat enjoying their liqueurs, "I've got my own phone. Remind me to leave you the number."

FROM *THE TIN FLUTE*
Gabrielle Roy

Where was the young man who had given her so many admiring glances yesterday? Florentine found herself watching out for him eagerly, although the memory of his bantering tone was still fresh in her mind. The noon-hour rush was in full swing.

The fever of the store communicated itself to her in a kind of irritation, mingled with a vague feeling that some day all this seething activity would come to a stop, and her purpose in life would become plain. It never occurred to her that she might meet her fate elsewhere than here, enveloped in the pungent aroma of caramel, between the tall mirrors pasted over with strips of paper announcing the day's menu, and to the crackling report of the cash register, a sound like the very expression of her frantic hopes. For her this place summed up the pinched, hurried, restless character of her whole life in Saint-Henri.

Her glance slipped past the five or six diners she was serving toward the front of the store—the restaurant was in the rear of the five-and-ten—and in the play of light on the nickeled panels, the glass and the tinware, her peevish smile attached itself aimlessly to sparkling objects here and there.

Her duties as waitress permitted her no leisure in which to dwell on the memory of what had happened yesterday, but in fleeting moments the face of the unknown youth came back to her again and again. Neither the clatter of the dishes, however, nor the shrill voices of the other waitresses as they called out their orders, could rouse her completely from her reverie, which from time to time sent little tremors over her face.

Suddenly she felt disconcerted, almost abashed. While she had been watching out for him among the crowd at the swinging doors of the store, the young stranger had seated himself at the counter and was calling her impatiently. She moved toward him, pouting. It was annoying to have him take her by surprise just as she was trying to remember his features and the tone of his voice.

"What's your name?" he snapped.

More than the question itself, his mocking, almost insolent manner put her back up.

"You'd like to know, wouldn't you?" she answered scornfully, but without finality, not as if she wanted to silence him. On the contrary, her tone invited a reply.

"Come now," he urged, with a smile. "My name's Jean. Jean Lévesque. And to start with, I know yours is Florentine ... It's Florentine here, Florentine there ... Florentine's in a bad temper today; you can't get a smile out of her. You see I know your first name. I like it, too."

Then he changed his tone imperceptibly and gave her a rather stern look.

"But you're Mademoiselle who? Won't you tell me?" he insisted with feigned seriousness.

As he moved his face closer she could read all the impudence in his eyes. Today for the first time she noticed his firm wilful jaw, the insufferable mockery in his dark eyes, and she was furious with herself. What a fool she was to have bothered about a fellow like that! She drew herself up so sharply that her little amber necklace rattled.

"Next you'll be asking me where I live and what I'm doing tonight," she said. "I know your kind!"

"My kind! What kind?" he mocked, pretending to look over his shoulder to see if there were someone behind him.

"Oh, you!" she burst out in vexation.

And yet that common, almost vulgar touch placed the young man on her own level, and displeased her less than his usual language and behavior, which, she felt dimly, put a distance between them. The smile returned to her face, a petulant, provocative smile.

"Okay," she said. "What'll you have today?"

But he continued to stare at her impudently.

"I hadn't got around to asking you what you're doing tonight," he answered. "I wasn't in that much of a hurry. Usually it takes me at least three days more to get to that point. But as long as you give me a lead ... "

He threw himself back in his revolving chair and spun around from side to side, his eyes narrowing as he examined her.

"Well, Florentine, what are you doing tonight?"

He saw at once that his question had upset her. She caught her lower lip in her teeth to keep it from trembling. Then with a businesslike air she pulled a paper napkin from the container, unfolded it, and spread it out in front of the young man.

She had a thin, delicate, almost childish face. As she struggled to get a grip on herself the small blue veins in her temples swelled and throbbed, and the skin of her cheeks, smooth, and fine-textured as silk, was drawn toward the almost transparent wings of her nose. Her mouth quivered from time to time. But Jean was particularly struck by the expression in her eyes. Under the high arch of her plucked and penciled eyebrows, her lowered lids concealed all but a hint of bronze, but he could see that the eyes were watchful, and yet extraordinarily eager. Then the eyelids fluttered open and the whole pupil became visible, full of a sudden iridescence. A mass of light brown hair fell over her shoulders.

In observing her thus intently the young man had no definite purpose in mind. She surprised him more than she attracted him. He had not planned his last words: "What are you doing tonight?" They had sprung to his lips without his being aware of it; he had tossed them out as one might test the depth of a pool with a pebble. However, the result encouraged him to go on. Would I be ashamed to go out with her? he wondered. And then the idea of restraining himself for such a reason, considering how little he cared for the girl, annoyed him and put him on his mettle. With his elbows on the counter and his eyes glued on Florentine, he waited patiently for her next move, as if they were playing a cruel game.

She stiffened under this brutal examination, and he saw her more clearly. Catching her reflection in the mirror against the wall, he was startled to see how thin she was. She had pulled the belt of her green uniform about her waist as far as it would go, but her clothes still hung loosely on her slender body. The young man had a sudden insight into the narrow life of such a girl afloat in the turbulent eddy of Saint-Henri. Like all the girls of her type, she had probably been scorched by the meager little fires of fictitious love in the pages of cheap novels.

His voice became sharp, incisive.

"Do you come from around here, from Saint-Henri?" he asked.

She twitched her shoulders, and gave him a rueful smile by way of response.

"Me too," he added with mocking condescension. "So we can be friends. No?"

He noticed that her hands were shaking, hands as fragile as those of a child; he saw her collarbones sticking out above the opening of her blouse.

After a moment she leaned sideways against the counter before him, trying to hide her uneasiness under a sulky air, but he no longer saw her as she was. He saw her in his mind's eye all primped up, ready to go out in the evening, her cheeks plastered with rouge to conceal her pallor, cheap jewellery rattling all over her skinny person, wearing a silly little hat, perhaps a veil, her eyes glittering with make-up, a flighty girl, bent on making herself attractive to him, Jean Lévesque. The thought went through him like a gust of wind.

"Then you'll come to the movies with me tonight?"

He was aware of her hesitation. If he had taken the trouble to state his invitation more politely, in all likelihood she would have agreed immediately. But that was how he wanted it: hard and straight, since he was inviting her in spite of himself, against his will.

"All right then. It's a date," he said. "Now bring me your famous special."

Whereupon he pulled a book out of the pocket of his overcoat, which was lying on the seat beside him, opened it, and immediately became absorbed.

A flush spread over Florentine's cheeks. She hated him for his power to disturb her deeply one moment and put her out of his mind the next, dropping her as if she did not interest him in the slightest degree. And yet it was he who had made all the advances in the last few days. She had not taken the first step. It was he who had aroused her from the torpor in which she had taken refuge from the disappointments of her daily life, it was he who had awakened her from the deep trance where suffering could not touch her, where she was alone with her undefined hopes. It was he who had given form to those hopes, now clear, sharp, tormenting as desire.

As she looked at him her heart contracted. She found him very attractive. To her he seemed the well-dressed young man, unlike the others she waited on at the store, dull salesmen or workmen with greasy sleeves and collars. He was a cut above the silly youths she ran across at the neighborhood cafés, juke-box joints where she and Pauline and Marguerite went dancing in the evening, or idled the hours away in a booth, nibbling chocolate and giggling at the boys as they came in. Yes, he was different from anyone she had ever met in the course of her timid, uneventful life. She liked the way his thick black hair bristled up from his forehead; at times she had to suppress an impulse to seize his wild thatch with both hands.

She had marked him out the first time he had come to the five-and-ten, and had schemed to wait on him. Now she longed both to run away from him and defy him at the same time, to prove that he meant nothing to her. Some fine day he'll try to make a date with me, she had said to herself with a strange sense of power in the hollow of her chest. And then she wondered: Will I take him up?

The other girls, Louise, Pauline, Marguerite, all except Eveline, who acted as manager, were always teasing each other about making dates with young men at the lunch hour. Pauline claimed that you ran no risk if the fellow called for you at home and took you to the movies. Then you had plenty of time to look him over and decide whether you wanted to continue seeing him. Louise had even become engaged to a young soldier she had first met at the restaurant. Ever since the war began the new recruits had shown considerable eagerness to form attachments before they went off to training camp. Friendships sprang up quickly and under altogether novel conditions, some of them ending in marriage.

Florentine dared not follow her thought through to the end. Even while reading, the young man wore a quizzical expression at the corners of his mouth that baffled her.

I'll show him, she thought, pursing her lips. I'll show him that I don't give a rap for him. But curiosity to see what he was reading overcame her momentary vexation. She leaned boldly over the open book. It was a trigonometry textbook. The queer shapes of the triangles and the polygons, the heavy black print of the equations, all of it totally incomprehensible to her, made her smile inwardly.

"No wonder you're so fresh," she said, "when you read stuff like that!"

And tripping over to the order phone she called out in a shrill, affected voice: "One thirty-cent special!"

Her piercing tone carried all over the restaurant, and Jean Lévesque felt the blood rush to his face. His eyes flamed darkly for a moment with resentment. Then pulling his book closer, he bent over it again, his face in his strong brown hands.

New customers were crowding around the counter in the usual noon-time rush: a few workmen from nearby factories, store clerks from Notre-Dame Street in white collars and felt hats, two Sisters of Mercy in gray cloaks, a taxi driver, and several housewives breaking up a shopping tour with a cup of hot coffee or a plate of fish and chips. The five waitresses were on the go constantly, colliding with each other as they darted about. Sometimes a spoon fell to the tiled floor with a hard, ringing sound. A girl would pick it up in passing, toss it into the sink with a grumble, and tear off with lowered head, leaning forward to gain speed. They were always in one another's way. Their brisk staccato steps, the rustle of their starched blouses, the click of the toaster when the toast popped out, the purr of the coffeepots on the electric plates, the buzzing of the kitchen phone, all these made a sustained clatter, a vibration as of summer, distilling vanilla flavors and sugary scents. One could hear too the stifled rumble of the malted-milk shakers, like the interminable murmur of flies caught in glue, then the tinkle of a coin on the counter, and the ring of the cash register from time to time, like a period. Although the swinging glass doors at the entrance to the store were covered with frost in fantastic patterns, here, in the rear, the heat was tropical.

Marguerite, a big fat girl whose naturally rosy cheeks seemed to be smarting from cold even in this hot-box, had charge of the ice-cream. She would lift the lid of the cooler, plunge the scoop into the cream and empty the contents into a large glass dish. Then she would squeeze a bit of whipped cream out of a pastry bag like toothpaste from a tube. Over this went a spoonful of marshmallow, caramel or some other syrup, the whole surmounted with half a maraschino cherry of an alluring red. In a twinkling the fifteen-cent sundae special, a favorite with the customers, appeared on the table, like a cool fountain on a burning summer day. Marguerite would pick up a coin, deposit it in the cash register, and return to create another sundae special. The procedure never varied, but Marguerite took as much care and innocent pleasure in building her masterpiece the tenth time as the first. Of peasant stock, she had only recently come to stay with relatives in the city, and she had not yet lost her illusions about the cheap glitter of the quarter. Nor was she surfeited with the wonders or the sugary smells of the restaurant. The animation, the flirtations going on about her continually, the atmosphere of pursuit and recoil, of halfhearted compliance, of temptation and daring, all this amused and delighted her, without troubling her deeply. "Florentine's boy-friend," as she designated Jean Lévesque, had made a great impression on her. And as Florentine went by, carrying a plate loaded with food, she could not help making her usual remark, with a hearty, kindly laugh:

"Your boy-friend's giving you the eye, eh?"

And licking her moist lips, which always seemed to taste of marshmallow, she added:

"I think he's smart, Florentine, and a good-looker, too. He'll come around soon."

Florentine gave her a smile of disdain. Marguerite was such a fool. To her life was a perpetual round of sundaes, at the end of which each one of the girls, without half trying, without lifting a little finger, would find herself engaged, married, in her wedding dress, with a little bouquet in her hand. As she approached Jean Lévesque, nevertheless, Florentine had the not unpleasant thought that the young man must really have shown her some special attention since a girl as dumb as Marguerite had noticed it and could tease her about it. But what a funny way to pay attention to a girl, she thought with a start, her face clouding over.

She placed the food in front of Jean Lévesque and waited for him to speak to her. But absorbed in his reading, he only murmured "Thank you," without raising his eyes; then, absentmindedly, he took his fork and began to eat, while she lingered, irresolute, finding his silence even harder to bear than his odd way of talking. At least when he spoke to her she had the pleasure of a retort. She walked slowly back to the other end of the counter to watch the hot dogs on the grill. All of a sudden she felt unutterably weary and depressed. Her body drooped against the edge of the sink.

God, how tired she was of this job! Waiting on rough men who made insulting advances, or else others, like Jean Lévesque, who made sport of her. Waiting on people, always waiting on people! And forever smiling, when her feet felt as if she were walking on a bed of hot coals! Smiling when her aching legs were about to give way with exhaustion! Smiling no matter how enraged and miserable she might be!

In repose her face took on a look of stupefaction. For the moment, despite her heavy make-up, the image of the old woman she would become was superimposed on her childish features. By the set of her lips one could foresee the wrinkles into which the fine modeling of her cheeks would dissolve. All youth, confidence, vivacity seemed to have fled from her listless, shrunken eyes, leaving a vacuum. But it was not only the mature woman that appeared portentously in Florentine's face; even more shocking were the marks of inherited debility and deep poverty that she bore. These seemed to rise from the depths of her somber pupils and spread like a veil over the naked, unmasked face.

All this passed in less than a minute. Abruptly Florentine straightened up, and the smile returned of itself to her rouged lips, as if it responded not to her will, but to some powerful reflex, the natural ally of her challenge to life. Of all the confused thoughts that had run through her mind, she retained only one, a conviction as clear and sharp as her congealed smile, that she must immediately stake everything she still had to offer, all her physical charm, on one wild chance of happiness. As she leaned over the counter to pick up some dirty dishes, she caught a glimpse of Jean Lévesque's profile, and it came to her with the force of a staggering blow, that whether she wished it or not, she could no longer be indifferent to him. She had never been so ready to hate him. Save for his name, which she had just learned, she knew nothing about him. Louise, who was a little better informed, said that he was employed at a foundry as an electrical machinist. From Louise too she had heard that Jean never went out with girls, an item that had intrigued her. It was a pleasing thought.

MOTHERING SUNDAY
Audrey Thomas

Hail Mary, Wounded art Thou among Women. That's what it means, doesn't it? Still, there in the French: *blesser*: to harm, to hurt, to injure, to wound. "*C'était une blessure grave.*" *Se blesser*, to wound oneself. In English we can trace the word back to *blod*. Hail Mary, Blessed art Thou among Women. All the Marys bleed.

I am sitting here in this elegant French restaurant, surrounded by mothers and daughters, mothers and sons, mothers and sons and daughters-in-law (who probably rang up and made the reservations and arranged for the corsage). Not many children around but then, this is not the kind of restaurant where one takes young children, not North American children. Families with young children are no doubt celebrating at McDonalds or Smitty's Pancake House. I had forgotten it was Mother's Day when I arranged to meet Lydia at this restaurant and I, as usual, was early. She, as usual, is very late. Perhaps she missed her train connection and will not show up at all. I'd hate to miss her—I'm hardly ever in Toronto—but sitting here surrounded by all these mothers is dreadful. Should I hold up a sign: I AM A MOTHER TOO or stand up and show my stretch marks? But then they would think—if she is a mother where are her children. Why is she sitting alone, corsageless, with no one to buy her an "Anna M" cocktail, concocted in honour of Anna M. Jarvis, the founder, foundress, of Mother's Day in America. A little card on the table explains the whole thing. Anna M. never had children of her own and died penniless and almost sightless, in a quiet sanitorium in Pennsylvania at the age of eighty-four. She devoted her life to Mother's Day and to her blind sister Elsinore. I wonder about Anna M.'s mother, naming a daughter Elsinore, especially when the other gets a common-garden name like Anna M. Something rotten in the State of Pennsylvania! "In a quiet sanitorium in Pennsylvania." I've worked in those places. Hardly quiet. Noisy and rowdy and the old ladies coming out with words you could hardly believe, throwing balls of shit at one another, puddles forming under their chairs. I didn't mind. I was young; it would never happen to me. I wonder if there were at least two pennies in her purse, to shut her eyes.

Several of the mothers are sipping their Anna M. cocktails—they look like Harvey Wallbangers. I am sipping white wine. I wish Lydia would hurry up; she and I are good together, we make each other laugh, egg each other on to say more and more outrageous things. The young no-hipped waiter (imagine *him* giving birth to anything bigger than a jelly baby) would be very quickly demolished by a combination of Lydia and myself. When he suggested an Anna M. cocktail Lydia would ask for a Bloody Mary or a glass of milk, as being more appropriate for the occasion. Who first came up with *that* name, Bloody Mary? Businessmen ordering it on airplanes without batting an eye, if you gave them a glass of blood they'd reach for the sick-bags pretty quickly. Or Bloody Caesar, who, like MacDuff, was from his mother's womb untimely ripp'd. No blood, no bloody Mary in the nativity accounts. Immaculate conception, immaculate delivery. We mothers know better, sitting here with our legs underneath the table, sitting here sipping our drinks, picking at the expensive food. Blood. A heavy word. No blood for months and then a lot. All cleaned up, fresh straw, fresh clothes, by the time the Wise Men came. In our church there was always a Christmas pageant and a white gift service on a Sunday near to Christmas. Children playing Mary, Joseph, Angels, Shepherds, Wise Men. "Gifts" for the poor children wrapped in white tissue paper and laid in front of the *tableau vivant*. All the parents loved it, especially the mothers. All the mothers wanted their daughters to be Mary.

The other day a young woman told me that, if you have the sperm, you can impregnate yourself with a turkey baster. I laughed and laughed and she was hurt. It was the turkey baster that made me laugh. Birds still involved in immaculate conceptions. Turkeys, such large, stupid delicate birds. Raised to be devoured at times of Thanksgiving and praise. Hail turkey, blessed art thou amongst birds. Turkeys didn't come completely dressed (meaning undressed) when I was a kid; my mother sat in the kitchen pulling out pin feathers after she had singed the bird, holding it over a candle, turning it. The kitchen smelled of burning feathers.

What do you do? Squirt the turkey-baster up you and then stand on your head for half an hour? (I don't really want to know.)

Where is Lydia? She knows the name of the restaurant, why hasn't she phoned? I could leave and go back to my hotel and wait for her there I guess; but I'm hungry and it's Sunday. We can't buy a bottle of wine and take it up to my room.

There are two carnations, one red, one white, in a crystal vase at each table. I wonder why it's always carnations—something to do with incarnate perhaps? The Word made flesh? That's another memory from my childhood, women standing on the church steps after the Mother's Day service, women wearing corsages of white or red carnations. White if the mother were dead, red if she were alive. But I don't remember us ever giving our mother a corsage of carnations. She probably told us not to. She had a habit of telling us not to do things: not to give her candy on Valentine's Day, not to give her birthday presents. I think now it was her way of asking for them but I didn't understand then. I understand, now, a great deal more about mothers. How they weren't, perhaps still aren't, supposed to ask for things. Unless they are useful of course—washing machines or microwave ovens.

Was Jesus a difficult child? Did he have tantrums, nightmares? Did he wet the bed? The Holy Ghost, the Original Big Bird, descends on her while she is sleeping and she wakes up pregnant.

(Lydia would probably add, "with maybe a spot of bird shit on the sheet.")

The original surrogate mother, and she doesn't even get to name the child. I wonder if he was a cult figure after he started preaching, he and his gang of twelve. We know that Mary and the other women followed him and the apostles "ministering" to them. But did the women steal bits of his clothes or snippets of hair, did they fight over who was going to bake the bread or hand him the honeycomb?

I think I'm a little oppressed by all this Mother's Day stuff, special drinks, special flowers. Shall I stay or shall I go? I don't feel neglected. When I get back home next week there will be cards and probably flowers, promises of breakfast in bed. But just now, alone in a room full of mothers and children I have some sense of what it must be like for those who never had children, never had that clear proof of their femaleness. See! See! I'm a mother; at least I've done something with my life. "Ocular proof."

Lydia's mother died when Lydia was fifteen. We talked about it once, whether that affected her and if so in what ways. Lydia ran the house for her father and younger brothers and sisters. She remembers her mother in a red-checked housedress with a big white collar. And a bib-apron over that. She was English and she wrote a lot of letters home. In England Mother's Day is called Mothering Sunday. She always wanted to send flowers to England on Mothering Sunday but never had the money. She died without ever seeing England or her mother again.

Lydia remembers that her mother cut out poems by Edna Jacques and stuck them on the ice-box. Lydia was very funny about Edna Jacques the Poet Laureate of the Kitchen. Even Nellie McClung admired her. The poems had titles like "A Mother at Night," "Small Deeds" and "A Mother at Christmas." I grew up in the States and had never heard of Edna Jacques. I think we had a similar person called Audrey Alexandra Brown. Last year Lydia found a copy of one of Edna Jacques's books in a second-hand store and gave it to me for my birthday. It's full of words like *bounteous* and *mayhap* and *laughter-tinted song*. The trouble is that although I laugh at Edna Jacques she does understand something about the wonder of watching little children. I've saved locks of "golden" hair, and early drawings, even a Mother's Day card from one of them

HAPY M
OTHERS DAY

I have no right to laugh at Edna Jacques.

I grew up during the Second World War. Mothers hung little silk flags in the front-room windows: a blue star on the flag if your son was fighting overseas, a gold star if he were killed or missing in action. Gold stars, in elementary school, were given for the very best, perfect or nearly perfect work. The teacher hung gold-star papers around the room. So gold-star mothers, and they were called that reverently, "Gold Star Mothers" were the perfect mothers, who had given up their sons to make the world safe for democracy. They would not have seen how they were part of the great myth, the old lie.

(I have just ordered another carafe of the house wine and some pâté and bread. "My friend has been delayed," I said brightly to my pretty no-hipped waiter. He doesn't believe me; he thinks I am a rejected Mother. He frowned when I ordered more wine. "It's all right," I said. "I'm not an alcoholic, I'm a drinker." Lydia will be here soon—she has never let me down. None of her children are at home any more, but perhaps she had an unexpected long distance call and missed the train. You can't cut people off when they've taken the trouble to phone you long distance.)

I went to see my mother last week. She is eighty-nine years old and lives in a cosy apartment in a senior citizens' complex near Boston. Every time I visit now she gives me something or shows me something that is "coming to me" after she dies. This time it was two lovely fans, one red silk and lace, one black, which had belonged to her mother. They are very fragile and I shall have to open them out, mount them and then frame them. Very fragile and very exotic, from a time when women carried fans on special occasions. We looked at old photographs and talked a bit, drank tea. Then in one box of bits and pieces which are to go to my sister and me my eye lit on a large oval frame, of some beautiful dark wood, cherry wood perhaps. I asked her what had been in it—I didn't remember it at all. She said, "Oh, do you want it? I was going to throw that away." I asked again whose picture the frame had been for. She said, "My mother." I asked her where the picture was now. She said, "I tore it up." Then she took the frame out of my hands and put it away in a drawer. She didn't offer the frame to me again.

Why? What had her mother done? I had always thought she loved her mother. I couldn't ask. It was something terrible and private, something between mothers and daughters, something Edna Jacques would never write about, the dark side of all this, the wounds as well as blessings.

"Well," I said, "I must be going now." I could see that she was tired, that we had run out of safe things to talk about. I have wounded her many times; she has wounded me. We don't talk about this. We send each other letters and greeting cards and presents; we worry about one another. We wonder.

"Well," I said, putting on my coat, "I'll write to you soon." We kissed the air and then she walked me to the front entrance. She looks twenty years younger than she really is. Women her age move through the over-heated halls pushing walkers or shaking with those hidden winds of extreme age.

"Goodbye," we call to one another through the glass door. "Goodbye, goodbye."

Here's Lydia coming in, shaking her umbrella, laughing. She sees me and waves.

"Don't have the Anna M. Jarvis cocktail," I say as she sits down, breathless and laughing. She smiles up at the waiter.

"What about a Bloody Mary?" and winks at me.

One of the mothers is celebrating her birthday. Her waiter is bringing in a cake. The whole restaurant starts singing, takes up the tune.

"Happy Birthday, Dear Mother, Happy Birthday to you."

"I missed the train," Lydia says, then looks around. "My God, look at all the mothers!"

"Did you bronze your children's baby shoes?"

"No, no. We didn't have the money. But I was definitely of the bronzed shoe school."

"Me too. Did you save things?"

"Boxes and boxes of things. But I wasn't as bad as a woman up the street. She saved all her children's milk teeth in a glass jar on the kitchen counter."

"Listen Lydia, I want to tell you something that just happened with my mother. Only let's order first. I'm starving."

We signal the waiter to bring the menus. I pour another glass of wine and begin.

RELIQUARY

Nadine McInnis

Crosses are vanishing
from above doorways and beds.
Instead, each of us lives
with a humming vault in our kitchens
the size of our own coffin,
its perpetual drone
like the ringing in the ears
of explorers before they freeze
or go mad.

This is a tall icy country
either in total darkness
or total light
with no line possible between.
Children put eyes to the slit,
pull slowly
to catch light snapping on.
Never are they thin or fast
enough

and the few who crawl inside
hurtle into their past
are found curled, blue chicks

feathered with frost, in eggs
that will never hatch,
and only melons
withering in the crisper
remember how they got there.

We were warned about this
even before kidnappers,
yet our crayon suns and flower bursts
were drawn to its magnetic pole.
Like mothers before me
I tape her feverish colours onto white,
a shrine to her quick vision,
a prayer that cold also preserves.

THE DISGRACE

Mary di Michele

But there's one disgrace we've never known:
we've never been women, we've never been nobodies
–William Arrowsmith.

A skinned rabbit sits in a bowl of blood.
In the foetal position, it dreams its own death.
I swell quietly by the warmth of the kitchen,
like the yolk that is the hidden sun of the egg.

The old wives and the new wives
are blabbering their gossip,
the intimate news of an idle moment.
Their children are blowing like seedclocks
in the yard. They are safe for now.
The girls are ready to be caught by the first
breeze and nestle in the grass.
Some of the boys will surely jump the fence.

On the first day I forget to play.
I am cramped in the corner like a snail
climbing the wall by the stove,

trying to sip camomile tea
with a blanket wrapped around my middle
to ease the first labour of blood.

My mother and aunts are eating
the unwritten stories of their lives
which they wipe away without a thought
and the crumbs on the table.

They all dine on the rabbit stew
together, good wives, good women, with an inch
of red wine in a glass carafe
brimming with secret desire.

This blood is anonymous and at times
gives off such a strong odour
that lettuce wilts in the hand,
and the new wine turns sour,
and the onions cry in their sleeves.

My blood is knotted into worry beads.
Deliver me, if you can, from the cup
that I am, the spilling cup.

The ladies, *le signore*, are ready to tell their stories
as my mother serves coffee and cake.
When they crack the whip, out of their closet
mouths come dancing familiar skeletons:

uncle Gianni, who made his wife suffer, (poor saint),
bringing in his mistress to live with the family,
her own room, for the slut, and the wife to play
the servant; he sent the children to school
with extra money for lunch, such a treat,
when their mouths were so tightly shut
they could not open them to bite,

Maria Luisa, my father's youngest sister,
went mad in her sleep,
she tried to kill the elder, Chiarina,

with a knife, she cut her own throat
in a hospital a week later
and I'm named for her,
the consequences to be revealed by my scars,

while Giuliano was named in the spirit
of a good joke by my father
after a Sicilian bandit
hung on the day he was born;
my mother didn't laugh then, but she smiles now,
as she tells the anecdote,
cutting another piece of cake,
pouring another cup of coffee,

Filomena, whose husband was sent to Ethiopia
to provide a repast for crocodiles;
she married his death,
then pined a long unrequited love for her own tragic dust,

and finally, of most recent interest, Anna's wedding night,
viewing for the first time the mysteries of a man's primordial appetite
for the blood he must claim as his own
and on the next day she had to study
the art of walking.

I am marking the day of my first bleeding
in red pencil in my work book.
I am ten years old.
Already they are plotting
a new and disquieting role for me.

Here is my initiation into the confessional of the kitchen
(will they stop my thinking?).
The men are in another room drinking grappa, smoking cigarettes,
while the hockey game minds its own business on the TV screen.
The men check the scores often, remembering their bets,
postulating the outcome of the series from a sophisticated knowledge
of the history and statistics of the league

Through the open doorway I can just see

a shadow school of the men's heads
bobbing like buoys in the white wash.
They think they are creating life in the living-room
while the dust of the outside world still clings to their shoes,
but even men, when they are common,
men of the trades: barber, plumber, electrician,
who make the real world because they lay
bricks for it, do not write their own histories.
They tell similar stories as the women
but with authority, with the weight of the fist
and the cry of the accordion.
However you will not read in books
the exploits of these family
men.

SEPTEMBER
Sharon H. Nelson

for Diana Ellis

We are thirty-five at least.
Unfooled by calendars, we know
the year starts now.

The first cool August night
we sniff the wind, perk up ours ears,
think of new shoes, new lipstick at the least,
think of pickles, jams, preserves,
the year turning, cycling,
an oval shape, a bow that draws
always to September, all ways from September.

We laugh into the phone
from opposite sides of the continent.
I have convinced you to freeze eggplant.
You have me hooked on canning tomatoes.
We are too busy, what with the year picking up its feet
and the harvest to put up, to write.

We correspond, like spoons, an old pattern,
and laugh at the anticipation and the work,
and wonder when will we be old enough
not to greet Labour Day Monday like two kids
almost holding their breaths with excitement
wanting to get to kindergarten,
wanting the leaves to fall so we can pile them,
wanting the clear beginning, the clean beginning,
the new jars washed and stacked and ready,
the new fruit gathered, washed, pared, prepared,
everything there, the year in all its fullness,
the year in all its favour,
the year fat and round and fleshy,
full and lush. We will be thin and colder than we want
quite soon enough.

FOOD
Bronwen Wallace

for Marty, and in memory of Jessie Glaberman

Begin where we all do
with milk. How I still like mine
straight from the cow, driving out
to a farm each week, through fields
dotted with Holsteins, the only landscape
I can understand. My dad says the stuff
that's really worth drinking's
squirted warm and straight from the teat
and I believe him, just as I know
his city life's the instrument
that pries that memory loose
from the history he hated, the narrow
caked path from pasture to barn
and the blistered sun at his neck
day after day. Just as I know
for me, too, it's more nostalgia
in the glass, as even the smallest farms
become factories, the cows hooked up

from udder to tank to truck
to pasteurization plant
and on (in just a few years, probably)
to what's become of beef or chicken, things
kept in buildings never opened to the sun.

Food. Or the politics of food. You see
I did learn what you tried to teach me, you two:
your house on Bewick Avenue, your table
where a union man from Bologna might meet up
with a woman from a feminist commune
in New Mexico or a kid from Oregon, on the road
for the summer, who'd heard about your place,
everybody hashing out their differences
over meals that went on for as long
as our appetites lasted and the wine held,
Jessie at her end, pushing her glasses up
with one hand, passing food with the other,
Marty at his, finger out, making some
theoretical point someone had overlooked,
living up to the joke we made of his habit,
as soon as he'd open his mouth, we'd laugh
and call out, "and then Lenin said ... "
loving him for it.

Just as I love you, Marty,
for that whole hot summer
when you taught me to read *Capital*
of all things, as I thought no book
could be read, cold theory warmed
by those hands of yours, the lines
that oil and grit had eaten there
part of what you were saying, just as the smell
that clings to hair and clothes gives off
the heat of a factory, the noise,
fights with foremen, meetings, wildcats,
always at it, "The working class
is revolutionary or it is nothing" –Karl Marx.
"But not a slogan," I can hear you saying,
"a statement of fact; either we'll manage

to change things or we'll disappear."
your finger out as you say this, the other hand
reaching for chicken or coffee, refusing
to separate food from what it costs.

Jessie, in the only snapshot I have
your mouth's open, of course, your face
blurred by what you were saying at the moment,
words freed as carelessly as the smoke
from your cigarettes, filling the air
and disappearing. At your end of the table
everything was always up for grabs;
"Spit it out," you'd cry, when we fumbled
for a straighter phrase, "don't be afraid
to say what isn't finished, what seems
crazy. Just say what you can;
we'll look at it together."
And we would. All of us,
peering into those dimmer, tangled
regions theory doesn't open on
and though I bet we'd argue still
about what got said those nights,
we'd all be hearing your voice
angry, laughing, leading us into them.
Oh, Jessie, it drives me crazy
knowing you died alone,
how you must have hated, struggled
and in another movement,
taken it, knowing we are always
alone in this, your shrug
—I can see it still—what I have
of you, your work
that widening of the wild zone
between the power to fight what happens to us
and the power to accept what is.

It's late afternoon in the old house on Bewick.
In the kitchen, someone's poking around
trying to decide what to have for dinner,
while in his new apartment

Marty follows an argument about Poland
from the stove, where he's making
his famous stir-fry, a recipe
I'll use myself tonight, with tomatoes
and zucchini from my garden, snow peas
from the guy in the third stall, second row
at the market, soy and ginger, Basmati rice
from I don't know where, and while we eat
I'll tell my family how I heard
on the radio today the future's
in kiwi fruit, a new type, hairless
and the size of a grapefruit, more vitamin C
than a dozen oranges and easier to ship.
I'll tell them how scientists
have developed an apple tree
shaped like a telephone pole, no branches,
fruit straight from the stem, for easier
picking and bigger profits and while we
take this in, women I've eaten with
are adding sour cream and red wine
to their pot roasts, as Jessie
taught them to. For all I know,
they're quoting Lenin and Marx,
maybe the FBI is right, subversion
is everywhere.
Oh, I know, I know, it's late
in the century, the revolution hasn't come,
the hungry go on, food costs the earth,
the work of getting enough
breaks us all, I know, I know,
but even so, the tomatoes
are red, ready to sting
my tongue, the smell of their vines
clings to my arms, Marty talks
with his mouth full, his finger
urgent as always, a woman throws
a handful of parsley in the pot, a taste
brings me up to her, and it's that
I'm telling for the moment, just
for now.

HOSTAGE
alice lee

today as any other day she sits in the morning silence of her kitchen the radio on the window sill an outside voice she reaches out and turns it on the announcer's voice echoes in the silence of the room echoes in the silence in her head the body found three days ago on the north side of the city has been positively identified as the remains of a woman reported missing several years ago however authorities are having difficulty locating next of kin her name will not be released her name will not be released emily thinks what a son-of-a-bitch it is the relatives have moved away if they had any brains in their heads they would have stuck around in case the woman was found emily thinks she should claim the body so at least the woman can have her name released but realizes this is a crazy idea she doesn't know what the hell has come over her to think such a thought she reaches out and changes the station

COOL WHIP AND OLD LACE
Lynn Neumann McDowell

It could be a Vermeer painting: A young woman in the large, spare kitchen with sunlight streaming onto the table, her chastely covered head inclined over a cutting board. Two other women, older, sit on a wooden bench against a white wall with yellow beans in the laps of their ankle-length blue-and-green plaid skirts.

Into this rustic tranquility bursts a young girl with a Swifts Premium box almost half her weight, rattling at "Tante Annie" in rapid German. Another young woman comes in waving an envelope pulled from another case lot of boxes, asking questions in loud German. One of the older women, Annie, turns to me with a puzzled look. "You wouldn't put cake mix in the freezer—would you?"

A man in his 60s, bearded and sturdy, strides in with a plastic-wrapped roast beef under his arm and begins recounting his adventures in comparison shopping to Annie, his wife and Head Cook of the Tchetter Hutterite colony, northeast of Calgary. "Did you bring vinegar for the beans?" asked the second elderly woman, his sister-in-law Susie.

"Ach," says The Boss, spying the stranger in his kitchen beside Susie. He sets down the roast and with a twinkle in his blue eyes extends his hand in welcome. "Everything is sour around here. Even the husbands!"

So this is the man who had answered my phone query about visiting the colony kitchen with the question, "What's to know about cooking? If you have potatoes, you peel them. If you have cabbage, you cook it." Today, after satisfying himself that I'm not yet another government employee (there's been a lot of them around lately), he goes off to run the rest of the farm, leaving the roast beef in Annie's custody.

Between the two of them, the sisters have for more than 20 years efficiently taken charge of not only the groceries The Boss brings home, but also the sauerkraut crocks, the walk-in fridge and freezer, a restaurant stove, an army surplus deep frier, a dining room for children aged 6–15 (younger ones are fed at home with food from the communal kitchen), an adult dining room, an arsenal of modern food preparation equipment, and a separate baking house with a commercial oven. In the context of this farm, it is no mean kingdom, replete with a big ring of keys.

"I was the Head Cook for 10 years and then my mother got a stroke," says Susie. "So I took my keys up and told the minister that I had to take care of my mother." Susie had noted with slight emphasis that she was of the *Tchetter* family. "So he took the keys and gave them to her." After five years, the interim arrangement started to feel permanent and Annie stayed on after their mother died. "Otherwise," Susie snapped a bean with a small grin, "I would still be there!"

Annie pours me a glass of ice tea and resumes her place at her sister's side. She explains that it is the baptized men of the colony who elect persons to fill the full-time positions which are held for life, such as Head Cook, Gardener, Kindergarten Teacher, and even Minister. Susie's present position is Selector of Cloth. Both sisters have two assistants at any given time. Both tell The Boss what is required, and he does the purchasing.

The girl who first burst in with the day's purchases flops down on the bench beside Susie. She rolls a long blonde forelock that has escaped from her kerchief and tucks it back in place. Miriam is celebrating her ninth birthday today. She kicks off her black lace-up shoes, and with a single efficient tug whips off her socks. Reclining against the wall with bare feet bouncing on the linoleum, Miriam recounts with cheshire smugness how she escaped garden duty this morning when her mother called her in to help in the kitchen.

Since it's her mother's week to help prepare the menu arranged by Auntie Annie, Miriam is also available to cut mountains of vegetables for stirfry (yes, and to grate cheese for pizza), to run errands, and to clean up after the 62 individuals who are fed from the kitchen three or more times a day. Miriam, who has performed these kitchen odd jobs since she was six, fills me in on the order of the daily kitchen routine and corrects her aunt on the details of a dietician's visit and advice after a colony-wide cholesterol test. ("I guess we know how to cook for ourselves," sniffs Annie when I ask whether the dietician recommended the margarine they are using in place of butter.) When she turns 17, Miriam's name will be slotted into place on the cooking and baking sides of the old wooden duty board that hangs near the bread slicer, and she will take one week in 10 as assistant cook, another week as baker along with the rest of the women.

There's doubtless a good reason why these women—aside from the Head Cook—retire from regular kitchen duty at 50. Relatives from larger colonies chide them that cooking for 62 is "just playing house," but Miriam's mother looks decidedly harried. She's been in the kitchen since 6:00 with her husband, who made the coffee and rang the bell, which began the day-long procession of adults and children through the kitchen complex. Breakfast dishes were barely done when the Kindergarten Teacher brought in the three-to-six-year-olds for their morning snack, and men, peckish from heavy outdoor labour, trickled through intermittently for a piece of bread or a cup of coffee while the noon meal was being prepared. True, the men do serve the food and clear their own places, and her husband sweeps the floor and sometimes helps with the dishes. But there are still pickles to make before supper, lunches to take to the harvesters, and supper must be ready to go right after evening church. Then kitchen clean-up and preparation for farmer's market in Calgary tomorrow, and if she makes it to the end of the week, she'll be glad to get back to the garden.

The garden. Perhaps more than the kitchen, this is the domain of women, the place where secrets melt in the sun and flow between the rows with never a man to know. Except for maybe the Gardener's husband, whose vocations are governed by the seasons and his wife's job. He is, in effect, assistant gardener in the summer and German school teacher in winter, ensuring that the children learn their prayers and Bible verses in the proper tongue.

"I would rather work in the garden than the kitchen," says Dora, a newlywed transplanted from Smokey Lake. She raises the old saying about the way to a man's heart, but says she doesn't believe it. She and the other women laugh at the suggestion that a woman is somehow less a woman if she can't cook. "There's some women who would rather work outside. It's just their nature," she explains, and some do get a reputation as better cooks than others. But cooking is part of a woman's job, just like gardening and butchering the legions of ducks and chickens every fall. It's a responsibility Dora feels toward the people who would be inconvenienced if she didn't shoulder her allotted part in communal life.

Causing such inconvenience may in fact be unthinkable. Like the grace that is said before and after each meal, the allotment of kitchen jobs and working together has spiritual significance. The text of Acts, Chapter Two, is fresh in the mind of Susanna, another newlywed who admits she'd rather be sewing with her new Pfaff machine. "We keep all things common, and everybody's together," she volunteers. "This is what the Bible says we should do."

The bonds forged in the communal kitchen are strong. "When you work with somebody, always you feel closer to them," observes Dora. Though she was not raised in this colony, she feels a special tie to Auntie Annie who is on duty every day, the constant in the hectic social centre of the colony. "To me she is just like our best friend. I can get along with her, and we do everything together. I think that's the way you're supposed to be with her. Otherwise, it's no use looking forward to cooking!"

And they do seem to look forward to their time with Auntie Annie: Dora the gardener, Susanna the seamstress, Susie the former Head Cook who at 65 still bustles about fixing lunches, laughing with her sister about their weekly childhood trips to the colony cobbler with shoes worn thin by "skating" on the creek in winter, about the tangy-sweet taste of pincherries touched by frost, about wild rosehip skins savoured like oranges.

A family—a colony—history is being passed on daily. There have been times of plenty, times to flee, times to begin again. But always there has been enough for God's children, the apple of His eye. "My grandfather used to say," Susie looks beyond, slightly above our heads, "when there is cabbage, and when there is potatoes, you will never go hungry." No, they have never been hungry.

These women know their lives are different; some of their favourite new recipes come from *The National Enquirer,* and they hawk their down pillows and saskatoons at city markets for a little personal pin money. But life on "the outside"—life without kitchen duty, where they would buy their own cloth, choose their own full-time job—is for most only a curiosity.

"Sometimes you think about it," says Dora. "But I don't think I would like it. You are born in here, and being by yourself and alone—I would never like it. If I'm at home alone for 10 or 15 minutes, I go and find somebody to talk to. Or if you want to go see a doctor, you just ask The Boss, and he pays all the bills, and you don't have to worry who will pay them." If she is sick, another woman will take her kitchen duty, and her husband will be fed. When she has a baby, another woman will be assigned to cook special food only for her.

"It's like the radio," chimes in Katie, the Kindergarten Teacher. "If you never had one, you never miss it."

I gather my things to leave, and Miriam presents me with a pound of frozen saskatoons, which I said I'd like to have for my father. He shares Susie's fondness for the wild fruit of a homestead childhood, a flavour uncluttered by modern luxury and taste innovations. A taste of the past. At two dollars a pound cleaned, I figure it's a fair deal.

"They make very good pies," says Susie. "You cook them with a little sugar and starch, and when the pie is done," her eyes light up with the thought, "you put a little Cool Whip on top!"

KITTENS

Irene Boisier

Twenty years later, Adelina still had nightmares about that house in the little village of Maipo. She saw herself walking from the entrance door through the string of rooms, crossing them one after the other, doors opening for her as she slowly went on, dragging her feet, hoping for something to happen that would pull her back, back to the entrance, back to the front yard, back to the road and the open air. But no, she had to keep walking through each and every room until finally, at the end of the house, she reached the kitchen.

She remembered that kitchen very well, every single detail in it: the grey, smoky walls, the grimy counters, the kerosene stove sitting on top of an old table, the strings of onions hanging from the ceiling, the barrel of honey in one corner, the tiny table and chairs for the children. And more than everything else she remembered the sink: a tin basin on a huge wooden table with a hole in it to let the water drain down to the *canaleta,* a small ditch carrying the used water through a hole in the wall to the rear yard.

How long had they lived in that house? The first time Francisco took her there she even liked it. At least she liked the way it looked from a distance, a long, horizontal shape, old and heavy with its Spanish tiles, marking the entrance to the village at the bend of the road. And she liked the honeysuckle and the palm tree and the entrance, and the rose bushes and the heavy wooden fence. They had been lucky to find a house and a piece of land in that little village where everybody had lived in the same place for generations. She would get used to living there; she could sew, she could raise chickens. Perhaps after a while they could buy a piano.

She felt so ignorant at that time about so many things. She still looked at the world with a feeling of wonder, and marvelled at other people's capacity to know everything and have all the answers. Like her mother, for instance, insisting that she had to marry Francisco.

"A good girl like you, so pretty ... It is the best way, Delita, it is the only way. Francisco is a good man; he will look after you."

Yes, he had looked after her. And they were happy with the two little children. But Adelina sometimes had this vague feeling of emptiness, deep down inside her, a hollow spot that, mixed up with her wonder, resulted in confusion and insecurity. So many things she didn't know!

If at least she could find a friend! But no, the first contacts with the village people had not been very promising.

"Buenos dias, señora, do you need someone to do your laundry?"

"My son is a good gardener, señora, he could look after your rose bushes ... "

"Patroncita, could you give me a coin or two? I haven't had any lunch ... "

Instead of a piano they got Chabela. It was Francisco's idea to hire a maid and Adelina gladly agreed: she was tired of doing all the house chores, tired of the children, tired of being alone. Chabela just came one day and knocked on the door, quiet, small, humble. Adelina savoured for the first time the feeling of being the *patrona.*

"How old are you?"

"Seventeen, señora—entering into 17, that is."

Younger than she, Adelina liked that.

Chabela was given a room opening to a small yard flanking the kitchen and close to the *casucha,* the toilet shed. A water tap and a barrel in the middle of the yard became Chabela's toiletry area, used also to wash the children when they got soiled from playing with the mud or the ducks in the back yard puddle.

Francisco seldom saw all this. He would rather stay in the sitting room where the windows were big and sunny, or with his bees in the orchard outside. Only the women and children stayed in the entrails of the house.

One of the things Francisco missed was the kittens. It was Chabela who first saw the cat hiding in Adelina's wardrobe. She made a bed for it with an apple box and old rags; she installed it in a corner of the kitchen, close to the children's table. The cat disappeared for a day and came back holding a kitten by the neck with her teeth, disappeared again, came back with another, until four kittens were deposited in the newly made kitten box. The cat then went to sleep in the box, and softly purred as eight small paws kneaded on its belly and two children touched the kittens and petted the mother with their clumsy and excited little hands.

It was not long after the kittens were born that Chabela approached her one day.

"Señora—Puedo hablarle?"

As Adelina went to the kitchen, Chabela withdrew and leaned for support at the old counter table. Small, shy, she looked tense and anxious as she waited for the *patrona* to address her. She was looking at the floor, fighting her tears.

"What is it, Chabela?"

"I can't tell you, señora. I don't know how to tell you ... "

From the superiority of her 23 years, Adelina looked at her. She could guess what the problem was, couldn't she? She had said something like that herself some time ago, hadn't she? That was why her mother had refused to keep her in the family home anymore, wasn't it? And made her marry Francisco.

"Tell me, Chabela ... are you by any chance pregnant? Is that it?"

"Yes, señora"

"Are you sure?"

"Yes"

"Have you seen a doctor yet?"

"No, señora."

The young girl didn't cry after all, she didn't move. Adelina felt very awkward, somehow the girl's shyness had tuned in with her own and made them both silent, strangers to each other, a young girl and her *patrona.*

The *patrona* took over.

"Do not worry, Chabela, it is going to be all right. We'll go to see the doctor tomorrow, have him do a checkup on you. You can go to sleep now."

"Yes, señora."

Adelina left the kitchen. She felt proud of herself. Her mother would have screamed scandal and kicked the girl right out of the house. It was surprising that

Chabela had been willing to tell her at all, so soon, when the pregnancy was not more than ... how long? She had forgotten to check that. Not too long, surely; the belly didn't show. She would ask her in the morning when they went to see the doctor. It would be a long walk from the village to the town, over an hour, unless they could catch the school bus; they had to get up very early and be ready in time to prepare breakfast for Francisco and the children. They would have to walk all the way back as the school bus made only a morning and an afternoon trip. They could stop by the drugstore in town and purchase whatever medication or vitamin the doctor might prescribe; vitamins for sure, Chabela looked rather pale and sallow.

She was already half asleep in bed when she heard the scream. Or thought she did. She wasn't sure what it was at first, it wasn't quite like a scream, it was more like a moan; no, not a moan either, it was very soft, as if suffocated under a pillow. She sat up in bed and listened: another one. They came from the kitchen.

And suddenly she recognized them. She had also screamed like that some time ago, in the hospital in Santiago, when Francisco had rushed there with her; except that she hadn't screamed right away, only later when the bag of waters had already ruptured and the contraction pains had become unbearable while the doctor was still away in a different hospital, attending another birth.

"Chabela!"

And then she had walked from one end of the house to the other, crossing the string of rooms one after the other, opening the doors one after the other, wishing to go back, back to her own room, back to the entrance door and to the open air. But no, she kept on walking towards the screams until, at the end of the house, she reached the kitchen. And there was Chabela, half kneeling, half bending down on the floor, her right hand in her mouth to muffle the screams, her left hand on her belly, the sticky liquid already coming down her legs, forming a puddle on the floor and streaming to the ditch under the sink.

"Francisco! Francisco! Get the doctor! Quick!"

No time to wait. Just pray that Francisco would wake up and rush to the doctor. She had to do something now. But what? Images came to her of old women talking about a pail of hot water, stories of Mapuche women delivering their babies all alone by the river, the mid-wife in the hospital saying push, push, now don't push anymore, the doctor holding a bloody mass of flesh and saying see? This is the placenta.

What to do, oh God, what to do? She knelt beside Chabela, gently stroking her hair and shoulders. She didn't touch the girl's belly; she couldn't even bring herself to look as it tightened with the contractions. Chabela, half-kneeling, half squatting, had her face hidden in her hands as she sobbed very softly, her face wet with sweat and red with embarrassment.

"Perdone, señora ... I couldn't get to my room ... "

"How long have you been like this?"

"It started this morning ... "

"Why didn't you tell me?"

"I tried, señora ... I couldn't ... "

And then it was Chabela's wet and sticky shirt, Chabela's underwear coming down, the strips of cloth tightly wrapped around the waist to hide the belly, the belly barely swelling after being released, pails and pails of water from the sink, masses of blood, masses of liquid flooding the pavement, draining out through the hole in the wall, mopped away. And the shrill noises made by the new creature.

"Is it over?" Adelina heard her own voice. "Is it over yet?"

"I need a knife," she heard Chabela whisper. "To cut the cord ... "

When Francisco and the doctor arrived two hours later they saw two boxes in the kitchen, one full of kittens, the other one with a baby, all of them wrapped in old household rags. Chabela, her body and clothes already washed at the barrel in the patio, made coffee for them as the doctor sat in the only chair in the kitchen and quickly examined the baby.

"The baby is okay," he said. "Boy, I'm so tired from this two-hour walk."

Adelina had her first nightmare that very night. But she did not hear Chabela collapse when, alone in the kitchen, she tried to lift the box and carry it with the baby inside to her own bedroom. Adelina only knew about it when no smell of coffee came from the kitchen as she woke the following morning.

"We'll have to get rid of her," Francisco said that evening. "We have no use for her. She lied about the baby. And besides, she will spend all the time with her child and neglect the household chores. Just look at the kitchen! It is dirty already."

He was right: Chabela did very little work the following days, so little that, by the end of the week, Adelina was already convinced. Her mother brought a new maid for her, an older woman who cooked like heaven and took care of everything. They moved out of the house after a while, when the money made from the land allowed them to rent a flat and send the children to a good school in Santiago.

Twenty years later, Adelina still had nightmares about that house. And until the day she died she had the feeling that life had not reserved any place for her.

THE COLLECTION

Brenda Baker

you say:
I want to cut out your lips
just your lips
like this

(his finger traces a line his nail cuts into my skin)
I will slice a perfect rectangle
they will be evenly framed
and I shall look at them always

in his kitchen
mustard yellow with dirty light
he tacks things on the wall

bits of paintings postcards
strips of cloth coupons
antique photos ticket stubs
fixed with straight-pins push-pins safety-pins
magic tape masking tape
bandaids bubblegum

positions are carefully considered
each addition fits neatly into the collage
kissing connecting covering the wall
all but for the small perfect rectangle
dead centre

and I say:
use a utility knife
it will make a clean job of it

COFFEE ON MARY HILL

UNMIXED GOOD

Su Croll

tea and candles come together   some days in december
we don't see the sun at all   those days my fingers ache
as they never ached at home

six to a bed we're never warmed

the cattle have strayed to the deeper woods
and must be found by their bells   a woman's a slave
to this country

the sound of chopping in the clearing
tells me he's home again   I can see his hunter's bag
is poor tonight   we'll take bread without beef for our suppers

fire took half our place last year

I can see his hunter's bag is poor and many mouths
make a large baking   winter is coming on
what are the fish seeing now

many mouths make hunger spread more thickly
I can't plan   the cellar is empty
the attic is empty

one of my boys went under the ice in the fall

how long will I be dead   waiting for that fish
waiting for that fish to push up
from the blue hole at our feet

the cattle have strayed   I already said that

how long will we be gardened under this frozen ground
how long will the rivers have nothing to give up
how strong is the hold of this winter

I guess there's no unmixed good in this world   you must roll it

and fold it as patience will allow you   then you must leave it
in the warmth to let it grow as it will

and out in the back he's humming low and sad   but I can't feed
a family on that   sun setting low over the trees   there are
wild dogs fleshing the winter garden   come back inside now

FROM *ROUGHING IT IN THE BUSH*
Susanna Moodie

Still confidently expecting to realize an income, however small, from the steamboat stock, we had involved ourselves considerably in debt, in order to pay our servants and obtain the common necessaries of life; and we owed a large sum to two Englishmen in Dummer, for clearing ten more acres upon the farm. Our utter inability to meet these demands weighed very heavily upon my husband's mind. All superfluities in the way of groceries were now given up, and we were compelled to rest satisfied upon the produce of the farm. Milk, bread, and potatoes during the summer became our chief, and often, for months, our only fare. As to tea and sugar, they were luxuries we would not think of, although I missed the tea very much; we rang the changes upon peppermint and sage, taking the one herb at our breakfast, the other at our tea, until I found an excellent substitute for both in the root of the dandelion.

The first year we came to this country, I met with an account of dandelion coffee, published in the *New York Albion*, given by a Dr. Harrison, of Edinburgh, who earnestly recommended it as an article of general use. "It possesses," he says, "all the fine flavour and exhilarating properties of coffee, without any of its deleterious effects. The plant being of a soporific nature, the coffee made from it when drunk at night produces a tendency to sleep, instead of exciting wakefulness, and may be safely used as a cheap and wholesome substitute for the Arabian berry, being equal in substance and flavour to the best Mocha coffee."

I was much struck with this paragraph at the time, and for several years felt a great inclination to try the Doctor's coffee; but something or other always came in the way, and it was put off till another opportunity. During the fall of '35, I was assisting my husband in taking up a crop of potatoes in the field, and observing a vast number of fine dandelion roots among the potatoes, it brought the dandelion coffee back to my memory, and I determined to try some for our supper. Without saying anything to my husband, I threw aside some of the roots, and when we left work, collecting a sufficient quantity for the experiment, I carefully washed the roots quite clean, without depriving them of the fine brown skin which covers them, and which contains the aromatic flavour which so nearly resembles coffee that it is difficult to distinguish it from it while roasting.

I cut my roots into small pieces, the size of a kidney-bean, and roasted them on an iron baking-pan in the stove-oven, until they were as brown and crisp as coffee. I then ground and transferred a small cupful of the powder to the coffee-pot, pouring upon it scalding water, and boiling it for a few minutes briskly over the fire. The result was beyond my expectations. The coffee proved excellent—far superior to the common coffee we procured at the stores.

To persons residing in the bush, and to whom tea and coffee are very expensive articles of luxury, the knowledge of this valuable property in a plant scattered so abundantly through their fields, would prove highly beneficial. For years we used no other article; and my Indian friends who frequented the house gladly adopted the root, and made me show them the whole process of manufacturing it into coffee.

Experience taught me that the root of the dandelion is not so good when applied to this purpose in the spring as it is in the fall. I tried it in the spring, but the juice of the plant, having contributed to the production of the leaves and flowers, was weak, and destitute of the fine bitter flavour so peculiar to coffee. The time of gathering in the potato crop is the best suited for collecting and drying the roots of the dandelion; and as they always abound in the same hills, both may be accomplished at the same time. Those who want to keep a quantity for winter use may wash and cut up the roots, and dry them on boards in the sun. They will keep for years, and can be roasted when required.

Few of our colonists are acquainted with the many uses to which this neglected but most valuable plant may be applied. I will point out a few which have come under my own observation, convinced as I am that the time will come when this hardy weed, with its golden flowers and curious seed-vessels, which form a constant plaything to the little children rolling about and luxuriating among the grass in the sunny month of May, will be transplanted into our gardens and tended with due care.

The dandelion planted in trenches, and blanched to a beautiful cream-colour with straw, makes an excellent salad, quite equal to endive, and is more hardy and requires less care.

In many parts of the United States, particularly in new districts where vegetables are scarce, it is used early in the spring, and boiled with pork as a substitute for cabbage. During our residence in the bush we found it, in the early part of May, a great addition to the dinner-table. In the township of Dummer, the settlers boil the tops, and add hops to the liquor, which they ferment, and from which they obtain excellent beer. I have never tasted this simple beverage, but I have been told by those who use it that it is equal to the table-beer used at home.

Necessity has truly been termed the mother of invention, for I contrived to manufacture a variety of dishes almost out of nothing, while living in her school. When entirely destitute of animal food, the different varieties of squirrels supplied us with pies, stews, and roasts. Our barn stood at the top of the hill near the bush, and in a trap set for such "small deer," we often caught from ten to twelve a day.

The flesh of the black squirrel is equal to that of the rabbit, and the red, and even the little chipmunk, is palatable when nicely cooked. But from the lake, during the summer, we derived the larger portion of our food. The children called this piece of water "Mamma's pantry"; and many a good meal has the munificent Father given to his poor dependent children from its well-stored depths. Moodie and I used to rise by daybreak, and fish for an hour after sunrise, when we returned, he to the field, and I to dress the little ones, clean up the house, assist with the milk, and prepare the breakfast.

MRS. B. (GERMANY) BORN 1908 (CAME TO CANADA IN 1957)

Inge Israel

Memories of what happened in kitchens? Well, what can I say? I was six during the First World War and was only allowed to go to school in the mornings. In the afternoons I was sent down the mine. What for? To work, of course! The coal mine. Ah, yes. It wasn't easy. But, somehow ... one worked. One had to! It wasn't healthy—but here I am still! A little the worse for wear, maybe. But I'm here!

And then, the Second World War ...

After that, it's incredible here! When I told them over there that I was going to Canada, they said I was crazy. "What d'you want to go over there for and drink out of those thick glasses?" they asked. But I didn't listen to them. I came. They wouldn't believe how much better it is—living as the Good Lord himself would in France!

When I arrived, I went to the Immigration Office. There were men and women there of all races and colours—Indian, Chinese, Black—you name it. So I looked up to heaven and I said "Lord, this is your people!"

But in the kitchen? Well, there were pots and pans ... and if there was food, we cooked it.

FROM "XMAS BAKING: A CHOOSE YOUR OWN MORALITY TALE"

Sarah Murphy

It was said of her when I first met her, and that was long ago and in the old neighbourhood, that she had never wanted, at any time, to exceed in length or breadth the size of a finger. Nor did it matter really what finger that should be, though she did develop a preference for Thumbelina, voyaging inside the wet ocean of her mouth, and Pointer who was a finger puppet and pointed at things it shouldn't or that she couldn't have, though with the accusing Daddy, Daddy we all called it back there, Daddy Finger, it was more a respect she felt. For the big one in the middle sticking up with its message, what would seem to her years later, by the time you met her, though of course she wouldn't say so, perhaps the only message from Daddy, from the essence of Daddy, that stand up and don't take no shit essence of Daddy that she, that Mommy, absent from her hand, never learned. Because there was only Ruby Ring, more a fancy woman like the redhead at the bar, cleaving to Daddy the way good women were supposed to though only the bad ones did. Without even any muscular independence, but tugged after him in all his activities, even wanting to rise when he did, though never allowed to participate in the major medium of exchange between all the kids in this neighbourhood, that was uniquely Daddy's privilege, standing tall to inform others where we wanted it stuck, or which way to turn it. The 'f' finger we called it too, as we said everything 'f', 'f' you and 'f' off and 'f' word, to avoid the consequences of the word itself, which is why it must have seemed strange to her: Daddy F. Finger, the 'f' like a good middle name.

Which left only Baby Pinkie, far too delicate and useless, she thought at first, so that only later, in that joke about sex where you tuck Daddy under and find that Ruby lies helpless, unable to even pick herself up off the table, with protest causing pain, did she learn that Pinkie could do what the far bigger Ruby could not, stand up for itself at least enough to wander a bit, never as far as Thumbelina, yet delving places no other could, ears or noses, or jars, or small burrows, hinges or other openings where it would go largely unnoticed. Which is why she settled on that name, the one you would know her by, Pinkie she had herself called, and enjoyed it, how small and silent and sneaky and able that name made her feel, out there on the edge the real outsider, left out and invisible more than opposing and independent, like the thumb, or Older Sister. Though the fact is that any finger would have done, she did even call herself Ruby for a while, and briefly tried to shine, while in moments of ambition she would take them all, as they would slap together openly, or more ominously fold into darkness, avoiding responsibility for themselves and their actions by becoming a fist.

And maybe this seems strange to you, especially since it is hard to vouch for the absolute truth of such a rumour, yet for all of you who so wonder at the brilliance of the work of her hands, how anyone could make or bake, put such spirit and life into the simplest of things, the wonderful creativity of her Christmas baking, of all the other cookies and cakes she makes for special occasions, while you sit in her kitchen, it should not seem so very peculiar, not with the way her fingers move across and into things. And while it might be obvious why, in this terrible and wonderful sinking into her extremities, she avoids her toes, trapped mostly in darkness, but even when allowed into the light, pinched and poked and compared too often to piggies who indulge in activities she has never enjoyed, not roast beef or going to market (she bakes better than she shops she always says) much less crying Wee Wee while running in any direction at all; still, even with the increase in her baking for the Holidays, it might not be quite so apparent that this feeling, along with the inward turning to silence that you have all noticed, should take her by seasons. That riding with the turning of the earth about the sun this impulse would pull her deepest at the time of the winter solstice, then let her go as high summer approached so that she could expand until she would not need her body at all but could be the shadow in the feather of the raven, a talisman encountered in the grass the first summer she noticed this waxing and waning in herself, so that Raven is still her secret name, the one she does not say, that releases her to float or fly or glide, noting the meaning of motion in the grass, or in the leaves, all those things that will often allow her to form another pattern, place upon one of her baked surfaces a perfectly formed leaf or petal or bract, Why, it's a work of art, some of you will say, complete with its veins, of holly or of ivy or poinsettia, or the image of a goose flying south, a snowy owl flying north: those things so admired.

While approaching winter would once more force her back, the bright spots in the hollow sky that was the night striking out at her, chasing her down, until she became the small and delicate light that might reflect from the eye of a cat at five o'clock on an evening in December when only the Christmas tree lights are lit. When she would feel herself wandering inside a space smaller than the span between her shoulders, herself the little light in the night of her body, tentatively flickering inside until she would fall down and down her arms to inhabit her fingers, with her eyes looking out from beneath the nails, to feel the colour in the texture of wood or plastic, the way they still see the flavour, the shape in the dough; and the rest stillness. Because she would know the outside was closed to her, that there was nowhere to go.

And to speak more clearly of the origins of the work her fingers have decided upon, I can tell you that it was one Christmas like that, still and waiting, to repeat not the sounding joy but the ongoing horror show, the night before Christmas when all through the house there was no Santa Claus, or even earlier caroling from door to door or around a large tree down in the town square, a friendly wassail after, an eggnog a hot buttered rum for the adults cocoa for the children, but drinks in abundance and shouts and spills and blows with presents opened, the fingers still nimble and quick as bunnies, to the smell of old alcohol and slurred speech and heavy breathing; when Mommy brought home, humming for the great deal she had gotten, for the first time, a tiny gingerbread house. Already half price on sale, what with waiting till the twenty-fourth having its advantages as you all know, and Mommy always was a better shopper than a baker, even Pinkie would say so, bought down at the neighbourhood supermarket, the one with its own bakery, where my mother and your mother and everyone's mother at one time or another must have worked. While Mommy, chatting constantly about such things, how there were coupons to cut and shopping to do and ends to be made to meet, the chopping knife going up and down, she did cook enough, staple fare she called it, the spoon stirring, between complaints about Daddy, called that one the best bakery about, only to be asked about what, and to have to reply, About about, that is, you know, Sweets, around.

Because Mommy had refused to buy a tree, not for the first time, Pinkie had asked why and she wasn't the only one, The tree, the tree, she had said, just two words, only to be told it was messy and expensive and dangerous, while Mommy moved her hands about her as if to clear a space, which let Pinkie know that Mommy was talking about other Christmases when the tree had been knocked over by just such a gesture, happy or angry, it didn't matter, it would be extravagant and violent in any case. Or left to dry, and dry and dry, until Easter bunnies and the equinox, when Pinkie would cease to let her eye-fingers wander its branches and watch it take on its natural size. And it would call to her, to take on her own, and to move with it, out the door and into the woods from which it had come, so that she would urge Brother to come with her, to be the Babes in the Woods, only to have him laugh (he probably knew the story and wanted no part of it) and tell her it wasn't from the woods anyway but from a tree farm, he agreed with Mommy that Christmas trees were useless, except for the presents under them, he was made of tougher stuff, like the presents he got, guns and robots and rocket launchers, while Mommy asked what anyone was doing farming trees for Christ's sake, well exactly for Christ's sake, Brother said, he knew how to sass, it was one of the things that made Daddy threaten him, though it did seem stupid enough, a farm with nothing on it anyone could eat, and he was hungry, always hungry, which was the problem for the Babes in the Woods too. So that it was good to know that someone could eat the the gingerbread house, even if Pinkie didn't want them to, she knew that the moment she saw it, the way she will still look longingly at her baking as it goes out the door, or say, No, don't eat that, of a special leaf or flower, something exceptionally pretty or solid or significant, even as she offers it to you, to make sure that you do. Because she knew somehow that this would be like special rations for her small daily voyage, something the Babes in the Woods didn't have, as she swore it her protection, sitting nearby and concentrating on it, throwing her web of stillness about it, that no one would knock it over or eat it, or break it, till Christmas was done. When they threw it away, saying it was too dry now to eat anyway. Except for the jujubes, which she and Brother picked off before the house went into the green garbage bag with the empty bottles and the tinsel.

While Mommy went on shouting about No tree, no tree this year, Hallelujah, no tree, until Brother winked at Pinkie and took the gingerbread house over to the planter with the Norfolk Island Pine, over there in the brightest corner of the old kitchen, a ridiculous thing from some island somewhere, Santa's reindeer might know or maybe Brother had figured it out from the way he spun the battered old globe in his hand when he wasn't using it as a soccer ball while he talked about all the voyages around the world he would make, Just like Daddy just like Daddy, farther than Daddy, by land by sea by air, he would say, the globe spinning faster and faster, farther than Daddy ever had working the rigs in Saudi Arabia or Venezuela or the North Sea driving his truck up and down and back and forth to criss-cross the continent flying his plane throughout the north sailing on the tanker around the world. Into space if he had to but Brother was getting out, out, way far OUT, the globe still faster in his hands as he leaned in over it as if he could fly out of the house with the centrifugal force he generated, while Pinkie would watch closing her hand into a centripetal stillness, with only Daddy F. Finger raising himself secretly behind Brother on her hand, beckoning him to stay, even if she knew he would go, just like he said, as far as Daddy, at least that far, while she would stay. Which she did of course, in that kitchen that is now her own, because that is the way of it, even when she left she stayed, occupying always the same position, her hands working the dough, the way her eye-fingers worked the gingerbread house, as Brother, singing Christmas carols, his voice registering somewhere between maudlin and sarcastic, decorated the tiny tree with real ornaments, the smallest they had. Then pushed the tree as close as he could to the house, so that the house was given shelter.

And it was true too that Mommy liked it when she turned from the stove, where she was making hash, Oh that's marvelous, she squealed out in the girlish voice she reserved for such occasions, her hands held together in front of her, A perfect Christmas, our own Christmas scene, and you could see her thinking it, Yes perfect. Away in a corner, rather than a manger, Christmas in a safe place, the kitchen always the house's safest territory, even when plates were thrown or broken it happened mostly in the living room or dining alcove, while Daddy laughed too, coming out of the living room where he'd been sitting letting her cook while he drank, and waited for the others to show up, That's great, Kid he said, clapping Brother on the back, You've decorated the tree to entice Hansel and Gretel, and then looking at Mommy, But who's gonna be the witch? and he laughed as hard as he could force himself to, probably remembering the way he had gotten Mommy the tree, and Pinkie shrank down, remembering too and feeling far too much like Gretel slowly fattening in her cage. It hadn't been a courting gift, those had come in long before, African violets mostly, with this tree a kind of joke for making up from a fight, Mommy did love plants, and he said it reminded him of her, Norfolk, Nor Fuck, he said, saying it not to Mommy but to Pinkie, who he'd pulled onto his lap, Nor Fuck, just like your mother, Nor Fuck Eye and Pine, No Fuck at least for him, while Mommy pined for the others, like that guy down at the bar, had she told Pinkie about him, or brought him around while Daddy was gone, no maybe not, just Eye and Pine, Eye and Pine down at the bar, he didn't think Mommy had the guts for anything else, while Pinkie just sat, and tried to be still while she let that solstice part that had shrunk so small wander, to be located right at that moment, not in her fingers, but floating, between her left lung and her duodenum, she liked that word, and was sure she had it right, it was the part that Rolaids (she thought it was Rolaids, though maybe it was Speedy, from Speedy Alka Seltzer, someone in the house was always taking one or the other) got out of so fast. The way she wanted to get out of this, but never could, she had to just let the words accumulate until the tiny part of her that she recognized floated among them, like Rolaids or Speedy among chewed food and stomach acid, or Carter's Little Liver Pills in the emulsified fat, picking its way between them, each word suddenly seeming larger than she was, far larger, even while the part of her that was Thumbelina, that could dress as a Princess, floated and feinted, and was Daddy's little girl, while her pinkies that she named herself for weren't even allowed to stick themselves in her ears, even if she knew they fit, and she had to hear it all.

With the drink of course behind it as Daddy held her in his lap and told her she wasn't like the old bitch, not like her at all, old Nor Fuck Eye and Pine, looking at all the young men, down at the bars and in the shop and even his friends who came over, it wasn't just the one in the bar, but all of them, eyeing them and pining for them while there wasn't a thing for him, not even a kiss when he got in dirty from the job, even if he'd been away for the longest time, days or weeks or months, just clean up Honey, clean up, before you make a mess, enough to make him not want it any more anyway, she understood didn't she, at least from Mommy, from the old bitch, or witch, the witch in the gingerbread house he told her that one time laughing, all bright makeup and bangles all enticement and then just the oven inside, to eat him up, his salary his savings the presents he'd bring, which he did, the nicest smallest dolls from the most far away places, and the plants. But Pinkie'd never be like that would she, she'd always be Daddy's little girl, wouldn't she, he would say as he held her tighter on his knee, squeezing and bouncing, it didn't matter which Daddy it was, except that there was the one who wasn't hers who winked and said, sometimes just to her and sometimes for Mommy to hear, that maybe he'd marry her when she grew up, rubbing his hand along her arm, she was perfect and gentle and good and not like the old bitch, she'd never run around would she, when her man was gone. So that she seemed always to be someone's little girl, his Princess, his Sugarplum, held on someone's lap, until all but the littlest Pinkie part of her felt like a pudding. A mushy overcooked jiggly pudding, jiggling and melting on his lap while her fingers twisted around in her own and Little Pinkie demanded of Daddy F. Finger, why was he saying this, why was he saying it to her, with never an answer and the words continuing, how she was better than all of them, the bitch and the witch and that Older Sister of hers, who was certainly going to get it when she got back from all that partying and running around. With older sister's parties in the old boarded-up house near the park, the whole neighbourhood remembers them, yet another cause for screams and blows in the middle of the night. Until Older Sister stopped coming home.

Which is when it was Brother's turn, he was going to get it, with the belt this time, if he didn't stop hanging out, and doing those things he did, Daddy knew what was going on, and he wasn't the only one. Which was true enough, I for one used to paint those signs on the walls with Brother, and hot wire cars too. So that Pinkie was the only one who didn't, get it, I mean, not as long as she was still, so very still, her eyes peeking out her fingers, and she listened, or pretended to, and she played nice. And if she was very good, very still and sweet, then no one else would get it either, because she just shouldn't be exposed to such things, belts falling through the air, fists pounding, plates breaking, hands slapping. Which means that is when she learned it, the trick of stillness, and of silence, and it was only the particular stillness, the particular silence, how sweet it would have to be, and how flavorful, to be hers, that eluded her. So that in the summers when Daddy was mostly gone, and Mommy was mostly busy, she would go out to look for it, and be the breeze on the wind, the raven feather shadow that passed and passed and passed and stored whatever it found for the coming of winter.

Which is why that year of the first gingerbread house in the kitchen wasn't really any different, there was just her shrinking consciousness and the conversation, always very much the same. And that small tree so suddenly celebrated, now delicately decorated, that tiny peace offering huddled so long among the African violets, served only to change Mommy's name from Nor Fuck Eye and Pine to the Witch with the Oven. Making Pinkie think it might be nice to bake real buns, not the babies they meant when they said someone had a bun in the oven, or to convince Mommy just to make little gingerbread girls, there might even be a mix on sale perfect for Mommy who just shopped then took a load off, drinking by the kitchen table, or fixing up whatever she could afford, that was as convenient as possible. Or made, because her own mother had taught her, every once in a while, a scratch soup, keeping the pot boiling, boiling and boiling, telling Pinkie what it had been like before when a few times a year all the women in some imaginary family (she felt so alone sometimes) or even town, maybe her own, as she best imagined it, had gotten together to cook, or to sew and to talk, and talk and talk, women's things, women's things Mommy said, though mostly it was the chili made with the canned beans and a conversation as endless as Daddy's, though at least with Mommy Pinkie could play and sit across the table not in Mommy's lap, while Summer Fall Winter and Spring, Mommy took her turn to tell Pinkie about the girl Daddy had picked up at the bar, though she wasn't a girl really, she just wore lots of makeup to hide her age, and dyed her hair flame red, brighter than that Christmas ornament said Mommy pointing. Brighter than that, and she laughed too loud, then said it again when Daddy got home, sometimes these conversations went by turns, You know your Mommy, You know your Daddy. With words, the chosen weapons for the first round, flying over Pinkie's head.

THE TABLE
Rosemary Sullivan

Nobody planned this
table stretching its broad grin
across the floor, loaded with lives.

It was the house. Some nights
it wants. We come
pulled by a stronger will,
unwittingly, to family
its geography of need.

Santiago's in the kitchen
hacking thin potato wafers,
crisp, ambiguous as memories,
placed like wafers on our plates.
They are an augury. We squirm,
and a thin laughter rises in the heat.

Adrianna watches the lampshade
swing a hex across the ceiling.
One night she tied her husband
like Gulliver to his bed,
eyes propped up with toothpicks,
while she took another man.
It was revenge he had to see.

Her son Sergito guards the door
where his father disappeared.
In his tiny mind the memory climbs.
He beats a drum in anger,
takes pennies from a jar,
holds them over open palms—
a practiced ritual—pulling back before the pennies drop. He knows
already to withhold.

Ricardo plays the guru of the kitchen.
If you painted a balloon with dots
collapsed it to one point,

that's space and time. The center
nowhere. Everywhere the center.
The universe contracted to a table.

We play at the illusion
of a moment. The house
erupts: oasis in our scattering.
We live as we die down.
We laugh as we hold on.

FROM *HALFBREED*
Maria Campbell

Our days were spent at school, the evenings doing our chores. Daddy was trapping from early October until Christmas, and again during the beaver season in spring. How we missed him! It was as if part of us was gone with him, and we were not complete until he had returned. I remember the times he came home, always on Christmas Eve. The food supply in our settlement would be very low at that time of year as the men were all gone on the traplines. However Grannie Campbell and my aunts would bring food they had been saving for a long time to our house. They steamed a pudding, which was called a "son of a bitch in a sack," made of raisins, flour, baking powder, sugar and spices. They made cakes with frosty icing, sprinkled with coloured sugar, and baked blueberry, cranberry, and saskatoon pies. The smells would be heavenly, because at that time of year our sole diet was wild meat and potatoes. There was no bannock as the flour was being saved for the holiday baking. On Christmas Eve, Grannie, Mom, Jamie and I always went into the bush for a tree. We decorated it with red and green crêpe paper, some ornaments Mom had from her mother, and strings of popcorn coloured with crêpe paper. There was an angel for the top branch, but no one put it there for that was Daddy's job. Mom laid out our best clothes while we all bathed in a washtub, and then she put us to bed. At ten-thirty we got up and dressed for midnight Mass. It was a thrilling time—outside we could hear sleigh bells ringing and people laughing and calling back and forth as they drove to church.

Right in the middle of all this Daddy would always walk in, with a full-grown beard and a sack full of fur on his back. First he swung Mom off her feet and kissed her, and then we climbed all over him. I remember that he always smelled like wild mink. He washed himself while Mom and Grannie put his sacks away, then we all dressed warmly and walked to church with Grannie Campbell. Cheechum stayed home and kept the fire going.

After Mass we talked around the big heater in the church, and friends and relatives all kissed each other. Then we'd all go home, for that was the one night families spent together at home. Daddy would tell us all the things that happened to him while he was on the trapline. While Mom tidied up and my grannies smoked their pipes, he put the angel on the tree, and we would say our prayers and go to bed.

Jamie and I always woke everyone up at five o'clock. In the living room our stockings were plumb full and overflowing with nuts and candy canes, oranges and apples—the only ones we ate all year. Under the tree there were gifts for everyone. Mom got a comb and mirror from Daddy; he got shaving lotion; and our grannies got cloth for new dresses. We were given blocks made and painted by Dad and Mom, homemade dolls which looked like the modern day "Raggedy Anns," and shoes from our grannies. Then Daddy made pancakes. That was the only meal he ever cooked while Mom was still alive. He made huge pancakes, and while we all stood around, wide-eyed and breathless, he would toss them in the air and catch them right back in the pan.

Christmas dinner was the highlight of the day. It consisted of meat balls rolled in flour, stewed moose meat, all covered with moose fat, mashed potatoes, gravy, baked squash and pemmican made of dried meat ground to a powder and mixed with raisins, smashed chokecherries and sugar. After that we filled ourselves with the pudding and cakes until we could hardly move.

All the families visited back and forth during the holidays. After supper, furniture was moved against the wall or put outside while the fiddlers tuned their fiddles. Soon they were sawing out a mean hoedown or a Red River jig, and everyone was dancing. Each family held a dance each evening and we never missed any of them. The hostess baked a nickel inside her cake and whoever got it in his piece held the dance the next night. We stuffed ourselves during those holidays until we hurt, because it would be a year before we would eat like that again. One thing about our people is that they never hoard. If they have something they share all of it with each other, regardless of good or bad fortune. Maybe that's why we're so damn poor.

MOTHER WITH CHILD

Leona Gom

She rocks the jar of cream
in her lap
like a cranky child,
tries to lull it
to some expected form,
as I see myself
rocked so often

on that tired lap.
Finally, late at night,
the cream thickens, clots,
she pours off the buttermilk,
gives me a glass.
Thank God that's done, she says,
and goes to bed.
I watch the pale hill of butter,
wonder if my own
murky childhood's end
met with such relief,
a sudden falling together
into one shape,
no more weary rocking, rocking
late into the night.

EATING AVOCADOS
Barbara Sapergia

Brandi sits across from me, staring at the centrepiece of fruit—Macintosh and Golden Delicious apples, soft ripe anjou pears, green grapes and the seedless purple kind with the unexpected crispness, bananas, kiwis, fat navel oranges, purple and yellow plums that glow as if they are giving off sun. Brandi herself is lovely, her long auburn hair framing her face in loops and tendrils; her face, with its soft golden down, calm and still; she looks like a Madonna who has decided not to get involved.

I serve the soup—homemade chicken and rice in dark earthenware bowls, croutons and melted cheese on top, smelling of sage and tarragon. We pick up our spoons. She dips hers in, takes small sips like a hummingbird, swallows. She looks up at me, trying to seem pleased, takes another tentative mouthful. I remember I mustn't stare, and start to work on my own soup. After all, it's delicious and I'm hungry.

* * *

She puts those crouton things in the soup, as if that's going to make me like it. Little hunks of dead-looking bread just floating there. She puts thick melted cheese on top, and around the edges of the bowl there's a ring of fat. Tiny drops of fat. Globules of fat. If any of that gets in my mouth, I know I'll be sick.

It's best not to smell things. There are too many smells, it confuses me. She's always trying to confuse me. Like she puts out a bowl of fruit, but she can't just use one kind, you could stand that—she throws in everything you can think of, all at once, in one bowl. Too many colours, too many smells.

I hate the skin on the apples. Like thin dry human skin, but all the colours are wrong. The kiwis have that awful hairy skin that makes me gag just looking at it. And the bananas are all mushy and soft, I can always smell them beginning to rot, even when she says they're perfect.

She looks at the fruitbowl as if she's created some kind of work of art. As if she'd like to sit down and eat them all herself. I can see her doing that, her teeth crunching through the apples, juice squirting into her mouth, dribbling down her chin.

She always serves the soup too hot, and then expects me to eat it. I try to swallow a spoonful a little bit at a time, but her staring makes me swallow too fast and I burn my throat. When it hits my stomach I feel like my stomach's puckering up. And then I get this taste in my mouth, like salt or blood. If only she knew what it's like. I try not to look at her. She's wolfing hers down like she hasn't eaten all week. Don't, I want to say, please don't.

* * *

I try not to look, but I can tell she's stopped. I hear soft breathing, then the clink of her spoon on the table.

"It's very nice," she says. "It's just that I'm not really that hungry."

I eat a few more spoonfuls, and then it's no good for me either. "I know what you mean," I say. "Let's just have the salad." I take the bowls of soup to the counter. I'll figure out what to do with them later. I turn the radio on to some soft classical music and bring on the salad. Romaine with avocado and artichoke hearts, oil and vinegar dressing.

She picks up the salad servers and doles out enough to feed a very small bird, say a chickadee. She arranges it on the plate, three pieces of lettuce and an artichoke heart. She considers it a moment as if she's a chef deciding on the best presentation. I feel like screaming: "Don't play with your food!" Instead I serve myself.

Sometimes I think, why am I trying so hard, and is that the problem? The more I try to tempt her, the more I try to make it look beautiful, the less she seems to eat. Why not just let up on it? But she's my daughter. It's my duty to feed her, as long as she's under my roof.

I guess there's no way Brandi can appreciate what she's got here. My husband has a good job, and I'm a secretary in a law firm. We have a nice home and car, better-than-average clothes, but food has always been our top priority. What's the use of keeping up with the Joneses, Randy says, if you don't eat well?

But what does it mean to her? We eat things I didn't know existed when I was a child. Avocados. I was in the world 23 years before I even heard the word. My aunt and I discovered them in the supermarket. We'd mash them on bread, squeeze on lemon, and salt and pepper them. My cousin Allison, who hated all green foods, watched us with fascinated disgust.

The avocado was sensuous and comforting as we watched my mother slowly dying, the other discovery of that year and one nobody wanted to talk about. Funny I should remember it now. A food bound up with a time and a place—1960 in my aunt's clapboard bungalow by the river, between visits to the hospital. Eating the rich flesh like some luscious new kind of butter, satisfaction a fat joy blotting out thoughts. Probably the closest thing I've ever done to taking drugs.

No use talking to her about those times. Brandi has never known anything like it. Avocados have always existed, always been plentiful. She's watching me now, serving my own salad, and I know without her speaking that she doesn't want it. She digs her top teeth into her bottom lip, unconsciously, pointy white teeth that look too juvenile for her age, which is 16. And I, who have never physically punished either of my children, would like to slap her, hard.

* * *

Oh God, just look at it. It's *glistening*. I don't like shiny food. It's only fat that does that, and I don't want fat. Why can't she understand? If I don't want it on my body, why would I want to eat it? And avocados! She wants to make me fat so she can keep eating this stuff and not feel guilty. Well, she can eat what she wants, but I won't do it.

Her body disgusts me. Her flesh. I can't stand her to touch me. God, she actually thinks she has a good figure. I'd be ashamed to have hips like that. Oh, and the way her stomach sticks out below her waistband when she forgets to suck it in. Why doesn't she do something about it? I would. But she can't. She likes food too much.

So she tries to make me like her. Always shoving food at me. Saying I need it, when she's the one who needs it and wants it all the time. Saying I should eat more to be healthy. That's a lie. Everyone knows it's not healthy to be fat. Even in school they know that much.

Maybe I could eat a piece of artichoke. If only it had another name.

* * *

"Brandi, did you go to school yesterday afternoon?"

"School!" she says. "I can't stand it any more. They always find some excuse to bug you."

"You didn't answer my question." I wouldn't be pushing, but I can see she doesn't plan to eat anything more, so there's nothing to lose. "Apparently you missed an appointment with the Counsellor."

"Why don't they take care of the kids with the real problems? I don't drink, and I don't smoke. I wouldn't do that to my body. Why pick on me?"

"Mrs. Becker thought you should see the Counsellor."

"Becker, that snotbag! The *health* teacher, for God's sake. She can't wait to light up in the staff room. I saw her!" Under cover of her anger, Brandi takes her plate over to the sink. She gets the Diet Coke out of the fridge, and swallows a big slug right out of the bottle.

"That's not the point, Brandi."

"It is to me," she says, and takes another gulp. "And she calls you up and you talk about me like I'm some kind of *case*. I bet it was your idea she should send me to the Counsellor." She lifts the bottle to drink again.

"It was not. And that's enough Coke!"

She drinks again, long and slow, just to bug me. "You guys think you can just send me anywhere. Don't I have any say?"

"Of course you do."

"You think you can make me do anything you want."

"I do not!"

"Don't you know I get scared?" She is edging away from the table towards the door, still with the bottle.

"What did you say?"

"Nothing!" she says.

"It didn't sound like nothing."

"What's wrong," she yells, "are you deaf or something? I said I get goddamn well scared!" And she lurches out of the room, whacking her hip against the table, Coke bottle in hand. I think of the bruise beginning to stain her meagre flesh.

Last year I would have run after her and tried to talk it through. I'm not that naïve any more. Also I'm still hungry. I'm going to have my lunch whether she does or not. Despite what she thinks, there is nothing to be ashamed of in a normal appetite. Or a normal body. And she's going back to school, I'll drive her myself. I'll walk her in the front door if I have to.

* * *

Rita drives me to school and actually gets out and watches while I walk in the door. I mean, as if I couldn't turn around and walk out a minute later. Rita's not all that logical. I like calling her Rita, it helps put her in her place. Calling her Mom makes me feel like a little kid, somebody who always has to do what she's told. Of course she doesn't let me call her Rita to her face. So I don't call her anything, and she hates that too. There's no pleasing some people, is there?

I can't believe I said I'd see the Counsellor. She phoned and got him to re-schedule it. Oh hell, may as well get it over with. They're not going to let up till I do. Of course Rita gets me here too early, so I have to sit here on this chintzy little couch staring at posters of fat students talking to sympathetic looking counsellors. What a bunch of crap.

The Counsellor is this guy, Mr. Kingsway, and he's so old and out of it, at least 50 or 55. Older than Rita, for God's sake. I hate even looking at him. His skin is like thick grainy paper, and it always looks dusty and grey. His beard starts growing in and you see those little black dots poking out, and you almost think you can *see* them growing. Before your very eyes. I swear to God. I mean, they talk about human rights all the time, why should I have to look at a guy that makes me sick? And I'm supposed to talk about my private life with someone like that?

"Have you given any thought, Brandi, as to what you'd like to do when you graduate? For a living, that is to say."

That's what he asked me last time. No kidding, that's how he talks. I mean, how am I supposed to know? As if I have any choice in the matter. He makes me want to scream. He asks me what I think my skills are, what I have to offer an employer. Jesus, I haven't got any skills, I can't even type. I'm not good at anything. I'm not good *for* anything. How do they think that feels? But they just keep playing their stupid games, asking their stupid questions, as if I just have to say "lawyer" or "brain surgeon" and it'll all happen just like that. And they wonder why you hate school.

"You can go in now," the secretary says. She's smiling, the kind that want to show they're on your side. I just sit. "I said, you can go in now," she says, as though I'm deaf or something. I look right through her, and then I get up and go in.

* * *

I'm going to be late for work, but at least I've got her back to school. For all I know she'll wait till I'm gone and walk right out again. If she wants to badly enough, I guess I can't stop her.

I wonder, does she try to ruin meals for me, or can she just not help herself? She imagines I don't know what she's thinking. I wish I didn't, but her mind's like a see-through raincoat.

Just once I started to see myself through Brandi's eyes. I don't know quite how it happened, but I began to think she really was the norm and I was grossly over-sized. My breasts, which I've always been proud of, looked flabby and soft like old sponge rubber. My hips started to remind me of softened lard, and my legs were like the pillars on an old Victorian house. I saw that I was monstrous and bloated, and images of fat—I mean as we see it on roasts and steaks and pork chops—kept superimposing themselves on my body. It was like Brandi's skull had suddenly gone soft and her thoughts were oozing into mine, and I felt I was going to be sick.

I was in a panic, but I knew I had to fight it. It was hard to fight, because I just wanted to empty my stomach and feel clean again. I made myself see an hourglass and the grains of sand slipping through it were those ugly thoughts. And then I was myself again and Brandi my painfully thin child.

She doesn't like anyone to see her without clothes. But it sometimes happens, and then I see how her bones fit under her skin, and I know the spine is not meant to protrude in that way. Her body seems strangely childlike, and yet healthy children don't look like her either. This leads me to a new idea about Brandi. Is it fear of maturity? Of sexuality? If it is, I don't know what Randy and I did to cause it. We like each other that way, always have.

Other mothers I know are terrified their daughters will get pregnant before they get through high school. I never worry about that with Brandi.

* * *

Kingsway sits in a high-back swivel chair. He swivels it towards me as I walk in and asks me to sit in the wooden chair across the desk from him. He's wearing his tweed jacket with the leather elbow patches. Someone must have told him it makes him look harmless and sympathetic. He doesn't fool me for a minute. His shave isn't holding up well. The little black dots are growing on his face. He has bits of cream-coloured grit at the corners of his eyes, dry and crusty.

"Hello, Brandi," he says. "I'm glad you could come after all."

"My mother thought it might be helpful," I say, playing his little game.

"Yes," he says, "I think she's worried about you." I just look at him. "Do you know why?"

Okay! He's decided to go on the attack.

"Uh, Brandi? I asked you a question."

"You're pretty free with first names, aren't you? How'd you like it if I called you Rex all the time? Eh, Rex?" That's his name, Rex B. Kingsway, no kidding. What got into his parents, I can't imagine.

He looks pained, then makes a big effort. A king-size effort. "Fine," he says, "if it makes it easier to talk."

"I couldn't care less, *Mr.* Kingsway."

"Brandi, we have to have some basis for discussion. You've got your parents deeply upset. And they're not imagining the problem. I've seen your medical report."

"Oh?" I say, "isn't anything private any more?"

Kingsway fights to keep the dignified, concerned look. "Your doctor says you're seriously underweight for your height and bone structure."

"That's what he thinks. I think I'm finally starting to look good."

"Your mother wants you to be well. Try to understand how frightened she is."

"Frightened? Rita? Don't make me laugh."

"Brandi, there's only one logical conclusion to starving yourself." He looks at me, wanting me to say it. I stare at the little black dots. I swear they're actually starting to crawl around on his face.

"Girls are dying this way," he says. "That singer, Karen Carpenter, for instance."

"She was stupid. I'd never let that happen to me."

"I'm glad you think so. But these things can get out of control."

"Well, I'm not out of control, so you don't have to worry. Tell Rita not to worry either. Can I go now?"

"There is the matter of the classes you've been missing. Your mother tells me you haven't been ill.

"Yeah, well she doesn't have to put up with my math class. Makes me sick to my stomach."

"So why take the chance of having to repeat a grade?"

"You mind your own business!"

"Brandi, please—"

"You don't know anything about me! Do you hear me? You don't know a thing!"

* * *

She now regrets calling the child Brandi. It seems too mindlessly cute, so wrong for this sick but determined child. They'd tried to give her a good start in life—everything she'd need to succeed. The name was like a symbol of hope and growing affluence, as if now people could even afford better names.

It had seemed to her that the parents of earlier generations had named their daughters to teach them the narrowness of their expectations. Verna. Edna. Betty. Mabel. Good solid names, perhaps, but with no glamour, no frivolity. Names that called girls to common sense and hard work; and to duty, first to parents and then to husbands. In the months before Brandi was born, she'd become sensitive to the names people were giving their daughters, and what she heard around her was Darcy and Tracie and Jennifer and Stefanie. Names that seemed to invite pleasure and carelessness. Names that were a message. Curl your hair, paint your nails. You will be looked after.

She'd wanted a name like that for her daughter; something to give her a head start in life. But now it seems to lack character. In the last year she's met two other girls named Brandy, as well as an Irish Setter called Brandywine and a Golden Lab called Brandee. Now even dogs have cute names. She resents the fact that people have chosen variations of her daughter's name for their pets, even though they obviously had no way of knowing.

What if we'd called her Caroline or Jane, she wonders. Would anything have been different? Sometimes she thinks it would have been. She herself has always been grateful her parents called her Rita. It seems to have saved her from the curse of dullness, at least in her own eyes. She remembers how it gave her the license to be a little different from the other girls. When she was a teenager, liveliness was admired in a girl. A certain perky optimism was the closest thing to being sexy that was allowed. The thing was to be a nice girl with a bit of spirit, but not too much.

Being Rita gave her a chance to be like that, and to be even a bit sexy too, and she'll always be grateful. She'll never know how her mother talked her dad into it. Robbie was always just a bit stuffy and unbending. She's sure he fought for Alice or Margaret or even Elizabeth. Or maybe, and she's never thought of this before, calling her Rita was his own small rebellion against Nana and the forces of the English establishment. What it's let her do is identify with her non-English side.

Of course Robbie had his own non-English side, she was forgetting that. His father, Eamon Conal, was Irish, a bright, strong, self-educated man who had somehow made Robbie into less than himself. Something cautious, inward looking, conservative. Except that he named her Rita. He'd given her that.

And she wonders, do we all turn our children into something less than ourselves? By giving them the things we never had? We think if we give them more, they'll be more. Only now it seems to her that it works the opposite way. She thinks of things she never had as a child. Television. Robbie wouldn't get one till 1959. She was 20 then, a grown woman. She remembers how slowly time seemed to pass when she was a child, and how she'd wished she could fill those spaces with Lucille Ball and Walter Cronkite the way some of her friends were doing. Now she's glad she had the long spaces, the feeling that she'd never reach 16 or 18, let alone 21. It felt like eternity, but it gave her time to think and dream.

Sometimes she wishes Sofie'd made her work harder around the house. Sofie always put schoolwork first; soon she'd had hardly any chores, because it was understood that she would always have homework to do. No one really seemed to notice that she almost never did any. Sometimes, though, Sofie'd get mad, when she'd do some petty household chore really badly. Then Sofie'd say "You're a useless tit, and I don't know what will become of you."

* * *

She sits at the back of the class. Mr. Abrams is talking about equations, writing numbers and letters on the blackboard. His voice drones on. It's too hot in the room. She can feel sweat under her armpits and it makes her feel filthy. She tries to focus on the board, but things seem to move, and she wonders if she needs glasses. She fixes her eyes on the "X," and watches it slowly slide down the board, then reappear at the top again. The blackboard is like a movie screen, only in black.

This is what they want her to learn. A bunch of stuff about "X." How to figure out what "X" is worth. Why, why, why? She needs a Diet Coke. She needs a big bowl of ice cream with mocha chocolate sauce dripping down the sides. "X" is growing, spreading its way across the board. It's been doing that lately. She can't imagine why. It always stayed put before.

Then she can feel them looking at her, the other students, they turn and stare at her with their big bulgy eyes, like a wave going out to sea that turns and tries to drown you. "X" is all over the place and Abrams is walking towards her.

"Brandi!" he says, "I asked you a question." No, please, no.

* * *

Randy's on the road a lot in his job, and she sometimes resents being left alone so much with their daughter. Ordinary home life has turned into a war zone; a minefield; a concentration camp. Lately she's been using her ingenuity to devise ways to avoid eating supper alone with Brandi. That is, to avoid being with Brandi while she refuses to eat supper.

Tonight Randy's away and Brandi's working on a school assignment in her room. She takes her a sandwich and a glass of milk on a tray, then takes her own to the living room in front of the television. She begins to eat, enjoying the food, hoping Brandi will take her own tray back to the kitchen and dispose of whatever food she's left on the plate, which will probably be almost all of it. She'll make a point of not looking into the garbage bin.

Despite everything, she hasn't been able to stop herself from trying to make the food nice. Her meals are delicious, as attractively presented as in a good restaurant. She has one highly satisfied customer, who isn't around a lot, and one incredibly picky one. "Is everything all right, miss?" she imagines yelling at Brandi.

She tries not to, but she often finds herself casting about for possible ways Brandi could live somewhere else. With someone else. She knows this is opposite to what most parents are trying for. She knows one woman who's afraid not to give her daughter everything she wants, because her daughter is always threatening to leave home. Sometimes she wishes Brandi would do that.

Tonight she's made open-faced shrimp sandwiches with a small side salad. The theory is that small amounts are less likely to revolt Brandi's sensitive appetite, and Rita has almost unconsciously started to cut back on her own as well. After all, she's going to be fifty this year, she has to watch her weight.

She's half-way through the news and the sandwich when they appear, the victims of drought in a far-away country. The sight of them used to make her feel hungrier, as if she had to eat and grow fat in case famine should come to her also. Now she can hardly swallow what's in her mouth. A woman's eyes look into the camera and seem to lock on hers. The woman has a child at her breast, and it is clear that there is no milk.

She hears a slight swish of movement and turns to see Brandi behind her, staring at the television, eyes bright with anger or tears. Brandi turns accusingly towards her. "See," her eyes seem to say, "I'm right." Right about what, she wants to ask. She puts down her plate, and feels a wave of nausea wash over her, mingled with a fierce physical rage. Another swish, and Brandi's gone again, and the remains of the shrimp sandwich look as appealing as fat pink worms in dirt.

* * *

She slams the door, starts to tidy the room. First the toss cushions on the bed. Each one has its own special place, as clear to her as if she had a diagram.

Then the books on the desk; she squares them up at right angles to the table edge and makes a minute adjustment to the study lamp. That's better, she can't stand a mess. The lamp is still wrong. She straightens it again; still not quite right, but she decides to leave it for the moment. Then a bad thing happens. She has a picture on the wall, of mountains, that she likes because it makes her feel clean and calm. The bad thing is that it's started to move, its colours pulsing lighter and darker like a heartbeat. The mountains look like giant breasts, blue-grey breasts heaving and throbbing. It's disgusting, obscene. She needs a Coke, why didn't she bring some Coke? Or some sugar. A little sugar would fix things up. Maybe it's getting out of control. No! She's just tired, it was a bad day at school. But the mountains are still moving. She looks at other things, and they stay still, although she's not sure about the light switch. Maybe it's moving too, inching its way down the wall.

* * *

Rita changes the channel. A woman is cooking an exotic looking dish. She flips the channel to a commercial for a fast food outlet with a salad bar. She doesn't usually watch commercials, but this is so beautiful. The light glowing through red and gold and green peppers makes her think of stained glass in a church. The lettuce, three kinds of it, seems to shine with an inner life. She flips the channel, and it's a beautifully roasted turkey and a mother smiling down at a clean fresh happy family. Everywhere she turns, she sees food. What does it mean any more?

Food is Sofie at the cookstove. Food is having a garden. Helping Robbie roast potatoes, pungent and smoky in the ashes of a bonfire. It's a box of MacIntosh apples in the winter, Japanese oranges at Christmas. It's a root cellar with tubs of carrots in sand, and burlap sacks of potatoes from Grandpa Lenchuk. Pies with criss-cross pastry tops. Pot roast in gravy. Cabbage rolls simmering in tomato sauce. Baba Lena's wild mushrooms fried in butter. Garlic, onion, herbs; juicy cherries; fat ripe olives.

Food is a microwave. A blender. Food is a processor. An oven with a black glass door. A package of dry frozen lumps zapped back to warmth and life, molecules dancing wildly through some process no one she knows really understands. Red apples that seem to shine too much or smell of unknown chemicals, no matter how long she washes them. Carrots without sweetness. Tomatoes like poorly-dyed pulverized cardboard.

Food is Mexican families sprayed by planes. Men, children, pregnant women, wet with the soft clinging mist of pesticides. Food is Indian families living in shacks to pick sugar beets. Food is having maple syrup for maybe the last time because the trees are dying from acid rain. Food is burning the tropical rain forest to get more land to raise cattle. Food is farmers leaving the land because they can't pay the bank. Food is people lining up at a food bank, which is not much like a food store and nothing like a bank. Food is a store. Food is paying the bank.

* * *

Brandi closes her eyes to shut the picture out, but she can still see it. She rubs her eyes with her hands, and the colours explode in her brain. Colours she's never seen in real things, colours that rake across her eyeballs like wire. Colours like grating, roaring noise. She knows the room is silent, tries not to scream.

* * *

Her work is clean work. Rita has followed her parents' advice and found clean indoor work, nothing heavy. Her husband is doing well in his job; her older daughter, a single parent, is okay. If Brandi makes it through the next few years, she may grow out of her problems. Rita is glad she has no other children.

Sometimes she imagines the ways it could be worse. In fact, she doesn't need to imagine, because real-life examples are all around her. Her brother in Edmonton has a child who can't pay attention to anything for more than five minutes and recently set the living-room drapes on fire. A neighbour down the street has a son who's into drugs and steals from his parents. Once, when his mother caught him, he told her to give him the money or he'd hit her; and she believed him and gave it to him. A friend has a daughter who got in with the wrong crowd, as her mother puts it, and is now a hooker down on the Strip. She has seen the girl on the street, and can hardly believe it's true. The girl looks lovely, says hello in the same slightly shy way she has always spoken to her parents' friends. It can't be true, and yet no one would make up a story like that about their own child.

And this is the consolation she sometimes looks for. The terrible things other children do that Brandi would never do. Brandi is neat and clean and always nicely dressed. Most of the time she is reasonably polite. Her room is absolutely, totally tidy, everything ironed, folded, hung, straightened, dusted, polished. And yet she knows that what Brandi does is worse. She thinks the other children have a better chance of reaching their 21st birthdays, although it's hard to be sure.

One thing is sure. A year ago, Brandi weighed 130 pounds. Now she weighs 89. She is 5' 6" tall. Her hair is thinner than it was, although she swears it isn't. She keeps her skin scrupulously clean, sometimes with several baths a day, but when her face breaks out, it heals very slowly. She used to run every day, but lately she doesn't, because she hasn't got the strength any more, although she claims it's just because she's sick of it. This at least is true. She is sick of it. She's getting A's in school, except for Math and Physics, which she's failing dismally. She refuses to talk about the future. Lately, she says she's going to stop going to see the psychologist at the mental health clinic. It is three months since the psychologist has felt able to suggest any sort of favourable outcome to Brandi's problems.

This child of hers. This child, this child. She sometimes forgets the child is 16 years old. Has tiny buds of breasts. Had her periods regularly from 12 to 15, then stopped. Her daughter hasn't had a period for over a year, she thinks. Wasn't that what happened in the concentration camps?

She thinks of herself at 16. Rounded, womanly; everyone thought so. She remembers how Nana looked at her, as if there was something cheap about it. But she hadn't dressed in a cheap or flashy way. She'd just had that look to her. Sensual, people would say nowadays. And she still has it. Brandi hates it, she can read it in her accusing eyes, and it makes her feel like a piece of over-ripe fruit that had once been good but is now past it. Brandi seems to think that the least she could do, in fact the only decent thing, would be to conceal herself as much as possible. "Those hips," she heard her mutter once, although Brandi'd denied saying anything. Maybe Brandi would've got along with Nana, she seems to have some of Nana's ideas. Thank God Randy still thinks she's sexy.

Brandi is unformed, unfinished, a reluctant fetus denying itself nourishment. Brandi is a sealed room, a high windowless tower; a science project she keeps always on display: "Teenage Girl, 1990." Brandi is a Judge without mercy; she has claimed the right to judge through her terrible victory over the flesh. Like some kind of medieval mystic.

Sometimes she hates Brandi, and wants to strike out at her. Other times she wants to take the child in her arms and comfort her, as if whatever it is can still yield to love and warmth and touch. Such moments are rare, and growing rarer. She feels she's coming to the end of her patience, the end of some kind of line. The moment is very close, she can almost see it. She can't name the day it will come, but it will be soon. And when it comes, she doesn't know what she will do.

Rita flicks the channels through myriad visions of people kissing, talking, fighting, driving cars at impossibly high speeds; through the commercials drenched in pulsing colours of people eating steaming hot pizzas, strands of cheese forever melting before her eyes, or joyously flipping the caps off their favourite soft drinks, marvellously refreshing and colder than glaciers. Everything throbs with brilliant artificial life. For a moment she thinks she hears a high piercing wail, and she presses the mute button. But there is only silence. She turns the sound back on and raises the volume.

FROM *HONOUR THE SUN*
Ruby Slipperjack

Camping, Summer 1962

Mom coughs outside the tent before her footsteps fade away again. It's a very quiet morning. I hear the lonesome cry of a loon, somewhere out on the lake. A few seconds later it's answered by another much closer to the tent. Mom would never make it as a loon. I hear her footsteps coming and the crash of wood on the ground. She pokes her head in the tent flap, rummaging around in the paper box in the corner for the matches.

I prop up onto my elbows and smile at her. She whispers, "Don't get up yet till I get the fire going. There are a lot of mosquitos out here." She ducks back out again.

I lay back down and pull up my knees, snuggling into the warm blankets. I sleep at the edge and my face is about a foot from the tent wall. I can smell the pine branches that we're sleeping on. The bottom of the tent wall is tucked and weighed down with rocks around inside the tent. A mosquito bounces along the tent wall and settles on the rock in front of my face. I put my hand out and squash it.

The fire crackles now and soon the smell of birch bark and wood smoke drift into the tent. Something small is scratching, scratching, then bounces off the tent wall in front of me. The canvas wall is a little loose between the rocks and I can see the imprint of the frog each time he bounces against the wall. I hold my hand against the canvas, my middle finger tight against my thumb, waiting for his next jump. Here he is. I let my finger go as hard as I can. Snap, the frog is gone. After a pause, he is back again. I look down the length of the tent wall and see one of my old runners. I nudge it up with my foot till I can reach it. The frog is still bouncing off the wall. I hold my shoe, flat side against the wall, waiting till he lands on the tent again. Whack. I got him good. The tent vibrates clear across the top centre beam. Maggie pops her head up behind me. "Wha ... what's that?"

Giggling I pull my shoe on and rummage around the pile of shoes for my other one. I step out into the fresh, clear morning air, then around the tent and into the bushes. After a battle with the mosquitos, I hurry back to the clearing.

Mom sits on fresh, broken pine boughs, making breakfast by the fire. She leans back, squinting her eyes each time the smoke sweeps around towards her. "The smoke just can't decide which way to go," she grumbles.

I pick up the soap and towel from the top of an old tree stump and head down to the lake. I slowly wash my face and hands. A mist hangs over the bay where the little portage is. We came here yesterday. Mom and Barbara came by canoe with the tent, groceries and camping stuff with Cora, Brian and Tony perched on top of the boxes and sacks full of blankets. Wess, Vera, Annie, Jane, Maggie and I walked the mile on the tracks to get here. We helped carry all the things across the portage and Wess and Mom carried the canoe over. Then Mom and Barbara made several trips with the canoe to get us all here to this island on the lake. Boy, our canoe was packed full.

The island is only about fifty feet from the main shoreline which is mostly swamp. There are some rocky slopes on the other side of the lake; some are quite steep. Here comes a train. I can see the tracks from here. Funny, I never even heard the trains that must have gone by during the night.

"You got the soap and towel?" Maggie comes walking down the rocky slope towards me. Rubbing her eyes and yawning, she squats down beside me by the lake. Slowly, she dunks both hands in the water and wipes her wet hands over her face. I hand her the wet soap. As she takes it, it squirts out of her hand and into the water. The soap sinks and slides along the rock, deeper and deeper. Maggie plunges her hand in quickly, trying to reach it. She loses her balance and falls over, her chest and shoulders sliding into the water. With a gasp, she scampers back onto the rock, dripping wet, but holding up the soap.

I start giggling and finally break out laughing. Oh, she looked so funny. Her wet hair is plastered to her head. After throwing the soap on top of the towel, she dashes back to the tent to change her shirt.

Mmmm ... I smell bacon and I rush up to the campfire. Mom has made raisin bannock, bacon and a big pot of boiled eggs. My mouth waters as Mom hands me my share of the breakfast. I find the nearest rock and settle down, enjoying every bite.

After breakfast, we wash the dishes and pans. The blankets are hung on a rope stretched between two trees. Then the camp settles down to some quiet, peaceful hours. Annie and Maggie are reading Annie's endless supply of comic books inside the tent. With Barbara's help, Mom is stringing up her newly finished fishnet. Beside the tent, Cora, Brian and Tony are building a miniature log cabin with twigs and dry sticks.

Mom sends Wess with the axe, and Vera, Jane and I to gather a pailful of pinecones. She wants to use them to dye her new fishnet. After an hour of tripping over brush, swatting flies and throwing pinecones at each other, we emerge from the bush with Vera carrying the pailful of cones. Our hands are black and sticky, the resin gluing our fingers together. Wess rubbed some of that sticky stuff over my left eye. Now my eyelid sticks every time I blink.

Giggling and pushing, we file past the fire where Mom has a tub filled with boiling water. Her fishnet is ready. She dumps the cones into the boiling water. She gives us each a dab of mosquito repellent to strip the resin off our hands. After washing our hands clean by the lake, we decide to have some tea.

I sit leaning against the tree with my tea cup, watching Mom stirring her pinecone brew with a long stick. Small puffs of clouds are slowly moving across the sky, sometimes covering the sun. Flies continually buzz around the campfire. Mom's satin-white fishnet lays folded in layers on a white sheet to protect it from the moss and twigs on the ground.

Wess and Vera are in the canoe calling us. I drop the cup by the tea pot and skip over the rocks to the lake.

"We'll pretend we're the train. Get in," says Wess.

"Where to?" he asks, after Annie gets in.

"Sioux Lookout!" she says.

"Where to?"

"Armstrong!" says Jane, settling down beside Annie.

"Where to?" shouts Wess again.

"Savant Lake!" says Maggie.

"Where to?"

"Fort William!" I step in, quite proud of remembering the name of that place.

"Sorry. You'll have to get off. We don't go there on this train," Wess shouts.

My mind scrambles for another town. "Okay, I'm going to Long Lac then!" I say and sit down beside Maggie.

"All aboard!" Wess shouts in his conductor's voice.

Mom yells at us from the campfire to be careful. Wess chuckles as the canoe is pushed away from the shore. Having gone only about the length of the canoe, he steers the canoe to shore. "Armstrong," he yells and points to the boulder by the shore.

"Aw-w-w, already?" says Jane, getting off.

Wess chuckles, "Well, Armstrong's not far, you know."

Off we go again; this time, he steers the canoe straight across the lake. Thoroughly enjoying the ride, I don't realize we are approaching a small, flat rock about two feet across, far from the main shoreline. I smile at Wess, who chuckles again and brings the canoe to a stop. He yells, "Long Lac!"

Well, what can I do? I have to get off. I step onto the rock which is only a couple of inches above the water.

The canoe turns and heads back to the island. I stand there, and glance at the bush behind me once in awhile. I can see them paddling around to the side of the island where they let Maggie off. Then I see the canoe disappear around the other side of the island. I stand there listening to all the little noises from the bush behind me.

Feeling dizzy from all the shimmering water around me, I try squatting on the rock. Soon my calves start to ache. Oh, I wish they'd come back. I try sitting down with my legs crossed in front of me, but the hem of my dress falls into the water on each side of me. The rock hurts my ankles and I almost lose my balance. Still no sign of the canoe.

Time passes. The mosquitos and horseflies from the bush have found me. I'm getting desperate. The wind has picked up and little waves are starting to lap at the rock in front of me, splashing my feet. I need to go to the bathroom.

Should I disgrace myself by yelling for help? Should I yell? I'll wait a little longer. More time passes by. I try standing up and stomping my feet but I almost lose my balance. I try sitting very still but my foot starts to fall asleep. More time passes. I can't wait any longer. I fill my lungs to yell. Then I see them picking up Jane. Slowly, the canoe approaches me. "Oh, thank you, thank you," I whisper as they come closer. Vera with her bright smile and curly head at the front of the canoe, is a welcome sight.

"What took you so long?" I ask meekly.

"Well, Long Lac is pretty far you know, so we had to stop for lunch first!" Wess answers with a chuckle.

Around the side of the island, Maggie comes out of the shade, stretching and yawning after a nice rest on a comfortable moss-padded clearing. We go around to the other side of the island. We come upon Annie stretched out on top a large boulder with a comic book over her face. Then we slowly drift towards the campsite. I am the first one out and head straight for the makeshift bathroom back in the bush.

When I return, Mom hands me a bowlful of macaroni in tomato sauce with a piece of bannock. I notice the new rust-coloured fishnet gently swaying in the breeze while it hangs in long sweeps over a rope strung between the trees. It looks silky soft.

Mom, in the shade under a tree, pounds a pile of lead sinkers apart to hold the bottom rope of the net. Beside her is a tub of multi-coloured floats Barbara has finished stringing. They will be attached to the top rope on the new fishnet.

After lunch, I run down to the lake and wash my bowl and spoon. Soon Maggie and Annie come to wash their bowls, too. We watch a big flat bloodsucker approaching in a steady wavy motion. "It probably smelled the food washed from our bowls," says Annie.

"How would it smell? I don't see a nose on it," I say.

"Maybe it just sees the pieces floating around," suggests Maggie.

"Well, he must have eyes for sure, because he seems to know exactly where he's going," says Annie.

I say, "You know, he looks like Crazy Bill's bottom lip." We all run up to the tent laughing.

Mom has decided to put rabbit snares in the marshy area across the bay. Wess is going with her to hunt for partridge. He's taking the small .22 rifle. Barbara will take them across in the canoe and come back to pick up Vera, Jane, Maggie and the little kids. They're going to the tracks to pick some late blueberries.

Annie has decided to stay in the tent to read her comics. Mom calls me over to her sewing bag and indicates the leftover spools of twine from her fishnet. "Look how much was left over," she says to me.

"Would that be enough for a little net?" I ask excitedly.

"Oh, it could be about two feet wide and about seven feet long," she says.

"Oh Boy! I'll start it right away!" I run my fingers over the satiny-smooth surface of the nylon twine.

I'll need a little rectangular piece of wood and a small spindle. Mom hands me a piece of cedar wood. I decide to get busy right away. Mom warns me to be careful with the knife before she heads down to the lake with Wess.

I love to carve things and I'm the knife and axe sharpener, when Wess isn't home. But I still manage to cut myself a lot. I must have over a dozen scars on my hands.

"Hey! I'm asking you if you're coming!" Barbara yells at me from the canoe.

"No. No. I'm staying here," I answer and make myself comfortable on the rock. I already see in my mind the small spindle that I am going to make.

I've got a sore neck. The rectangular crossbar I've made is about an inch and a half wide; that's how wide the squares are going to be. I've sanded it smooth so that the twine doesn't catch. The spindle I've made is about five inches long and about an inch wide, with a long pointed tongue in the middle. I've sanded and smoothed the inside, all along the tongue around the sharp curved tip and down to the nicked flat bottom. The red stains along one side are from the small cut on my middle finger.

The girls came back awhile ago with a pot of blueberries. The branches of the pine trees above me interlock together and part again, gently swaying in the breeze. I hear a long whistle from the shore. That's Wess's signal that they're ready to come back. Barbara heads down to the lake and into the canoe to pick them up.

I sit up again and start winding the twine on the spindle. Starting from the bottom, I bring it up; loop around the tongue; down the bottom and around. Faster and faster I go. The spindle gets fatter and the twine climbs higher and higher up the tongue. There, it's full!

I'm done and here comes Mom, twigs clinging to her hair which has escaped from around her scarf. A pleased look crosses her face when I place my new crossbar and full spindle beside the shiny white nylon spools on her sewing bag.

"Oh, you've finished them," she says smiling.

"Yep!" I answer, grinning, quite pleased with myself.

Wess snags my hair with the protruding sights of the .22 gun, when he passes by me. "Oops!" he chuckles.

Mom and Barbara go to check the fishnet. I lie down with Annie who just woke up from a long nap. I look at one of the "Archie" comics. Maggie lies sprawled on the other side, giggling and turning the pages of a "Sad Sack" comic. With Wess in there, our comic reading quickly turns into a pillow fight. My ears burn from a whack on both sides of my head. I dodge out of the tent. Mom is starting to fry fish in the two frying pans. The sun has already gone down behind the trees.

Vera and Jane are getting the bedding down from the line and into the tent. Cora is grouchy and tired. Brian and Tony are almost leaning on each other while they sit waiting for their supper.

I sit down under a tree, watching them and listening. Barbara has just put down her sewing—a baby bonnet? Gee, it looks pretty small. My heart fills with love as I watch my mother, there by the fire, swatting flies away from the food. Her hair is very tangled now and blowing in a fine fuzz all around her head. She's asking Jane for a long piece of wood by the fire. As Jane pulls it, the end flips up and knocks the teapot over. Barbara is mad. She has just made the pot of tea. I study Barbara for a moment and decide her belly must be getting fat.

At last, supper is ready and we're all having our fill of fish, potatoes and bannock. The wind is completely gone now. I sit there thinking we should all chew at the same time, so there'd be some silence. I turn around and face the lake. It's calm and peaceful. Almost as part of the nature all around us, the voices grow quiet, turning into a low drone mixed with the twitters of laughter.

I sit there daydreaming, having long since returned my plate to the pile by the fire. Maggie and Annie are washing the dishes by the fire. The little ones have gone to bed. Mom sets the last log in the campfire for the night. I linger by the fire watching the flames greedily devour the dry wood until it is almost burnt out.

I stand up and brush the twigs off my dress. After a big stretch and a yawn, I shuffle along to the tent. Everyone's already jostled to a comfortable spot when I poke my head in. Mom sleeps by the door so I look along the row of bodies until I spot a space at the end, beside Jane. I start gingerly at first, until I hear the first, "Ouch!" Quickly removing my foot, I get another, "Ow!" Then in rapid succession, it is "Ouch! Awoo! Hey! Watch it!" Stepping and slipping on feet and toes, I finally make it to the end, where I drop down quickly before someone throws a shoe at me. Jane giggles beside me, as I take off my shoes. I pull the covers over me and stretch out on my back.

Mom, grunting and sighing, settles down on her bedding beside the tent door. Quiet settles over the group as she digs in her bag. She clears her throat and reads from her worn Cree prayer book and a chapter from the red Bible, a nightly ritual. Small lights flicker across the tent front from the dying campfire outside. The reading is done and the nightly jokes and stories start. Mom tells a legend of two sisters who went on a journey. They had looked longingly at the brightest star and that star came and took them up to where they found an old woman fishing from a hole in the sky. They asked her to let them back down to earth with her fishline. My eyelids grow heavy as Mom's voice drones on and on ...

FROM *THE TENT PEG*
Aritha van Herk

I stand at the head of the long table that Thompson built this afternoon and I ladle, I spoon, I dish out steak and salad, vegetables and bread and butter, baked potatoes and sour cream. Thompson grins when he sees what I've made for this first supper.

"Meat and potatoes night, eh?"

"Thought I'd get off on the right foot," I say. "Besides, I haven't unpacked all my spices yet."

"I can hardly wait," he says. "Curry's my favourite."

Down the length of the table Jerome scowls but says nothing. He has moved in with Mackenzie and put Thompson with the helicopter pilot, so he feels guilty enough to restrain himself. And now they are all seated, two rows of masculine heads bent over melmac plates, silent except to reach for the salt, to clatter a knife on the oilcloth. I thought oilcloth didn't exist anymore, but there it was in the supplier's in Yellowknife, and of course I had to buy a length to cover the table.

They are so silent, absorbed while they eat, men are. Mackenzie looks at me and smiles, then returns to his plate. I can see the maps unrolling in his head, he's studying the contours of the mountains in the shape of the food he's eating. He's glad to be out here, away from town, the transition accomplished. This is his world, he moves effortlessly, the moss under his feet natural and yielding. The men obey him instinctively, Jerome blusters and shouts, but Mackenzie is in control as surely as he seems awkward and unassuming in town.

His world it is, and I have to halt, catch myself at the strangeness of this place. Where are we? The middle of a mountain range in the Yukon where I doubt any man has been before and, if so, left no trace, nothing behind. The mountains and the moss echo no residue of humans at all. And me, what am I doing here, a woman pretending to be a cook, pretending to have the nutritional welfare of these men foremost in my mind when all I wanted to find was silence, a relief from the cacophony of sound, of confession that surrounded, that always impinged on me. I didn't want their secrets, my ear not receptacle enough for ordinary words, let alone confession. I do not practice absolution.

Indeed, I have my own fear and my own doubt and my own confession to make, if there were anyone to listen. In the lengthening dusk I watch nine mouths chew and swallow, I watch nine pairs of eyes cover me and then look away. We are in the middle of the Yukon mountains with only tenuous radio contact to the outside world and I am on my own with or against them. At my own desire, at my own folly.

And quite suddenly I'm afraid. Me, self-contained but slight and alone and, yes, fearful, balanced against the anger and heft of nine men. With only the dubious position of cook to protect me.

I wanted this; I schemed to get here. And I think of walking across the uneven ground to my huddled tent, of lighting the Coleman lantern—but, no, every movement you make shows itself through the transparent tent walls. I may look like a boy, but I will have to undress in the dark every night.

And yet when I look at their faces down either side of this rough table, I see the same faces I have always seen, the same men I have always known. Bearded or clean-shaven, angular or smooth, they are after all only men. I have no reason to be afraid. I cannot be afraid or they will smell my fear, and I will certainly be lost, at their mercy. Keep them at bay with kettles, with pots and pans and wooden spoons, keep them on their knees with scalding water and merciless soups, keep them confused with the hieroglyphics only I can read in flour.

And now, searching for some source of strength, I think of Deborah, her bundle of faggots resting beside her as she reaches out a comforting hand. Deborah my friend, singer of joy and sorrow. We have more than once shored up our doubts and our losses together. Saving each other from ourselves, a woman's eternal lot.

She envied me coming here, retreating from the precast world. But when I told her it was easy, she smiled and shook her head. And of course she was right. It would be impossible for her, beautiful and soft and full of light, with that deep, broad voice. They would have no choice but to destroy her. It's easier for me, a girl shaped like a boy, with a boy's sharp angles.

Nine men. They are finishing now, shoving away their plates and scraping back their folding chairs and lighting cigarettes. I should have made a rule, no smoking in the cooktent. But it's too late now, and even though this is going to be my kitchen, it is already invaded.

Mackenzie clears his throat and looks at them, one by one. There have been few introductions. I hardly know their names. Now I can see he's going to say something, begin the summer officially, although we actually began it days ago, every one of us when we left wherever to come up north.

They are a miscellaneous lot, an odd assortment, not what I would have expected. I thought of geologists as solid, bearded men who smoked pipes and resembled one another. But as they turn to face him, expectant, I can see that they are hardly similar at all.

Mackenzie speaks without preamble, he cannot be pompous. "Well, I guess everything is pretty well set up. We have to finish building the shower, but Hearne, you and Cap can do that tomorrow."

"What do we need a shower for?" asks Jerome sourly. "The lake's full of water."

"That lake hasn't warmed up since the ice age," says Mackenzie. "Makes camp a lot more bearable if a guy can have a hot shower once in a while. They're easy enough to build. Other than that," he looks at the men steadily, "breakfast is at seven, and you're all expected to be up by that time. After breakfast everyone will be given the day's work. Also, every day two of you will haul water for J.L. She's got enough to do cooking."

"Hey, I thought the cook hauled her own water," someone says.

"Not in this camp," says Mackenzie pleasantly. "Now, you've all been assigned a tent, it's up to you how you arrange that situation. If you really can't bear who you're bunking with, we'll try to arrange something. But I don't want to hear about any fighting. Oh, and by the way, those camp cots may seem uncomfortable, but get used to them. If you sleep on the ground you'll get rheumatism." He pauses, surveys them for a long moment as if their faces are maps. "We're supposed to be looking for uranium here. We'll be working on the claims the company's optioned and we may do some staking, if we find anything good. Questions?"

They shake their heads and I can see on their faces that desire to be out on the mountain, hammering boulders, walking the ridges. They all want to be the one who finds it, who discovers something, they will fight for that privilege.

And me, I clear the dirty dishes from the table, step around their feet and heat a pail of water to wash up with. There is something comforting in the familiar work, in my hands' movement from memory, an orchestration we women grow up with. Why does it seem that we're never taught how to do this, we simply know, we know the smoothest, most efficient way of making food and giving food and clearing up the remains of food, nourishers always. And, when we are angry, we have a tendency to break, yes, dishes. Deborah once said that our lives are like the outer edge of china plates, sometimes smooth and sometimes scalloped, sometimes chipped, but always with an edge, always circular, ever-returning.

And me up to my elbows in soapy water scrubbing congealed food off melmac plates, rinsing them, stacking them in the remembered ceremony. By the end of the summer I will have washed more plates than I have in my entire life. I didn't count on that. I thought only of the making, the creating, the cooking. And discover I will spend more time washing dishes than I ever will cooking.

And before I can go outside and shut myself into my tent, I will make lunches, two dozen sandwiches buttered and sliced and wrapped, two dozen cookies and nine apples and all of them in brown bags lined up on the table waiting for the morning. Already I am tired. I only want to wrap myself in that down-filled sleeping bag and dream, dream lapped in the silence and the unhindered sweep of the moss and the mountains.

FROM *IN SEARCH OF APRIL RAINTREE*
Beatrice Culleton

I was taken to a small farming community further south of Winnipeg on the outskirts of Aubigny, to the DeRosier farm. It was a Friday afternoon when we arrived. While Mrs. Semple talked with Mrs. DeRosier, I studied my new foster mother with great disappointment. She was a tall woman with lots of make-up and badly dyed hair. If she had been a beauty once, the only thing left of it now was the vanity. Her voice was harsh and grating. The more I watched her, the more positive I became that she was putting on an act for Mrs. Semple's benefit. I wondered why Mrs. Semple couldn't figure that out but then I thought it was okay as long as Mrs. DeRosier gave me a good home.

After my social worker's departure, Mrs. DeRosier turned to me. I looked up at her with curiosity. She went to the kitchen drawer, took out a strap and laid it on the table near me. She told me the routine I would be following but in such a way that it made me think she had made this speech many times before.

"The school bus comes at eight. You will get up at six, go to the hen house and bring back the eggs. While I prepare breakfast, you will wash the eggs. After breakfast you will do the dishes. After school, you'll have more chores to do, then you will help me prepare supper. After you do the supper dishes, you will go to your room and stay there. You'll also keep yourself and your room clean. I know you half-breeds, you love to wallow in filth. You step out of line once, only once, and that strap will do the rest of the talking. You don't get any second chances. And if you don't believe that I'll use it, ask Raymond and Gilbert. And on that subject, you will only talk to them in front of us. I won't stand for any hanky-panky going on behind our backs. Is that clear? Also, you are not permitted the use of the phone. If you want letters mailed, I'll see to it. You do any complaining to your worker, watch out. Now, I'll show you where your room is."

I was left alone in a small room at the back of the house. It was cold, smelled mouldy and felt damp. There wasn't even a closet, just nails sticking out all over the walls. The Dions had given me a new set of suitcases and I opened one up and started hanging a few things on the nails. I stopped and sat on the bed. The mattress was soft and warped. Self-pity was not good for one's spirits, Maman Dion had told me, but right now, I felt sorry for myself. Mrs. DeRosier had said, " ... you half-breeds." I wasn't a half-breed, just a foster child, that's all. To me, half-breed was almost the same as Indian. No, this wasn't going to be a home like the Dions'. Maybe if there were other children, they might be nice. Most people I'd met when I had stayed at the Dion's had been nice enough. With this thought, I finished hanging up my clothes, looking forward to the arrival of Raymond and Gilbert, who I thought must be at school.

I was waiting at the kitchen table in order to meet them. Mrs. DeRosier was in the kitchen too, but she only glared at me as if to warn me to stay quiet. I saw the school bus from the kitchen window and thought how nice it would be taking a bus from now on. Four kids got off, two older boys around thirteen or fourteen and a girl and a younger boy. I was hoping that they would like me. They all walked in but the two older boys walked by without looking at me and I heard them going up the stairs. The younger boy and the girl eyed me contemptuously. The boy said to Mrs. DeRosier, "Is that the half-breed girl we're getting? She doesn't look like the last squaw we had."

The girl giggled at his comment.

"April, you may as well start earning your keep right now. Here, I want you to peel these potatoes." Mrs. DeRosier got out a large basket of potatoes and put them down in front of me. I was sure that the two children must be Mrs. DeRosier's very own. They made themselves sandwiches, making an unnecessary mess in the process. When I finished peeling the potatoes, Mrs. DeRosier told me to clean up their mess. Mr. DeRosier came in at suppertime and it became apparent to me that Mrs. DeRosier towered over him not only in size but also in forcefulness of personality. He and the two boys who had changed into work clothes, sat on one side, Mrs. DeRosier was at the head and Maggie and Ricky and I sat on the other side. The only talking at the table was done by the mother and her two children. I had finished my milk and reached for the pitcher to pour myself another glass.

"You're not allowed more than one glass," Maggie said in a whiny voice. I froze, my hand still on the handle, waiting for Mrs. DeRosier to confirm that statement or say it was all right. I wondered if I should give in to this girl, then realized I had no choice because Mrs. DeRosier simply remained silent. Slowly, I withdrew my hand from the pitcher and looked over at the mother and daughter. Maggie had a smug look on her face. I wanted to take that pitcher of milk and dump it all over her head. At other meals she would make a show of having two glasses of milk herself.

When Ricky finished eating, he burped and left the table without excusing himself either way. The other two boys had also finished eating but remained seated until Mr. DeRosier got up to leave. Then they followed him outside. Mrs. DeRosier put the left-overs away and indicated I was to start on the dishes. While I washed and wiped them, Maggie sat at the table and watched. I wondered why this family was so different from the Dions, especially those three. So much malice, so much tension. It seemed to me that it was a lot easier being nice; after all, the DeRosiers were Catholics, too. How I wished that my own parents would rescue me and right this minute would be a good time. I finished wiping the last pot and put it away. I started for my bedroom, relieved to get away from Maggie's watchful eyes.

"You're not finished," Maggie said in a bossy tone. "You didn't even sweep the floor. I heard you half-breeds were dirty but now I can see that it's true."

"You didn't do anything yet. Why don't you sweep the floor?"

"Because it's not my job. My job is only to see that you do yours. So get the broom!" Maggie hissed at me.

I stood there for a minute, looking down at Maggie. She was still sitting, very composed, very sure of how far she could go. Helpless fury built up inside of me but I was alone here, unsure of what my rights were, if I even had any. So I went to get the broom. After sweeping the floor, I went to my room. I had nothing to do but think. Was it only this morning I had felt loved and cherished? Now, I had been told I would have to earn my keep. I knew that Children's Aid paid for my keep. And I didn't like that word 'half-breed' one bit! It took me a while to get over all these new things I didn't like so I could get ready for bed and say my prayers.

Praying could bring me comfort, Maman Dion had told me. I had memorized the Lord's Prayer in French and English but I had never really thought about the meaning of each sentence. Now, I said it slowly.

"Our Father, who art in Heaven, hallowed be Thy Name. Thy Kingdom come, Thy will be done, on earth as it is in heaven. Give us this day our daily Bread. Forgive us our trespasses, as we forgive those who trespass against us. And lead us not into temptation, but deliver us from evil, Amen."

I would have to forgive these people their trespasses and no doubt there would be many. 'But, hold on there, God', I thought. 'I don't have any trespasses for them to forgive. So how come I'm going to have to forgive theirs?' I looked for the answers in the talks and the Bible readings at the Dions. I remembered the saints and the martyrs. They had been tested. Maybe I was being tested. Maybe what I had to do while I was here was turn the other cheek. When I went to sleep, I was feeling very saintly.

Saturday morning, Mr. DeRosier rapped at my door, telling me I was supposed to go for the eggs. It had been windy all night and I had not slept well in my chilly room. I sleepily got dressed and went to the kitchen. No one was there but I saw a pail by the doorway and supposed I was to use that. It was still dark outside and it took me a while to find the chicken house. There were deep drifts of snow which had been whipped up by the wind overnight. Another thing I decided was that I didn't like winter anymore. Not as long as I lived on this farm. I gathered the eggs, got nasty pecks from the hens that were too stubborn or too protective. As I floundered through the snowdrifts, my mouth watered at the thought of breakfast, but when I entered the house, no one seemed to be up. I was still cold and very hungry but I didn't dare touch anything. I washed the eggs and found that a few had broken and many were cracked. I worried while I waited for Mrs. DeRosier. A few hours later, she came down in her housecoat and she looked a whole lot worse without her make-up.

She started to put some coffee on to perk and noticed the eggs still drying in the trays.

"What the hell did you do with these eggs? They're all cracked. I can't sell them that way!" I jumped up when she screamed. She picked up a few of them and threw them down on the floor in front of where I was sitting. She went on ranting and raving, not wanting my explanations. Finally, she told me to clean up the mess and she started breakfast.

When everyone had eaten, she and her two children got ready to go to town. She left me instructions to wash the floors and clean the bathroom after I finished the breakfast dishes. I thought to myself that if Ricky had been a girl, I would have been just like Cinderella. When I finished my assigned chores, I washed out my own room, trying to rid it of the musty smell. I had a few hours to myself before they came back, but when they did, Maggie, with her boots on, walked all over the kitchen floor and I had to wash it again.

FROM "TEETH"
Cathy Ford

"I cannot always be a child crying in the dark."
–from *Magdalene* by Carolyn Slaughter

1

tongue against teeth
feet versus shoes
teeth
the pressure to get out
talking
you hold me like history
story of the cellar

the outhouse had no prestige
the change began
in the root cellar
like history

the stairs down wooden
precious electric light
there was one

the stairs creaked
the stairs shadowed
it was too steep to change
direction
the declaration made

must continue

you
hold me
a function of mechanism
gone full light
seldom
does the long thin light chain
silver break
that must be security

2 everyone was there
the winterhouse supply
jars and jars and jars
plums
tin lidded
tomatoes pushed against the glass
red

you did not hurry down the stairs

the waiting face of the venison
or chicken
gelled
noses eyes
slimed
flat
pickles dilled
green and onioned
flattered in panicking small girls.

3 you have to wear shoes
the cellar is damp

—under the house—

footsteps creak above
scrape of kitchen chairs
terror in the open cellar door
the door could admit another

uncle
or slam shut
a three storied house is full
of drafts

the stench is the worst

A SASKATCHEWAN KITCHEN

Rose Miller

The kitchen is a place I remember very well as a child. I lived in a kitchen for 10 years of my life.

When I was nine years old I was an orphan. I was born to an unwed mother. By the time I was four, I had acquired two younger brothers, Bruce and Harvey. Harvey had only lived a short time when he was diagnosed as having T.B. My mother also had T.B. This was during the early 1940s when tuberculosis was rampant and there were sanitoriums everywhere. My brother, Harvey, and Mother both died within six months of each other. So my brother, Bruce, and I were alone.

We were living in the home of a man named Alfred. We weren't Alfred's children, so he didn't want to raise two snotty-nosed little waifs who weren't his. He sent us packing down the road with the few clothes we had tied in pillow cases on the ends of little 'hobo-sticks'.

The creek by our house had flooded, so we waded through water up to our necks. We arrived at our neighbours' about one-half mile down the road with our 'hobo-sticks,' all our clothes soaking wet, looking like two skinny, drowned rats. I handed them a note, written by Alfred, which explained to these people why we were there. They had no choice, so they took us in.

The lady was nice to us, but the fear of T.B. was so bad that she explained how she couldn't keep us because her grandchildren were coming to visit her. The man was a pervert, and would put his hands in my underwear every chance he got. I have no idea why he did this or what he was looking for. Over the years I would be wakened up in the night with this happening to me ... men in their long red flannel underwear draped over me. I say 'men'. because I went through a series of foster homes, basically all the same.

Finally we were sent to a home with two ladies: an old lady we called Gramma and an old maid daughter who lived with her, too, whom we called Aunty. The Aunty was very nice, but she, too, was controlled by the Gramma. The Gramma was like the old witch in Hansel and Gretel. She sure wasn't your usual Gramma with milk and cookies. In fact, two of the main foods I remember there were lumpy cold oatmeal porridge, which I ate seven days a week, 365 days a year, for 10 long years; and cold greasy fried potatoes. Or sometimes soup or stew with big lumps of turnips or cabbage. Here we lived in the kitchen for 10 years. We weren't allowed in the living room; the kitchen was our home.

Let me tell you what this kitchen looked like. It was a big old shed that had been hauled from a farm and joined onto the rest of the house. It had cheap linoleum on the floor and wallpaper on the walls. The furniture consisted of a big stove that burned coal in the winter and wood in the summer. There was a reservoir on the side for hot water, and an old kettle on the top with more hot water. It had an oven in the bottom, and a warming oven on top. The only other pieces of furniture in the kitchen were a sink in the corner where we washed our hands and faces each morning (it was really a basin in a cupboard), a wooden table and four old wooden chairs.

I spent a lot of my life on one of these chairs—doing homework or reading. I read every Nancy Drew book she ever wrote, also *Huck Finn* and *Tom Sawyer*. When I wasn't reading books I was hauling rainwater in the summer, or ice or snow in the winter to keep the reservoir filled. Bruce and I also cut wood for the stove, brought in the coal, shovelled snow, cut grass with a push lawnmower—and we had a big yard.

We were allowed to go to school, but we couldn't socialize with our friends; we had to always come straight home from school, do our chores, then sit our skinny little butts in the kitchen until bedtime—which always came very early. I used to lie in bed and pretend I was very rich and lived with Kings and Queens and had lots of servants and everything was wonderful.

We had to use an outside biffy (toilet) winter, summer, spring and fall. All we had for toilet paper was an old outdated catalogue. In the 1940s those catalogues had rough pages, so when I only had to pee I wouldn't use it. I would just pull up my drawers and drip dry. (I really did wear drawers, white or red—down to the knees, elastic waist, very ugly).

On Sunday night we filled big washtubs on the stove so there would be wash water for Monday morning in the old wringer washer. The night before, this same old tub was put into the middle of the kitchen floor and filled with warm water so Bruce and I could have our regular weekly baths.

One Monday morning I came downstairs, as always planning to just sit and choke down my lumpy cold porridge, when I was hit by a big stick across my back. When I turned to see why this time, a pair of my long drawers were pushed into my face—because of all the 'drip dryings' on them. I decided this was the last beating I was going to take for this, so every Sunday night I would gather up all my dirty undies and wash them out by hand in my basin; I would dry them under my mattress in my room, so by the time they got put into the wash pile—no drip-dry pee stains. I never told Gramma, and I doubt if she ever figured out how my drawers were so clean on wash-days.

KITCHEN SECRETS

Laura Vocat

When I was young, my father and mother both worked, so I was sent to a babysitter's. There I spent most of my time in the kitchen. It was the only place I was comfortable. It was the only place I belonged. I did not belong in the bedrooms with the babysitter's children, I did not belong in the living room with breakable things, I belonged in the kitchen.

My first babysitter was Shannon's mother. She was a dark-haired, sturdy woman with brightly painted red lips. She always smiled and she never got mad and she never yelled.

Shannon's mother's kitchen was dull. It had dark brown brick walls but it was still happy like Shannon's mother. It was happy because of Sheldon, the dalmation. He ate scraps that fell on the kitchen floor, food Shannon and I passed to him under the table, and bread crusts that Shannon's mother cut off our sandwiches.

I only stayed in the brown kitchen for a short time because Shannon's family was transferred to Edmonton. I was transferred to a kitchen up the street.

This kitchen was yellow. It belonged to Mrs. Usher, a thin, red-headed, stone-faced woman who didn't smile, didn't laugh, and didn't like babysitting me. Mrs. Usher's kitchen was the opposite of Shannon's mother's kitchen. It was also the opposite of Mrs. Usher. The Usher kitchen was covered with flowered lemon yellow wallpaper and pale yellow tiles.

No one spoke during lunches in the yellow kitchen, they just ate. No spotted dalmations trotted through the yellow kitchen. Nothing trotted through the yellow kitchen. No one laughed in the yellow kitchen. No one smiled in the yellow kitchen. No one dropped a scrap in the yellow kitchen.

Food in the yellow kitchen was yellow too. Fluffy yellow scrambled eggs, golden omelettes filled with ham and cheese, big yellow-pupilled egg eyes on toast, yellowy-grey boiled eggs with rust speckles. Premature chickens. Always warm, always yellow.

Yellow air filled the yellow kitchen. It curled its steamy fingers up my nose, down my throat and into my stomach. Deep into my stomach the yellow fingers crawled. They squeezed my stomach, forced waves up my throat.

Yellow is the colour my stomach hates most.

Mrs. Usher knew my stomach hated yellow, that was one of the things my mother told her before I started going to the yellow kitchen. This didn't matter though because this was the yellow kitchen. Day after day, I sat at the white table in the yellow kitchen and watched. I watched the white table as though it were about to disappear. I watched the Usher children shovel forkfuls of yellow down their throats. I watched thin sticky yellow strands ooze down their chins. I watched yellow eyes disappear into their hungry pink mouths. I watched and I waited.

I waited for the day the yellow would disappear. I waited for the day I wouldn't have to see yellow and hear Mrs. Usher say, "You eat what I make or you don't eat at all!" That day finally came.

Yellow disappeared into a sea of peanut butter. For the first time I ate in the yellow kitchen; spongy white bread piled thick with smooth brown butter. I am positive Mrs. Usher didn't think my 10-year-old stomach could hold that much.

Mrs. Usher learned her lesson. I could eat more peanut butter sandwiches than she wanted to feed me. I never saw peanut butter sandwiches in the yellow kitchen again. Instead, the yellow returned.

One day, about three months after my arrival in the yellow kitchen, my mother had an argument with Mrs. Usher. She said Mrs. Usher was a bitch and she hated "that woman." Since my mother decided she felt the same way about Mrs. Usher that I did, I told her about my yellow lunches. I was promptly removed from the yellow kitchen.

The yellow kitchen was soon replaced by another brown kitchen. This brown kitchen belonged to Mrs. Bauer (who I called Mrs. B.). Mrs. B. was a lot like her kitchen; drab. Mrs. B. was very thin, had polio in her left leg and had scraggy brownish-grey hair, a wrinkled face, and smoky yellow teeth and fingers.

Mrs. B. knew my stomach hated yellow, so I never saw yellow in her brown kitchen. I did see many other things which I didn't like though. I was a very fussy eater and was allowed to refuse things I didn't like at home. Not at Mrs. B.'s. The rule was, "Eat what Mrs. B. makes you."

The reward for following the "eat everything" rule was dessert. Dessert was usually Dad's Cookies. My favourite was the soft chocolate chip kind with the small "x" baked into the top. Since I was allowed to eat as many cookies as I wanted if I ate all of my lunch, I usually took two packages of four cookies. I used to grab the cookies, stuff them into my mouth and chew until my mouth could no longer move. This resulted in a lumpy greyish-brown paste, which I stored in my mouth until I met my friend Joanne at her house nearby. Joanne and I would walk a little ways, then I'd open my mouth and let the paste plop onto the sidewalk. It made Joanne sick. I thought it was cool.

Mrs. B.'s kitchen soon became the one place in her house where I was safe. I wasn't safe when I was watching *The Flintstones* at lunch, I wasn't safe after school when I watched *Another World* with Mrs. B. I wasn't safe because I could be sent downstairs to play and I wasn't safe downstairs.

Mrs. B.'s basement was a lot like the kitchen. It was drab and brown. I hated the basement. In the basement, bodies flew onto beds, Mrs. B.'s son ground and groped, screams were never heard.

I spent five years trying to hide in the brown kitchen. My mother never had an argument with Mrs. B., so I never told her about the basement. Finally, I was old enough to leave the brown kitchen.

For the first time, I was allowed to go home for lunch, alone. No more yellow, no more drab kitchens, no more hiding. Best of all, no more babysitters.

I liked our kitchen because it wasn't drab and it wasn't yellow. It had one brick wall with tan bricks, one wall with tan wallpaper and the other walls were painted beige.

I liked going home for lunch because for the first time I was going home, to my house. My house, where I belonged. I belonged in the kitchen, I belonged in the living room, I belonged in the basement and I belonged in the bedrooms.

COFFEE ON MARY HILL

L.A. Martinuik

you know charlotte next door.

[pause. fill kettle.]

well i was talking to her, she came over to the fence when i was outside you know the problems she has, she's always really depressed and there's social workers around all the time. and they keep her drugged, i'm sure.

anyway, she says they're going to put her in the hospital and take away her kids and put them in foster homes. i don't think the little kids know at all, but the social worker told this to her daughter. over the phone. can you imagine?

hearing that over the telephone? and you've already been in and out of group homes and foster homes, and

i don't think the oldest knows. he's had so much to deal with.

well i could see taking *him* in but i sure don't need those other kids. it'd be just too much.

[pause. pour water into coffee filter.]

anyway so i said to her, charlotte you've got to fight this. they'll get you in there and they'll drug you and shock you and how are you supposed to get better when you're lying there trapped in the hospital and knowing your kids are all over hell.

and she just sortof nodded. i mean, she has no energy at all; all this makes her really weak.

anyway, so when i phoned you to come over i just wanted to know if you had any ideas about how you get it so you can prevent somebody from having to go in the hospital. and i know you know the people at the transition house and i thought maybe they would know, or, anyway i just thought

anyway i had to go do the shopping but i said to her to come over after and we could talk some more. so she came over and i made us a cold drink of lemonade.

well apparently this is just a temporary thing, so it's like she'll be there for a couple of weeks so she can have a complete rest. she signs herself in and then signs herself out again, and she has to do it like this because she can't afford to have the social worker there all the time.

and that's what she needs right now is to have someone be there all the time.

so as far as the kids, they'll come back with her; they'll just stay somewhere for a couple of weeks.

[pause. pour coffee]

but you know, they're just using her.

like, she's been on this one medication for a year, and it seemed to be working just fine you know, like you see her out and she seems okay

and then they switch her onto something else, and it's like, why did they do that? and she says well it was something new they wanted to try out

so i just said oh, well, that's really nice, isn't it. they're experimenting on *you*. they don't care if you get helped or not, they just want to see what the drug does.

and i know that's what they're doing up at riverview, those patients, you know sometimes they'll send in certain patients to do work with us in the laundry, and sometimes they're just happy and fine, and then sometimes they're just doped right out of it, shuffling around. and i know they just go ahead and switch the drugs around to see what will happen.

[pause]

there's the social worker now.

HUNGER OF ANOTHER KIND
Beth Brant

In 1945, the day Margaret Hill turned nine years old, her mother was murdered. A hit and run, the constable called it. Lily was crossing the street in town when a car closed down on her, running her over, then running out of town. Hit and run.

The white men in uniforms brought her mother's body to the house she shared with Uncle Douglas and Delilah, her grandmother. Limbs twisted and broken, face covered in blood, Lily was unrecognizable.

Uncle Douglas sobbed and raged over the body of his younger sister. He told the men in uniform he'd kill the driver of the car if he ever found him. The men looked embarrassed and uneasy, anxious to get away from the display of emotion emanating from Uncle like hot wires that snake and dance in the aftermath of a storm.

"Take it easy, Doug," the constable placated. "It won't do any good to get all riled up."

Uncle slumped into the chair, screams bouncing in his head as he wondered where on earth an Indian could get justice and the answer was an echo—nowhere, nowhere.

Delilah was silent. Pointing to the kitchen table, her finger instructing the men to lay the body of her daughter on the wooden planks, she was silent. The men left the house, casting glances back at Uncle. Delilah went to her daughter, taking off Lily's shoes, the sturdy brown shoes found in the mission box at church, and stroked her daughter's feet.

Margaret had watched the procession and could not believe this was real. She felt like she did when she was dreaming—outside the events that were happening, not believing this was her mother, her beautiful mother who carefully rolled her hair into a pompadour every day and wore bright dresses and jewellery, who painted her fingernails and toenails with red varnish, who applied lipstick with a brush, who was alive. Yesterday, Lily had promised a special surprise for Margaret's birthday. Lily had sat with Margaret on her lap and taught her a new song about sitting under an apple tree. Yesterday, Margaret's world was small and contained within the circle of mother, grandmother, and uncle. Now she saw a huge hole grabbing at her, waiting to pull her in.

"Mama?"

Uncle looked up at Margaret. He held out his arms to her and she went to him, but her tears were stuck somewhere inside and she could only let Uncle hold her while she waited for the choking feeling to subside.

Delilah still stood at the kitchen table touching her daughter's feet. "You'll help me get your mother ready," she told Margaret. "We'll need to get the others."

"Jesus Christ, let the kid be!" Uncle cried. "She's just a kid."

"Don't take the Lord's name in vain," Delilah said absently, "she'll need to help. Go get the others."

But the others had already heard the death news and were now making their way into the small house, bringing their presence and other gifts for Lily—a piece of braided sweetgrass, a pouch of tobacco, a bottle of whiskey to pass around. The men sat with Uncle, unscrewing the cap of the bottle, talking in low voices. The women ringed themselves around the kitchen table, touching Lily, touching Delilah, trying to hug Margaret who stood like stone.

"Child, bring us some water."

Margaret went outside and pumped water into the bucket. She carried the heavy pail back to the kitchen, almost stumbling up the steps. On the kitchen table lay her mother, stripped of the bloody rag that used to be her favourite dress. The women had straightened Lily's legs, which were broken and hung at odd angles from her torso. Margaret brought the bucket of water to the women, who dipped cloths into it and began to wash the body. The water soon turned red and Margaret was sent out to get clean. As she dumped the water on the earth she thought of the water as her mother, her life seeping into the hard earth, making little rivers trickling off into the weeds. A Lily river, Margaret thought. A river of Lily. Margaret pumped the water, her brown braids swinging back and forth. She looked up at the sky, the cold, dark clouds hovering around the house. She pumped and sang, "Don't sit under the apple tree with anyone else but me," her thin, girl voice matching the rhythm of the pump.

Inside the house, Margaret once again brought water to the women, who dipped and washed, who applied salve that smelled like mint, who worked silently. Margaret stood off to the side feeling as if she were in a dream. She had seen her mother naked lots of times but never like this—her breasts small and flat, covered with scratches and bruises. Her pubic hair, matted and blood-soaked. Lily's delicate hands curved into hooklike claws, the red varnish on her nails chipping and peeling. This wasn't her mother, Margaret thought. This wasn't her mother.

She looked at the men sitting around the wood stove. They were quiet except for the occasional shout of anger from Uncle. He paced the tiny room, his slick, black hair falling loose from where he had tucked it behind his large ears. Uncle's face was frightening to Margaret. She had always seen him laughing, or telling funny stories, his face screwing into shapes that would make her laugh. Today, his face was that of a stranger; angry, bitter lips pulled back into a snarl over his gums.

Yesterday, Uncle had held her hand as they trudged to the Methodist church for Sunday service. He had grumbled, as he always did on Sundays, because Delilah insisted they all go to church. Lily and Delilah walked on ahead and Uncle had held her hand and complained about the minister—"Can't tell a decent story if his life depended on it." The hymns—"Why do they have to sing every damn verse of those songs? And they sing like a funeral march! If they could just speed things up a bit, I wouldn't mind so much. Margaret, your grandmother is a hard woman, to make us do this every damn Sunday of every damn week!" And in church when they started on verse five of

The Old Rugged Cross, Uncle had looked at Margaret and whispered, "You'd think the man would be finally dead by now after four verses." She had giggled and hid her face in the hymnal and Delilah had given her a sharp look. Lily had smiled at her brother and winked at Margaret and gone on singing verse five in her clear, strong voice.

They had walked home and eaten their dinner of potatoes and beans, Uncle and Lily drinking tea by the quart, reusing the leaves and boiling the last bit of flavour from them, Delilah sitting by the stove, mending some piece of clothing and asking Margaret to read from the Bible. Margaret had read a story about a Samaritan helping somebody who lay in the road because nobody else would stop and give aid. She didn't know what a Samaritan was but she was happy reading out loud. Margaret loved to read. She dreamed of someday owning books and being able to pick one up at any time and read to her heart's content. The only book they had in the house was Grandmother's Bible, and Margaret poured over this volume every day.

"That was a good story," Uncle remarked after Margaret had finished.

"It was more than a good story," Delilah said, "it was a lesson. We should always stop to help people who are in need. There are rewards for helping others."

"I guess that's why there ain't any Samaritans around here. They know we can't give out any rewards," Uncle snickered into his hand.

Lily laughed, "If you see any Samaritan, grab 'im quick, before he changes his mind!"

Delilah sighed. "Read another story, Margaret. The one about Joseph's coat of colours."

Margaret looked back at the kitchen table. Delilah was beckoning to her. "Come. Come wash your mother's face. We'll make her pretty again. You'll see. Come."

Margaret took the cloth and went to where her mother's head rested at the head of the table. The women were massaging the mint-scented salve on Lily's arms and legs. They had straightened her crooked fingers and her hands lay at her sides, shining with grease. As Margaret brought the cloth to her mother's face, the sobs that were waiting in her chest came rushing out. Tears from her eyes spilled on Lily's face, mingling with the water from the cloth. The women crooned and continued to rub grease on Lily's breasts, her abdomen, under her arms where the black hairs curled and shone from the salve. Delilah touched Margaret's head. "That's right. See, her face is getting pretty again, just like I said. You're doing a good job. Your mother is pleased you're making her pretty again."

As Margaret washed her mother's face, she could see Lily's features becoming visible. Aside from a long scratch on her right cheek, the face was lovely as ever, almost like she was sleeping, Margaret thought. She cleaned Lily's forehead, pushing back the black hair. She touched her mother's eyelids, the dark lashes brushing against her fingers. Delilah had a brush in her hand and began untangling Lily's hair and brushing it smooth as it hung over the edge of the table.

"I'll fix her hair Grandma. I watched her do it. I know how."

Margaret took the brush and drew it through her mother's hair. Rolling puffs on either side of Lily's head and securing them with the hairpins Delilah held in her hand, Margaret worked to get it just right, just the way Lily would have done it. She lifted her mother's head to attach the black snood that held the rest of Lily's long, glossy hair. One of the women held out the jar of grease and Margaret lightly smeared it on Lily's face, caressing her mother's features, her nose, her lips.

"She needs her lipstick, Grandma. The red kind."

Delilah brought it to her and Margaret outlined Lily's full lips, struggling to keep within the lines of her mother's mouth. The women had stopped their work and were watching Margaret, leaning over the face, applying the red colour to the lifeless mouth. Delilah reached toward Margaret, "That's good child. It looks fine."

"No. It has to be just right." She painted the lips, making quick little strokes like she'd seen Lily do, using her little finger to spread the bright red colour. "There." She pulled away from the table and studied her work. "There."

"She looks real pretty, Margaret. You did a good job." Delilah took hold of Margaret's hand but Margaret pulled away.

"We have to get her dress. The one with the red and black squiggles. She liked that one." Margaret walked swiftly to the bureau and began pulling out drawers. Gathering her mothers underpants, slip, and dress, she walked back into the kitchen and Uncle lurched in front of her, taking hold of her shoulders. "Margaret. My little Margaret. We'll find the one who did this. I'll kill him for sure. We'll find him!" Uncle's face was contorted with grief and anger. "Your mother, she was the best," the tears pouring out of his eyes, "even if she went around with white men and pretended she wasn't Indian, she was still the best." He took his hands from Margaret's shoulders and raised a fist into the air. "I'll get him. I'll get him."

"Douglas! That's enough." Delilah's commanding voice sliced the air.

Margaret took her mother's things into the kitchen and handed them to Delilah. The women rolled the body over, pulling on the underpants, the slip. Delilah tore the dress with the red and black squiggles and fit it around Lily's body, slipping her arms into the dress and tucking the rest underneath her. She was almost ready. Opening Lily's mouth, Delilah inserted the small piece of braided sweetgrass, then closed the mouth, sealing the red lips together.

The women gathered their jars and cloth and men and left the house, murmuring their condolences and promises to come and sit with Delilah. The house was silent.

Uncle sat by the stove, still staring into the coals. "Mother?" Delilah went to him and took him in her arms. He cried, "She was the best, my sister."

Margaret looked at Lily on the kitchen table. She pulled out a chair and sat beside her mother. After a while, Uncle and Delilah came and sat beside her. They sat there all night long.

In the morning, Margaret woke to find herself in Delilah's arms, a blanket covering them both. Uncle was making tea, his body stooped over like an old man's, instead of the 35 he was. Margaret looked over Delilah's shoulder to see if Lily was still there, if maybe it had been a dream after all. But there she lay, stiff and unmoving, her red lips, her black hair, arrayed on the oak table. Delilah moved and opened her eyes. "Well, it's morning. Got to start cooking. People will be coming." Margaret got off Delilah's lap and stumbled into the the bed she had shared with her mother. She lay down and went back to sleep. She didn't dream.

She woke to the sound of the minister's voice. "I'm so sorry, Delilah."

Uncle lifted the curtain around the bed and sat down beside her. He whispered, "Had to get away. Can't stand the voice of that man." He lit up a cigarette. Margaret could hear the voice of Delilah and that of the Methodist minister, but couldn't make out the words. "We'll just wait till he's gone," Uncle said between puffs of smoke. They soon heard the door close and Delilah's, "Douglas? I need some help here." Uncle grinned and put out his cigarette, saving the butt in his pocket. "Got to chop some wood. Wanna help?" Margaret shook her head no. He put out his hand and touched her hair. "Keep going, kid. It's the only way."

Margaret smoothed the bed and went into the kitchen, avoiding the body on the table. Her grandmother was stirring the corn soup in a large kettle. She smiled at Margaret. "It'll be better today. Every day gets a little better. Your mother was just like you when she was little. Serious about everything. She was a good girl, like you."

"What did Uncle mean about Mama pretending not to be an Indian?"

"He didn't mean anything! Just the liquor talking. Your uncle likes his drink too much."

"How much is too much?" Uncle asked as he hauled wood into the kitchen.

"Never you mind. Just don't upset the child." Delilah continued stirring the soup.

"He doesn't upset me, Grandma." Margaret went to Lily's body and touched her mother's hair.

"Enos will be bringing the coffin soon. Reverend Jameson will be doing the service. You go and get yourself ready. I'll do your hair." Delilah dampened the coals under the kettle.

Margaret opened the bureau drawer and got out her good skirt and sweater—the grey pleated skirt with the suspenders that buttoned in the back and her grey sweater that Delilah had knit from a cast off found in the mission box. She had unravelled the wool from the man's sweater and rolled it into a ball. With her knitting needles she had made Margaret an almost-new sweater. Margaret got dressed. Delilah came to brush her hair and plait the braids that hung down her back.

"I used to do this for your mother. Only her hair was coal black and yours is brown like sparrows' wings."

"Why do I have brown hair and not black like Mama's?"

Delilah stopped braiding. "That's because your father didn't have black hair. You must take after him."

"Who was he?"

"Why are you asking that now? Didn't your mother explain all that to you?"

"She just said he died in the war. She didn't tell me he had brown hair. Why wasn't his hair black too?"

Delilah resumed braiding. "Because he was a white man."

"Is that what Uncle meant when he said that Mama went around with white men?"

"Your mother ... is dead. I'll have no disrespect in this house towards your mother."

Margaret was silent, her head bursting with questions she couldn't ask. She knew that tone of voice from her grandmother. It meant she had to keep her mouth shut and not ask anything more.

They heard the door open and Delilah hurried out to greet Enos and the other men bringing the pine box to lay her daughter in. Delilah lined the box with an old quilt and the men lifted Lily's body into the box.

"Wait!" Margaret ran to the box, holding a red satin pillow trimmed in gold fringe—*Niagara Falls* embroidered on the top in blue silks.

A souvenir, Lily had called it. "A souvenir of my big trip to the Falls. But the best souvenir I got was you," and Lily had hugged Margaret.

Margaret got on her knees and placed the pillow under Lily's head. "There. You can take her now."

Uncle smiled his lopsided grin. "You done good, kid. She'd like that pillow under her head. She sure looks pretty, don't she?" He turned to Delilah, "You go on ahead, Mother. Me and Margaret, we'll follow."

Delilah hurried out the door to catch up to the men carrying the pine box.

Uncle reached into his pants pocket and pulled out a small package wrapped in tissue. "This is your birthday present from your mom. Thought you might want it today. She looked all around for this. Wanted to give you something special for being nine years old. Lily said there was something about being nine. Like it was the beginning of some kind of special thing. I guess for you it is."

Margaret unwrapped the tissue and in the middle of the paper was a small locket on a chain. "It's beautiful. It's a locket like I saw in a movie. See, you open it up and you can put small pictures inside." She opened the small hinge and Lily's face was smiling at her. Margaret started to cry, huge gulping sobs that shook her whole body.

Uncle hugged her, his own tears wetting the top of her head. "She was the best, wasn't she? Let me put it around your neck. God, it looks real pretty on you, Margaret. You're gonna be a looker like she was."

"Grandma said my father was a white man. Does that mean I'm not an Indian any more?"

"Where'd you get an idea like that? Jesus Christ! Your grandmother is a case for the books. You're a little half-breed, kid. Real special. Lily thought so. I think so. And your grandmother thinks so too. She's just a hard woman sometimes. Goes to church too much. But hell, guess there ain't much else to do in this place. Your grandmother is disappointed in her son. That's me. It rubs off in odd places, but she's a good woman, and you're a good girl."

"Why would Grandma be disappointed in you, Uncle?"

"Aw kid, I'm not much. Drink too much, fool around too much. I'm 35, kid. Not going anywhere." Uncle's face twisted and he ran his hand through his hair.

"You're the best uncle in the world," Margaret cried and she hugged the man to her.

"I'd do anything for you, you know that?" he said. "Lily always said you were the best thing that ever happened to her. All I know is you're the best thing that happened to me, my little half-breed. You're gonna grow up special. I can feel it. You can read and write. You're real smart, Margaret. That's a gift. I'm real proud of you. So was Lily. She used to tell me that all the time. God, I'm gonna miss her! But we got a piece of her right here. You. And you got a piece of her, right there in that necklace. Ain't we lucky?"

Margaret stared down at her locket. "I'm still an Indian?"

"Hell yes! Anybody says different, you let me know. I'll straighten 'em out." Uncle laughed and pulled her braids. "We better get going. We'll see her out real good, Margaret. We'll see your mother out real good!"

He took her hand and they walked down the road, the locket bouncing against her sweater.

The funeral was too long. Uncle Douglas was right. Reverend Jameson, wanting to give comfort to these people he would never understand, not in a million years—talked, preached, tried to get through to the faces that studied him so politely. To his dismay, the old people came and chanted over the coffin, the women's wrinkled skin and clear eyes daring him to say a word—which he didn't. They sang their songs, spoke prayers in Mohawk and everyone took a last look at Lily who lay in the pine box. Margaret adjusted the pillow under Lily's head and tucked in the few hairs that had come loose from the pompadour which rose so majestically from her mother's head. Delilah kissed her daughter, Uncle took his sister's hand and kissed it. The coffin was nailed shut. They carried the pine box into the cemetery behind the church, and lowered it into a hole dug for such a purpose. The people began a song, Uncle's voice rising above the others. They sang Lily into the earth, into another place where she would be in peace. Margaret stood surrounded by her people, Uncle and Delilah holding her hands, their strong grips keeping her safe. She felt the cold in the air, the coming of winter.

Back home, the women were busy cooking. The men stood by the wood stove, passing a bottle from mouth to mouth. Some went outside to smoke and tell stories. They brought forth memories of Lily they had been saving for this moment. Old Joseph recalled the time he had taught Lily to step dance. She was his best pupil and had won all the contests at the fair. Uncle told the story of how Lily had been sent to the field by Delilah to pull weeds. She had been five years old and had heard music coming from the ground. She had started to dance and in the process of dancing had not only trampled the weeds, but Delilah's burgeoning potato bean crop. All was forgiven when the girl had carefully replanted each small, green plant—including the weeds! It was true, they all agreed, Lily was one of a kind, the best.

Margaret wandered through the groups of men, the children playing outside. The noise and confusion was soothing to her as she wondered what her life was going to be like without Lily. She wiped her tears with the edge of her sleeve and touched her locket. She thought about growing up, what it meant. What it meant to be an Indian. It might mean that people hated you for reasons known only to them. It might mean that people could run you over with a car and nobody would care. It might mean that Lily died because she was an Indian, even though, as Uncle said, she pretended not to be one.

The food was ready. Delilah called to Margaret. She went inside the house and there, on the kitchen table where her mother had lain, were plates and platters of food. Like some miracle in the stories Margaret read aloud. Food. Scalloped potatoes resting in milk, pools of oleo floating on the oval slices. Two kinds of jello moulds—this treat usually reserved for Christmas. Orange jello, blended with carrots and black walnuts picked from Ida's tree. Red jello, stuffed with groundcherries. Each imposing mould set on a prized plate, a special piece of china. In the kettle, Delilah's corn soup, thick and rich with rabbit meat, white beans, turnips and lyed corn. The soup was choking with the hominy, the broth so thick the men joked about using forks and knives instead of spoons. There were green beans and wax, squash baked with maple syrup. There were onions, creamed whole with salt and a touch of the precious sugar to keep them sweet. Plates and plates of fried bread, grease draining and soaking onto coarse, white cloth. Hunks of dough, fried in lard, the outside crisp and brown, the inside heavy and doughy. Dishes of pickled beets and corn relish sat here and there on the table.

Delilah said grace, "Our heavenly father, bless this food we are about to receive. In Jesus' name we ask it. Amen."

An old woman spoke in Mohawk, thanking the Creator for giving this food, for giving this day, for giving Lily a chance to walk with her ancestors.

Uncle took Margaret's hand and talked about his obligation to Lily's memory and to her daughter. Tears ran down his twisted nose as he recited the words.

Delilah took Margaret's other hand and said, "Of all the gifts that came from Lily, this is the greatest of them all. Let us eat."

The people each took a plate, holding it to their stomachs like a shield or a gift. Food—always received with gratitude and appetite—especially at death. The plenty of the table on this day staving off hunger of another kind.

THE LADY OF THE HOUSE

THE HOUSE ON HAZELTON

Miriam Waddington

Once long ago I lived in a tall narrow house on Hazelton Avenue. It was there I learned to cook.

Hazelton in 1937–38 was not the street of boutiques, art galleries and million dollar condominiums it is today. It was an old residential Toronto street. The back windows of its houses looked down on a crazy criss-cross of older streets crowded with little stucco houses. And Yorkville, which bordered Hazelton, was another such residential street, except that its houses were newer.

I was then an out-of-town student in the second year of my undergraduate studies at the University of Toronto. Before World War II Jewish girls didn't usually think of living in residences such as Whitney Hall for the simple reason that they would not have been welcome there. At that time my family was living in Ottawa, a city that had no university of its own. My parents decided that they would pay my fees and give me a monthly allowance so I could study in Toronto.

I had rented a room in the fall in a rooming house near the university, but when I returned from a student conference in Winnipeg that December I found that my landlady had packed my things and rented my room to a man because, as she said, men were less trouble.

I had caught a bad cold at the conference and by now I had a fever as well as a cough. I knew I wasn't fit for class or anything else. I went to the women's medical service, which in those days, consisted of a doctor and an elderly nurse. Miss Donald, the nurse, was a small energetic person with a much wrinkled skin and noisy false teeth. The doctor decided I needed four or five days in the residence infirmary and a warm place to live afterwards. When I explained that I was between rooms and had no place to go, Miss Donald looked me over, meditated for a minute or two and then made me the following offer: I could have my room and board in the house she shared with her sister Angela if I would shop and cook the daily breakfast and evening meal as well as Sunday dinner. We would all share the table-setting and dishwashing. I confessed I didn't know how to cook a full meal, just a few individual dishes. Miss Donald assured me that would be no problem; she would teach me.

After a week in the infirmary my cough subsided and I moved into the house on Hazelton Avenue. It was a yellow brick house with a large living room and a bay window that looked out into the street. There was a dining room and a large kitchen with an adjoining pantry, and also a back kitchen where the sisters kept their coal. My job would be to shop on my way home from the university and to cook the dinner.

There were no food stores on Avenue Road but there was a Pickering Farms on Yonge Street at the corner of Yorkville. My Miss Donald, called Birdie by her sister, kept a purse with the housekeeping money in the top drawer of the sideboard. No one as far as I knew, ever counted the money in that purse, but Birdie replenished it at regular intervals, and there was always enough money for our groceries.

For the first few weeks either Birdie or Angela came with me to show me what and how much to buy. They also directed me to two cookbooks that lived on a shelf in the kitchen pantry. One was *Mrs. Beaton's Cookbook,* and the other an old edition of *The Boston Cookbook.* Between them they explained everything.

Apart from cooking and helping with the washing up, I had no other duties. Saturdays were free as on that day the sisters laid a fire in the living room and had high tea from the tea wagon instead of dinner. For their tea, Angela, who worked as a librarian, used to bring home little jars of jellied chicken which she bought at a delicatessen near her library branch.

The sisters were devout Anglicans and on Sunday mornings they went off to church while I stayed home to cook the dinner. I loved those Sundays when I had the house to myself. My Miss Donald, Birdie, showed me how to make steamed suet puddings, and her favourite was a cottage pudding with pieces of preserved ginger as well as suet chopped into it. Individual dishes were easy enough to make, but I had to learn how to time, organize, and prepare a full course meal so everything would be synchronized, cooked but not overcooked, simple yet nutritious. The rule was soup, meat or fish, two vegetables—one underground and one aboveground, potatoes or rice, dessert and coffee. I served the coffee in a china coffee pot and we drank it out of delicate demi-tasse cups, beautiful and very old.

The sisters, like everyone else during the depression were economical. Since I was Birdie's responsibility she had to show me how to save money on food. For example, she taught me how to make meatballs without eggs by using a white sauce instead. Before I came to live on Hazelton I had never heard of white sauce, or suet either, but the white sauce trick came in handy during the war, after I was married and food was rationed.

One Sunday it happened that there were no fresh vegetables to go with the roast. What to do? I racked my brains and both cookbooks, and was finally driven to create a dish from what was at hand. Talk about stone soup! I took some onions, parboiled them, scooped them out and stuffed the shells with rice, which I had boiled separately, the onion centers, and seasoning. Then I opened a can of tomatoes I found in the pantry, mashed them up with a fork—we had no blenders or Mixmasters—and poured the tomatoes over the stuffed onions, all of which I then put into a casserole and baked along with the roast. I was proud of that dish and the sisters praised my ingenuity.

I didn't always get praise; I had to be careful to mash and pound the turnips and potatoes so Angela wouldn't complain of lumps, and I had to salt the vegetables while they were cooking just enough and not too much. Angela believed that salting them at the table was bad for her arthritis and perhaps she was right, although in those days no one thought salt made any difference one way or the other. As for arthritis—I had never heard the word before I came to the Donalds'. Either my parents were healthy or they didn't complain.

Every second Tuesday an old cleaning woman who had been with the family for years came to do the skivvying. I never saw her without her woolen tuque, one of those hats whose colour has faded, but whose material has taken on the individual shape and character of its wearer. Each of us got one clean sheet and one pillowcase every two weeks; the sisters would have thought it an extravagance to change both sheets at the same time. Mrs Williams, as she was called, scrubbed the three sheets by hand on a scrubbing board in the back kitchen, all the while muttering away to herself. She was often still there when I got home from classes, my arms full of books and groceries. There she was, bent over the old-fashioned galvanized iron washtub scrubbing and muttering, muttering and scrubbing. She never answered my greeting but kept on talking to herself. I'm sure she was well over sixty, and I thought then how hard her life must be that she should still be bent over a washboard scrubbing in her old age.

The sisters had season tickets to the symphony concerts in Massey Hall. They went to Massey Hall as regularly as they went to church, and just as in church, they sat in the same seats their parents had occupied during their lifetime. I don't know how much they knew about music, but they knew everything about the musicians and their instruments. Angela especially, noticed every mannerism and every hesitation, every change in the position of each player and in the sound of each instrument. On the morning after the concert Angela was always full of news about substitutions, absences, falterings and changes in the handling of the instruments.

I was seldom home Saturdays when the sisters had high tea in front of the fireplace, and my Sunday afternoons were usually spent reading in the old reference library on the corner of St. George and College. I knew little about their social life and they were equally ignorant about mine, which that winter was not very active. I didn't feel free to have boys call for me at the Donalds'. I wasn't sure if I should invite them in when they called, although I was sure that they couldn't come in when they brought me home. So I spent my evenings after dinner studying in the front room library upstairs.

Life picked up in early spring when the snow began to melt on the lawns of Hazelton. Birdie and I would go to market Saturday morning and return with rhubarb, beets, and occasionally expensive imported green peas still in their pods. Birdie was an expert at making pastry, and together we would make round succulent apple and rhubarb pies. They were quite different from the ones my mother made. Her pies were baked in large 9" x 12" cake pans and the crusts were made of cookie dough. Birdie also directed me to Mrs. Beaton's recipes for charlottes, custards, and gelatine puddings with all their variations—desserts neither made nor eaten in my European mother's circles. For them, desserts meant sponge cakes and fruit compotes.

Then there were soups. I learned that the genius of a tasty soup lay in the use of leftovers and spices, and was amazed to discover that you could make a soup stock from the bones of the roasted chicken that had been eaten for dinner the night before. The motto, waste not want not, was taken seriously in our household. Other of Birdie's sayings and popular wisdoms are still deeply engraved in my memory: exhortations like, *wipe stains up promptly, never put off for tomorrow what you can do today, a penny saved is a penny earned, a watched pot never boils, look before you leap, if gold rusts what will iron do;* still echo in my mind.

Birdie had one extravagance; she had an old Persian cat who usually sat on her lap during dinner and must have slept at the foot of her bed at night. This cat, whose name I have forgotten, ate most of our leftovers, but his mainstay was the fish and hamburger Birdie bought and cooked especially for him.

As spring progressed Birdie worked in her garden. I was delighted to see familiar bulbs come up and bloom around the front and side of the house—scilla and crocus, hyacinth and early tulip—but I was amazed to see Birdie picking ordinary after-rain mushrooms out of the lawn which she brought in for me to cook. We ate them every day that spring; all the same, I have never trusted myself since to pick mushrooms out of my own lawn.

Easter Sunday with the sisters was something special. At that time of the year I was deeply involved in studying for my final exams, for in those days every course had them. Birdie cut and brought into the house branches of japonica with its exotic orange flowers, as well as bunches of daffodils. The sisters had gone to church early, and now the breakfast table was full of colourfully wrapped presents. For me there was a book, a string of imitation pearls, and a coffee mug, blue with doves flying around the border. I thought of it as my peace cup. For the cat there was a toy; for Angela new white gloves, and for Birdie an airy pastel-coloured shawl. And there were cards with decorous messages to go with every present.

On that sunny Easter morning Birdie's eyes shone with goodwill and her false teeth clittered and clacked more than ever. She paid me what I now realize was a high compliment considering that my background, interests and age were very far removed from her own Anglican upbringing and spinster state. "I'm glad you came and cooked for us," she said, "I thought we would never find anyone like Kathleen, the missionary nurse who lived with us last year." I blushed and stammered my thanks. Dimly I realized that was my evaluation, and that I had passed.

After that year I never saw the sisters again. The next autumn one of my younger brothers entered the engineering course at the University and we shared an apartment where my cooking came in handy. Yet I still feel a deep gratitude to Birdie. She saved me from pneumonia, she gave me a home, and taught me how to harvest the good that is in every food, including Toronto lawn mushrooms. Because of her, I have always had a japonica bush in my garden. It's true that the frost kills the blossoms on the top branches, but every spring, at the bottom of my japonica, close to the earth, exotic orange flowers burst into bloom. At such times I remember Birdie and the tall narrow house on Hazelton where I first learned to cook.

FROM *DANCING IN THE DARK*

Joan Barfoot

A lifetime of thoughts in those twelve hours. All of it was clear, if not comprehensible.

"I'm sorry, Edna," said the woman's voice. "But I thought you ought to know." Explaining everything. "They were kissing. What other explanation could there be?"

My glossy living room. The couch on which I was sitting, the couch on which Harry and I sat together. Where I held his hands and traced his fingers and believed they could do anything. (And they could.)

The chair from which I'd sometimes watched him, still amazed that he was in this room and that I was in this room with him.

All the other rooms now out of sight, my perfect home; except that the vacuum cleaner was still sprawled upstairs waiting, work unfinished. That nagged a little. But not right now. To go back upstairs and flick the switch, restart the motor, look beneath the beds for dust, push carefully into corners, not right now.

Downstairs was finished. After all the years, it was truly finished, the cleanness frozen. No more holding the toaster over the garbage, dislodging crumbs, and wiping the counter beneath it. Or drawing a cloth across the windowsills, or picking up a cushion to punch it fresh. No more dirty dishes or smudged windows or bits of dust in the corners of shelves. It had not seemed possible to ever finish; but here it was, done now.

The new gold-flecked white wallpaper had my full attention.

The house was airless. Once, Harry shouted at me because we were out of lemonade. He was angry because it was so hot, a heavy, stifling day, and maybe for other reasons, too. He went out and bought an air conditioner. We did not quarrel again because of heat, but the windows had to be kept shut. It disconnected the house from the world, and one might be startled, struck, by walking out the door into a different atmosphere. This was not a different atmosphere, however, but no atmosphere at all; the air sucked out leaving me holding my breath.

Pain, yes, of course. Odd, though: I could tell the pain was there, but could not quite feel it. It left a hole instead of a presence of pain. Quite a different sort of pain from skinning a knee in a fall, or from cutting a finger on paper. A gap of pain. Shocks like lightning behind the eyes, and weightlessness, a whipping away of solidity like a tablecloth from beneath a setting of dishes, so that I might rise and float into the air, away, or crash.

Time like a stop watch: the action halted at the finish. Forty-three years. So busy, time filled or put in, time in which to do things or time by which to have things done, time for home-comings and different little tasks and leavings, time for coffee or for waking up, time passing, time running out, time gone.

Time suspended like the air. Only the gold-flecked white wallpaper timeless and airless to hold onto. If I fixed on it firmly, I might not vanish.

No need to go through it year by year, moment by moment, like a photograph, it could be taken in at a glance. But cruel, a staring into the sun, a blazing on the eyeballs, after keeping the head down for so long. The eyes, unprotected and naked, were easily scorched.

Two phone calls in a day. The second the familiar trusted voice, but tinny, like a poor recording, down the line. No need to move, the arm reaches out on its own accord, no need for the eyes to wander, the arm lifts, flexes, and the ears hear the warm voice that is no part of this. Like those queer moments of seeing from the corner the two of us in bed; or stories I have read of people dying, a watching part moving away, shifting off, looking back with distant disinterest at the heavy shell of body now unrelated. His voice wholly a mystery now, if not the words.

"I'm sorry, Edna," he is saying from so far away, another life, some other level altogether. "But I'll make it home at some point."

"Yes."

"Is something wrong? You sound funny."

"No."

Did he use the pause to tell himself it was all right to be free? That there was no need to pay attention? He must have needed many times to reassure himself, or how could he have kept on with what he did?

"Okay then, if you're sure. I'm sorry. Tomorrow I'll definitely make it home for dinner. Listen, you're sure everything's all right?"

"Yes."

Even to me, my voice sounded odd; as if it were coming from outside, no internal resonances.

"I'll be as early as I can. It's this damned job."

"Yes."

The remote muscles of the arm on their own again, replacing the receiver without a fumble, no need to look. So many things can be done without a glance, it seems; so what need is there for twenty-odd years of vigilance?

The important thing to watch was the gold flecks on that white wallpaper, the light changing on it, afternoon moving into evening, sun from a new direction and fading. If the light went out entirely, there would be no seeing those gold flecks; and if I could not see them I would lose my balance, topple, slide, dissolve. There would be no holding me.

In the grey dimness of late evening, my arm reached out again, thumb moving for the switch on the table lamp and finding it, the light flaring on. It was possible, if still dim, to see the golden flecks; the main outpouring of the light on me now, but enough reflecting across the room to where I needed it.

There was a certain warmth, I could feel, from the light.

I wanted to keep very still, apart from that necessary move. I needed to be careful, because I was precious and fragile like a piece of transparent china, and could easily be tilted out of place and broken.

Sounds changed like the light. They, too, were far away and outside, like my voice. There were bird songs, until it got very dark, and cars on the street. Sedate here in this proper neighbourhood, no peeling rubber or screeching brakes. Lights flashing, reflected from cars or the houses near by. In those other houses people moved from room to room, came home, went to the bathroom, watched television, or trudged upstairs to bed. Even with the windows closed, I could smell steaks barbecuing in the early evening. All those people doing all those familiar things. Things I might have been doing yesterday. Everything now so changed that each move they might be making, each move I had once made, just yesterday, all of it so ordinary, normal, was unimaginably exotic. A different world I was in now, and I could see only the reflections of their lights.

Not lonely; remote. This was so far away that to have been lonely would not have been so distant. It would have been a connection of some sort.

All of it gone as if I read or watched it.

I learned to walk, standing only to my mother's thighs, looking up, up at the lines beneath her chin, the hard setting of the jaw, a throbbing in the neck; a smell about her of clean laundry and hard work. And my father's sad eyes, and their voices over and across me. Tiny Stella, bland baby eyes closed: my mother and father united once, staring down at her. I was beside them, looking up at them. Had they stood over me that way, together and wondering?

Hair and make-up and menstrual blood. Dances and music and easy feet and longings. The passion of mirrors and pillows. Hearing Harry's voice for the first time, and later lying down beside him, surveying his long and narrow body as if he were sunshine. This was no mirror and no fantasy, but completion, purpose, end.

There were poets and dark-skinned men; but this was in my apartment and in my bed and his hands blotted longings as if they were tears, and the cloth of his body wiped mine clean, and soothed it.

I could not have done less in return. He contained me: all the people in our life, all the magazines and quizzes and recipes, the scrubbed floors and shining dishes and matching dinners, all the wine and laundry and supermarket shelves' all the vacuumed rugs—in one slender body, all of this.

Gone like the air, astonishing blow.

Darkness all around, except for the brightness on me, reflecting on the wall.

Lights outside flicked off, and there were few headlights to sweep the walls any more. Only the lamp and the dancing, glittering, golden specks.

I might be motionless forever. I might never move a muscle. I might sit and breathe and die. I could be still, I had often been still, although not like this, not frozen. But this was my whole life here, breathing in and out until it stopped, watching the golden flecks.

I might know everything now. I might see clearly. There were forty-three years here, not hard to know all about them. Except for why, of course.

I saw through myself like a glass; but could no longer see Harry at all.

There was a crackling on the gravel driveway he kept saying should be asphalted; but never did. Rare for him, procrastination, except he said he thought gravel might be less slippery in the winter. The rumbling of the garage door going up, slamming car door, garage door down. Such familiar sounds. Sounds that on other days I had leapt up for, a springing in the stomach. Tonight there was no one in the hallway taking a last glance into the mirror, checking hair. Some time earlier I must have taken my last glance and not recognized it.

They key was quiet in the lock. Oh, I had the senses of bats to hear so sharply through doors and walls.

The front door swung open and there were footsteps, and it clicked shut. Solid door, closing with a clunk, always safe behind such a door, no intruders, no one seeing in.

A quiet padding of footsteps upstairs. Above me I could hear him like a thief. Water ran and toilet flushed. Doors opened and shut, feet moved more quickly. A voice, the friendly ordinary voice but at a slightly different pitch, was calling, but so far away. Feet moving faster, and without efforts to be quiet, not to disturb. Running down the stairs and the voice louder. It called my name with a question mark, but I was all silence inside.

He was moving around and then he was in the living room and the footsteps stopped abruptly. I could feel the foreign presence. I was safe though, if I did not look and if I kept quite still.

He would have been wise to go away, but he wouldn't have known that, of course.

Two long legs in front of me—could I have leaned forward and caught her scent? I could see past them to the wall and held to that.

But the two long legs bent and lowered, a trunk appeared, chest, neck, face, hands so close, on my knees, face earnest and concerned, and altogether it blocked the view. I peered and peered, but couldn't see through that face, so handsome and fearful. The golden flecks danced for a moment in his face, but faded. Impossible to hold them. The familiar face unfamiliar, strange and bewildered, mouth moving in a babble.

I could hear my thoughts. I thought, "It does not all end here in this face. That is wrong, a mistake."

Without a place to look, the loss of balance, toppling, sliding dissolution, began.

The muscles trembled and were tender, the legs were weak, standing after so long a time. How rigidly they must have held themselves for all those hours. But some core in there to hold them up, to move them, a foot shifting with the impulse of this leg and then the other, this is what walking comes down to, again and again. The voice was loud, shouting and why, I was not deaf? I just wasn't listening.

What was it he wanted so badly? Not me, and too late for that anyway. I could feel his hands and fingers, well-known admired hands and fingers, clutching at my arm, my shoulder, trying to restrain. Not to hurt, not to be unfriendly, just a force to hold me back.

But my, I was strong. He could not begin to match me now. I could brush him off like a fly.

Although my skin could still feel his fingers when they were gone, dents and wounds like burn marks, cigarettes stubbed out in the pores.

My feet were moving to the kitchen, the light and yellow kitchen. The light was on —he must have looked for me here already. Here was the table where recipe books were read, cigarettes smoked, coffees drunk, meals planned, meals eaten, wine uncorked, and glasses raised. The smiles exchanged across the table hovered over it, the lying angels. All the lying moments in each kitchen tile and cupboard. Every thread of yellow curtains and each drop of yellow paint a lie. Each tap on the sink and each element on the stove, all the chairs and the two plants, each green leaf on both the plants a lie.

Dark outside the window above the sink. So many hours spent here staring out, while hands did other things: washed dishes here in this sink, and dried them. Cleaned vegetables and pared them, peelings from potatoes, carrots, onions, dribbling in. All the mouthfuls and forkfuls of food prepared here in this room. To fuel the lies.

False vitamins and phony colours. Beside the window, above the sink, a rack of wedding-present teak-handled sharp steel knives. Five: the smallest for paring, the largest for carving. The middle one sharp for tomatoes and other delicate things.

I am turning, and see him again. Now he is more than frightened. Not concerned-frightened, but terrified, I see, and backing away. His hands are reaching out towards me and the sounds are much louder and higher-pitched, shouting on a different level. The hands do not reach for me, but against me. Something new here, the voice and the expression.

I am so strong. I have never been so strong before. I wonder why I didn't know I could be stronger than he was?

It does not go into him so far that it is necessary actually to touch him. The softness is pleasing and surprising, and I experiment with it again; several times more. It is a little like digging a trowel into soft earth in the spring to plant a flower. Once there is some hard impediment, like a root or a rock, but it's easy to twist around that, back into the softness.

It is the way I once thought making love would be: a soaring loss of consciousness, transcendence, and removal. I have gotten out of myself at last—so this was the way; and I am joined and free. This instant is wholly mine, and I am so free and light, tiny and light, a helium being.

The white daisy clock on the kitchen wall, with its yellow petal hands reaching from the yellow centre, it goes so slowly, slowly, in the silence. The moment is only a moment. His face and hands have vanished, and the moment disappears as well.

But now I know it is there; I have proved that it exists.

The silence rings and echoes and the hands of the clock are slow.

It is like resting my head on Harry's shoulder afterward.

Outside in the black, I hear voices, some shouting. The silence stops ringing. I find myself holding the tomato knife stained brighter than the fruit. Under the tap the stain washes off red and thick and glossy, catching onto fingers and fluttering away under the hard blast of water. I slide my fingers up and down the blade until the red is gone and the shining silver shows through again. The wooden handle, with the carved indentations for fingers to grip, is harder: the red does not come out of the grain so easily.

It is dried, and replaced where it ought to be. There are small stains and smudges in the ridges of my fingertips and my palms, and I wash my hands clean and wipe them on a towel.

I could move through this house blindfolded, or blind. I step back to the living room, the familiar room where the lamp still glows on the gold-flecked white wall. It is different now; the waiting is finished. I sit down to try to pick patterns from the swimming golden flecks.

Much better than cooking the perfect meal, or shining the perfect crystal. I have accomplished something here, I have found the moment.

HAVE YOU EATEN YET: TWO INTERVIEWS WITH CHINESE CANADIAN WOMEN

Rita Wong

The common Chinese greeting "Have you eaten yet?" is not only what mothers say to their children, but how friends of either gender greet each other. Food is connected with caring, as well as with social norms such as good manners. Within the Chinese Canadian community, there is such a variety and difference between Canadian-borns and recent immigrants, between dialects, villages, families. The interviews are just an introduction to these traditions.

Special thanks to Tammy Wong and Cindy Yeung, both of whom helped with the interviews and translation.

Margaret

This interview actually took place in the living room, but I later visited the kitchen at the restaurant where Margaret works and spends much of her time. The restaurant kitchen was large, had at least four woks going, walk-in fridges, huge rice cookers and two friendly cooks who were busily working away. The restaurant is a family business (owned by Margaret's husband) and this was reflected in the kitchen's comfortable atmosphere. While the facilities could have been cold in another context, the human presence in the kitchen made the room a lively place where you could move and talk quite easily. We spoke mostly in English, with a smattering of Cantonese/Toisanese.

The contrast between today's modern kitchen and the one Margaret grew up in was striking: from icebox to walk-in fridge, from having a tree stump for a cutting board to having big wide steel and wood counters. Another contrast was that the cooks in the restaurant were male, while the cook at home is usually female.

M: I was born in Winnipeg; I guess my first memory of the kitchen was on the farm where I grew up. We had a wood stove, so it was really hard work trying to get a meal. I remember helping my sister in the kitchen when my mother was out working in the fields; I'd run out to the field and fetch snow peas, cabbage, carrots, whatever. I'm 68 now, so that'd be a long time ago. It was a big kitchen, an old-fashioned house. I get a lot of my cooking from remembering the way my mother cooked, and that's the way I still cook some of the old Chinese dishes. Like stewing lamb with *foo juk* (strips of bean curd), red beans ... Stir-fry vegetables are still cooked the same way, only the ingredients change.

My mother was usually out in the fields working, so she didn't cook that much, except at regular mealtimes. Nothing special like some people cook, cook, cook.

R: So you'd use the wok on the stove?

M: No, we didn't have woks when we were kids. We just had big fry pans and pots. That wood stove was so hard to work! After my sister got married, I had to cook by myself sometimes, since my brothers would rather work in the field. Once I got the rice cooking on top of the stove, I'd chop the meat, and by the time I'd done that, the fire would have gone out since there was no one else to help me feed it.

R: Was it hard to get Chinese ingredients like ginger back then?

M: We were able to get them; they used to import them, bring them over by ship. The ginger wrinkled, but it was still usable. And garlics are grown over here.

R: I'm just thinking that even in the past few years, there are so many more fruits available in Canada.

M: Right, a lot more ingredients. But then, we used to be able to get the dried mushrooms, the *hoong do* (dried sweet red berries), and *foo juk*—anything dried like that. We could buy and store and use whenever we needed. We grew a lot of our own fresh vegetables too—*gai lan* (Chinese broccoli), *bok choy*—you name it, we had it.

R: Were there special days, meals?

M: New Year's—there's always something special for New Year's. My mother made *cha siu bao* (pork buns) and *siu my* (pork balls) and things like that for special occasions. We kids helped, if we were around.

R: I always wanted to learn how to make *joong* (rice and filling wrapped in leaves) the way my grandmother does.

M: I learned that with a friend, just a few years ago, right here in Calgary. I can't do it by myself, but I can do it alongside somebody else.

R: Those are the fun dishes, the ones that you can do with someone else, or in a group.

M: Like my *siu my* and my dumplings. I learned from watching cooks in the restaurant, or from cookbooks. I have tons of cookbooks, though I don't always use them. I'll try a recipe and if I like it, then I'll improvise.

R: Were many recipes passed down through generations or from your mother?

M: No, the old folks didn't have recipes—they just sprinkled a bit of this and a dash of that ... Oh you know, taste it. They did it so often, I guess they just knew exactly what to do.

R: How did you learn to cook?

M: Just by watching people or asking them how to do it. Before I got married, I used to cook burnt rice, pancakes that were half-cooked; I was terrible. My mother used to say that I made "three-level rice"—the bottom was burnt, the middle soggy and the top uncooked.

R: My dad always has to have rice for dinner; his day's not complete without it.

M: Now that I'm married, it doesn't matter, because we're all Westernized. We usually have rice quite often, though. My husband's brother was like that—it was terrible; they were eating rice for breakfast, rice for lunch, rice for dinner.

R: Do you use a rice cooker?

M: I do now; I didn't use to. You can't burn it, it always comes out all right now.

R: What are some of your favourite dishes?

M: My family really likes roast pork. I get a Boston butt, plug it full of holes, and fill it full of garlic. It's not traditional Chinese stuff. Our cooking is half and half—half Chinese and half Western. So we barbecue, bake pies. I like to bake cakes and cookies, get fat. (laughter)

R: I don't remember very many desserts, just the red bean soup, the tofu fa ...

M: Right, Chinese people as a rule don't have desserts—by the time you finish your meal, you're too full.

R: Did you find your cooking style changed after you were married; did you have to adjust to a different family's cooking style?

M: No, not really. The only way I could cook was by remembering what my mother did, and then I learned new dishes along the way. My mother was a good cook. She'd

go over to neighbours and friends; she learned how to bake bread just from someone telling her. She couldn't read or write, but she had a good memory, I think, because of that. So she'd memorize all this stuff, come home and bake bread.
R: You said you worked in a restaurant?
M: Off and on. My husband had a take-out restaurant at one time and we hired all the cooks, so you'd just watch the cooks. I didn't cook in the restaurant, but I asked for the recipe if I liked something they cooked. That is, they'd show me what to do, and I'd write it down. I learned how to make crispy skinned duck.
R: We've never figured out how to do that in our own house.
M: It's not the same. You haven't got the equipment to do it with. It's the method: you have to have a big wok full of boiling water and you have to dunk the whole duck inside the water for a few seconds, and you can't do that at home. You haven't got a pot big enough. And you can't hang it up somewhere and let it dry.
R: What about the men in your family? Were they allowed in the kitchen; did they cook?
M: My brothers all learned to cook outside of the home. They worked in restaurants.
R: But they didn't cook at home?
M: No, never. Being on the farm, they had too many chores outdoors.
R: After they learned to cook, did they do so at home?
M: Yeah, sure. They cooked for their families. Their wives didn't have to cook when they were at home. My husband doesn't do that; he never learned to cook. When I think back to my generation, my uncles, they used to live in laundries, they had to do their own cooking. Their wives were in China. Many men were without their families; they had to learn to cook.

Today, our son and daughter and their friends—both girls and boys cook to some extent; they cook together, let's put it that way. There isn't just "you cook and I'll sweep" or something; it's "we'll cook and we'll sweep." They seem to get along, get together and do things, whereas in the older generation, it was more defined; the women did the women's work, the men did the men's.
R: I guess there weren't that many women here to do "women's work."
M: Not in Canada, no. But in China, the men wouldn't think of going in the kitchen to cook—no way!

A lot's changed. Our son, when he got married, they had twins; he did the washing, the cooking, the floors. He didn't do that at home! I thought that was really great, that he was good enough to help—it's a lot of work with twins. So, he learned.
R: Do you see the kitchen as being central to the house?
M: We do; my husband would not buy a house unless it had a good big kitchen. He wouldn't eat in the dining room if you paid him. The only time we use the dining room is when we have company; he's not comfortable there.
R: Do you bring company into the kitchen?

M: Yes, my intimate friends. We all sit in the kitchen and talk; that's what my husband likes. He'd rather sit in the kitchen and talk to people.
R: What changes do you see in the cooking, the traditions?
M: Well, I find that home cooking is really village cooking. When you come out to the city and the restaurants, it's all commercial. Now it's from all parts of China—Cantonese, Mandarin, Szechuan ... We used to have shrimps in lobster sauce; you go to Chinatown now, they don't even know what you're talking about. But I taught my kids that dish; they still cook that way. I give them recipes, they can do it on their own. Black bean and garlic, they like that.

I often wonder how people in China can cook—they don't have wood, they don't have coal—not in the Southern part. They just go out and cut straw and grass and use it for fuel. My husband used to say—I don't recall it—he said they had a brick stove and the wok would go on top and there'd be a little hole on the bottom where you'd feed the dried grass into it. The whole house would be full of smoke—no chimneys.
R: Was your husband born in China?
M: No, we were both born over here, but he went back when he was small. So, he's seen what the village is like. I was only seven when we went "back" to China; we stayed there for a year, and were only in the village for about two weeks.
R: What's your attitude towards cooking? Is it a creative act, or something you do because you have to?
M: I like the creative side; I like to garnish, make something that looks nice. I only do that if the family gets together, and we cook a big dinner. At the moment, I'm helping at the restaurant and babysitting at the same time, so I don't have much time.

I like cooking, it's fun. If you get together, you know, with a group of people. Sometimes my daughter comes home, and we cook together. When my sister was still alive, we used to go over to her house. We have a big family; everybody'd go over and help somebody cook this dish, and somebody would cook another ... fifty, sixty people in our house all the time. Really social. It brings our family together; we enjoy cooking together. We have a good time. That's the only time you get to see everybody. All our family's children are all grown up and if we get together, we congregate in somebody's house, and we all cook or barbecue. That's how we get to see friends and family all at once. We go to Toronto ...
R: To cook?
M: Yeah, we do! One time, we went to Toronto. My husband's brother lives there, and I have cousins there. One of my cousins is married to a girl who has nine kids in her family, and their kids ... The only way we could all get together was have a barbecue. We took the steaks from Calgary. At that time, we got filet mignon at $3.99 a pound. I haven't seen it like that again. So we used to stack a box full and go to Toronto, cut it up and get everyone together, have a barbecue, play ball ... We had lots of fun.

Mrs. Wong

Mrs. Wong is 75 years old; she came from China to Canada, via Hong Kong, over 20 years ago. She speaks the Toisan dialect that is common in her generation. The interview took place in her daughter's kitchen, a cozy, modern looking room. Mrs. Wong's own kitchen is quite comfortable, and has a strong smell from all the cooking that is done in it; it is the first room you encounter walking in from the much-used back door.

Her daughter Tammy helped with the interview while taking care of her two baby daughters.

R: What are your early memories of the kitchen in China, in the village?
Mrs. W: In the village, in the morning, you'd have to boil water, make tea, wash dishes. After this, you'd go to the vegetable garden (which was not always right beside the house; it could be a short walk away), bring the vegetables back and wash them, and then it would be time to cook a meal. You'd use sweet potato (*fan see yup*), shrimp paste, wintermelon, they really liked that, dried shrimp ...
T: What were your impressions the first time you went into the kitchen?
Mrs. W: The first time in the kitchen? It was like that; anytime you go into the kitchen, that's what you do—wash, clean ... As a child, I didn't have to cook. When I was 12, my brother married, so there was my sister-in-law to help cook. Whatever my mother cooked, I ate.
R: Did your mother teach you to cook?
Mrs. W: She did not teach me to cook; she cooked. She didn't have to teach me; I learned by myself. It was too crowded in the kitchen. When I was 14, my second sister-in-law came to live with us. My mother and sisters-in-law would cook, and I would set the table.
T: When did you learn to cook?
Mrs. W: After I got married. As a child, there was my mother, and two sisters-in-law in the household; I didn't need to cook. I made clothes, pillowcases ... Before I was married, there was a house just for the daughters. (Drawing with her hands, she shows that her husband and his brother's family had separate living quarters, separate kitchens, but shared a large dining room/living room where they ate together everyday.) Meals were twice a day—at nine in the morning and then at four. When I first started, I didn't know how to cook and I burnt the rice a lot.

I was married at 19. There was my sister-in-law, Ah Mu, my mother-in-law, grandmother, and a maid (*moi niu;* poor families sold their daughters out as servants/maids) to help with the housework.

In the morning, Ah Mu would cook the rice and I would cook the other dishes. At night, I would make the rice, and she would cook the dishes.

She would cook in her kitchen and I would cook in mine. Then, we'd bring the food into the dining room and the whole family would eat together there. There were over 10 people.

T: Did you use tinder or straw to cook?

Mrs. W: We used grass to cook rice, tinder to cook dishes. There was one wok and one pot for cooking dishes. If you wanted to save money, you would put a small pot in the oven's fire under the wok. (One fire to cook two things; this was possible since the oven was like a big box with a fire in it and a hole on the top for the wok to go into.) Most people had to steam food since you could cook more things that way. The person who cooked the rice also steamed the food. The person who made the dishes also made the soup.

If you had money, you used beef, cooked it up with roots and bean curd preserve; if not, you used shrimp paste. Green bean leaf (*ow gok yep*); I really liked to eat that with shrimp paste.

Food was served in a *fot tau* (approximately an inch-high dish) and moved in a *foong lam* (a big multilevel bamboo food carrier).

After cooking, eating, washing the dishes, sweeping up, if you wanted, you could sew clothes, knit.

T: Did you have much time for these other things?

Mrs. W: It took about an hour to cook a meal. You could find time to sew after your work was done. (T. looks sceptical; this hour estimate does not include running around buying and picking food.)

Initially, I didn't have to help in the fields; later, when we had land, I went and helped in the fields and grandmother would do the cooking. We'd plant rice in March, April, harvest in June. There were two harvests a year. I'm used to gardening. (She keeps a large and varied vegetable garden in her back yard in Canada.)

R: What would you consider the centre of the house?

Mrs. W: The dining room was the centre of the house. There were four big tables in it. The kitchens had a table in each of them. Each table held about ten people; so you could fit 40 people in the dining room, 60 in the house altogether.

T: What was your mother's kitchen like?

Mrs. W: Every house is the same (as her husband's). My mother's house was built when I was around six years old, so it was reasonably new. My husband's house was newer, built a year and a half before I got married.

The house had two levels. There were pipes, so you could pour water from the second storey and it would flow outside.

Our well was close to the house. Some people had to go to the river for water, which was very far. There was a time when people were putting things in the well, so a cover and lock had to be put on top. It wasn't as convenient as it is here. Here everything's convenient.

R: Could you talk with friends in the kitchen?

Mrs. W: There was a table in the kitchen where you could sit and talk. But I spent more of my time upstairs or by the doorstoop, where it was brighter. (The kitchen was downstairs.) My brother-in-law's granddaughter went back and took pictures, you can see the upstairs sitting area has tile.

The water was stored in the living room, between the two kitchens. You had to walk to get water in the house.

R: What did people like to eat?

Mrs. W: Stir-fry taro root with black bean and beef; you cook this in a big wok and spoon it up when it's done. In the village, eggplant and clam meat was good. *Han toy* (a green vegetable), *fan guut* (a root) are good. The Vietnamese like *fan guut*. Another popular dish was big yellow bean sprouts with pork intestines. Chicken feet, squash, fish, chives (*kew choy*), preserved turnip. The turnip preserve here in Canada is different. During the fall, in the village, we grew sweet potatoes, *bok choy, gai choy, gai lan* (Chinese broccoli).

R: Did you grow much fruit?

Mrs. W: Very little. If we grew fruit, it was for sale. It was hard to grow fruit where I lived; there was guava and *loong ngan* (dragon eyes). Generally, at this time of the year (June), we had sweet potato leaves, green bean leaves, *gow gay* (a vegetable with small green leaves; grows easily and almost anywhere) and *han toy*.

Fruits and vegetables had to be bought daily at the market, since there was no refrigerator back then. We'd go buy them around 12:00 to 2:00 p.m. daily, while beef, pork and clams were bought around 8:00 or 9:00 a.m. The market also sold fish, shrimp, frogs ... In China, you could only get chicken at certain times; here you can get it year-round.

It's easier to cook in Canada. Although it doesn't always taste as good here; the frog legs here are frozen, don't taste any good.

Meat was abundant in China, but only if you had money. If no one sent any money home from overseas, there wasn't any way of making money since most people sewed for themselves. Here you can wash dishes for money, be a chambermaid. Women here can make money and spend it any way they want. In the village, you had to depend on money being sent home. The work—farming, sewing, cooking—was just for ourselves.

R: Do you enjoy cooking?

Mrs. W: If you get used to doing something, you get to like it.

R: Did you teach Tammy to cook?

Mrs. W: (laughter) No, what's to teach? I didn't need to be taught either. I cook what I like to eat. I like cooking.

R: What are your favourite dishes?

Mrs. W: I like bird's nest soup, shark fin soup; I just brought some fins home to make it. The soup with *foo juk* (strips of bean curd), dried oysters, white nuts in it.

R: What are the popular holiday dishes?

Mrs. W: In the village, for New Year's, we'd make pigs' feet, soup with dried oysters, *faat choy* (seaweed; its name suggests good fortune in Chinese) and *foo juk*. Steamed goose, steamed chicken, steamed taro root with bamboo shoots, bean curd, *faan guut*, carrots ... There was one dish—a sour stew with turnips, garlic, pork intestines and wine vinegar—that we made for holidays; no one in my family here likes to eat that. Here, you can eat what you want. Though I do know some people who make that here. For New Year's, you can steam taro roots with sour turnips and it smells really good.

For New Year's I also make *ti doy* (deep fried brown dough balls filled with sweet red bean paste), *fukin nan yen* (small round white dough balls that go in soup), *gai loong* (salty white crescent-shaped dough with meat inside), *ning gok* (steamed yellow cake).

For special days in the village, we often had bean cake and bean sprouts; the bean cake symbolizes fortune for your sons and the bean sprouts symbolize growth. My father-in-law in Hong Kong sent us sea cucumbers too. If you had money, then you'd have abalone. Most people had *faat choy*, dried oysters, *foo juk*, vermicelli ... Some people liked to eat *guo dong* (*joong* in Cantonese—sticky rice with filling, wrapped in leaves).

R: When did you leave the village?

Mrs. W: I left for Hong Kong around 1952, 1953; I would have been in my 30s then.

T: Would friends come and help out in your kitchen when you had parties or celebrations?

Mrs. W: In the village, in China, of course. To make sweets, you'd have to have help. At home in China, it was easy to ask people to help out; you'd get together, talk.

T: And now, no one helps out.

Mrs. W: Here, no one helps out. Everyone's busy working (for wages). Who has time? In China you had to make your own flour, grow your own rice, work the fields. It was really hard. It's less work (in the kitchen) here.

R: Do you use recipes at all?

T: (laughter) Recipes? No.

Mrs. W: It's in my head; I cook what I want when I want.

R: Would men ever help in the kitchen?

Mrs. W: In China, very rarely.

R: Did you cook in the (Canadian) restaurant where you used to work?

Mrs. W: No, I just cook at home. At the restaurant, I washed dishes.

R: Were the cooks male or female for the most part?

Mrs. W: Both, it depends on who wanted to do what.

T: But it is more often men that are cooks.

R: What did you do in China if there was nothing to eat?

Mrs. W: Let's see, I was married at 19 ... (counting to herself through the 20s). That would be when we had to run from the Japanese during the war. That was a very difficult time. We had to run here, run there. There was nothing to eat. We had our rice-fields, so there was a little; if you didn't have enough, then you asked for help from others. Unhusking the rice was really hard work. Sometimes there were sweet potatoes, taro roots, other roots you could make into flour ... Since there wasn't enough rice to make flour, you'd use roots if you could get them.
T: Apart from cooking, did anything else important happen in the kitchen?
Mrs. W: Not really, you cook and eat, cook and eat. Wash the dishes, clean up.
T: You know why these questions are hard for them to answer? They don't really have much of a view of relationships and things like that. For their generation, it's all pretty basic. In the kitchen, you cook and stuff like that, and that is how your daily life went, in a routine. They very seldom look at relationships between people and events.
R: It's funny how Chinese people usually greet each other by saying "Have you eaten yet?" instead of something like "How are you?"
Mrs. W: Manners demand this. Eating is the most important thing for Chinese people. In the village, you would make some tea and have a talk. When Chinese people want to chat, you would drink tea (*yum cha*) and eat. In China, when someone enters your house, you offer them some tea. This is polite. If you don't do this, you don't have manners. It shows you have concern, are thoughtful. Older people will always offer you something to eat, to drink.

In the village, if you had time, you'd make sweets to offer guests. Here, you can buy things in the Chinatown bakeries.

FROM *ITSUKA*

Joy Kogawa

Blind alleys, cul-de-sacs, "No Trespassing" signs. What remains for me of the two years following Uncle's death is a desperation of dead ends in my efforts to reach Stephen. A waiting, watching, screaming season of lies.

Obasan's health deteriorates steadily throughout the fall and winter of 1972. There are times when it feels criminal to leave her alone and I ask her repeatedly to come and stay with me in my house in Cecil, but she will not. Her house, she says, needs care. So also does she. Her short-term memory bank is almost depleted.

"What reason? Forgotten," she says with a chuckle when she catches herself wondering what she started out to do. After supper one night, she can't remember that she has just eaten. All her old pots are ruined, blackened and burnt by forgetfulness. The sturdy old rice pot as well. I take a chisel and hammer to it one Saturday night to try to budge the burnt prunes which are one soldered mass of coal lumps welded to the bottom. The next week she searches so persistently for the old pot that I dig it out of the garbage and give it back to her. The kitchen, her queendom, is finally crumbling from her control and turning into a mine field of taps and stove knobs and freezing pipes needing to be constantly checked. It's not a situation that can continue.

I go and sit on the square wooden box cistern cover outside the kitchen door and think about what to do. The box is a humble throne in a new springtime of weeds—purple flowered thistles, crab grass, a few carrot fronds with rat-tail roots. Uncle's world has become a scratch patch.

The rage within begins its slow emergence that winter as I drive back and forth through the early blizzards and the freezing snow. The night of the freak storm, I'm trapped in a snowdrift for five hours and finally get to Granton at 2:00 a.m. after inching along in a parade of cars following a snowplough. Obasan is asleep and there is water all over the kitchen floor from a tap that has been left on to keep the pipes from freezing. She forgot to unplug the drain. We need help. I drive her back with me to Cecil. She wants to return the next day.

Two weekends after this, I arrive to find the kitchen sink overflowing again and Obasan asleep in a luke warm bathtub. I carry, drag her unresponsive body the few shuffling steps to her bed. A marathon.

All that wind reaping Alberta winter, I phone for people to stop by, I drive over the squealing snow, from Cecil to Granton then back to Cecil, stumbling into my unmade bed in the early still dark morning. Then groggy at 9:00 a.m., I sleepwalk into the classroom to face the upturned faces of the children with their thousand unanswerable questions.

One weekend before Christmas I drive home to find there's been a power failure. The furnace is out. The water pipes have burst under the sink and flooded the cupboard. I find Obasan squatting with soggy cardboard cartons of food, jelly powders, salt and cereals piled on a stool while the water seeps over the floor and under the stove to a low spot from where it drips into the dirt cellar below.

It's utter idiocy working with her in the house that weekend. Hank drops by with the milk and stays to fix the pipes.

"This ol' house gettin' ready to meet the saints eh?" he says giving his head a quick shake.

"Guess so."

Obasan is trying to salvage the unsalvageable. Nothing is ever to be discarded or destroyed. Plastic bleach bottles are waste paper baskets and plant trays. Mandarin orange boxes are covered stools. Even the hems of her slacks are not cut but are rolled under till they form a heavy clump of cloth at her ankles. There seems to be an inability to let go. Or a sense that usefulness is inherent in every material thing. Perhaps it's also a type of tenderness, a concern for earth, a treasuring of every tentative little thing. Unlike Pastor Jim she does not divide the world into the saved and the lost.

The cold she catches that weekend will not let her go and develops into pneumonia.

"She's a very sick lady," the new young doctor at Granton says.

As I drive her to the hospital in Lethbridge, I'm unaware that she has begun her long last haul.

ITALIAN SPAGHETTI

Joan Clark

"Brr, it's cold out there," Tom said. "I'd better light the fire." He came into the kitchen and set the scotch and the wine on the countertop. There were red dimes on his cheeks and frost at his temples. The frost made him look distinguished.

Leslie was standing at the sink hulling strawberries.

"Not yet," she said, too sharply. "We only have those paper logs I made from newspapers. And what's left of the packing case."

The packing case was what their books had come in when they'd moved here to Toronto in the fall.

"It's okay. I brought in some wood scraps Old Man Proctor said we could use."

Old Man Proctor was their landlord. They lived in three rooms on the top floor of his rambling house. The apartment was drafty and gloomy but Tom found it within easy walking distance of the university which meant Leslie could use their old Ford to get to her school out in Oakville. Leslie had fixed the place up with a sisal rug, boards and bricks, strategically placed plants. She didn't mind these frugal measures as long as they were temporary. She liked to think of her life in stages: right now she was in her scrimp and save stage. This attitude also helped in tolerating Old Man Proctor who, perhaps because the rent was low, seemed to think it within his rights to snoop in their apartment when she and Tom were out. Once Leslie came home early from school and found the diaphragm she had left drying on the bedroom window sill had been moved—this was when the pill had first come on the market and Leslie didn't want to risk the side effects so she and Tom were putting up with the diaphragm instead. Another time she came home and found Old Man Proctor in their bathroom opening the medicine chest. He said he was checking for dry rot and Leslie thought that was a strange place to look for it. Moreover the old man had a teenaged granddaughter named Fay who thought she could sing. She came over late Saturday afternoons and endlessly practiced showtunes on his grand piano. Before Christmas it had been songs from *Fiddler on the Roof.* Leslie didn't think she'd ever recover her fondness for "Sunrise, Sunset" since the granddaughter had strangled it. After Christmas

Fay had moved on to *Showboat.* She had a small part in her school's spring production, Old Man Proctor had proudly informed Tom when he'd gone down to pay the rent. The smallness of the part had not dampened Fay's enthusiasm for learning the entire musical score which she sang off key.

> *Fish gotta swim, birds gotta fly*
> *I'm gonna love one man till I die*
> *Can't help lovin' that man of mine.*

Every Saturday her flat nasal voice travelled up the heat register to the third floor seeking them out. She had not yet shown up this Saturday afternoon. Leslie was hoping Fay would get it over with earlier than usual today so their dinner guests wouldn't be subjected to the unwanted distraction but so far she hadn't turned up. With any luck the girl had come down with laryngitis.

Leslie finished hulling strawberries and put them in the fridge. The strawberries were a winter treat flown in from Florida or California. They were expensive. Leslie was sure their dinner guests, Richard and Nancy, wouldn't be able to afford them. She had splurged on them to fancy up the main course, spaghetti with meat sauce, which was cheap. That was one of the reasons she was serving it; the other was that it was supposed to be popular with kids or so she gathered from TV commercials which she watched infrequently when she and Tom visited their parents in Halifax. Nancy and Richard were bringing their kids, Paul and Charlotte. Leslie wasn't all that enthusiastic about the kids coming: by Friday afternoons she'd had enough of teaching garrulous school children, she looked forward to weekends without kids. But Nancy had said there was no money in their budget for babysitters so they had to bring them.

Leslie decided to make the most of it. She had brought colored paper from school and made placemats: a rooster for Paul, a bunny for Charlotte, which she put on the cardtable in the kitchen. She had also made them a centerpiece of toothpicks and jelly beans and bought them each a coloring book and crayons to keep them occupied while the adults visited in the living room. For the adults she had bought a red-checkered tablecloth to put on the kitchen table and dribbled wax over the sides of an empty wine bottle to create the Italian *ristorante* atmosphere.

"Tom, can you give me a hand with this table?" she said. "I want it in the living room."

Tom was sitting on the sofa, shoes off, reading the sports news, the weekend papers spread around him.

"Sure," he said obligingly. He set the paper aside and stood up.

It irked Leslie that he had gone right in and sat down without offering to help her first, that she always had to ask him to do things. With teaching and keeping up this place she had more to do than she could manage. Didn't he notice that she never had time to sit down and read the newspaper?

Tom took one end of the kitchen table, Leslie the other and they carried it into the living room.

"Careful," Leslie warned. She didn't want the tall candle she had stuck into the wine bottle to tip. When the table was in place in front of the window Tom said, "Anything else?"

Leslie looked at him. His trousers were rumpled, his shirt tail was out and bare toes showed through his socks. He saw her frowning at his feet.

"Relax. I'll put on my shoes when the doorbell rings."

"Aren't you planning to change?" Leslie said.

"I hadn't planned on it. I showered this morning," Tom said. He sat down and picked up the sports page.

So Leslie put the chairs around the table. She tidied the wood scraps Tom had dropped in front of the fireplace. Then she picked up the loose newspaper sections and folding them noisily, tucked them under the sofa.

"There!" she said.

Tom kept on reading.

Back in the kitchen ripping the lettuce, Leslie thought that Tom could afford to be casual about this dinner party because he'd never met Nancy and Richard. There was more at stake for her. Nancy and she had been room mates at university before Nancy had become pregnant with Paul and left in her third year to marry Richard. It was important to Leslie to renew this friendship not only because she knew so few people in Toronto but because from the little she'd seen of Nancy since moving here, she perceived Nancy as someone who needed friends, badly tied down as she was with two kids and with another one on the way.

From the living room she heard the sound of Tom shuffling into his shoes. He came into the kitchen, put his arms around her waist and kissed her on the neck.

"Ummm," he murmured, "you taste good."

"Not now, Tom."

The doorbell rang and Leslie ducked under his arms and ran for the door. Their four guests crowded into the tiny hallway, the kids behind their parents. Leslie and Nancy hugged each other. Leslie felt Nancy's swollen belly between them; in the month since she'd last seen her, Nancy had ballooned out. Richard kissed Leslie, his five o'clock shadow bristly against her cheek. Then he and Tom, who was watching all from the kitchen, shook hands formally. The children pushed past them into the living room and looked around.

"Where's the TV?" Paul said. He was dark and solemn like his father.

"Shame on you," Nancy scolded him. "You didn't come here to watch TV. Besides you're not allowed to watch TV except on Sundays and you know it's Saturday."

"What is there for me to do then?" Paul challenged her.

At five years of age, Leslie noticed, he had perfect enunciation; better than most of the grade one-ers she taught.

"I have coloring books and crayons," Leslie said.

"We stopped at the library on our way here and got out new picture books," Nancy said. "All right, children, take off your coats and hang them up. Then you can look at these books. They're brand new. You'll be first to use them. Isn't that lucky!"

Charlotte took off her coat but Paul made no effort to take off his.

"Get a move on, Paul," Richard said. "Remember what we told you about on the subway. It's a privilege for you to be invited into the McIntosh's home. You can show your appreciation by behaving yourself."

Richard had a deep ministerial voice. It was his voice that had first attracted Nancy to him. She'd met him when he'd come to their campus with a debating team from a nearby university. She thought he had a sexy voice, she'd told Leslie in their room afterwards. This was true: Richard's voice was deep, compelling. Leslie could feel herself being pulled toward him, to a man physically huge, larger than life; not this short lean man with a narrow face, high forehead and small eyes.

At the time Nancy had met Richard, he was studying for the ministry. When they were married he told Nancy this: though they were becoming man and wife he would always love God first. Nancy had accepted this as one of Richard's high principles but the declaration had weighed heavily on Leslie, who was their maid of honor, when she was told this. It had carried with it a sense of doom, a warning that try as she might Nancy would never get past being a handmaiden. Yet Leslie admired Richard: she admired a person with convictions, someone who was willing to take a stand even if it was wrong. This was one thing that troubled her about Tom. He was so reasonable, so without an axe to grind, so willing to listen to someone else's point of view that Leslie sometimes wondered if he had one of his own. It didn't occur to her that his point of view might be an amalgam of other people's.

Paul had taken off his coat and dropped it on the living room floor.

"Pick it up," Richard said.

The boy obeyed. Richard certainly handled his son firmly. In school Leslie had children of permissive parents to cope with. Some of them refused to co-operate no matter how politely they were asked.

"Would they like to use our bed to read on?" Leslie asked.

"Thanks but I'd rather keep them here where I can watch them," Nancy said and shepherded them toward the fire, told them to sit on the floor and handed each child a book.

Paul took his book and headed for the bedroom.

Richard signalled him back. Paul dropped his knees to the floor but he didn't look at the book. He stared moodily into the fire.

"Maybe they'd rather color instead," Leslie said. She went into the kitchen and came back with the coloring books and crayons. She handed them to the children.

"What will you have to drink?" Tom said.

"A little wine," Nancy told him.

"Richard?"

"Scotch if you have it."

This was a switch for him. When he was courting Nancy he wouldn't touch liquor because his mother had been an alcoholic. Leslie supposed this sort of socializing went with selling insurance.

"So how's business?" Tom called from the kitchen.

Leslie was astonished Tom would bring up the subject of insurance. After they had been married a month, a bulky envelope arrived by registered mail. It was an investment portfolio Richard had made up for them even though he'd never met Tom. Tom had thrown it into the wastebasket. Here he was leaving himself wide open for questioning.

"Fine. Fine." Richard shouted back. "Record sales last year. By the way did you ever get the portfolio I sent you? I tailored it especially for your needs. I do a lot of student portfolios."

Tom came into the room and handed Richard and Nancy their drinks.

"Yes, but we're not ready for that yet," he said easily. "Someday maybe, but not now." He went into the kitchen for the other drinks. When he returned he said, "But you can tell me what you think I should look for a few years from now." Tom sat on the sofa beside Richard and waited for him to take over the conversation. He was quite prepared to do this, to let someone else do all the talking.

"I lucked in on a tremendous sale," Leslie told Nancy. "A gift shop on Eglinton that's closing out. I found that red-checkered table cloth half price." She waved toward her Italian table, then listed off the sale items in case there was something Nancy could afford. Since picking up their friendship this was the sort of thing they talked about: fabric sales, food stamps, recipes for leftovers; they could go on for hours about domestic trivia. They took pleasure in talking about how they shamed store managers into giving generous refunds for stale bread and woody bananas. Nancy was more serious about this than Leslie who regarded it as a bourgeois game that was fun as long as she didn't take it too seriously. But Nancy thought nothing of walking two miles to return a head of rusted lettuce. She dragged her kids all over Toronto tracking down bargains. Every penny saved went to pay off the loan from Richard's father who was a lawyer. Richard had borrowed the money while he was in university before he had found out about his father's mistress. Now that he had disowned his father he couldn't pay back the money fast enough. He and Nancy still had no furniture but slept on the floor, sat on cushions and trunks. Their one luxury was the TV. Nancy managed these deprivations with proud defiance, a determined gaiety meant to ward off sympathy.

But Leslie felt sympathetic nonetheless. She was sure a dinner party, even a modest one like this, was a rare outing for Nancy. Leslie sipped her wine and listened to Nancy. She was talking about a supermarket where she bought groceries by the case. While she explained the advantages and disadvantages of buying in bulk, Leslie saw Paul slip quietly out of the room and go into the bedroom, Charlotte following. Nancy didn't notice. She had moved on to a description of a course she was taking from the extension department on household money management. Since neither of them had much money to manage, Leslie could not sustain interest in the subject for long. She cast around in her mind to find some way of breaking new ground between them or at least reviving some of the old. She recalled the time she and Nancy had organized their Italy or Bust raffle. They had taken an art course together and were determined to go to Florence to see Michelangelo's *David*. Nancy had been so much fun in those days, willing to do anything on a dare. And you could always count on her: she was loyal. Leslie didn't think different lifestyles and husbands need interfere with old friendships: she still thought of marriage as a separate institution.

Charlotte came into the living room and announced she was hungry so Leslie got up and went into the kitchen to boil water for the spaghetti. Nancy followed.

"What can I do to help?" she said.

"You can pour the kids' milk," Leslie said. "Or there's apple juice if they'd prefer that. I set up this table especially for them."

"Why, you've made placemats and a centerpiece," Nancy said. "They'll be thrilled."

"Well I wanted them to have a good time," Leslie said. "Us too."

"There's one thing I should mention. We like the children to eat with us. Would you mind if we moved the placemats into the living room?" Nancy said this so quietly, so easily that it took Leslie a few moments to realize she did mind.

But she was conscious of being the gracious hostess so she put it obliquely, "You know the old saying: when in Rome, do as the Romans!" And she didn't move the placemats.

But Nancy persisted. "It's just that they might carry on if they're sitting separately. And once you've established family policy on something it's important to be consistent. When you have children you'll understand what I mean."

When *I* have children I won't drag them everywhere, Leslie said to herself. I won't foist them on other people. I won't let them take over my life. But she stalked into the living room and unset the table.

"Let me help," Nancy said.

"No," Leslie said sharply, "you go sit down. You're here to enjoy yourself."

When Leslie pulled out the extra table leaf she noticed that the new tablecloth was too short, the table edges showed at either end. She transferred the placemats to the ends to cover up this discrepancy and put the jellybean centerpiece beside the waxed wine bottle. So much for atmosphere. But then the incongruities of the table setting struck her as comical and she snickered—at them and her own pettiness. She lit the candle.

She looked at Tom and said, "Could you pour the wine?"

She thought he looked relieved to be asked.

Richard took the children into the bathroom to wash; Paul had black crayon on his hands.

After they were seated, the couples opposite each other, the children at either end, Tom poured the wine. The salad and bread were passed. Leslie got up and handed round the plates of spaghetti and meat sauce. While they ate Richard regaled them with a story about last summer's vacation which they spent in a pup tent in the pouring rain. As a child, he said, his parents had always taken him to expensive hotels for holidays and dumped him with a babysitter so he thought of camping as a novelty. Richard had a talent for description; it was he who wrote cheerful descriptions of the year's activities in a mimeographed Christmas newsletter as if he was determined to assuage the unhappy Xmases of his childhood.

"Can we go camping next year?" Charlotte asked, her words squashed in with the spaghetti.

"Don't talk with your mouth full," Nancy said.

Charlotte swallowed obediently. She was a cooperative child, blond and sturdy like her mother.

Nancy turned to help Paul, who had eaten a piece of bread and was sitting with his hands in his lap, his spaghetti untouched.

"You'd better start eating or you'll get behind," Nancy said. "I can't eat this," Paul complained. "It falls off my fork."

"Certainly you can. All you have to do is use your fork and spoon together." Nancy picked up his fork and spoon and put one in each of his hands. Then using her hands to guide his she said, "You take your fork and hold it against the spoon winding the spaghetti around like this, see? Isn't that easy?" she popped the spaghetti into his mouth. "That's the way they do it in Italy!"

"Why doesn't he cut it with a knife?" Leslie said. She had seen Charlotte cut hers. "It does slide off the fork."

"Nonsense," Nancy scoffed. "He hasn't even tried it yet."

Paul made a half-hearted attempt at twisting the spaghetti around the fork holding it jerkily against the spoon, but when he failed he dropped both utensils onto the plate, sat back and stared at his lap. Nancy had dressed him in a suit, probably a cast-off of Richard's made over. He looked like a sullen old man.

"Did Tom tell you he changed his thesis topic?" Leslie said and without waiting for an answer prompted, "Tell them, Tom"

Tom had eaten his spaghetti but had left his wine. He was leaning forward, elbows on the table, eyes averted, far away. He did this sometimes when the going got rough, retreated to some lonely place, a northern wilderness where no one could follow. Leslie dreaded this retreat.

Tom came back.

"With the necessity for better ecology escalating every day, I decided to concentrate on environmental engineering," he said. He went on expanding, explaining. Richard asked good questions and together they took up fifteen minutes. During this time everyone had finished the spaghetti except Paul who still stared into his lap.

"Eat your spaghetti," Richard said.

"I can't."

Paul poked a strand of spaghetti into his mouth with a finger then sucked it inward with a satisfying slurp.

"That's enough," Richard said. "Eat it properly the way your mother showed you."

"Why don't I take some off his plate?" Leslie suggested. She felt she should do something to make up for the mistake of serving spaghetti. If she'd known it was going to be this much trouble she'd have settled for hot dogs.

"I probably gave him too much," she said and reached for his plate.

Richard put out a restraining hand.

"No," he said. "He'll eat it. He's just being stubborn."

Leslie looked at Tom but he'd retreated again. She was angry at him, at Richard and Paul. It was clear father and son were locked in a stalemate. What were the rest of them supposed to do while this silly game was being played out? Sit and wait for the kid to eat? Well she wouldn't. She got up and carried the plates into the kitchen.

Nancy gave Charlotte a jellybean from the centerpiece, then she turned to Paul.

"When you finish your spaghetti you can have some of these candies for dessert," she said gaily.

Leslie bristled. Wasn't that ridiculous. Once a kid dug himself into a hole as deep as Paul's it took more than bribery to get him out. You didn't need kids of your own to figure that out. She spooned out limp strawberries, added cream and passed them around. They were eaten in silence. The candle burned low. The fire went out. Leslie brought in coffee.

Tom stood up. "I'm taking my coffee to a more comfortable chair. Anyone care to join me?" He looked at his wife.

Leslie left the table. Then Nancy and Charlotte got up. Leslie noticed Nancy's hand shaking when she picked up her cup. Coffee spilt onto her maternity dress, no doubt one she had made especially for tonight. Why didn't Nancy say something to Richard? Paul was her son too. Why didn't she take the whole knotted mess of spaghetti and throw it into the garbage? Paul still made no attempt to eat but sat hitting his shoe against the table leg.

"Paul," Richard said, "Mrs. McIntosh did not prepare this fine meal in order to have it thrown into the garbage. Not only is your refusal to eat a waste of good food but it is bad manners." Richard looked at his watch. "I'll give you ten minutes. Now you either clean up your plate or I'll take you into the bathroom and give you a beating with my belt."

Now that he had played his hand Richard stood up, picked up his coffee and started toward the living room sofa.

Tom was sitting in a basket chair. Leslie heard him say, "Not in my home you won't."

She was amazed that he would say anything so rash, to make a move before the winner was declared. There was still a chance, however slight, that Paul would finish his spaghetti. Tom wasn't waiting for that possibility: he'd been pushed too far. Leslie felt a peculiar thrill, strongly sexual, watching him. In their eight months of married life she'd never seen him dig in this way.

Richard stopped in the middle of the sisal rug. He turned his head sideways. There was a half smile on his lips, a smile of incredulity.

"What did you say?"

Tom got up out of the basket chair and faced Richard.

"I said not in my home you won't."

Richard stopped smiling. The tips of his ears were red.

"Are you telling me how to bring up my own son?" He looked like he might hit Tom.

Tom folded his arms across his chest.

"No, I'm not," he said quietly. "I'm merely telling you what I won't permit in my own home."

As the two men stood there staring at each other Leslie heard a tinny nasal voice—very faint—coming from downstairs.

Fish gotta swim, birds gotta fly,
I'm gonna love one man till I die.

And she started to laugh. She couldn't help it. Old Man Proctor's granddaughter was at it again. Leslie sat down in the basket chair. She was laughing so hard she had to hold onto her sides. Tears streamed down her cheeks. She didn't dare look at Tom.

Richard gave her an injured look. Very carefully he set his coffee cup on the mantlepiece. "In that case we'll go," he said. He motioned for Nancy and Charlotte to follow and jerked a thumb at Paul who had his head down, a replica of his father's earlier smile on his face.

All three followed Richard into the hall and put on their coats.

Leslie pulled herself together and went into the bedroom for the library books, the coloring books and crayons. One of the new library books lay open on the bed. A thick black line had been crayoned across the shiny page.

After she had carried the books down the hall and given them to Nancy, Leslie got the candy centerpiece from the table and handed it to her as well.

"Don't forget this," she said. "I'd like the kids to have it."

"No thanks," Nancy said stiffly. She turned and walked into the corridor.

Oh come *on,* Leslie felt like saying. Isn't that going too far? Instead she tried to apologize. "I'm sorry about the laughing. It was that girl downstairs." Leslie's voice faltered. "It's hard to explain."

Still Nancy said nothing but stood, feet planted stolidly apart, eyes downcast, on her bulging belly.

As Leslie looked at her old friend an incredible sadness swept over her, a heavy weight that came with wondering how much time this family, including the unborn child, would have to spend living down Richard's unhappy childhood.

"Good luck with the baby" Leslie said, "and everything."

"Thanks," Nancy finally said. And they were gone.

Leslie went into the living room. Through the heat register she heard Fay's whiny voice reaching for the high notes.

> *When he goes awaaay, it's a rainy daaay,*
> *But when he comes home again ...*

Tom was at the fireplace crumpling up newspaper, piling on wood scraps, relighting the fire. He looked awkward, hunched over, his shirt tail coming out of his trousers, his hair ruffled. Leslie watched him rummage in his pocket for a folder of *Eddy* matches, typically ignoring the box of elegantly long matches she had placed on the mantlepiece. She thought of going into the bedroom, taking the diaphragm out of her jewelry box where she had hidden it from Old Man Proctor's prying eyes, putting on her sheer nightgown, but that was all she did—thought about it. She walked over to her husband and unbuttoning his shirt and unzippering his trousers, she slowly undressed him. Then she made love to him in front of the fire, on the untidy heap of clothes she had dropped on the floor.

LISTEN

Daphne Marlatt

He was reading to her, standing on the other side of the kitchen counter where she was making salad for supper, tender orange carrot in hand almost transparent at its tip, slender, & she was wondering where such carrots came from in winter. He was standing in the light reading to her from a book he was holding, her son behind him at the table where the amber light streamed from under its glass shade bought, she had, for its warm colour midwinter, tho he had called it a cheap imitation of the real thing. Under it, her son was drawing red Flash & blue Superman into a comic he was making, painstakingly having stapled the pages together & now with his small & definite hand trying to draw exact images of D.C. Superstars and Marvel heroes none of them had ever seen except in coloured ink. But he was reading to her about loss, excited, because someone had named it at last, was naming it even as he read it, the shape of what he felt to be his own, recognized at last in words coming at him from the page, coming to her through his emphatic & stirred voice stumbling over the rough edges of words that weren't his, even as he was embracing them. Lost, how dancing had lost touch with the ring dance which was a collective celebration—she was standing with the grater in one hand, carrot in the other, wondering if the grating sound would disturb him. She wanted to hear what had stirred him. She wanted to continue the movement of making salad which, in the light & the Lowenbrau they shared, was for once coming so easily, almost was spring stirring round the corner of the house in a rhythm of rain outside she was moving in, barely knowing, except for the wetness of walking home—hand in hand, he was saying, a great circle like the circle of the seasons, where now people barely touch each other, or at least with the waltz they used to dance in couples & then with rock apart but to each other, whereas now, he caught her eye the dances we've been to you can see people dancing alone, completely alone with the sound.

Lifting the carrot to the grater, pressing, watching flakes of carrot fall to the board, she felt accused in some obscure way, wanted to object, thought up an obscure argument about quadrilles being collective in ballrooms where all the guests were invited, their places in the collectivity known & symbolized by their places in the dance. But now, & she recalled the new year's eve party they'd been to, almost a hundred people, strangers, come, or people don't know each other in a city the way they do in a village, but it wasn't really that, or that only glanced off what the book was saying about husbandry & caring for the soil. The whole carrot was shrinking into a thousand orange flakes heaped & scattered at once, the whole carrot with its almost transparent sides shining in the light, had ground down to a stump her fingers clutched close the the jagged edges of tin, she saw her fingers grating, saw blood flying like carrot flakes, wondered why she imagined blood as part of the salad ...

Listen, he was saying, this is where he's really got it. And he read a long passage about their imprisonment in marriage, all the married ones with that impossible ideal of confining love to one—"one cannot love a particular woman unless one loves womankind," he read. Listen, he said, & he read her a passage about the ring dance, about the participation of couples in the one great celebration, the "amorous feast that joins them to all living things." He means fertility, she said, thinking, oh no, oh back to that, woman's one true function. He means fertility of the earth, he said, he means our lives aware of seasonal growth & drawing nourishment from that, instead of material acquisition & exploitation. Listen, & he read a passage about sexual capitalism, about the crazy images of romance that fill people's heads, & the sexual "freedom" & "skill" & the "me-generation" on all the racks of all the supermarket stores.

Using her palms like two halves of a split spoon, she scooped up the heap of carrot flakes & set them onto a bed of lettuce, dark, because it was romaine, torn into pieces in the wooden bowl with other green things. Dance. In & out. She watched the orange flakes, glistening again in a sea of oil, dance in & out among the green she tossed with real spoons, each dipping into the dark that lay at the heart of, what, *their* hearts, they had, the other night, sunk into bed at the end of the party, drunk & floating, their laughter moving in memory through the night as they lay wrapped in the warmth of what everyone had said & how they moved away & toward each other & loved in very obscure ways. & they had made love to everyone in each other, & *to* each other, falling thru & away from each other. Listen, she said, as the rain came up & she set the salad on the wooden table underneath the lamp.

PRESERVATION

Shirley A. Serviss

The cold room in her parents' cellar
holds shelves of pickled carrots, sealers
of canned crabapples, raspberry jam in old
mayonnaise jars. Onions tied with bindertwine
hang from the low ceiling.

Two deep freezers are filled with roasts
wrapped in brown paper, homemade bread
in plastic bags, apple pies in foil
stacked in soda biscuit boxes.

The cupboards in her city apartment
are bare but for a few tins of asparagus,
crabmeat and mushrooms. Her fridge
holds nothing but yoghurt, coffee,
and sometimes French wine.

"We called you Saturday night," her mother would
say on the phone, "and before church Sunday morning."
"I'm sorry you missed me," she has learned
to say rather than offer explanations.

Once, she had married
to please them, but her marriage
changed in unexpected ways like potatoes sprouting
too soon for spring, grew mould like black
currant jam, rotted like pumpkins.

Now she does not know what the future
has in store, can not anticipate
meeting her needs with dill pickles,
or Mason jars filled with pears.
Still, she packs a pudding made from suet
in her suitcase to take back to the city.

JOY SULUK, 37, ARVIAT, N.W.T.
– Interviewed by Laurie Sarkadi

You can almost see the wind from Joy Suluk's kitchen window in the summer as the Hudson Bay curls and crashes in a sea of whitecaps. With no trees and few man-made impediments, some days the wind whips through Arviat, on the Bay's northwest shore, with such ferocious power it forces people to walk at seemingly impossible angles. From another window you can see Joy's sister's house, where a small puppy wobbles on playful new legs. It is fitting that Joy, a 37-year-old adult education trainee at Arctic College, lives so near her family because she draws great spiritual strength from her own five children and their Inuit heritage.

In her kitchen, a spacious, airy room with trendy dark blue countertops and clean, eggshell cupboards, Joy discusses the difficulties of being a 90s Inuk; daydreaming of trading in her microwave and modern-day securities for the harsh, yet uncluttered life her grandmother knew on the tundra.

Joy Suluk

I hate the kitchen. Like I said, I really don't like cooking, but when you have friends it's a really great place to sit. And also I used to visit the world in my kitchen, until I got my computer. I've got pen pals all over the world and I'd write from my kitchen table. I use it as a desk and it's close to coffee and tea.

Everybody cooks. The girls cook, Luke (my husband) does, it depends on who's the creative one of the day, but mostly it's me because I do it out of duty because I know my family needs to be fed. I don't hate it, but I don't exactly like it either. We're starting to use the microwave a lot and make instant food.

We love Chinese food my style with caribou and vegetables and bannock. I love bannock when we're out hunting.

I can't live without caribou. I just can't. Even when we have lots of store-bought foods, if we don't have caribou often I get tired more easily and I get heartburn. I used to think that my grandmother was making it up when she said she used to get heartburn if she didn't have caribou and I used to think I could live without caribou but I can't. You can do a lot with caribou. I could eat caribou every day and not get sick of it—you know when you eat chicken every day you get sick of it—although I can't say the same for fish. The best way I love caribou is eating it when it's frozen. But I love cooking outdoors.

Our camp is at Austin Point, just north about an hour's canoe ride. Our cabin is at a small point. It's quite flat, lots of rocks and you can hear the sea (Hudson Bay) from both sides and when you look towards the land there's a great big hill and just before you reach the hill there's a flat area where there's dried clay and it's really smooth.

When we're not fishing out in our cabin we usually go out some other place and use a tent. Usually it's just behind the hill. As long as I don't see the houses I'm O.K.

(On the land) I have a stove made of stones with a grill over it and for firewood we use dead bushes that have washed up and they're really dry and the smell, it doesn't smell like when you're in smoke, it's not very pleasant, but when you're cooking outside the smell doesn't bother you. In fact, you love it and the smell of bannock. You have to go through it in order to understand.

And I can feed the fire with wood forever. Even if I'm not cooking I love feeding the fire and you barbecue caribou and fish and you don't need dishes except for the tea. I guess I love it because I don't have to wash dishes. You're cooking and you have children playing and they don't seem to fight so much and it's really satisfying to hear them enjoying themselves. You're giving them something that you can't give them in the community, and you think about your cooking.

If the weather's bad, I use the Coleman. I love making bannock in the tent. You light up the Coleman, put flour in the bowl, add salt and baking powder and water and you just stir it, not watery, but like a paste and you put lard in the frying pan, heat it up and cook it like a pancake. I love it when it's nicely browned, not black. When you're done you take a piece and put peanut butter and strawberry jam on it and eat it with tea and sugar.

I like making stew over the Coleman stove, caribou with onions, potatoes, carrots and a dried chicken soup mix. You don't need very much. You make do with nature. You use what nature gives you. You just need a pot, matches, a frying pan, a tea kettle and cups and bowls for the stew.

I love the land. I want to live on the land. When you're out, you're yourself, you can be who you want to be.

There's a point where children start drifting away from you and if you don't watch yourself you're going to lose them. You just keep after them and tell them they're welcome to come and how nice it is out there and now my oldest one is starting to come back, starting to come with us. I think there's a point where they want to be alone and they're not satisfied with going out. But they do come back. At least my oldest one did. For two years she wouldn't come to our camp, but last weekend she asked if she could come along, which was really nice, and she actually enjoyed herself. Before, if we took her she would complain that it's boring and there's nothing to do and she wants to come home, but we went out there a whole day and she never complained.

She's not a cook. I guess she took after me.

I don't remember anything about the kitchen (of my grandmother's, where I grew up), but I do remember the smell of bannock and my grandmother cooking outside. Like, we used to live in tents and igloos. When we moved here we lived in a shack and she used to make bread in a wood stove.

One time when we were living in a tent and she decided to bake the bread, she stuck too much wood in the cookstove and she was inside the tent and when she came out she could see the sparks coming out of the chimney. She took a bucket—she used to wear long dresses and a shawl—she took a bucket and I can just see her running to the roof of the house, it was quite low, and going up the roof and pouring the water down the chimney. I can just see her dress flapping. That bad day of baking, I remember.

And I remember her making dried meat and while she was doing that she boiled caribou legs and head over a fire outside in this great big pot. I guess that's why I like cooking outside because it reminds me of when I was a little girl.

It's the same smell that I smelled when I was a little girl. It's funny it doesn't change.

It's very different (today). We've got an electric stove and then we got a microwave and we've got running water. Most of the stuff I use for cooking, it wasn't there (before).

I spent a lot of time with my grandmother, that's where I learned most of my language and about the land. When she was cooking, sometimes she had a visitor and they would talk and I would sit and listen.

I think I was born at the wrong time. I would love to live way back then. Sometimes I wish I could change my life with my great-grandmother. She'd flip. Don't you ever wonder, like if you were born in the 1800s and all of a sudden you switch places with somebody. You would know because you heard about them, but that lady wouldn't know it, she wouldn't have experienced it yet, and all of a sudden she's in this house with running water and electricity. I do a lot of daydreaming.

It was hard (hunting and living off the land), but I think what we go through today is even harder, just as hard, because we've got all these pressures. It's harder mentally because they didn't have to worry too much about everything that I worry about now, because they worried about where their next meal will come and how you're going to keep warm. But when I worry, I worry about my children getting into drugs that they didn't have before or that somebody might persuade them to steal. I guess that happened before, but there wasn't much to steal at that time. I think it's harder mentally now. Don't you think?

And when I talk to my grandmother—I talk with her a lot—and when she talks about the old days she gets this look when she remembers. It's a look of fond memories. Even though they say life is hard, you can tell they'd love to go back and you don't blame them. This is our time and their time was back then. That's when they got educated about life.

I like living out on the land because I don't have too much stuff. Like when I'm here, I've got lots of things, things I don't really need, but things that give me pleasure for a short time. When we're out camping, we've got no choice but to talk. That's why I like to bring my kids out there, to communicate with them.

MORNINGS LIKE THIS

Pat Jasper

Mornings like this, cold and damp
with steam rising from the slush,
she would call, bragging
that her daffodils were up.
She'd take time out to check
a cheesecake in the oven
with a broomstraw.

The phone hangs silent on its wall cradle
as I flip through her old recipe box:
a life history indexed on three-by-five cards,
the well-used ones blotted with lemon juice

or smears of something that looks like soy sauce.

Here's one for the *Snow Cream*
we used to make as kids:
milk, vanilla, sugar
and fresh-fallen snow, stirred
with a wooden spoon til thick.

The faces of old friends and neighbors
hover like ghosts from a culinary graveyard:
Helen Wise's Pickled Beets
—her son won the state spelling bee—
Mrs. Yinger's Sweet Potato Pie
—the widow down the street who
kept getting her purse stolen—
one from Mr. Morgan who
used to mow our lawn.
Filed behind its proper tab, each
in a different hand, my vegetarian sister's
Eggplant Parmesan, my sweet-tooth sister's
Mandarin Orange Jello and my dependable
Barbecue Sauce.

Recipes with ingredients casual
and humorous as my mother:
Stove Pipe Bread baked in coffee cans
calling for handfuls of flour,
Shrimp Scampi made with
as much shrimp as you can afford,
instructions for *Strawberry Shortcake*
to pile on the whipped cream.

She hung on through April, too weak
to check the wild spring growth
that overran her garden. This far north
the daffodils came up long after hers
were in yellow tatters, bloomed
heartlessly into June.

I settle on *Authentic Pound Cake*

and turn the oven on to preheat.
Warmth begins to fill the kitchen.
The phone rings. I jump
but it's only my sister.
The one with the sweet tooth.

THE TAMING
Dorothy Livesay

Be woman. You did say me, be
woman. I did not know
the measure of the words

until a black man
as I prepared him chicken
made me listen:
—No, dammit.
Not so much salt.
Do what I say, woman:
just that
and nothing more.

Be woman. I did not know
the measure of the words
until that night
when you denied me darkness,
even the right
to turn in my own light.

Do as I say, I heard you faintly
over me fainting:
be woman.

IN THIS KITCHEN
Kristjana Gunnars

in this kitchen there is none of me   a place of noise and bad manners   where the one son drinks his leisure coffee listens to Tom Waits and Lou Reed on the ghetto blaster reads Robert Priest's The Mad Hand and discusses Soviet astronauts' conversations with Alberta ham radio operators   where the other son brings the telephone discusses skateboard problems with the rest of the world   makes plans to sell one board send back another buy a third with the refund   where the father holds forth on philosophical issues for the benefit of young minds while eating bread   where the mother   in this case me   is usually silent wondering where all the minds at the table are off to and following sometimes with pride sometimes with suspension but wondering will I ever write the poem let alone get my head together for the novel I promised the Canada Council

this is just a family an average family of loves and apprehensions not something you'd want to trade in necessarily but a state of being and this kitchen is mostly a place of meals I did not cook and floors I did not sweep and pots I did not wash and shelves I did not wipe and when I come home on library day after writer in residencing it is a place of grease and chaos where no hand has been except the noisy and ill mannered one where food has been ripped from the cupboards and torn into crumbs over tables and floors and consumed in haste between urgent telephone convos   where I become the disconsolate army surgeon slowly lifting broken items back into place and I must be dreaming in this kitchen there is none of me

SUNANDA
Jagruti Dholakia

Sunanda was born in India and was raised in Bangladesh. Her father owned tea plantations. Their big business gave them a good lifestyle. They had many servants but the kitchen was considered to be a place where a woman rules or controls. Her father believed that mother should cook the food, as good thoughts and good values can be transmitted only by mother to children while cooking the food and feeding the family. It was a process of nurturing. Being staunch Hindu, she believed that touch of food with holy feelings and prayers can make food divine and thus God will bless the whole family. She believed that good simple nutrifibre, wholesome food can nurture good moral values in the family.

Her mother died when she was three years old; as a result, her elder sister had to look after the family. At the age of 10, Sunanda began helping her sister in the kitchen. Her sister was a patient teacher, which made the learning experience creative and innovative.

Sunanda believed that cooking can be learned by observation and every woman can be a successful cook if she observes her mother carefully. She took the entire responsibility of the kitchen at the age of 17. Her large extended family, along with the children who lived with them, were given the opportunity to develop their talents. She believed that kitchen was the place she could put her soul into and make her family happy and healthy. Being a democratic and enlightened mother, she raised her daughters and sons alike. She did not push her daughters to help her in the kitchen; rather, she allowed them to choose their activities as they liked. One of her daughters preferred to concentrate on studies whereas the other loved to work in the kitchen. Both daughters focused on education and learned cooking by observation. They entered kitchen at the age of 22.

By living in an extended family she shared her work with her sister-in-law which was quite relieving and enjoyable. At family weddings and festivals women used to get together and cook. This was the happiest time for them because, while cooking, they sang songs and shared feelings during the whole night. On certain occasions men also joined women in cooking which made cooking not only enjoyable but also a uniting force.

Being confident in cooking, she never hesitated to cook in another's kitchen. She believed that one can always learn new methods of cooking and bring variety to food preparations. Her willingness to adapt new methods made her life less stressful.

Sunanda never worked outside the house because her family was rich and never needed her financial support. She was raised in a traditional family and so never thought of becoming a professional woman. She loved her "housewife" role and believed that whatever one would become, cooking should be done by oneself. However, she never undermined women who did not cook because of riches or jobs. She believed that cooking should not become a standard to judge women's potential, qualities, or goodness as women have to play many other vital roles to keep the family together, happy, and progressive.

However, in a traditional setting she believes that kitchen is the safest and most confidential place for major decisions to be taken. It is the only place where the family gets together to discuss family issues without interference.

She feels that lifestyle has changed tremendously now. The traditional beliefs and norms such as: without taking a bath/shower one is not allowed to cook, children cannot touch mother while she is cooking etc. are not followed strictly.

PROFILE OF AN UNLIBERATED WOMAN

Miriam Waddington

I was a dish
to be eaten off
to be broken
I suppose to
fall wherever
I fell I wish
I had been
more (or less)
breakable I
was blank
white un-
patterned
and I had
only the usual
contrariness
the irritating
resistance of
all inanimate
objects.

SURVIVAL WORK

Lee Maracle (prepared with Maria Baptiste and Lainy Lea Greyeyes)

It's funny how there is such emphasis on women being in the kitchen. Some think the negative. For me, it's so old, so understood, that it seems natural.

For us it was never an imprisonment—survival work—like chopping and hauling wood must have been for the boys. But the kitchen was more than that for me. It still is. I don't quite know how to describe my qualms about women who don't like cooking, doing that kind of work. It isn't the cooking I love—only fools enjoy washing dishes—though my mother swears she likes it. Solitary, she always said. Alone time. It isn't the work. The kitchen is like the heart of the home. If the body is ailing no one would suggest you cut out the heart, and yet, because there is illness in our homes women want to cut the kitchen out of their lives.

The kitchen was where I really saw my mother, heard her thoughts and came to understand her. Women can be alone in a crowd of people in the kitchen. It's like that even now. My mom regrets the harshness of our childhood, and every now and then I can see she wants to talk and we retreat to the kitchen. She washes dishes and I rinse and put them away, slowly, while she hums out her sorrowful memories, her children, working away, fending for themselves, me playing mom to four little kids.

As a child, it never dawned on me that life was hard. There were no conveniences then, everything was done by hand from grinding corn meal to making our own peanut butter—everything. Clothes were washed by hand and hung out on the line or hung up inside the porch on one of those wooden foldouts. How much each family would need, who had new children, whose kids were teenagers and eating more, we planned our work according to how much food was needed to bring us through another year. There was one occasion when no one had much more than bannock and tea.

It was a rare day when there was no bannock and tea. I do recall the odd occasion when the tea got used twice though. Generally, if we ran out of store tea lots of kids were ready to pick wild tea—mint, comfrey, Labrador or the like. Springtime rolled around and the dandelions were ready for picking, salmon berry shoots, mint leaves and fiddleheads—that was salad. I still pick fiddleheads, blanch them and melt them with butter—sautéed.

Everything was kind of slippery in our community then. I remember Dad when he fell out of work—not fishing—he cooked, cleaned, or did whatever to keep himself busy. If there was nothing to build, then there was something to clean. Even us kids. We had this old galvanized gray tub. Three times a week we all got cleaned up. The canning kettle would be on the stove, filled with water heating up to boil and the tub was half full of cold water. Mom would heave them around, or Dad, depending on who was there. One by one we jumped in and one of our parents, usually Mom, scrubbed us up. I don't suppose Mom thought it was such a gay time, but we loved it. We were all ticklish so it made it hard for her to wash our necks. We'd be jumping and dancing around, scrunching down our heads so she couldn't reach our necks, and giggling like crazy—that happened in the kitchen. When Dad was out of work, he was right there next to her, drying us up and laughing too.

I never actually taught my daughters to cook. We expect our children will remember what they need to know through watching or helping out. We never had anyone standing up there classroom-style and droning on about *it's time for cooking lessons.* My second daughter, not too long ago, was moaning one day that she didn't know how to cook. I told her, "My gawd, girl, you've been standing beside me in the kitchen, cutting up vegetables for years. Weren't you watching what I did with them? Didn't you see me stick them in a pot, not even once?" She laughed and said she was too busy listening to me talk to myself. She figured it out though, and now she is a pretty good cook—I am not sure if she just grew up or if being with her new man just naturally led her to domestic work.

There is an order to us working in the kitchen. When I was younger, before I had children and after I wasn't little anymore—between 10 and 20—I used to help out with the cooking wherever we were, tending the children or cleaning. No one told me I had to, but I think these things get passed on through watching others and kind of mastering who does what in the back of your mind—subconsciously. My kids don't have children and they are pretty big, so wherever we go they pitch in. If I am visiting someone my own age and we have teenage kids, they busy themselves serving us; if there are a lot of women, young and old, and no men, my husband and sons will start feeding us; sometimes if it's a more formal occasion and I want to show off, I cook. I expect my kids to help but not my company. Nothing is ever said, everything just kind of works itself out—like the same sense of order belongs to all of us. Some of our people are different, only women cook and in some of the younger families, the men share all the work. Now that my daughters are older they get to join the women more often.

In First Nations communities nothing seems to be preplanned or pre-determined. Everything depends on what you think/feel is expected of you. Planning is felt, order is sensed. You walk into the kitchen and look at your host and you know, she looks tired, or she looks like she wants to talk—with you—and you respond accordingly. Every home seems a bit different. That doesn't bother us because we can see the order of the home as soon as we walk in the door. In fact, we know that other Canadians don't know how to look and see the lay of the land. They'll come into your kitchen and ask if they can help. We never tire of laughing about that.

Nothing has changed for me except things are a little easier and a whole lot less desperate. I still pick huckleberries with my brother, blackberries sometimes with my kids, and put up fish and fruit. But now, if we run out, we can go to Safeway or IGA. It is more for pleasure and just good eating than it used to be. I don't think I will ever quit food gathering. When my brother and I go picking huckleberries, we reminisce, laugh and just generally talk about how we feel about life, family, folks. We even talk about the world, our philosophy and how the world would be better off if people just did things our way, thought the way we do about the world. What's the contemporary word for that—therapy—First Nations style.

There are foods out there in the bush that my body really needs, like fiddleheads, or certain medicines. You can buy fiddleheads, but those crazy people charge a fortune for them. A little bitty jar costs a lot of money—and of course, you can't buy any of the medicines we use. Besides, picking is social for us, like visiting in the kitchen. I know two, three times a year I come up for gatherings with writers in Penticton or Terrace, or to plan something. First thing the women do is go out and pick berries if it's summer. Once I was late getting in. I didn't want to wake Jeannette Armstrong up, so I stayed in the motel here and went straight to the office in the morning. (I try not to be late for work.) I waited for the women. I sat in that office for three hours before

Delphine, Jeannette's sister, told me they were all out picking berries. Well, I teased them when they got back after what seemed like forever. I told them I was jealous. I think the meeting went better for them having gone up the hill to gather food.

Once in Terrace, Ola and some white women organized a women's gathering. In the morning before the workshops started one of the Native women said the huckleberries were ripe. Pretty soon all the Native women were rummaging around in the kitchen, looking for bowls or containers, and heading up the hill. We talked and laughed, about some of the things our different Nations had in common, culturally. It seems like every time we get together we tell about our ways and dig around for things our different peoples have in common and we do it best when we are working around the kitchen or out picking berries. I think we see things more clearly when we are outside on a hill, plucking fat berries and swatting at mosquitoes and thinking about eating or preparing food. There must be some connection between planning and eating. Anyways, turns out the white women were angry about us later. Called us 'isolationist'. After the conference, a debate took place by mail among them about the nature of our participation and whether or not it was negative and divisive. They were upset about how we were able to hang out together as though we had known each other a long time. No one told them to stay in the lodge.

When I first moved to the city I left all those traditional foods behind. I got sick and went back to the hills behind my home and memories came back. I had such fun. I wondered why I had left it behind. Maybe you need to be hungry to appreciate your own foods and the food gathering process. The first time I realized there wasn't enough money to carry us through the month, there I was gathering dandelion leaves, camomile, comfrey and vetch peas and making salad—eating grass, my kids said. They still tease me about that. They tell their friends when they were small and hungry I used to make them eat grass. My kids would say, "What are these?" and I'd say, "Never mind, just eat them, they're good for you." To tell the truth I don't remember the names for some of the things we still eat.

I only cooked for a living once. It was for a family of white people in South Vancouver. I was 13 years old, though I don't think the woman realized I was that young. I had to babysit her three children all day—cook for them, etc.—and at night I cooked the main meal for the whole family. By the time we were five years old we knew how to watch people and see how they acted before we did anything dense. Well, I knew these white folk were different; not having been in any white people's homes, I wasn't sure just how to act, but I made out like I knew what I was doing anyway. Cooking for the kids wasn't too bad; they were fussy, saying they didn't like this or that, but I ignored them and fed them what their parents told me to. I didn't mind cooking for them, but I did not like cooking for their parents. I am not sure why. It wasn't that I had to work for someone else. I had done that in various farmers' fields. It wasn't that. All the cooking was done in the kitchen—alone. No one came by for dinner or even coffee. The eating was done in the dining room and the table was pre-set (by me). The meal was served by the father. A portion was handed out, pre-determined by the dad, and second helpings were unheard of. On top of all that, no one could leave until her plate was empty. The children were not allowed to talk. I presumed that meant me too. Once in a while the man and woman would argue. In front of us.

Maybe because I was a stranger—a stranger to their ways—we never got to be friends. They were friendly enough, treating me like some long lost buddy or something, but I knew they were strangers in a way none of my own folks were. I was aware that I was not at home, nor in the home of anyone like me.

I had to decide on what to cook based on what I imagined their sense of eating to be—eating is so intimate and cultural. They didn't eat the same as we did. I didn't recognize half the stuff in the cupboards. What is Mr. Ragu anyway? There was a lot of instant this and instant that that I had no idea how to prepare.

She told me what the dinner menu was, pork chops on Monday, roast beef on Tuesday, etc., and I was supposed to dream up some way of cooking it. Never in my life had we ever eaten that way. You gathered food all during the spring and summer, gathered whatever spices you could and tried like the devil to make it different and interesting each time you made it. No one had 'recipes' and I knew I couldn't read a cookbook to save my life. There I was standing in the middle of the kitchen, all the cupboards open, saying "Let's see what we got here, what am I supposed to do with all this stuff?" They ate a lot of pork, which I didn't like, and beef, my second least favourite food. When she said 'chops' I got a little confused. Chop was something you did with an axe to wood. Pork chops and applesauce (out of a store-bought jar, of course). My idea of fruit and meat is huckleberries and venison or salad and moose. I faked it. It took me half the day to make up some applesauce—later they showed me the canned goods. They never complained, but the formality of dinner was very uncomfortable for me. At home there are usually a dozen or so people sitting around yammering away, half the people not listening to the other half. It was like they, these white people, couldn't wait to finish their meal and get down to some serious TV watching. I think they don't like talking to each other much.

After dinner the woman would get on the phone and talk for ages to her friends—electronic visiting, I called it when I told my sisters what it was like there. We had a lot of pretty good laughs about those people and their ways.

He was kind of mean to his kids too, though I don't think he thought himself mean. The first day he asked me if all the children had eaten all of their breakfast and lunch. Theresa, the middle daughter, had not eaten her mush. Thinking he was just curious, I told him the truth. After dinner he goes into this strange ceremonial performance talking to his bird—a cockateel—and makes out like the bird tells him Theresa didn't eat her mush and then he punishes her—spanks her and sends her to bed. She hates the bird and tells the bird off before going to her room. I never told him the truth after that. What a ritual. Their sense of ceremony was weird.

That experience shaped me, somehow. Even though there are lots of things I would rather do besides cooking, or eating for that matter, I could never 'hire' someone to do my cooking. But then, I have never been able to bring myself to a "beauty shop" so someone can fiddle with my hair. Grooming and survival work seem to be intimate, too personal to imposeon someone else in your own home. It isn't like a restaurant. I think people who don't like doing their own cooking should go and eat at a restaurant. I have never felt resentful about spending so much time in the kitchen. We have a sense of pride about 'feeding the people' and our folks always treat the cooks good.

The kitchen is the heart of our homes. To have some stranger wander around banging your pots and pans in front of your face would be like watching someone do your laundry or something. It wouldn't feel right.

I know a lot of young women feel differently, feel there shouldn't be so much emphasis on women being the only ones who have to do the cooking and cleaning. Life is different now, it isn't like our men have to spend a lot of time building the family furniture and hauling firewood; and the jobs they do have don't seem as difficult as they used to be. Not even longshoremen work without machines. And women work. We all work all day; few of our families are structured so that the man works and the woman stays home. Young people are working out a new way of sharing, but I wouldn't like to lose the intimacy, the closeness of family and friends in our kitchens in the process.

Life has changed and we have to change with it. But I don't think that means getting rid of the way we relate to each other, it just means coming to a new sense of cooperation. Now when I go home, we all seem to organize ourselves, cleaning up and cooking, and then we sit down and really enjoy the meal, report the day's news—gossip—and share a few laughs. No one thinks I am solely responsible for doing the physical labour of preparing the meal, but at the same time, I have not lost my voice in the family. My counsel, my advice has weight in my family. My family prefers it that way. I don't make any internal family decisions without consulting my family, but in the end, I plan with the full knowledge that my word has tremendous weight. I feel most comfortable, safe, in our environment the way it is. I think my daughters, young as they are, feel that way too. No one had to teach our fathers to share in the work: they knew that gathering wood used to be part of food preparation, and cooking is just another part of that process. Since it isn't necessary to gather wood anymore, young men will have to learn to cooperate in new ways. Just because my father gathered wood to help my mother cook, didn't mean he was her boss and she had no voice in the family; likewise, because a man helps with the cooking and cleaning ought not to erode the voice of women.

I don't think we are as hung up about the decision-making process and the work process as a lot of white people. I mean everyone has to eat, so everyone gets busy. We also take each other's advice more seriously, respect each other's words. If someone wants to do something in a certain way, it is given careful consideration, particularly if that someone is the woman in whose home you are. We don't care whose name is on the mortgage documents, the home still belongs to the woman.

It is important that when we change, we change the things that aren't good and keep the things that are. Our sense of cooperation, the sense that food is not personal property but a gift of creation that everyone is entitled to have. These things are important to our humanity. I would not like to visit my daughters by telephone and have to arrange an appointment to visit them and eat some of their food. That would upset me. It would destroy our families and erase our culture if the kitchen ceased to have its old meaning for us.

MRS. V. (RUSSIA) BORN 1917 (CAME TO CANADA IN 1947)

Inge Israel

Came to Canada in 1947. In Russia, didn't cook—worked in fields all day, dog-tired at night, just took a handful of corn and fell asleep. Always gave husband one spoonful of turpentine in food. Is healthy. Children too—two drops turpentine in milk when small. Every day. Big men now. Strong. Daughter too. Best have three children. If something happen with one, two left.

Here, in Canada, have nice house, good kitchen—everything there: water; big stove. Not cook on stove—is nice, clean, shiny. Have other stove in basement. There, cook, fry, make cake. Kitchen stay nice, clean.

Son married now. Has nice house, good kitchen. Is terrible! *He* cook! *He* wash dishes! Everything! No good! Is *man*, son-of-a-gun!

Daughter married too. Big house. Big kitchen. Is happy. Good husband. He *cook.* He *wash dishes.* Everything!

SPRING CLEANING

Sandra Birdsell

They were sitting in the kitchen, Lureen Cooper and Marlene Paquet, waiting for their friend, Bobbie, to arrive with a bottle of rum. Marlene had chased the kids out into the chilly spring to play beneath the heavy clouds and telephone wires slung low from rugged cross-bars and glass condensors. They were enclosed in the kitchen which smelled of pine disinfectant, chlorine bleach. Their wash rags lay in a heap in the sink, shredded and torn. Around them on the gleaming enamelled walls were dull rectangles of oxidized paint where pictures once hung. Just hang the pictures back up in the same place, Lureen had advised. But Marlene thought she would paint over the spots tomorrow.

Lureen watched as Marlene rolled cigarettes for them with prunish-wrinkled fingers. "What do you think, should I invite Bernice and her old man to the party?" Marlene asked as she handed Lureen a too-thick cigarette which would split its seams.

"It's your party," Lureen said. What she really wanted to talk about with Marlene, while they waited for Bobbie to return with the bottle of rum, was what she would cook for Easter.

"Sure, it's okay for Claude to say invite them," Marlene said. She flicked tobacco from her tongue. "But guess who's going to have to put up with Bernice coming over every day? Claude? Because you know as well as I do, once she gets her foot in, it'll be game over." Lureen listened with growing impatience. She admitted that this Bernice and Mike thing was puzzling but she was tired of discussing it.

"Well this is it," Lureen said, mimicking Bernice, who inferred she knew everything there was to know and waited patiently for them to realize it. Well this is it, Bernice said with a slight smile on her anemic bony face as she examined a fleck of dirt beneath her fingernail and chewed it loose. Lureen understood the look Bobbie and Marlene gave each other when Bernice said that. They wanted to smack Bernice across the mouth. Marlene joked that Bernice was such a terrible housekeeper that when Mike went to pee in the sink, there were always dishes in it. Bobbie had dubbed Bernice, "The Creature From the Black Lagoon," because Bernice's large ears stuck through her thin dark hair and she stored her bottom dentures in a junk drawer in the kitchen. Lureen suggested that Bernice's smugness was ignorance.

Sounds of shooting and dying erupted suddenly from the living room. They had left the television set turned on for the kids who all day wandered out the front door and in the back every few moments. They had rid the closets and cupboards of the things that tended to collect during the winter, the mismatched socks and empty sanitary napkin boxes. Now that the spring cleaning was complete, they wanted to enjoy their rum in peace and so they made a plate of sandwiches, set it out on the back stoop and hooked the door. From the window, Lureen had a perfect view of a block of sagging garages, battered garbage cans or sometimes Bernice, bent over and clutching her grapefruit-sized stomach as though she was afraid it would fall out, picking her way into their bitch and brag afternoon. I bleed like a stuck pig, every month, Bernice explained her swollen stomach, her constant anemia. They can't do nothing about it.

"Ever notice how Good Friday is always like this?" Lureen asked because she wanted to stop talking about Bernice. She referred to the smoke-coloured sky, water dripping from the eaves. "It's always so gloomy."

"Hah. You just think so because the kids are home," Marlene said. She sent a cloud of smoke up towards the ceiling and frowned. "Dammit. Will you look at that? I think we missed a spot." She got up and dabbed at the door frame. "You're wrong," she said. "It's not always gloomy. It was sunny last year. I remember because I took the kids out to Aunt Sally's Farm at the zoo. Claude was away. As usual," she said and threw the rag back into the sink.

Marlene Paquet was not French, but a Mennonite. Lureen Cooper wasn't English. She hated it when people thought she was. One of the things she disliked about being a Cooper was their lack of customs. Just ham for Easter, she had complained to Marlene, that's all. Dull and boring. There were no coloured eggs or Paska bread with icing letters spelling out, "He is Risen."

One of the kids began pounding at the door and then kicked sharply.

"Jesus." Marlene jumped up and went out into the back yard to settle an argument. The kids, five of them, were a collusion of bicycles and wagons. They gathered around her. Bobbie's boy had seized the opportunity of her absence to act up.

"You're not my mother," he said to Marlene. "You can't make me."

"Sheesh, kill him," Marlene said when she came back inside. "What's keeping her, anyway?" Reward yourself, Bobbie said. Its the only way I can force myself to do this crap, meaning the walls and ceilings. They smoked their cigarettes and waited for her to return. Lureen felt ground-out like the weather because Larry, her husband, was also away, as usual. He was away building a business. Well so long, he'd said to her one day. You won't be seeing much of me for awhile because I'm going to be busy building a business. Those were not his exact words but she liked to work things down to one basic line. And for once, she'd told them, Larry kept his word. She hadn't seen much of him since then, but telephoned him every afternoon to ask how it was going. She imagined him building the business, brick by brick, with a "Leggo" kit. Larry inquired, how was it going with the kids? Be sure Jamie stays away from the models, he said, referring to his electric train in the basement. And make sure they eat right and wear their mitts. Tell them this and that, he said and she felt like a telephone answering service. She enticed him into long conversations about the kids. She recited pieces of information which she read in the newspaper. She asked him questions. Who really shot JFK? she asked. And why do you think all those women went and jumped from bridges when Marilyn Monroe died? Even though Larry was just around the corner, she sometimes thought it was as though he'd gone to China for the week and stumbled in every Saturday afternoon suffering from jet-lag. Yellow-faced and surly, he greeted her as though he had a mouth full of broken glass. He curled into a ball in the centre of the bed and slept until Sunday afternoon. While Larry built his business, she categorized and labelled and thought and dusted furniture with stained underpants.

"She's here. Finally," Marlene said as the front door slammed shut. "What in hell kept you?" she called.

But it was not Bobbie. Bernice tiptoed into the kitchen from the living room in her fuzzy bedroom slippers, walking as though she were avoiding puddles. She pulled her sweater around her sunken chest.

The kids had betrayed them, Lureen thought. Yeah, she's home, they probably said. She's not doing nothing.

"It's me," Bernice said and stepped onto the braided mat. She shook one foot and then the other like a rain-soaked cat. She surveyed the room with her deep-set eyes, in search of betrayal, exclusion.

"I don't usually use the front door," Marlene said. "Usually I have the couch in front of it." Marlene's husband, Claude, was a travelling salesman for a tool company. While he was away, she washed walls and arranged furniture. She arranged it according to the seasons, around the flow of cool air in summer and away from icy winter drafts that coated wall sockets with frost.

"I didn't come the back way because I was across the street, at the store," Bernice said. "I wasn't busy and so I thought I'd drop by. So what have you guys been up to?"

"Working our butts off doing spring cleaning," Marlene said. "Love your timing. We just finished."

Bernice crossed her arms over her chest and surveyed the room. "Smells like a soap factory in here," she said. "You sure wouldn't catch me doing no spring cleaning."

"Must be nice," Marlene said. She ground out her cigarette and lit up another.

"I clean," Bernice said. "But I do it bit by bit. When Mike's off, he gives me a hand with the big jobs."

"Good for Mike."

Lureen had been thinking about the folly of their work binge while washing walls. Although she would never come out and say it, she thought Marlene's Mennonite background had not been entirely done away with when it came to the housecleaning thing. She had been thinking of writing an article for *Chatelaine* on how not to have to do spring cleaning. How they were being foolish and driven and shouldn't worry if grease from cooking coated the set of good dishes on the top shelf. Wash them as you need them, she was going to say. Or do as she did, cover them in Saran. Come Easter, she would drag Larry out of bed, whip the Saran off the good dishes and serve up his ham on clean pink thistle and pussy willow plates. But it ticked her off that someone like Bernice might have caught on.

"Anyway," Lureen said loudly. "As we were saying. This guy I'm reading, Velikovsky, makes a lot of sense."

"Uum," Marlene said. "As you were saying." She contained her smile in the tiny muscle which jumped beneath the mole beside her lip.

"I mean, when you think about it, that bit in the Bible about the Red Sea parting."

"God. The Red Sea. I never think of it."

"But you would if you could make sense out of it and I think a cosmic event happening just at the same time as the sea parted is the answer. It's the same thing as the quick-frozen mammoths. A possible explanation."

Bernice shook loose her slippers and inched towards a kitchen chair. They ignored her.

"I always figured it had to be something other than the ice age that caused the mammoths to be frozen instantly. Some of them even had buttercups in their mouths."

Bernice parked her sharp rump on one corner of the chair and leaned forward with her elbow on her knee. "Well this is it," she said.

"What is it?" Marlene asked.

"What she said," Bernice said. "A cosmic event. It had to be." Because her bottom teeth were missing, Bernice's jaw jutted forward unnaturally. Lureen thought she wasn't so much a creature from a lagoon. In her stretch black ski pants, she resembled a daddylong-legged spider.

"Coffee?" Marlene asked abruptly. "Or don't you have time? I don't want to force you."

Bernice picked at a cuticle. I quit wearing my teeth because they hurt, she said once. If Mike doesn't like it, then to heck with him is what I say. She crossed her legs and swung her foot. "Mike's off today," she said and smiled. "It's his turn to look after the kids."

Lureen walked home from Marlene's feeling light-headed because of the rum. Pressed against the fence around her yard was the litter of winter uncovered, newspapers, wrappers of all sorts coated in a powdery dust. She disliked this dreary in-between season after the snow had melted, exposing the grit and garbage which was also entangled in the chokecherry bush. The bush was the only nice thing about her yard. She wondered how it came to grow there against the fence. She had looked it up in a book, chokecherry, and learned the fruit was used in pemmican after being pounded into mush. She read many books, biographies, television-repair manuals, child-rearing books, cereal boxes. She was proud of herself. She understood the language of the Bible and Shakespeare and income tax forms. She knew the women resented her books because once Marlene had asked her, what are you trying to prove, anyway? Sometimes, she wondered if they talked about her in the same way they did Bernice. She carried the frozen farm chicken Marlene had given to her because she complained to them over their rum about having to cook ham once again for Easter. You can have your Paska bread, Marlene said. There's just too much else that goes along with it. Customs give your kids something to be depressed about when they grow up, she said. But when Lureen looked at her children running around the yard, she felt a pang of doubt. That maybe she was cheating them by not teaching them about Easter. She missed the smell of the bread baking, the toadstool-shaped loaves crawling up and out of their cans and collars of wax paper. She missed the Easter baskets. Her sisters took turns making them, decorating them in mustard yellow and purple crepe paper. Even now, her mother was probably rolling coloured eggs across newspapers to dry and planning Easter baskets for the youngest ones still at home and for the grandchildren who would be there for Sunday dinner. Only now, her mother shaped the nests from Rice Krispie cake and the grass was dyed coconut and so everything, the baskets included, was edible.

"I'm sorry." Larry said when she telephoned him. "But there's no way I can take the weekend off." The sound of the air compressor chugged and clanked in the background. Her chest tightened with the sound of his voice. When he came home, just the sight of him getting out of the car jumped forward to meet something in the centre of her eye. Even though he often looked frowsy, rips in jeans, every new shirt initiated with a smear of grease, buttons yanked loose or tears snagged where he had brushed against sharp pieces of metal, still, she was captured by the sight of his thick, yellow, too-long hair, the methodical slowness of his movement across the yard to the house.

"I promised this guy I'd have his car ready to go by the weekend and I'm way behind. I'll have to stay here until it's finished." He sounded as though he had a cold. He was allergic to something he used in the shop.

"Come on, it's Easter weekend."

"So?"

"Well, we should do something."

"Why?"

"For the kids. It's a holiday and most people do something on a holiday."

"They'll survive. I have to do what I have to do."

She felt anger rising. "What you want to do, you mean."

He ignored her. "So, what's new?"

"Not a hell of a lot. I'm reading a book."

"What's it about?"

"Oh, this guy. He claims that the oil and gas deposits actually came from the sky. From the tail of a comet that passed close to the earth." Saying it made it sound silly. When she'd read it, she felt it made sense. Now she didn't know.

"Oh. Science fiction?"

"Kind of."

"Say." He hesitated for a moment. "What kind of do is Marlene having anyway?"

"The usual. Neighbourhood people. She said to come around eight."

"I don't think I'm going to make it," Larry said. "You'll have to go without me."

Lureen resisted the impulse to throw the telephone against the wall. "That's just great."

"I'm sorry, but I just got to get this car done."

Now that the kids were in school and had to be in bed early, Lureen missed not being able to go down to the garage to sit and drink Cokes and watch him when he had to work late. She missed crawling around the inside of the cars, pulling loose torn headliners, side panels, helping him make it new. He whistled when she was there and told jokes or else they worked without speaking, finding their rhythm in the country and western music he listened to. She missed the satisfaction of seeing pieces fitting together, the jars of nuts and bolts whose placement in the metal jumble Larry had memorized or knew instinctively.

Because she and Larry had moved seven times in six years she arranged furniture once and it stayed that way until the next move. Although they had moved frequently, they had not moved far. From one small town to another. Larry changes his jobs as often as other people change their socks, was what she told the women, but it was no longer true. They had not moved for two years. And she no longer helped put together the metal puzzle. Now she had to think about things like spring cleaning and cooking ham for Easter.

"This is quite a nice place you've got here," Mike said at Marlene's party.

"Get him," Marlene whispered and nudged Lureen in the ribs. They had seen Bernice's husband only from a distance before. He had come to the party dressed in a suit and tie. He was tall and very blond and did not look like a mailman. Lureen thought there was something young and earnest in the stiff wave above his forehead, his glossy shoes. He had sprayed them with *Amway Shoe Glow,* he explained when Claude commented on the glassy look of them.

"They're the same shoes he wears on the route every day," Bernice said. "He's nuts to spray them because his feet can't breathe."

"And you wouldn't enjoy it very much if they did," Mike said without a trace of annoyance.

Lureen thought of the contrast, Marlene's hand-made, pinchpleated drapes and the grey blanket Bernice had nailed up to her front window. When you sit at her table, don't lean forward, Marlene had warned. There's so much crap on it, you'll never get your arms loose. Marlene stood in the doorway watching as Mike admired the furniture Claude pointed out, their new raisin-coloured freizé couch with its glittering silver threads, the colour television set with remote control. Marlene had opened up the gateleg table and covered it with a linen cloth and set out food. Lureen knew Marlene was looking for signs of envy or dissatisfaction. "Hey, is what you do Iegal?" Mike asked Claude. "This is terrific," his good-natured smile never wavering.

"Oh, Marlene's a real work-horse," Bernice said and told them how early in the morning she had seen sheets on Marlene's clothesline.

Mike shook his head and sat down beside Bernice on the couch. He put his arm around her shoulders. "Sure can't say that about you, can we mother?" he said.

Bernice laughed. "You wouldn't catch me doing anything at that hour. Not until I've had at least a pot of coffee."

Which Mike probably made and brought to her bedside, Lureen thought. Marlene raised her eyebrows. Mike was an enigma, Lureen realized. He had stepped over some line. Last winter he made a skating rink for the kids in the neighbourhood and skated with them. Carried their own around on his shoulders. On his days off he hung out the laundry, did the shopping, painted cupboards. I'll bet he's a fruit or pervert of some kind, Bobbie had said and while they laughed, nevertheless, they watched from the window for evidence and found none.

Bernice wore the same black baggy sweater she had on yesterday and the fuzzy slippers. Marlene wore a long black skirt and a peach satiny blouse knotted at the waist. She had gathered her auburn hair up into a French twist. Lureen wore her only dress, pink, of some nubby material which she bought in Eaton's. It was a good thing they weren't going home for Easter she decided, because another of her family's customs was that everyone bought or sewed a new dress for each religious holiday. Claude, who she could tell had been drinking long before they arrived, began to talk to Mike about hockey. Lureen didn't know any of the men well. They had an unspoken agreement that if a husband came home unexpectedly, they all left immediately. They spent their time discussing the men's likes, dislikes, comparing. They spring-cleaned, read, kept the kids quiet on Saturday mornings and stayed attractive. Except for Bernice.

Lureen found a corner and nursed her second drink. Several other couples arrived and each time the door opened she thought of Larry. Above the kitchen door, a crucifix and the Christ were impaled in agony, an insect specimen under glass for their inspection. Lureen realized, as she listened to the jokes, the laughter, that her mother would disapprove if she knew that Lureen had gone to a party on Easter Weekend. Of the crucifix, her mother would say, that's the problem. The Catholics leave him hanging. Lureen's mother, who was a Mennonite like Marlene, didn't believe in crucifixes being hung anywhere, but she had a plaque in the kitchen that one of the kids made at a summer camp and decorated with pine cones and macaroni which said, "By Grace Are Ye Saved." Which means, her mother said, that you don't deserve it. Claude's sardonic laughter grated on her ears. He had told the same joke three parties in a row now. When Claude got drunk he would take out his dentures and drop them down into his drink so no one would take it when he went to the bathroom.

"Hi guys, better late than never," Bobbie said as she stepped into the room and all conversation was suspended. Wayne had picked Bobbie up at work and she hadn't bothered to go home and change but had come to the party in a black, pleated miniskirt, fish-net stockings and go-go boots. She pulled her head-scarf free and her platinum hair fanned out across her back. "Did I miss anything?"

"This is Mike," Bernice said.

"Well, what a surprise," Bobbie said and shot a look at Lureen which said, is she kidding?

Claude jumped up. "What are you drinking?"

"I'll help myself," she said in her throaty voice. "I'm not crippled."

"I can see that."

Lureen felt the bald hunger in the men's eyes as Bobbie left the room and for a moment, she resented her.

Only Mike seemed unaffected, and Wayne, Bobbie's husband, who was dark and silent. When he sat down, he crossed his legs and folded his arms across his broad chest. "Once a Month Wayne," Bobbie complained about their sexual activity during their bitch and brag afternoons. Lureen thought Wayne was the perfect example of a man who would go berserk and shoot his family on a quiet Sunday afternoon and everyone would be surprised. He was a polite man who kept to himself, they would say when interviewed.

"That's a real nice outfit," Mike said.

"I couldn't see myself in a get-up like that," Bernice said.

"I guess not." Claude laughed loudly.

"Get Bernice," they heard Bobbie tell Marlene in the kitchen, "her idea of dressing up is to wear pantyhose under her ski pants."

Bernice swung her leg up and down, up and down. Mike leaned forward and said something. She shrugged his arm from her shoulder. "You don't have to say that," she said, "I know what I look like."

Bobbie came back into the room and handed Wayne his drink. She hesitated and then went over to the couch and squeezed in beside Mike. "I've been serving drinks all night," she said. "What's one more?" She smiled at Mike and put her hand on his arm. "I guess you would know all about sore feet," she said.

Wayne shifted in his chair and cleared his throat. Bernice smiled at him and continued to swing her foot up and down. "Know why you wouldn't catch me in a get-up like that?" she asked and everyone stopped talking to listen.

"Some people care what they look like," Wayne said.

"Nope," she said, "it's because I'm made like Phyllis Diller. My legs don't go up that far."

The guy's obviously retarded, had been Bobbie's sullen comment when the women had washed up the dishes following the party. Lureen pulled the pink dress over her head and threw it onto the bed. Retarded. Clueless, all of them, wanting to hide behind such a statement. She'd wanted to explain it to them, the matter of grace. It's grace, she should have said. Bernice has grace. She stood still, listening as a car passed in the lane. Although it was almost midnight, Larry was still not home. She stood looking out the window for a moment at the row of houses behind the fences, in front of them the telephone poles and the lines that connected her to Larry. She liked the telephone poles. They reminded her of gardens and woodpeckers telegraphing messages between the lines of time-splintered wood. She imagined her mother's street, silent and white beneath the moon. Her mother was crawling about on her hands and knees or reaching for a suitable hiding place for the Easter baskets. She saw the frosted Paska bread, lined up on the table, one for everyone. She wiped her eyes on her underslip. She stood in the hallway and listened to the quiet sound of her children breathing. And then she went into the kitchen and put the chicken back into the freezer. She took out the ham. Tomorrow, she would try something new with it. Marlene had suggested, stick it full of cloves and baste it with beer.

LIVING ALONE

Susan Glickman

Not such a hard thing to do
if you have the right appliances.
A radio is essential: that voice in the background
eases you into the day
like a breakfast egg into water.
For that, of course, you need a stove,
a pot, a spoon or two—
one of those beautifully turned pepper-mills, preferably teak.

If you stay in the kitchen it's amazing how much space
you can fill:
a coffee-grinder, blender, garlic press,
all manner of intricate knife.
Emergency rations: instead of baked beans
smoked oysters, a bottle of brandy.

These things taste best at 2 a.m.
when the rest of the house is cold.
You wake up dreaming you're asleep in the fridge,
there's so much white space beside you.

BRAZILIAN HOUSE
P.K. Page

In this great house white
as a public urinal
I pass my echoing days.
Only the elephant ear leaves
listen outside my window
to the tap of my heels.

Downstairs the laundress
with elephantiasis
sings like an angel
her brown wrists cuffed with suds
and the skinny little black girl
polishing silver laughs to see
her face appear in a tray.

Ricardo, stealthy
lowers his sweating body
into the stream
my car will cross when I
forced by the white porcelain
yammering silence drive
into the hot gold gong
of noon day.

BORROWED BEAUTY
Maxine Tynes

In Service. I grew up hearing those words. As a little girl in my mother's kitchen I would hear those words. In Service.

"She went In Service."

With little-girl ears where they shouldn't be, bent to lady-talk. That scary, hushed, exciting lady-talk between my mother and women who came to see her. Tea and talk. Lady-talk.

In Service. Mama and Miss Riley. Mama and Aunt Lil. Mama and Helen. Helen. The one grown-up person we were allowed to say the name of without a Miss or Aunt in front. Helen. I loved to say her name and feel her velvet hats. Tams. She always chewed Juicy Fruit gum.

It was always the same. Talk of dark and mysterious women things, softly spoken. Lips would burble tea in cups. Eyes would roll slowly or point sharply when certain things were said, names were named. Sometimes talk of Mama's In Service memories; of her grandmother, a ten-year-old girl being sent in from the country, from Preston, to be In Service. Talk of Aunt Lil and, sometimes, with her. Laughing Aunt Lil, with hair like fleeting movie-star dreams. Aunt Lil, who always included laughing in her lady-talk. And Miss Riley, who never did.

These conversations always seemed to carry their own colours. This one—scary, smoky black, light, misty grey. Lady-talk. "Children should be seen and not heard." "Keep in a child's place." I was afraid of those hard red sentences Mama always had ready during lady-talk. I had to go where they couldn't see me. But in a small house the scary grey-black mist of lady-talk can always find you.

In Service. Sterling silver, glowing in the dark-and-sunlight words to me. Like the lone brass button always at the bottom of Mama's button box, when I would sneak the polish to it, to bring back the shine. The Mysteries of In Service were all confused and glowing with parade dreams and uniforms marching by in a flash of things shiny and formal.

"Yes, girl, she went In Service when she was ten."

"It was right after I went In Service that Uncle Willy died."

"She was In Service for years."

"She died In Service."

My little-girl mind imagined shiny, wonderful things, not clearly defined. Not knees sore from years on hardwood floors. Not hands cracked, dry and painful, callused and scrub-worn. Not early-morning walking miles into town to start the day off right with morning labours for some family. Not always going to and coming from the back door. Not "speak when you're spoken to," see and don't see, hear and don't hear, in case you anger them and they let you go. Not eating their leftovers in the kitchen alone. Not one dollar a day for back-breaking floors, walls, dishes, furniture, windows, washing, ironing, sweat-soaked labour. In Service.

"She died In Service." That describes Helen. I was allowed to say her name. Velvet tams and Juicy Fruit gum every night in Mama's kitchen. When I was little, I was allowed to stand by her and feel her tams. When I got older, she'd be there every night, watching me cry into cold dishwater.

And still the tams were there. The ruby, the emerald green, the midnight velvet blue of them glowed richly against the grey-black, soft and woolly head. Sometimes she would reach up, too, to finger that soft glow, almost as if to make sure that lovely part of her was still there. Helen's hands against such splendid velvet were like wounds, flags of the world of drudgery that were her days.

Helen was someone's girl, this never-married Black lady, already in middle age by the time I was old enough to know her. Somebody's girl. Not in the romantic notion of being somebody's girl (friend). Helen was some white lady's girl, some white family's girl. She came to our house every night as if it were a target, an end point to her day, to sit in our kitchen with a cup of tea, to read the paper. She never took her coat off.

The lady-talk would start. Mama and Helen. It was always about Helen's lady—the woman she worked for. "My family." "My Missus."

Helen "lived In Service," which added to the mystique of it all. My little-girl mind imagined something with a faint glow. Not a room off the back. Not a living away from your family. In a house, a bed that was never yours.

Through my window I could see "Helen's house" not far from my own. On Sunday walks with one or other of my older sisters, seeing "Helen's house" was to see a dream, or at least a storybook page. "Helen's house," huge and golden yellow, with a fence and a yard that held what in later grown-up years I would know as a gazebo. But then, surely, that wonderful little in-the-yard house was where she lived, behind cool, dark green lattice. Helen's house. So different from my own, so squat and brown and henlike. My house, teeming with the dozen of us. My house, which Helen fled to each night; to maybe, for a little while, be a little of what my mother was, and did and had. Mama, with hands on her own dishes, on her own child.

Helen had eyes that were always friendly. I would see them peek behind her tam, even as she sat and sipped her tea and waited for it all to happen every night. Waited in the wake of the dark and tiny storm of activity that hummed along after Mama; a whirlwind of shooing the creeping horde of us; of moving through clouds of flour from baking; of ironing; of putting up late supper for Daddy; of watching and listening for Daddy; and finally settling down to braid my hair and have tea and lady-talk.

Sometimes Helen would bring a shopping bag full of clothes with her to show Mama. Clothes—cast off, not new—that her lady had given her. Clothes and hats. Velvet tams. Helen. Mama and Helen and lady-talk.

What did a little Black girl know, touching a velvet tam over hooded and frightened eyes? Helen. Perhaps she knew and feared the loneliness of her own life, circled round and round her like an echo; loneliness circled round and worn close, fitting her like the coats and tams from her shopping bag. Perhaps the secret mystery and the fear should hide deep in her eyes from me, from my little-girl eyes watching Helen bring the secret of In Service each night. This world, this life, this loneliness all too real for her. A dark and female mystery still for me.

Helen. Driven like a magnet to somebody else's kitchen, somebody else's child. Helen. With careworn hands, handing me the future luxury of dreams, and thoughts, and "I remember Helen," and the awful mystery of In Service unravelled now from the whispers of lady-talk, found now in the voice of these words.

Looking back, I know she was saving me. They all were. Helen. Mama. Miss Riley. Aunt Lil. My sisters. Known and unknown Black women. Armies of Black women in that sea of domestic service. With unlikely and unowned addresses. Waiting for buses on prestigious street corners. Carrying back bits and remnants of that other world of In Service in shopping bags, and wearing the rest in coats and velvet tams.

HOW I MET MY HUSBAND

Alice Munro

We heard the plane come over at noon, roaring through the radio news, and we were sure it was going to hit the house, so we all ran out into the yard. We saw it come in over the tree tops, all red and silver, the first close-up plane I ever saw. Mrs. Peebles screamed.

"Crash landing," their little boy said. Joey was his name.

"It's okay," said Dr. Peebles. "He knows what he's doing." Dr. Peebles was only an animal doctor, but had a calming way of talking, like any doctor.

This was my first job—working for Dr. and Mrs. Peebles, who had bought an old house out on the Fifth Line, about five miles out of town. It was just when the trend was starting of town people buying up old farms, not to work them but to live on them.

We watched the plane land across the road, where the fairgrounds used to be. It did make a good landing field, nice and level for the old race track, and the barns and display sheds torn down now for scrap lumber so there was nothing in the way. Even the old grandstand, boys had burned.

"All right," said Mrs. Peebles, snappy as she always was when she got over her nerves. "Let's go back in the house. Let's not stand here gawking like a set of farmers."

She didn't say that to hurt my feelings. It never occurred to her.

I was just setting the dessert down when Loretta Bird arrived, out of breath, at the screen door.

"I thought it was going to crash into the house and kill youse all!"

She lived on the next place and the Peebles thought she was a countrywoman, they didn't know the difference. She and her husband didn't farm, he worked on the roads and had a bad name for drinking. They had seven children and couldn't get credit at the Hi-Way Grocery. The Peebles made her welcome, not knowing any better, as I say, and offered her dessert.

Dessert was never anything to write home about, at their place. A dish of Jello or sliced bananas or fruit out of a tin. "Have a house without a pie, be ashamed until you die," my mother used to say, but Mrs. Peebles operated differently.

Loretta Bird saw me getting the can of peaches.

"Oh, never mind," she said. "I haven't got the right kind of a stomach to trust what comes out of those tins, I can only eat home canning."

I could have slapped her. I bet she never put down fruit in her life.

"I know what he's landed here for," she said. "He's got permission to use the fairgrounds and take people up for rides. It costs a dollar. It's the same fellow who was over at Palmerston last week and was up the lakeshore before that. I wouldn't go up, if you paid me."

"I'd jump at the chance," Dr. Peebles said. "I'd like to see this neighborhood from the air."

Mrs. Peebles said she would just as soon see it from the ground. Joey said he wanted to go and Heather did, too. Joey was nine and Heather was seven.

"Would you, Edie?" Heather said.

I said I didn't know. I was scared, but I never admitted that, especially in front of children I was taking care of.

"People are going to be coming out here in their cars raising dust and trampling your property, if I was you I would complain," Loretta said. She hooked her legs around the chair rung and I knew we were in for a lengthy visit. After Dr. Peebles went back to his office or out on his next call and Mrs. Peebles went for her nap, she would hang around me while I was trying to do the dishes. She would pass remarks about the Peebles in their own house.

"She wouldn't find time to lay down in the middle of the day, if she had seven kids like I got."

She asked me did they fight and did they keep things in the dresser drawer not to have babies with. She said it was a sin if they did. I pretended I didn't know what she was talking about.

I was fifteen and away from home for the first time. My parents had made the effort and sent me to high school for a year, but I didn't like it. I was shy of strangers and the work was hard, they didn't make it nice for you or explain the way they do now. At the end of the year the averages were published in the paper, and mine came out at the very bottom, 37 per cent. My father said that's enough and I didn't blame him. The last thing I wanted, anyway, was to go on and end up teaching school. It happened the very day the paper came out with my disgrace in it, Dr. Peebles was staying at our place for dinner, having just helped one of our cows have twins, and he said I looked smart to him and his wife was looking for a girl to help. He said she felt tied down, with the two children, out in the country. I guess she would, my mother said, being polite, though I could tell from her face she was wondering what on earth it would be like to have only two children and no barn work, and then to be complaining.

When I went home I would describe to them the work I had to do, and it made everybody laugh. Mrs. Peebles had an automatic washer and dryer, the first I ever saw. I have had those in my own home for such a long time now it's hard to remember how much of a miracle it was to me, not having to struggle with the wringer and hang up and haul down. Let alone not having to heat water. Then there was practically no baking. Mrs. Peebles said she couldn't make pie crust, the most amazing thing I ever heard a woman admit. I could, of course, and I could make light biscuits and a white cake and a dark cake, but they didn't want it, she said they watched their figures. The only thing I didn't like about working there, in fact, was feeling half hungry a lot of the time. I used to bring back a box of doughnuts made out at home, and hide them under my bed. The children found out, and I didn't mind sharing, but I thought I better bind them to secrecy.

The day after the plane landed Mrs. Peebles put both children in the car and drove over to Chesley, to get their hair cut. There was a good woman then at Chesley for doing hair. She got hers done at the same place, Mrs. Peebles did, and that meant they would be gone a good while. She had to pick a day Dr. Peebles wasn't going out into the country, she didn't have her own car. Cars were still in short supply then, after the war.

I loved being left in the house alone, to do my work at leisure. The kitchen was all white and bright yellow, with fluorescent lights. That was before they ever thought of making the appliances all different colors and doing the cupboards like dark old wood and hiding the lighting. I loved light. I loved the double sink. So would anybody new-come from washing dishes in a dishpan with a rag-plugged hole on an oilcloth-covered table by light of a coal-oil lamp. I kept everything shining.

The bathroom too. I had a bath in there once a week. They wouldn't have minded if I took one oftener, but to me it seemed like asking too much, or maybe risking making it less wonderful. The basin and the tub and the toilet were all pink, and there were glass doors with flamingoes painted on them, to shut off the tub. The light had a rosy cast and the mat sank under your feet like snow, except that it was warm. The mirror was three-way. With the mirror all steamed up and the air like a perfume cloud, from things I was allowed to use, I stood up on the side of the tub and admired myself naked, from three directions. Sometimes I thought about the way we lived out at home and the way we lived here and how one way was so hard to imagine when you were living the other way. But I thought it was still a lot easier, living the way we lived at home, to picture something like this, the painted flamingoes and the warmth and the soft mat, than it was for anybody knowing only things like this to picture how it was the other way. And why was that?

I was through my jobs in no time, and had the vegetables peeled for supper and sitting in cold water besides. Then I went into Mrs. Peebles' bedroom. I had been in there plenty of times, cleaning, and I always took a good look in her closet, at the clothes she had hanging there. I wouldn't have looked in her drawers, but a closet is open to anybody. That's a lie. I would have looked in drawers, but I would have felt worse doing it and been more scared she could tell.

Some clothes in her closet she wore all the time, I was quite familiar with them. Others she never put on, they were pushed to the back. I was disappointed to see no wedding dress. But there was one long dress I could just see the skirt of, and I was hungering to see the rest. Now I took note of where it hung and lifted it out. It was satin, a lovely weight on my arm, light bluish-green in color, almost silvery. It had a fitted, pointed waist and a full skirt and an off-the-shoulder fold hiding the little sleeves.

Next thing was easy. I got out of my own things and slipped it on. I was slimmer at fifteen than anybody would believe who knows me now and the fit was beautiful. I didn't, of course, have a strapless bra on, which was what it needed, I just had to slide my straps down my arms under the material. Then I tried pinning up my hair, to get the effect. One thing led to another. I put on rouge and lipstick and eyebrow pencil from her dresser. The heat of the day and the weight of the satin and all the excitement made me thirsty, and I went out to the kitchen, got-up as I was, to get a glass of ginger ale with ice cubes from the refrigerator. The Peebles drank ginger ale, or fruit drinks, all day, like water, and I was getting so I did too. Also there was no limit on ice cubes, which I was so fond of I would even put them in a glass of milk.

I turned from putting the ice tray back and saw a man watching me through the screen. It was the luckiest thing in the world I didn't spill the ginger ale down the front of me then and there.

"I never meant to scare you. I knocked but you were getting the ice out, you didn't hear me."

I couldn't see what he looked like, he was dark the way somebody is pressed up against a screen door with the bright daylight behind them. I only knew he wasn't from around here.

"I'm from the plane over there. My name is Chris Watters and what I was wondering was if I could use that pump."

There was a pump in the yard. That was the way the people used to get their water. Now I noticed he was carrying a pail.

"You're welcome," I said. "I can get it from the tap and save you pumping." I guess I wanted him to know we had piped water, didn't pump ourselves.

"I don't mind the exercise." He didn't move, though, and finally he said, "Were you going to a dance?"

Seeing a stranger there had made me entirely forget how I was dressed.

"Or is that the way ladies around here generally get dressed up in the afternoon?"

I didn't know how to joke back then. I was too embarrassed.

"You live here? Are you the lady of the house?"

"I'm the hired girl."

Some people change when they find that out, their whole way of looking at you and speaking to you changes, but his didn't.

"Well, I just wanted to tell you you look very nice. I was so surprised when I looked in the door and saw you. Just because you looked so nice and beautiful."

I wasn't even old enough then to realize how out of the common it is, for a man to say something like that to a woman, or somebody he is treating like a woman. For a man to say a word like *beautiful*. I wasn't old enough to realize or to say anything back, or in fact to do anything but wish he would go away. Not that I didn't like him, but just that it upset me so, having him look at me, and me trying to think of something to say.

He must have understood. He said good-bye, and thanked me, and went and started filling his pail from the pump. I stood behind the Venetian blinds in the dining room, watching him. When he had gone, I went into the bedroom and took the dress off and put it back in the same place. I dressed in my own clothes and took my hair down and washed my face, wiping it on Kleenex, which I threw in the wastebasket.

The Peebles asked me what kind of man he was. Young, middle-aged, short, tall? I couldn't say.

"Good-looking?" Dr. Peebles teased me.

I couldn't think a thing but that he would be coming to get his water again, he would be talking to Dr. or Mrs. Peebles, making friends with them, and he would mention seeing me that first afternoon, dressed up. Why not mention it? He would think it was funny. And no idea of the trouble it would get me into.

After supper the Peebles drove into town to go to a movie. She wanted to go somewhere with her hair fresh done. I sat in my bright kitchen wondering what to do, knowing I would never sleep. Mrs. Peebles might not fire me, when she found out, but it would give her a different feeling about me altogether. This was the first place I ever worked but I already had picked up things about the way people feel when you are working for them. They like to think you aren't curious. Not just that you aren't dishonest, that isn't enough. They like to feel you don't notice things, that you don't think or wonder about anything but what they liked to eat and how they like things ironed, and so on. I don't mean they weren't kind to me, because they were. They had me eat my meals with them (to tell the truth I expected to, I didn't know there were families who don't) and sometimes they took me along in the car. But all the same.

I went up and checked on the children being asleep and then I went out. I had to do it. I crossed the road and went in the old fairgrounds gate. The plane looked unnatural sitting there, and shining with the moon. Off at the far side of the fairgrounds, where the bush was taking over, I saw his tent.

He was sitting outside it smoking a cigarette. He saw me coming.

"Hello, were you looking for a plane ride? I don't start taking people up till tomorrow." Then he looked again and said, "Oh, it's you. I didn't know you without your long dress on."

My heart was knocking away, my tongue was dried up. I had to say something. But I couldn't. My throat was closed and I was like a deaf-and-dumb.

"Did you want a ride? Sit down. Have a cigarette."

I couldn't even shake my head to say no, so he gave me one.

"Put it in your mouth or I can't light it. It's a good thing I'm used to shy ladies."

I did. It wasn't the first time I had smoked a cigarette, actually. My girl friend out home, Muriel Lower, used to steal them from her brother.

"Look at your hand shaking. Did you just want to have a chat, or what?"

In one burst I said, "I wisht you wouldn't say anything about that dress."

"What dress? Oh, the long dress."

"It's Mrs. Peebles'."

"Whose? Oh, the lady you work for? Is that it? She wasn't home so you got dressed up in her dress, eh? You got dressed up and played queen. I don't blame you. You're not smoking that cigarette right. Don't just puff. Draw it in. Did nobody ever show you how to inhale? Are you scared I'll tell on you? Is that it?"

I was so ashamed at having to ask him to connive this way I couldn't nod. I just looked at him and he saw *yes.*

"Well I won't. I won't in the slightest way mention it or embarrass you. I give you my word of honor."

Then he changed the subject, to help me out, seeing I couldn't even thank him.

"What do you think of this sign?"

It was a board sign lying practically at my feet.

SEE THE WORLD FROM THE SKY. ADULTS $1.00, CHILDREN 50¢. QUALIFIED PILOT.

"My old sign was getting pretty beat up, I thought I'd make a new one. That's what I've been doing with my time today."

The lettering wasn't all that handsome, I thought. I could have done a better one in half an hour.

"I'm not an expert at sign making."

"It's very good," I said.

"I don't need it for publicity, word of mouth is usually enough. I turned away two carloads tonight. I felt like taking it easy. I didn't tell them ladies were dropping in to visit me."

Now I remembered the children and I was scared again, in case one of them had waked up and called me and I wasn't there.

"Do you have to go so soon?"

I remembered some manners. "Thank you for the cigarette."

"Don't forget. You have my word of honor."

I tore off across the fairgrounds, scared I'd see the car heading home from town. My sense of time was mixed up, I didn't know how long I'd been out of the house. But it was all right, it wasn't late, the children were asleep. I got in bed myself and lay thinking what a lucky end to the day, after all, and among things to be grateful for I could be grateful Loretta Bird hadn't been the one who caught me.

The yard and borders didn't get trampled, it wasn't as bad as that. All the same it seemed very public, around the house. The sign was on the fairgrounds gate. People came mostly after supper but a good many in the afternoon, too. The Bird children all came without fifty cents between them and hung on the gate. We got used to the excitement of the plane coming in and taking off, it wasn't excitement any more. I never went over, after that one time, but would see him when he came to get his water. I would be out on the steps doing sitting-down work, like preparing vegetables, if I could.

"Why don't you come over? I'll take you up in my plane."

"I'm saving my money," I said, because I couldn't think of anything else.

"For what? For getting married?"

I shook my head.

"I'll take you up for free if you come sometime when it's slack. I thought you would come, and have another cigarette."

I made a face to hush him, because you never could tell when the children would be sneaking around the porch, or Mrs. Peebles herself listening in the house. Sometimes she came out and had a conversation with him. He told her things he hadn't bothered to tell me. But then I hadn't thought to ask. He told her he had been in the War, that was where he learned to fly a plane, and now he couldn't settle down to ordinary life, this was what he liked. She said she couldn't imagine anybody liking such a thing. Though sometimes, she said, she was almost bored enough to try anything herself, she wasn't brought up to living in the country. It's all my husband's idea, she said. This was news to me.

"Maybe you ought to give flying lessons," she said.

"Would you take them?"

She just laughed.

Sunday was a busy flying day in spite of it being preached against from two pulpits. We were all sitting out watching. Joey and Heather were over on the fence with the Bird kids. Their father had said they could go, after their mother saying all week they couldn't.

A car came down the road past the parked cars and pulled up right in the drive. It was Loretta Bird who got out, all importance, and on the driver's side another woman got out, more sedately. She was wearing sunglasses.

"This is a lady looking for the man that flies the plane," Loretta Bird said. "I heard her inquire in the hotel coffee shop where I was having a Coke and I brought her out."

"I'm sorry to bother you," the lady said. "I'm Alice Kelling, Mr. Watters' fiancée."

This Alice Kelling had on a pair of brown and white checked slacks and a yellow top. Her bust looked to me rather low and bumpy. She had a worried face. Her hair had had a permanent, but had grown out, and she wore a yellow band to keep it off her face. Nothing in the least pretty or even young-looking about her. But you could tell from how she talked she was from the city, or educated, or both.

Dr. Peebles stood up and introduced himself and his wife and me and asked her to be seated.

"He's up in the air right now, but you're welcome to sit and wait. He gets his water here and he hasn't been yet. He'll probably take his break about five."

"That is him, then?" said Alice Kelling, wrinkling and straining at the sky.

"He's not in the habit of running out on you, taking a different name?" Dr. Peebles laughed. He was the one, not his wife, to offer iced tea. Then she sent me into the kitchen to fix it. She smiled. She was wearing sunglasses too.

"He never mentioned his fiancée," she said.

I loved fixing iced tea with lots of ice and slices of lemon in tall glasses. I ought to have mentioned before, Dr. Peebles was an abstainer, at least around the house, or I wouldn't have been allowed to take the place. I had to fix a glass for Loretta Bird too, though it galled me, and when I went out she had settled in my lawn chair, leaving me the steps.

"I knew you was a nurse when I first heard you in that coffe shop."

"How would you know a thing like that?"

"I get my hunches about people. Was that how you met him, nursing?"

"Chris? Well yes. Yes, it was."

"Oh, were you overseas?" said Mrs. Peebles.

"No, it was before he went overseas. I nursed him when he was stationed at Centralia and had a ruptured appendix. We got engaged and then he went overseas. My, this is refreshing, after a long drive."

"He'll be glad to see you," Dr. Peebles said. "It's a rackety kind of life, isn't it, not staying one place long enough to really make friends."

"Youse've had a long engagement," Loretta Bird said.

Alice Kelling passed that over. "I was going to get a room at the hotel, but when I was offered directions I came on out. Do you think I could phone them?"

"No need," Dr. Peebles said. "You're five miles away from him if you stay at the hotel. Here, you're right across the road. Stay with us. We've got rooms on rooms, look at this big house."

Asking people to stay, just like that, is certainly a country thing, and maybe seemed natural to him now, but not to Mrs. Peebles, from the way she said, oh yes, we have plenty of room. Or to Alice Kelling, who kept protesting, but let herself be worn down. I got the feeling it was a temptation to her, to be that close. I was trying for a look at her ring. Her nails were painted red, her fingers were freckled and wrinkled. It was a tiny stone. Muriel Lowe's cousin had one twice as big.

Chris came to get his water, late in the afternoon just as Dr. Peebles had predicted. He must have recognized the car from a way off. He came smiling.

"Here I am chasing after you to see what you're up to," called Alice Kelling. She got up and went to meet him and they kissed, just touched, in front of us.

"You're going to spend a lot on gas that way," Chris said.

Dr. Peebles invited Chris to stay for supper, since he had already put up the sign that said: NO MORE RIDES TILL 7 P.M. Mrs. Peebles wanted it served in the yard, in spite of bugs. One thing strange to anybody from the country is this eating outside. I had made a potato salad earlier and she had made a jellied salad, that was one thing she could do, so it was just a matter of getting those out, and some sliced meat and cucumbers and fresh leaf lettuce. Loretta Bird hung around for some time saying, "Oh, well, I guess I better get home to those yappers," and, "It's so nice just sitting here, I sure hate to get up," but nobody invited her, I was relieved to see, and finally she had to go.

That night after rides were finished Alice Kelling and Chris went off somewhere in her car. I lay awake till they got back. When I saw the car lights sweep my ceiling I got up to look down on them through the slats of my blind. I don't know what I thought I was going to see. Muriel Lowe and I used to sleep on her front veranda and watch her sister and her sister's boy friend saying good night. Afterwards we couldn't get to sleep, for longing for somebody to kiss us and rub up against us and we would talk about suppose you were out in a boat with a boy and he wouldn't bring you in to shore unless you did it, or what if somebody got you trapped in a barn, you would have to, wouldn't you, it wouldn't be your fault. Muriel said her two girl cousins used to try with a toilet paper roll that one of them was the boy. We wouldn't do anything like that; just lay and wondered.

All that happened was that Chris got out of the car on one side and she got out on the other and they walked off separately—him towards the fairgrounds and her towards the house. I got back in bed and imagined about me coming home with him, not like that.

Next morning Alice Kelling got up late and I fixed a grapefruit for her the way I had learned and Mrs. Peebles sat down with her to visit and have another cup of coffee. Mrs. Peebles seemed pleased enough now, having company. Alice Kelling said she guessed she better get used to putting in a day just watching Chris take off and come down, and Mrs. Peebles said she didn't know if she should suggest it because Alice Kelling was the one with the car, but the lake was only twenty-five miles away and what a good day for a picnic.

Alice Kelling took her up on the idea and by eleven o'clock they were in the car, with Joey and Heather and a sandwich lunch I had made. The only thing was that Chris hadn't come down, and she wanted to tell him where they were going.

"Edie'll go over and tell him," Mrs. Peebles said. "There's no problem."

Alice Kelling wrinkled her face and agreed.

"Be sure and tell him we'll be back by five!"

I didn't see that he would be concerned about knowing this right away, and I thought of him eating whatever he ate over there, alone, cooking on his camp stove, so I got to work and mixed up a crumb cake and baked it, in between the other work I had to do; then, when it was a bit cooled, wrapped it in a tea towel. I didn't do anything to myself but take off my apron and comb my hair. I would like to have put some make-up on, but I was too afraid it would remind him of the way he first saw me, and that would humiliate me all over again.

He had come and put another sign on the gate: NO RIDES THIS P.M. APOLOGIES. I worried that he wasn't feeling well. No sign of him outside and the tent flap was down. I knocked on the pole.

"Come in," he said, in a voice that would just as soon have said *Stay out.*

I lifted the flap.

"Oh, it's you. I'm sorry. I didn't know it was you."

He had been just sitting on the side of the bed, smoking. Why not at least sit and smoke in the fresh air?

"I brought a cake and hope you're not sick," I said.

"Why would I be sick ? Oh—that sign. That's all right. I'm just tired of talking to people. I don't mean you. Have a seat." He pinned back the tent flap. "Get some fresh air in here."

I sat on the edge of the bed, there was no place else. It was one of those fold-up cots, really: I remembered and gave him his fiancée's message.

He ate some of the cake. "Good."

"Put the rest away for when you're hungry later."

"I'll tell you a secret. I won't be around here much longer."

"Are you getting married?"

"Ha ha. What time did you say they'd be back?"

"Five o'clock."

"Well, by that time this place will have seen the last of me. A plane can get further than a car." He unwrapped the cake and ate another piece of it, absent-mindedly.

"Now you'll be thirsty."

"There's some water in the pail."

"It won't be very cold. I could bring some fresh. I could bring some ice from the refrigerator."

"No," he said. "I don't want you to go. I want a nice long time of saying good-bye to you."

He put the cake away carefully and sat beside me and started those little kisses, so soft, I can't ever let myself think about them, such kindness in his face and lovely kisses, all over my eyelids and neck and ears, all over, then me kissing back as well as I could (I had only kissed a boy on a dare before, and kissed my own arms for practice) and we lay back on the cot and pressed together, just gently, and he did some other things, not bad things or not in a bad way. It was lovely in the tent, that smell of grass and hot tent cloth with the sun beating down on it, and he said, "I wouldn't do you any harm for the world." Once, when he had rolled on top of me and we were sort of rocking together on the cot, he said softly, "Oh, no," and freed himself and jumped up and got the water pail. He splashed some of it on his neck and face, and the little bit left, on me lying there.

"That's to cool us off, Miss."

When we said good-bye I wasn't at all sad, because he held my face and said "I'm going to write you a letter. I'll tell you where I am and maybe you can come and see me. Would you like that? Okay then. You wait." I was really glad I think to get away from him, it was like he was piling presents on me I couldn't get the pleasure of till I considered them alone.

No consternation at first about the plane being gone. They thought he had taken somebody up, and I didn't enlighten them. Dr. Peebles had phoned he had to go to the country, so there was just us having supper, and then Loretta Bird thrusting her head in the door and saying, "I see he's took off."

"What?" said Alice Kelling, and pushed back her chair.

"The kids come and told me this afternoon he was taking down his tent. Did he think he'd run through all the business there was around here? He didn't take off without letting you know, did he?"

"He'll send me word," Alice Kelling said. "He'll probably phone tonight. He's terribly restless, since the War."

"Edie, he didn't mention to you, did he?" Mrs. Peebles said. "When you took over the message?"

"Yes," I said. So far so true.

"Well why didn't you say?" All of them were looking at me. "Did he say where he was going?"

"He said he might try Bayfield," I said. What made me tell such a lie? I didn't intend it.

"Bayfield, how far is that?" said Alice Kelling.

Mrs. Peebles said, "Thirty, thirty-five miles."

"That's not far. Oh, well, that's really not far at all. It's on the lake, isn't it?"

You'd think I'd be ashamed of myself, setting her on the wrong track. I did it to give him more time, whatever time he needed. I lied for him, and also, I have to admit, for me. Women should stick together and not do things like that. I see that now, but didn't then. I never thought of myself as being in any way like her, or coming to the same troubles, ever.

She hadn't taken her eyes off me. I thought she suspected my lie.

"When did he mention this to you?"

"Earlier."

"When you were over at the plane?"

"Yes."

"You must've stayed and had a chat." She smiled at me, not a nice smile. "You must've stayed and had a little visit with him."

"I took a cake," I said, thinking that telling some truth would spare me telling the rest.

"We didn't have a cake," said Mrs. Peebles rather sharply.

"I baked one."

Alice Kelling said, "That was very friendly of you."

"Did you get permission," said Loretta Bird. "You never know what these girls'll do next," she said. "It's not they mean harm so much, as they're ignorant."

"The cake is neither here nor there," Mrs. Peebles broke in. "Edie, I wasn't aware you knew Chris that well."

I didn't know what to say.

"I'm not surprised," Alice Kelling said in a high voice. "I knew by the look of her as soon as I saw her. We get them at the hospital all the time." She looked hard at me with her stretched smile. "Having their babies. We have to put them in a special ward because of their diseases. Little country tramps. Fourteen and fifteen years old. You should see the babies they have, too."

"There was a bad woman here in town had a baby that pus was running out of its eyes," Loretta Bird put in.

"Wait a minute," said Mrs. Peebles. "What is this talk? Edie. What about you and Mr. Watters? Were you intimate with him?"

"Yes," I said. I was thinking of us lying on the cot and kissing, wasn't that intimate? And I would never deny it.

They were all one minute quiet, even Loretta Bird.

"Well," said Mrs. Peebles. "I am surprised. I think I need a cigarette. This is the first of any such tendencies I've seen in her," she said, speaking to Alice Kelling, but Alice Kelling was looking at me.

"Loose little bitch." Tears ran down her face. "Loose little bitch, aren't you? I knew as soon as I saw you. Men despise girls like you. He just made use of you and went off, you know that, don't you? Girls like you are just nothing, they're just public conveniences, just filthy little rags!"

"Oh, now," said Mrs. Peebles.

"Filthy," Alice Kelling sobbed. "Filthy little rag!"

"Don't get yourself upset," Loretta Bird said. She was swollen up with pleasure at being in on this scene. "Men are all the same."

"Edie, I'm very surprised," Mrs. Peebles said. "I thought your parents were so strict. You don't want to have a baby, do you?"

I'm still ashamed of what happened next. I lost control, just like a six-year-old, I started howling. "You don't get a baby from just doing that!"

"You see. Some of them are that ignorant," Loretta Bird said.

But Mrs. Peebles jumped up and caught my arms and shook me.

"Calm down. Don't get hysterical. Calm down. Stop crying. Listen to me. Listen. I'm wondering, if you know what being intimate means. Now tell me. What did you think it meant?"

"Kissing," I howled.

She let go. "Oh, Edie. Stop it. Don't be silly. It's all right. It's all a misunderstanding. Being intimate means a lot more than that. Oh, I *wondered.*"

"She's trying to cover up, now," said Alice Kelling. "Yes. She's not so stupid. She sees she got herself in trouble."

"I believe her," Mrs. Peebles said. "This is an awful scene."

"Well there is one way to find out," said Alice Kelling. getting up. "After all, I am a nurse."

Mrs. Peebles drew a breath and said, "No. No. Go to your room, Edie. And stop that noise. That is too disgusting."

I heard the car start in a little while. I tried to stop crying, pulling back each wave as it started over me. Finally I succeeded, and lay heaving on the bed.

Mrs. Peebles came and stood in the doorway.

"She's gone," she said. "That Bird woman too. Of course, you know you should never have gone near that man and that is the cause of all this trouble. I have a headache. As soon as you can, go and wash your face in cold water and get at the dishes and we will not say any more about this.

Nor we didn't. I didn't figure out till years later the extent of what I had been saved from. Mrs. Peebles was not very friendly to me afterwards, but she was fair. Not very friendly is the wrong way of describing what she was. She never had been very friendly. It was just that now she had to see me all the time and it got on her nerves, a little.

As for me, I put it all out of my mind like a bad dream and concentrated on waiting for my letter. The mail came every day except Sunday, between one-thirty and two in the afternoon, a good time for me because Mrs. Peebles was always having her nap. I would get the kitchen all cleaned and then go up to the mailbox and sit in the grass, waiting. I was perfectly happy, waiting, I forgot all about Alice Kelling and her misery and awful talk and Mrs. Peebles and her chilliness and the embarrassment of whether she had told Dr. Peebles and the face of Loretta Bird, getting her fill of other people's troubles. I was always smiling when the mailman got there, and continued smiling even after he gave me the mail and I saw today wasn't the day. The mailman was a Carmichael. I knew by his face because there are a lot of Carmichaels living out by us and so many of them have a sort of sticking-out top lip. So I asked his name (he was a young man, shy, but good humored, anybody could ask him anything) and then I said, "I knew by your face!" He was pleased by that and always glad to see me and got a little less shy. "You've got the smile I've been waiting on all day!" he used to holler out the car window.

It never crossed my mind for a long time a letter might not come. I believed in it coming just like I believed the sun would rise in the morning. I just put off my hope from day to day, and there was the goldenrod out around the mailbox and the children gone back to school, and the leaves turning, and I was wearing a sweater when I went to wait. One day walking back with the hydro bill stuck in my hand, that was all, looking across at the fairgrounds with the full-blown milkweed and dark teasels, so much like fall, it just struck me: *No letter was ever going to come.* It was an impossible idea to get used to. No, not impossible. If I thought about Chris' face when he said he was going to write to me, it was impossible, but if I forgot that and thought about the actual tin mailbox, empty, it was plain and true. I kept on going to meet the mail, but my heart was heavy now like a lump of lead. I only smiled because I thought of the mailman counting on it, and he didn't have an easy life, with the winter driving ahead.

Till it came to me one day there were women doing this with their lives, all over. There were women just waiting and waiting by mailboxes for one letter or another. I imagined me making this journey day after day and year after year, and my hair starting to go gray, and I thought, I was never made to go on like that. So I stopped meeting the mail. If there were women all through life waiting, and women busy and not waiting, I knew which I had to be. Even though there might be things the second kind of women have to pass up and never know about, it still is better.

I was surprised when the mailman phoned the Peebles' place in the evening and asked for me. He said he missed me. He asked if I would like to go to Goderich where some well-known movie was on, I forget now what. So I said yes, and I went out with him for two years and he asked me to marry him, and we were engaged a year more while I got my things together, and then we did marry. He always tells the children the story of how I went after him by sitting by the mailbox every day, and naturally I laugh and let him, because I like people to think what pleases them and makes them happy.

THE LADY OF THE HOUSE

Julie Emerson

Come in, everyone comes in the back door, not just the reporters. That's mint: it smells so nice when you brush against it, but I have to keep it close to the house or it would get out of control in the garden. This is really my dream kitchen, it's so big. I had the centre island for the appliances put in and James—he's a decorator friend of mine—talked me into using real butcher block counters. It's kind of impractical compared to an arborite counter, but it has a nice natural look. It's good for chopping. You feel liked a professional cook, though that's the last thing I'd want to be since I hate to cook. That's why I have this big freezer. I make three of four pies at a time. The same with casseroles. There are so many pot-lucks and community suppers to go to, as you can imagine, and I always have to bring something. Now you probably think I'm a little crazy to have a piano in the kitchen. But I love it. I like listening to my daughter Ellen practicing. She keeps me company when I'm cooking. I even like listening to her play scales. I used to play the piano some, but not anymore.

* * *

We've had so many guests in this dining room. I keep the names of all our guests in my little file and I write what we had for dinner, and which table linens I used, too. That way I don't serve the same people chicken three times in a row! Ellen is going to put all the information on our home computer for me. I love this table: it has three extra leaves, so it seats 15 people. Last weekend we had 12, mostly people who work for Paul. He just had to tell them his news about Ottawa. Some of the men he's known longer than he's known me. He went to university with them, he's always spent a lot of time with them. When they come to dinner, I always try to have a more balanced conversation, not just all politics. They're not very social; you have to draw them out. These chairs with the cabriole legs are Queen Anne. James and I chose the seat covers to pick up the orange in the painting, but then he always says he doesn't know anything about art. The art and decorating is my department. I found this chandelier when we went on holiday and I carried it all the way back on the plane, carried it on my lap so it wouldn't break. I put the little shades over the lights; I think they look much better covered. This floor was in terrible shape before, so James and I had it stripped and sanded and bleached. It really brightens up the room. I'll tell you, this room is full of light now, but it used to be so dark and gloomy. James and I had such a time getting it into shape. When we finished, we went out to celebrate and had lunch in a nice restaurant.

* * *

Here's the living room, and that wing chair, by the way, is one that John Davies always sat in—he was an MP for the longest time, and at one of our parties he sat there and knocked his red wine over and I had to have the whole chair slipcovered. I didn't mind that much. I matched one of the colours in the chintz on the sofa, it's a sort of neutral colour. The loveseat is called a double camelback because of the two humps. It's really quite comfortable; I do want people to feel comfortable here. I've had reporters just sink right into the down cushions on the sofa and lean back and look like they never want to leave. I get interviewed a couple of times a year for things like the lifestyle section of the newspapers. The reporters plump down on the sofa and put their tape recorders there on the coffee table and drink, oh they always drink, out of my Waterford crystal glasses of course, and first they tell me I'm such a valuable partner to Paul, and then they say, as if it's something really daring and I'm supposed to be flattered, that I should run for political office myself someday. I just thank them, but I think, how naïve, how little they know about what it's all about. I mean it's so much work. And our home is so important. Oh, that vase on the shelf is by David Yamada. Isn't it a nice colour? I think it enhances the other colours in the room; it's so subtle it doesn't compete with them. You can see the carpet is a much paler version of that colour. I had the wall-to-wall installed right after we moved in. It would be the devil to keep clean, but I don't allow shoes on it. That's my rule: everybody has to take off their shoes before they come into the living room. And if you saw the pile of shoes out there sometimes, from all these important people, you'd laugh. Once my son did hide someone's shoes—I won't tell you whose—but I grounded him for a month for that. Yes, I'm the one who does the disciplining at home. Paul just wouldn't do it. In any case, I like the house to be a peaceful place for him to come home to, a place to rest. He has so much on his mind. All the problems of being in government would be too much for a person after a while if he couldn't forget about them at home. Paul used to let it all get to him, but now he can relax more. He likes to sit there in the leather chair in front of the fire. So while he's away, you might say I just keep the home fires burning. That's where I answer the letters and pay the bills; the desk opens out from the antique bookcase. It's Victorian.

* * *

James and I had those cupboards built to hold all the towels and sheets, and we put more cabinets under the vanity. See how much storage space there is? The tiles go with the wallpaper and the curtains; you can get everything coordinated these days. This old bathtub is my luxury. There's nothing I like better than a nice, hot bath to help me relax, all by myself. But the kids used to come in when they were little, since I couldn't really lock the door, and sometimes Paul comes in and talks to me. It's kind of funny, me lying in the tub, and Paul sitting there all dressed. You feel like splashing him. As a matter of fact, I was in the tub and he was sitting there when he told me about this new position he's got in Ottawa.

* * *

This is the kind of four-poster bed with a canopy that I always wanted. The bedspread is the same fabric as the bed curtains and the dust ruffle, but you see it's quilted. James suggested having the throw pillows in raw silk. We knocked out a wall to have enough space for the grouping with this rattan daybed. You see how the wicker's wound around and tortured into all these little spirals, I painted it white with a brush, but I should have sprayed it. The drapes are handpainted silk, but they're lined so they're not see-through. Having some privacy is important, as you can imagine, in my position.

We have two closets: one for me and one for Paul. I organized Paul's so all his clothes are colour-coordinated in sections: the shirts next to the suits they go with, and the ties next to them, so he wears the right colour tie with the right suit. His wardrobe was a disaster before I started doing this. He must be a little colour-blind; lots of men are, you know. He uses that mirror in the antique frame. I put the telephone table right under it when I noticed him dragging the phone over so he could look in the mirror while he was talking. He was sort of practicing his expressions; he has to look good for the TV cameras. They have to look like they're on top of things and like they're concerned even if it's some petty problem like ones they've heard a hundred times before, and believe me, he has. He tells me what's going on. In our big bed here, we talk about everything. Of course sometimes we do more than talk. In bed. But you have to understand, the kind of job he does is very tiring. He's away a lot, too. Personally, I like sex well enough, but it's like eating a peach: very nice when it's available, but when it isn't, then I don't miss it. I like a man who treats me nicely, and Paul is a gentleman. He's very affectionate. When you see us on election night at campaign headquarters, and the returns are in and we won and everybody's shouting that they all love Paul, and he's so happy that he gives me a big kiss, well that is real, that is really it. I get so excited I go all red in the face. About the shade of that rosy colour in the carpet. Oh yes, that's a dhurrie carpet.

* * *

What's this sign? KEEP OUT. THIS MEANS YOU! I'm afraid my son's room probably looks a bit too lived in to show you, anyway. He won't clean it up. I have a girl in once a week and she does the heavy cleaning and a once-over of all the rooms, but she doesn't touch his. Now Ellen keeps her room tidy, even her old dollhouse, that used to be mine. Ellen always makes her bed; her great-aunt sewed this quilt. She likes our canopy bed, so I hung this swag over hers, like one of those French campaign beds. I love a light blue room, it's so feminine. My mother did Ellen's first bedroom. You see, Ellen was early, and I hadn't finished the baby's room. My mother had come to stay for a few weeks, and she wallpapered it in little blue and white flowers and she got it all ready. When she came to see me in the hospital, she didn't say a word. Then I came home with Ellen wrapped in a little bundle, and there was her room, all done, as a surprise. That was before we bought this house. I've fixed up every room of this house; I love it. I enjoy decorating. Some people say I have a talent for it. I worked in James' store for a while. At first it was interesting, but then it got boring sitting in the store all day. Afterwards, I had to race to pick up the kids and then make dinner or go to some function with Paul as usual. Paul liked the idea of my working. My salary was just pin money, though. I prefer to stay home. It's important to have a stable environment for the family, for Paul. I don't want the kids to have to move. I don't want them to have to leave everything that's familiar to them. This house.

* * *

Here we are again. The kettle must have boiled dry; it's a bit warm for tea, anyway. Don't you think it's hotter than usual? At least it's not Ottawa; the summer there is unbearable. Maybe I should put one of those nice ceiling fans over the table. A white one. No, it would be too low. Paul's so tall it would cut his head off. Oh no, just imagine what the tabloids would do with that! And last night Paul was standing right there, right where it would go. He was talking to Ellen about moving to Ottawa, and he said she has to get used to the idea of a new school, and we'll have a new house, and we all have to get ready to move. Well, I'm not. Getting ready to move. I'm not moving.

MIXED MESSAGES

KITCHEN TERRITORIAL

Susan Ioannou

Her kitchen.
KEEP OUT.
Plump and pink-aproned,
Ma puffed through aromas,
stirring up, straining.
Preserving pots crowded the stove.
Steam whitened windows
until high quart baskets'
apples, peach, pear, plums
gleamed into cellar jars
row after row.

Her kitchen.
DON'T TOUCH.
Across the scrubbed tabletop,
strudel she tugged thin
enough to read newspaper through.
Canisters spilled out
fat raisins, brown sugar.
Fill-and-fold-over-pinch-up
fingers flew.

Her kitchen.
STAND BACK!
the hot oven door screeched.
Grease skipped and stung round our Sunday-night roast.
Potatoes glowed golden, and onions transparent,
while sweet baby carrots frothed in red juice.
Turn-prod-baste, elbows jerked,
working fatted strings loose.

Her kitchen.
Not mine.
Over and over,
Don't touch. Stand back, girl. Keep out!
"But, ma, when I marry,"
I'd whine from the doorway,

"I still won't be able to cook!"
Flouring bread dough,
she thumped through a whirlwind,
"You read? Buy a recipe book."

CHEMISTRY
Rhea Tregebov

Do I remember the black woodstove,
its heavy lids lifted to the roar inside?
My mother's mother, like that.

* * *

Burnt water: the funny story
of how my father taught my mother to cook,
kitchen orphan, her mother denying her
even instruction.

* * *

Smell the old-woman smell,
the deep smell of yeast, which is alive.
Gifted, her monumental, fleshed arms
command strudel dough to rise,
to ripple thinly, forcefully across the tabletop,
the finest, the whitest linen.

* * *

Dinner spoiled, my mother's anxious pots tremble.
Every Friday, she cannot cook for her mother,
every Friday every offering disdained.

* * *

It is a peculiar love cooked them, flesh to seared flesh.

HOW TO MAKE PASTA

Irene Guilford

The formica table top in my mother's kitchen is a perfect circle around which, within which, we work, my mother, my grandmother, myself. It is brown, smooth, glossy, hard. There are black squiggles embedded beneath the surface, beneath the hard plastic shine that my mother wipes and wipes clean with hard, pushing strokes. The opaque streaks evaporate quickly, steadily, and of their own will.

We are making pasta, I am making pasta, for them. I have brought my pasta machine, a chrome contraption that cranks with a handle. It hangs heavy, pulls at my wrist when I lift it onto the table, and I like the feel of the push I must make to hold it erect. I have bought exactly the one recommended in my Italian cooking course by Bonnie Stern. I am going to make them *Pasta Primavera* because of the thin strips of pepper, yellow, red, and green, and the way the cream clings to the noodles, a thick cream, rich and indulgent.

The pasta machine is clamped to the formica table top and now I am mixing the dough. I unload a cup of flour right onto the table, make a well in the mound and break in an egg, tilt in a bud of salt from my palm, dribble a thin thread of oil and watch it flow down the yolk into the flour. Then I begin to mix with a fork, starting in the centre of the egg and working in the flour from the edges. I can hear and feel the fork scrape against the table top as I scrape at the flour under the slithery egg mixture. My grandmother clucks and almost shakes her head, but she watches. I know she thinks I should be using a bowl, not the table.

My mother is bustling, no not bustling, the Lithuanian word is better, *triusia,* keeping herself busy. She is at the sink, at the stove, putting dishes away, moving around between sink and stove with purpose, with importance. She glances at my grandmother. I start to feel confused, I don't know what it is, but I see that my grandmother is watching my mixing in the flour with intent and I feel a slight stirring inside me, a vagueness as I keep at the dough. I put down the fork, wipe the tines downward between my thumb and forefinger and flick the sticky bits into the pile of dough, then start to knead. It is sticky, yolk-yellow. My grandmother smiles at this. She watches me sprinkle a light flour over the dough and knead, sprinkle and knead, until it is no longer sticky. The pieces on my hands have dried into gritty scales that I rub at fiercely to loosen them. My mother is at the sink.

Come and watch this, I say, for I am going to feed the dough into the pasta machine and start the first step of the cranking cycle. There are two phases, and I know the first one is fun, but the second one is the best. I am saving that one. The dough has gone silky in texture, silky and stretchy and slightly glossy, just like Bonnie said it would in class although you don't believe it when it is a sticky wet mass of dough.

My mother puts down a pot she's been washing and wipes her hands dry on the tea towel, then hangs it up and walks over to the table, glancing over her counters, checking herself from picking up something or starting something else. I wait by the table. My grandmother waits and watches. My mother finally settles, we are all around the formica table.

Watch, I say, hearing more excitement in my voice than I'd like, for I don't want to still be a child.

I flatten the dough with the heel of my palm, pushing out the outsides until it is a thick, large cookie. Then I feed it into the machine's metal lips, shiny wide rollers that have been greased with vegetable oil and operate like smooth ball bearings. They catch the dough and pull it down, squeezing it thin like the wooden rollers on old washing machines used to squeeze flat all the wet clothes, making big wrinkles and folds and I used to laugh at them coming out the other end, so collapsed and uncaring in their appearance, allowed to be that way.

I crank the handle in an up and down circle, my right hand bringing it up and rising over the top, then falling down the side, while my left feeds through the stretchy dough. It is becoming even more silky, almost satiny. My grandmother watches, leaning over towards me. My mother lets me know that she is making herself watch, I can tell from the way she's breathing, the artificial brightness on her face, but I don't mind too much because now I am going to show them the big treat, the last part of step one, when the rollers are set to the closest notch and the pasta stretches so thin that it becomes long like a ribbon. Bonnie said one of her guest teachers always draped the pasta in and around the chairs of his students as he worked. And now my pasta is stretched thin and my grandmother's eyes widen for she has never seen this and she watches me lift my hand high up into the air up above my head to hold the ribbon off the floor until the last tip of tail flicks out of the machine.

I can feel the struggle within my mother, how she tries to keep the smile on her face, how she wants to take a step away from the table but I take my time at cutting the long ribbon into four shorter strips, watch the wobble of the wavy pasta wheel, for now I am about to show them the second step, the secret, how the strips are made into noodles.

I inch the edge of the pasta up to the teeth, tamping it down along the edge the way you feed a rumpled fabric under the foot of a sewing machine. I move the crank handle to another hole and when I start to turn, thin strips of noodles, threads, dangling like a fringe of hair appear under the snout of the pasta machine and my grandmother lets out a gasp, claps her palms with a smack, holds them together and rolls her eyes upwards.

Look, look I want to say to my mother.

Vuje, vuje, says my grandmother, her voice full of wonder.

But wait, I have something else, I say as I gather the fringe like a curl and lay it gently on its side on a dinner plate.

I move the crank handle into the final hole, settle another strip of pasta, swept through flour to keep it from sticking, along the teeth's edge. This time, there are broad noodles, wide and flat, even, swinging with more weight as they drape from below the pasta machine's lip like a fringe of felt, like the fringe on a jester's skirt.

I am wiping the formica table now, sweeping up the flour and dough balls that are left with the side of my hand.

Don't throw those away, my grandmother lunges for the tiny dough balls. There are a couple the size of peas, but most are like lint on a sweater and she picks them out of the flour dust.

Kukliai, she says with a singing dip, dumplings.

She looks through cupboards for a glass jar to save them in.

Here, says my mother as she pulls out a plastic sour cream container from a top shelf.

I boil the pasta in my mother's shiny steel pot, soften the crisp peppers in butter in her cast iron skillet, then mix it together. The final step, I sprinkle parmesan cheese in a wide circle, embarrassed at my own flourish.

Pasta primavera, I say as we sit at the table to eat the soft pasta, the yielding coloured peppers, the drip-thick cream.

My grandmother is murmuring as she eats. I know my mother is making herself sit there. She twirls her fork, looks at but doesn't see her dish, says nothing, and I think, she hasn't even heard the name of my dish. She gets up, goes to the cupboard for a container to store the leftover pasta.

Naudok stikline, my grandmother is scraping together the pasta remains, use glass.

Now they are arguing, both standing back from the circle of the table, standing on the table's other side, facing one another. They are like two animals, teeth bared, that I have stumbled on in a forest clearing. Their voices are shrill, my mother is haughty, laughing, and I am shocked at how she scalds, that she doesn't care that I see. My grandmother's voice is warning, threatening but not yet let go. My mother turns to me, drags at me, invites me to join her ridicule. I feel as if I am going to throw up. She turns back to my grandmother who now lets go, is lashing forward.

Then my grandmother turns to me, *Nu Irena,* what do you think?

But before I can answer, she is facing my mother again. I can feel my head sink between my shoulders, my ears trying to bury themselves where they won't have to hear.

Stop, I finally screech, and they pause a moment, stunned, then both turn to face me from the other side of the table, beseeching me, pulling at me, talking together at me.

I will hear no more, I shriek. My face is hot and I am breathing hard. They both flash me looks of betrayal, each having thought my silence a support of one against the other.

I WISH YOU HAD FLOWN
Anna Mioduchowska

I still think you should have run away from
home Mama children and all
one rainy afternoon laundry
boiling on the stove damn the laundry

now the stove's a different model you are
at the end of your term children
grown laundry boiling still

FROM *THE BOX GARDEN*
Carol Shields

We have scrambled eggs on toast for lunch, Martin, my mother and I. In this household, guests have never been frequent: occasionally when we were children my Aunt Liddy, my mother's older sister who lived in the country, would come to spend a day with us. And there was a second cousin of our father, Cousin Hugo, who owned a hardware store, a large fat man with wiry black hair and curving crusts of dirt beneath his fingernails. And once a neighbour whose wife was in the hospital with pneumonia had been invited for Sunday lunch, an extraordinary gesture which remained for years in my mother's mind as the "time we put ourselves out to help Mr. Eggleston." Always on these occasions when guests were present she would serve scrambled eggs on toast.

Doubtless she considered it a dish both light and elegant. She may have read somewhere that it was the Queen Mother's favourite luncheon dish (she is always reading about the Royal Family). Certainly she is convinced of the superiority of her own scrambled eggs and the manner in which she arranges the triangles of toast (side by side like the sails of a tiny boat), for she always compares, at length, the correctness of her method with the slipshod scrambled eggs she has encountered elsewhere.

"Liddy doesn't put enough milk in hers and I always tell her that makes them rubbery. If you want nice, soft scrambled eggs you have to add a tablespoon of milk for every egg, just a tablespoon, no more, no less. And use an egg beater, not a fork the way most people do. Most people just don't want to bother getting out an egg beater, they're too lazy to wash something extra. They think, who'll notice anyway, what's the difference, but an egg beater makes all the difference, all the difference in the world. Otherwise the yolk and white don't mix the way they should. Liddy always leaves big hunks of white in her scrambled eggs. And she doesn't cut the crusts off her toast. She thinks it's hoity-toity and a waste of bread, but I always save the crusts and dry them in the oven to make bread crumbs out of them afterwards so there's no waste, not a bit; you know I never waste good food; you'll have to admit I never waste anything. Most people won't bother, they won't go to the trouble; they're too lazy; they don't know any better. And I always add the salt before cooking, that makes them hold their shape, not get hard like Liddy's but just, you know, firm. But not pepper, never pepper, never add pepper when you're cooking, let people add their own pepper at the table if that's what they want. Me, I never liked spicy food like what the Italians and French like. And Greeks. Garlic and onions and grease, and I don't know what, just reeking of it in the subways these days, reeking of it; I don't dare turn my head sideways when I go downtown. Toronto isn't the same; not the way it used to be, not the way it was way back."

We eat lunch in the kitchen. Martin is quiet. So am I. Our forks clicking on the plates chill me into a further silence.

"Hmm, delicious," Martin says politely.

"Yes." I agree, forcing my voice into short plumes of enthusiasm. "Really good. So tender."

Afterwards she washes the dishes and I dry. *Always take a clean tea towel for each meal. It may be a little bit extra in the wash but when you think of the filthy tea towels some people use ...*

I yearn desperately to talk to her; to say that, despite my foreboding, I have been rather taken with Louis Berceau, that I am immeasurably pleased that he and she have found each other and she will no longer have to endure the loneliness of the ticking clock, the sound of the furnace switching on and off, the daily paper thudding against the door, the calendar weeks wasting, the reminders of time slipping by which must be unbearable for those who are alone. But the words dry in my throat; if I only knew how to begin, if only I could speak to her without shyness, without fear of hurting her. Instead I poke with my tea towel into the spokes of the egg beater.

"Don't bother drying that," she turns to me, taking it out of my hands. "Here," she says, "I always put it in the oven for a little, the pilot light dries it out; the gears are so old, I've had it since just after the war, it was hard to get egg beaters then. Cousin Hugo got it for me from the store. I don't want the gears to rust, they would if I didn't get it good and dry. I've had it so long and it will have to last me until—"

Until what? Until death? Until the end? That is what she means; the words she couldn't say but which she must have recognized or why did she stop so suddenly? I have never thought of the way in which my mother thinks of her own death. No doubt, though, she has a plan; she will do it more neatly, more thoroughly than her sister Liddy, better than the neighbours, more genteely than Cousin Hugo, more timely than our father; no one will laugh at her, no one will look down on her.

Still, it may be that she is a little uncertain: the way she plunges into vigorous silence over the scoured sink hints at uneasiness, an acknowledgement at least of life's thinned reversal, of the finite nature of husbands and egg beaters and even of one's self.

RUTH'S POEM

Helen J. Rosta

Harold's voice awakens me—not that he's talking loudly. I rise slowly, sluggish from the unaccustomed afternoon nap and oppressed by the humidity; I don't want to face him yet. In the hall, I hesitate at the living room door and look over this gathering of Ruth's friends and acquaintances.

Jenny's husband, Ken, is pouring drinks. Harold stands by the fireplace, holding his. He's in conversation with a woman Jenny's age (I catch the word "investment"). My eyes search the room; he hasn't brought his wife, new wife—what's her name?—Andrea.

"Tasteful of him," Ruth would have said, the words muffled, slurred a little. I can imagine her standing here, muttering, "Just look at him—posing like some goddamned mannequin, elbow on the mantelpiece, drink in hand, belly all sucked in." Ruth's way of getting around him looking so good.

That is, if she weren't crying out betrayal. Lamentations jumbled with fragments of poetry. "'What thou among the trees hast never known.' How could he do that? How could he do that me? How could he?"

A comfortable murmur fills the room. Someone laughs. I hurry to the kitchen.

"Aunt Lynne, glad you're up!" Jenny exclaims. "We can use another hand."

Ken's mother is trimming crusts from slices of white bread. She lays down the knife and we lean into an embrace. Her cheek is warm and she smells softly of flowers. "We'll miss her."

"If Mother had lived," Jenny says firmly, "she'd have been miserable. Third degree burns. Skin grafts."

Martha Hamilton neatly severs the crust from a square of bread. "Jenny said you were exhausted. The early flight and the time difference."

Jenny takes a bowl of vegetables from the refrigerator, dumps them onto a plate and nestles a carton of prepared dip in the middle of the pile.

"Where's your rolling pin?" Mrs. Hamilton asks.

"Don't have one. I use a wine bottle. What do you need a rolling pin for anyway?"

"Aren't we going to make pinwheel sandwiches?"

"Those dinky little jelly roll dooies? We don't have time."

"But they look so nice. I could have helped you with them last night."

"Last night I was running around like a chicken with its head cut off. What's wrong with ordinary sandwiches? Salmon salad, egg salad, devilled ham." Jenny slides a table knife across the counter. "Here, Aunt Lynne. You spread."

"I could have—" Martha Hamilton lifts critical eyebrows and glances at me with an "if she'd been my daughter" air.

I spoon a dollop of egg salad from the bowl and turn to Jenny. "Ken told me your mother left most of her things in the house when she moved into the Condo."

"Took the clothes on her back and a few odds and ends. We called the movers after the house was sold." Jenny slices a sandwich into diagonal halves. "It wasn't like her."

"No." Remembering, after Mother died, the suitcase of Spode—remnants from Father's side of the family—that Ruth had hauled back East.

"She was using the saucers under plants," Ruth had said disapprovingly. "Antique china, irreplaceable." And later. "You'd likely ruin it in the dishwasher." But she'd had a few drinks when she said that.

"Ken mentioned," I say nonchalantly, "that the chap who bought the house was impressed with your mother's books and music and art collection."

"Impressed isn't—the word. He went on and on about what an interesting woman had lived there. He wished he'd known her."

Ruth's kindred spirit? I put a face on the man, a gentle, scholarly face, and install him in Ruth's house—not just the house in Rosemont, in all the houses where she'd lived with Harold.

In their first house, perched above the mining town. "A company town," Mother called it. Even the house belonged to the company, an aerie for young, rising executives.

I was 10 the summer my mother and I visited. Ruth was 22.

That summer, Ruth held a tea for Mother: silver tea service and pinwheel sandwiches, slices of white bread flattened by rolling pin and filled with cream cheese that Ruth had tinted in delicate shades. She'd found the recipe, complete with colour illustrations, in a magazine called *Woman's World Weekly*.

"Pretty," Mother said as she helped Ruth arrange the sandwiches on trays covered with doilies, "but a lot of fuss."

Jenny reaches for the last egg salad sandwich, slices it and sets the halves atop the heap on the platter. The heap quivers and she steadies it with both hands, Mother's hands, square-based and sturdy, not the narrow elegant hands of my sister.

I wipe the table knife on a paper towel and am spreading devilled ham when Ken sticks his head into the kitchen.

"How's the food coming? Should I plug in the coffee?"

Mrs. Hamilton looks up from the cake she's cutting, opens her mouth, closes it and glances at Jenny.

"I guess so," Jenny says. "It'll take awhile to perk."

Ken gets a bottle of sherry from the refrigerator and uncorks it. "I see they've spirited you into the kitchen," he says to me. "I thought you were still resting."

He picks up the paper towel and wipes the mouth of the bottle, avoiding the smudges of egg salad. "A lot of them have brought pictures. They're passing them around and reminiscing."

He holds the wine against the light. It's honey-golden, like the amber necklace Ruth brought back from Denmark the first time she and Harold went abroad.

I have the snapshots she sent my parents, names, dates, descriptions inscribed neatly on the backs: "Helligandshus, the only medieval building in Copenhagen." "Gefion Fountain, the Goddess Gefion with her oxen plowing an island out of the soil of Sweden." "The Little Mermaid gazing sadly into the sea—looking for her lost family or her lost soul? Perhaps both." Museums, churches, monuments, Ruth or Harold (occasionally both of them) in the foreground.

The pictures are in the family album along with other glimpses of my sister. Ruth, the only child—infant, toddler, schoolgirl. Ruth, the leggy 12-year-old, cradling the baby, me.

To me, she was always a grown-up, the woman in the photographs on the mantle: Ruth in cap and academic gown, Ruth in veil and wedding gown. The pictures were taken within weeks of one another.

Perhaps there was a graduation celebration but it's the wedding I remember, cool, vaulted church massed with flowers, the solemn procession, Ruth on my father's arm, moving ever so slowly, so stately down the aisle. And afterwards the reception in a banquet room of the Regency Hotel, green velvet drapes tied back so that you could see the valley below. For a moment, Ruth stood there with Harold, her hand on his arm, looking out.

Mother watched them with tears in her eyes. "My first-born little girl," she said.

A waiter passed, balancing long-stemmed glasses on a silver tray. Father took two glasses and handed one to Mother.

"Drink up," he told her. "There's nothing like champagne to kill the pain."

In later years, I heard the rumour that Harold's parents had paid for the wedding and wondered if my father's pain was a big, expensive wedding he couldn't afford, or, as he would have put it: he couldn't "foot the bill."

Ken gestures with the sherry bottle. "Would you ladies like some?"

"No," Mrs. Hamilton says. "We'll be in shortly."

I want to ask him for a scotch and soda, something medicinal, but immediately envision Mrs. Hamilton's critically raised eyebrows. Not that I can really blame her.

Jenny hands Ken the platter of vegetables and gives him a light shove. "Get a move on. They can start with this. Tell them sandwiches are coming up."

The year Jenny was born, Harold bought the summer cottage.

By then he'd been transferred East and was moving up in the company, not Rosemont yet—that was still a few years away.

Although the house on Riverside Drive was air-conditioned, Ruth wrote about escaping to the "wonderful cool of the lake. Baby loves it here; all smiles and chuckles.

"The cottage is marvellous. It overlooks the water and is finished in local wood and stone so that it seems to be part of the landscape. I scoured antique stores and have found some pieces that fit right in—pine table and chairs, a wonderful old washstand—

"Please come and stay with us this summer—and that includes my stick-in-the-mud father. Dad, you must come to see your adorable granddaughter!"

My father didn't go with us. "Tell her to book a flight this fall and bring the baby home. Harold can afford it," he added.

The lake was a women and children preserve. That summer, I was 15 and in love with Lester Nelson, a senior back home who didn't know I existed. Nevertheless, I spent a lot of time thinking about him, sitting on the beach and gazing over the water with a vague, but painful, longing in my chest.

When the men came down on weekends, there were parties, but to me, the men, aside from being married, were old and the parties were about as dull as our daily routine: Ruth reading, or reciting poetry to us when she wasn't fussing over Jenny, and Mother fussing over Jenny.

Even Ruth admitted the parties had shortcomings. "The men," she complained, "talk business and the women talk babies. Not that Jenny isn't a perfectly adorable subject."

The other subjects were food and drink: how to barbecue a steak, create a perfect dry martini (pass the martini cork over the gin bottle) or judge a wine. Ruth had taken a wine-tasting course and talked knowingly of bouquet, balance or a foxy taste—which was something bad.

She prepared dishes she called pâtés and terrines to go with the wines and she set her table with hand-made ceramic plates and bowls and a centrepiece of wild flowers.

I watched Ruth's preparations closely, planning to emulate her when I married Lester Nelson. I knew I couldn't count on learning the fine details of entertaining from my mother; our cabin at Lake Anne was the repository of frayed tablecloths, mismatched cups and saucers and chipped plates.

Mrs. Hamilton wouldn't have approved. But on the other hand, Ruth (although she wouldn't appreciate Jenny's slapdash style) would agree with Jenny about pinwheel sandwiches. Only Ruth had called them "silly." I was watching her cover a terrine, Canard à l'Orange, with a thick layer of Madeira aspic when she suddenly looked over at me and laughed, "Remember the time I made those silly little pinwheel sandwiches?"

The remark surprised and puzzled me: up to that moment I had thought pinwheel sandwiches elegant and they had been high on the list of skills I considered essential to my culinary repertoire.

I remove a paper cup from the stack beside the coffee urn and am slowly filling it—putting off meeting Harold—when he comes over and lays an arm across my shoulder, giving it a light squeeze.

"Ken told me you just got in this morning."

"Jenny called. Last minute thing. There wasn't any funeral service."

"That's the way Ruth would have wanted it."

How do you know what she wanted? But I don't say that; I nod and sip my coffee.

Harold draws a cup. "Morley's somewhere in Asia," he says in an off-hand manner. "We haven't been able to reach him."

"They told me."

Morley must be a keen disappointment to Harold—a slap in the face—his only son renouncing all worldly goods and now sitting on a mountaintop in Asia, meditating himself to a higher spiritual plane.

Harold might have accepted that of Jenny—although he wouldn't, of course, like it—but Jenny's turned out to be the practical, no nonsense one. Efficient, even when it came to handling her mother's cremation and throwing—the word seems apt—this reception in her memory.

I'm compelled to talk about Ruth. "The manager heard her scream," I say. "Her clothes were on fire. No one seems to know how it happened."

He stands there, swishing the coffee in his cup, not saying anything and I regret my choice of topics because I know what he's thinking. "She was probably drunk."

Probably. I've often wondered when the before dinner drink became morning's vodka and orange juice. Does he know?

It couldn't have been that day at the lake when she looked up from her book and exclaimed, "Listen! These have to be the most sensuous lines in the English language:

O for a beaker full of the warm South,
Full of the true the blushful Hippocrene,
With beaded bubbles winking at the brim,
And purple-stained mouth."

But it had started long before I found the empty vodka bottles—all mickies—which she'd dumped in my garbage before she left for home. And it was long before she and Harold came through on their way to his engineers' convention and he took her, stumbling and incoherent, from my house and put her into the car. "I have to be on time for that reception."

It was only an hour's drive; she couldn't possibly sober up.

I want to ask him, "Why did you do that, why did you drag my sister to that posh reception and parade her in front of your colleagues?"

When I was with her I'd try to cover up, feeling anxiety akin to panic at the saliva thickening voice, the slackening mouth, anticipating the raised voice, the sudden burst of anger—like the evening in Cload's after her second trip to the washroom. I never returned to that restaurant.

Harold's eyes shift from mine and I notice their tension, his unease. He wishes I would ask about his wife—how is Andrea? Then he could talk about the present, his retirement, their travels.

Ruth planned they would travel when he retired. She gathered brochures, maps, travel magazines and talked at length about the architecture, museums and treasures of the great cities of the world, creating, as she spoke, an image of her and Harold making their cultured way around the globe. She didn't take into account the stumbling, incoherent Ruth of the posh reception, or the Ruth who mistook for food the paper doily on her plate.

If we could talk honestly, I would tell Harold there were times I felt for him—like that evening at Cload's when she slushed her food, sawed at the paper doily and abused me for some imagined wrong.

I might even admit it was inevitable that he'd find someone else, although I wouldn't have thought of Andrea, the unhappily married next-door-neighbour who, in moments of Ruth's lucidity, cried on her shoulder.

Ruth certainly didn't perceive any threat in a woman Jenny's age; Andrea was like a daughter.

After Harold moved out, Ruth started phoning me long distance in the middle of the night, rambling and repetitious calls riddled with sobs and lost thoughts.

Night was always the worst time for her: at my house, sleepless and full of vodka, she'd run into the yard and wail.

I lived on the edge of panic, alert to shuffling in the guest room, footsteps starting down the hall. I hated her then.

But sometimes, before she started on the vodka, she'd turn to me with puzzled eyes and ask, "How could that happen to me?" And then my sorrow for her was absolute.

Harold lifts his chin and glances over the room, wearing the arrogance captured in a snapshot taken at my house, chin lifted, lips crimped, blue eyes looking out from under half-lowered lids.

I often saw that expression turned on Ruth, even the first summer at the cottage. My mother saw it too but both of us pretended that we didn't. Not that I understood—or wanted to.

Harold lowers his chin and his face looks softer, almost gentle. No doubt his

Andrea face—acknowledgment of her 30-year advantage—no scathing glances, cutting words driving her in tears from the dinner table.

Scenes that no one spoke of.

Only once, going home on the train, my mother alluded to them. "Harold's so demanding," she said. "And Ruth tries so hard to please him. Wants to live up to his standards, I guess." She paused and gazed out the window.

The morning sun washed the prairie grass with subtle mauves and tawny shades of brown. I pressed my face against the glass and waited.

My mother sighed. "I wonder if things would have been different if she'd married Anthony Carter. He worshipped the ground she walked on."

Anthony Carter was a dim presence in my mind.

"He sang, didn't he?"

"Yes. He had a beautiful baritone voice. And he played the piano. Don't you remember those Chopin waltzes he used to play?"

On my 30th birthday, Ruth and I shared a bottle of wine under the white lilac tree in my mother's garden.

"You're catching up," she said and I realized then that the 12 years between us were no longer so great; now we could be sisters.

"Mother's worried you'll never marry."

The lilac blossoms were luminous, and heady with fragrance. I twirled my glass slowly, trying to catch moonlight in the wine.

"Maybe sometime. Maybe never. She shouldn't worry."

"No," Ruth said, "she shouldn't. But I guess she's still operating on the theory a woman needs a man to look after her. Anyway, marriage isn't everything. *THOU still unravish'd bride of quietness.* Your poem." She set her glass down and began to recite:

> *"Bold Lover, never, never canst thou kiss*
> *Though winning near the goal—yet do not grieve;*
> *She cannot fade, though thou hast not thy bliss,*
> *For ever wilt thou love, and she be fair!"*

"I don't know about that unravished bit," I said. "There was someone."

But Ruth picked up her glass and began talking about poetry, reciting lines. As if words were a shield.

"She loved poetry," I say to Harold. "Especially Keats. She used to quote Keats all the time to Mother and me."

"Yes, she liked poetry," he replies, looking uncomfortable. "She could recite it by the mile but I'm afraid I never had an ear for it."

"There was one I called Ruth's poem. I don't know why. Maybe because of Anthony Carter. Ruth said he had a beautiful baritone voice.

Perhaps the self-same song that found a path
Through the sad heart of Ruth, when, sick for home
She stood in tears amid the alien corn ... "

He touches my arm with his fingertips and begins to edge away.

I want to say, and then there's the line, *"That I might drink, and leave the world unseen and with thee fade away into the forest dim"* Not with you, Harold. She wanted to fade away with the nightingale.

But I shake his hand and we say goodbye.

After this reception, when the dishes are washed, bottles collected and the paper cups thrown into the garbage, we'll sort through Ruth's personal belongings. Jenny showed them to me this morning: dresses, scarves, underwear heaped on the basement floor. The furniture, paintings, books will be appraised and sold at auction. Jenny doesn't want them. "Too much trouble," she said.

POLONAISE
Erin Mouré

Today I am the Polonaise my mother imagined,
devastating, but able to cook cabbages.
Knowing the uses of salt brine, & its smell in the air
at the sea, slightly industrial, mixed in
with the noise of birds, as noise is,
as smell is,
like my grandmother's hands that were the mark of
her profession, not separate from what she did,
none of these senses can be separated from the other,
Mrs. Farmer, Ma'am.

I don't speak a single Polish word,
except for *baba**

The table with its few grains of rice spread out near me, the knife with red jam
on it, a food reduced to colour, the light coming in the window
through the blind so beautiful I wish
I had a prism held out
to pull apart the colours

A stapler, addresses, a newspaper selling houses, homes

it says

A photograph of the novelist whom I loved, she was so
beautiful & harsh to me, sometimes
The picture of her in the country yard, the legs of her pants rolled,
the sunlight making her expression vanish

I think we should all stop drinking alcohol.
As a generation it will be our protest against the government,
an economic sanction against the forces of production,
including governments.

I'll tell you this much: the blue of the eyes
fades eventually.
Mine & my mother's eyes were once the same colour.

& it's only getting up in the morning that's devastating, my hair red
halo & in the fridge when I open it,
cabbages.

You knew it would end this way.
You knew I would come to the cabbages.**
Look at them, they are heavy & full.
You wouldn't have read this if I could not show them to you.

** Grandmother*
*** The cabbages were grown by the novelist, who comes from Montréal, not Poland*

THE WOMAN'S TESTIMONY
Sharon H. Nelson

we have been betrayed in america
betrayed by america
our jewboys no longer love us
they will not marry
a girl who makes excellent yeastdough

you have destroyed our art forms, taken away

the stuff of which we make our lives
you learned from other women
breasts are upturned
bellies flat
bodies long and lanky

how we suffer
your short and dumpy darkhaired women
saddled with america
saddled with nightmares of america
of never being
tall enough blonde enough light enough straight enough

we cannot feed you
you have taken the pots we inherited from our grandmothers
you have taken the recipes we inherited
and make us rewrite them
because you cannot read hebrew
because you do not want other women to look down on you:
to see a jewish nose is all right
to see your jewish eyes is all right
to suck your jewish cock is all right
but to see a jewish belly that is not all right

we die for you
we lie in our beds in the night fat and lumpy
and weep because you cannot love us
you, grandsons of men who loved our grandmothers
as vessels loaded heavy with the names of god

you slap our faces
we are not good for you
we are dark and private
doctors tell you
to break with us
break away from
the doughy arms the doughy food the constipation
dark and private women make in the brain

and then you dream

some myth of america
some myth of poland
starving hungry belabored poland
foul poland defiled poland dismembered poland
some ideal where
the chickens were fatter the fish were firmer the
prunes were plumper the raisins were sweeter

and when we serve you
such ritual delicacies
you will not eat

but in your dreams you come
back to the dishes your grandfathers dreamed to eat
that dream extending their bellies to america
that dream extending their shrunken bellies to america
not for themselves, not for their sons but for you

now you choose
to go hungry
hating progress
hating america
wishing
no one had ever
discovered america
wishing
women with shaved heads pendulous breasts would
put the plate on the table in order not to hand it to you
and you could eat of that mystery
eat and be filled

now you go hatless
dreaming of *shtreimls*
dream of fat ducks fat carp fat capons

you say we
are suffocating you suffocating you making you sick

we cannot cook for you
we are not good for you

you cannot eat

it is all because of us because of us because we are
too like our grandmothers unlike our grandmothers
:from this you make books

EATING CAJUN

Katherine Beeman

Eating
I feel at ease
the fire, pots
knives, table
between us—
shared

More juices than one
loose my tongue
cooking, not thumbs,
makes us human

We come now
from the same tribe.

LOVE WASN'T ALWAYS

Susan Musgrave

You've been out back butchering
all week. I cleave the heart and fry
the last of the black boar in hog's grease
until his blood weeps. You like your piece
done so there's something for your teeth
to sink into. I watch you eat
and later, when you sleep, your body
smelling of jerked meat and the juice
that's been pent up in me all week

I lie beside you thinking

love wasn't always this way with us—
ugly as love you called the one sow
who wouldn't die quickly on the slab
the way you wanted her to, trusting you—

love wasn't always this way. Sometimes
I thought it could last, like the first time
I came to you innocent as air

and you were waiting there.

PASTRY HOOK
Judith Stuart

Feeding grey dough into the mixer
she's surrounded by marriage:
his children   their noise
a narrow kitchen.

One slip—
dull   clogged with flour
the gold band on her finger
catches the bright
        revolving
          hook
tears flesh
plucks at fine bones.

She has always expected today
or another just like it ...
it's the absence of pain
that stuns her.

KITCHEN MURDER

Pat Lowther

Everything here's a weapon:
i pick up a meat fork,
imagine
plunging it in,
a heavy male
thrust

in two hands
i heft a stone-
ware plate, heavy
enough?

rummage the cupboards:
red pepper, rape-
seed oil, Drano

i'll wire myself
into a circuit:
the automatic perc,
the dishwater, the
socket above the sink

i'll smile an electric
eel smile: whoever touches
me is dead.

FROM *THE SACRIFICE*

Adele Wiseman

The warm wind of a summer night, tugging persistently at Abraham's beard, pulled him gradually out of his stupor. Slowly he raised his head and looked around him. He pushed himself away from the fencepost and took a few steps forward. He stopped again irresolutely. Where? The stars, distant and cool, posed indifferently in the sky. There was no command. Only the wind, threading the hair on his face, whispered teasingly of life.

Gradually his surroundings assumed a familiar shape. His eyes focused on a window on the top story of a familiar house. There came to him the whole puzzling aspect of his life to which she, this woman, seemed strangely related. Hadn't she lurked always in the shadow of their new life in the city? A shadow moved now, past her lighted kitchen window. Somewhere must be the thread to unravel the knotted skein. Others had been led. He would trust. He would follow. He would even, if necessary, demand.

He crossed the street. He started the long climb up the stairs. He was tired in every part of him, and every separate movement seemed to require his complete concentration. He labored upward under a growing heaviness, as though he were carrying his whole life on his back up an endless flight of stairs. With each step the burden grew heavier, the stairs longer, the object dimmer, and the need greater. Slowly his limbs carried him. Several times he had to stop to catch his breath. But he could not remain for long in the vacuum of no movement. He pushed immediately on again, for it was absolutely necessary to reach the top, as though something important, after this arduous journey, must await him.

He stood for a moment in the dark of the landing, uncertain, with no more stairs to climb. Automatically then he groped for the doorbell. The sharp clamor of the bell was startling. He began to ask himself what he was doing here, but the incipient question lost itself in the dream familiarity of the moment. It had occurred to him at various times in his life that a scene seemed to welcome him back, as though he had been and was come again. All of it, Laiah's face framed in the doorway, the instantaneous change of expression from frightened suspicion to surprised pleasure, nudged for a moment at his memory, as though this had been promised or foreseen, and was gone. What remained was her immediate presence, the way she pulled him, after one swift glance behind him at the door across the landing, into the apartment, and his own surprise and lack of surprise that he should be here.

"Oh!" Laiah gasped, leaning for a moment against the closed door and holding tightly onto his arm with one hand. "You gave me such a fright. People don't usually ring my doorbell at this time of night. But come in, come in." She moved along beside him into the light of the kitchen. "You're welcome any time. I always tell my friends that they can drop in whenever they wish. But did you lose the key? Well, never mind ... " Laiah could feel that she was prattling but could not, for the moment, attend carefully to what she was saying and deal with her internal feelings at the same time. The surprise, yes, she could have dispensed with the instant of fright when her doorbell had suddenly rung at this time of night. But his sudden appearance, disturbed—she could see he was disturbed; it must have been a struggle for him; she could understand that too. But here he was. She could hear herself chattering on, " ... midnight snack. Sometimes I can't get to sleep without it, would you believe it? Every time—it seems to me that every time you see me I'm eating. That's where the weight comes from. But I was just saying to myself that in the old country we didn't care about weight, did we? Everything was more natural there."

Inwardly she exulted. He had to come! All of a sudden the weight that she was talking about seemed to fall away from her. Her body felt an internal glow of pleasure such as she had not known since—oh, since a time that might return again. She could feel herself almost blushing under the disturbing steadiness of his eyes, and her own eyes slipped modestly to focus on his beard. Her fingertips tingled to caress that beard, and the tingling spread, an almost invisible shudder, through her body.

Was this love that she felt? She had asked herself this question before in an ironic way when she realized how seriously she had begun to take what she called her "teasing" of him when they had tea together, a teasing which consisted of finding out, of probing to see what he felt and could feel. Not love, she had insisted then, but a kind of game. What else could you do with a man who took you so rigidly at your word? She had urged him to sit and talk sometimes, so he sat and talked sometimes. Often she had had to laugh afterward. But then it had occurred to her, wasn't this a sign of respect for her as a person? Well, now he was ready for more, and now, in an excess of grateful emotion, she was willing to let it be love, let it be anything as long as she could go on feeling this way—young, alive, ready again to show the world. She had scarcely stretched out her finger really, she felt now, and he had come—not just anybody, this man. Look how he suffered from it, his face strained, his eyes dark—for her.

Laiah's eyes moved with pitying tenderness over his face. She had an impulse to lean forward and whisper those words, as though he might recognize and respond to them. "Little daughter," her bearded master had whispered as he had crawled in beside her on the stove. "Little father," she had whispered. But this was no Russian landlord to give her a pair of shoes and a hat with a feather. He would give her back more, all that had been taken since and all that had been freely given. Laiah felt suddenly, voraciously hungry.

Abraham waited, not quite sure in his mind what he waited for, not quite clear in his mind what he was here for. Her vivacity confused him. It was not what he had expected. What had he expected? While she was making a whole pile of sandwiches, as if she expected guests at this time of night, he looked around him, examining the tiny kitchen, then turned his gaze through the door into the darkness of the bed-living-room and the hall, as though perhaps someone or something hid waiting there. Nothing. He faced the sandwiches again, which Laiah was urging him to eat. He noticed with a craftsman's twinge of disapproval that she did not wipe the bread knife when she finished slicing a tomato, but left it on the table with tomato juice and seeds clinging to it. He couldn't eat, but watched her orange lips fold themselves over a sandwich like separate, living, predatory things. Laiah, chewing, shook her head and made sounds to indicate that the sandwich was good and to encourage him to eat.

Abraham shook his head again, picked up the knife, and with a paper napkin wiped it carefully dry. Beyond his uncertainty and his feeling that for some reason he had been brought into an alien place, he was conscious of a special awareness, of a reaching out of his senses. Sensations impinged on him sharply and separately. His eyes brooded on her face, on the masses of orange-auburn hair that lay on her shoulders now in little-girl fashion. This was so far removed from his own life, and yet—Her words had never sent him weeping into the streets. He felt an uprush of resentment against Ruth, and immediately a counterwashing sense of his own guilt, his own degradation.

"You won't have anything to eat or drink?" Laiah repeated. "Well, I won't press you." She wiped the breadcrumbs away from her mouth and pulled her chair closer to his corner of the table so that her knee brushed against his. Why didn't he speak? It flashed across her mind that he must have waited until his daughter-in-law and grandson were asleep and then sneaked out. How this must have been growing in him. And she hadn't even gauged it, really. She had thought that maybe—But who could tell, with him? Well, this secrecy was fine for now, for now it was all right. Later on—Already she could see herself dropping by the butcher shop to look in on her husband. Who would say anything to her in the kibitzarnia then? She might even consent to play a game occasionally if they would bite their vulgar tongues. And on the High Holidays she would go with him to the new synagogue they were building in the heights, to worship before the miracle Torah that her stepson had saved. She would sit with the richest women in town. But all that for later. For now—Laiah stretched her arms back; her breasts heaved forward momentarily. Then with a sigh she dropped her arms, wriggled her shoulders slightly, and leaned toward him, smiling.

"Well, Avrom, you've come to see me." She looked sideways at the table and added tenderly, "At last." Her voice was low, resonant. No use to be coy. He had come to her, distraught, disturbed. She would show him that she understood.

The words caught at his mind. He withdrew his eyes from her breasts, glancing at her guardedly, searching her face. Laiah put her soft hand over his, which toyed restlessly with the handle of the bread knife. "Yes," she began again as Abraham turned his eyes to her hand, which moved gently on his own—a soft, opulent hand with an odd red freckle here and there. The underlying throbbing in his fingers, on which was now superimposed the caress of her hand, seemed to draw all the nerves of his body to that hand. But this seemed to be taking place apart from him. In another region entirely his ears strained for her next words.

"Yes," said Laiah softly, caressingly, her words playing, like her hand. "I've waited a long time," she said a little chidingly.

"You have waited for me?" Now it seemed to him that she was beginning to reveal herself. If he listened now, if he could seize the right moment to ask the right question—It had been done in stranger ways. Something about this woman ...

How tense he was! All she had to do was to lean over and pull his beard, and she would be in his lap in a minute. No, not yet—not with him. "Those times you've come here and sat with me for a few minutes, I could see that you knew, that you had felt it too, underneath. Further back even, from the first time I saw you in Polsky's shop, I could feel it. There was an affinity between us. I've always known that we'd be friends someday, good friends—maybe even more. Polsky"—Laiah gestured with the hand that had lain on his own—"even Polsky was—" She shrugged. "How could he understand me really?" Laiah said this with satisfaction, and her hand dropped back onto Abraham's hand and squeezed it slightly.

"You've known?" he repeated as though to himself. "You've waited?"—through all those years when he had suffered and labored and sweated to rebuild? He began to be afraid. Something he had expected, something he had wanted to know. Now he felt suddenly that it was late at night; he wished suddenly that maybe she wouldn't go on. All this turmoil in one part of him, while another was deathly still, intent, listening.

"How often I've thought to myself this last little while," Laiah continued when he said no more, "what a crazy world we live in. All this time that we've known each other, you and I, aware of each other; how often we've moved toward each other a little bit, feeling that somehow there was an affinity, that we were made to come together." Still he was silent. "I'm not hiding anything from you, Avrom. I know you must have heard stories. I was married once—better not to talk of that now. What do people understand? And besides, can you say"—she faced him challengingly—"that there are things you don't regret?"

"You have never had any children?" he said.

The statement—she didn't know whether it was a question or a statement—seemed so totally unrelated that Laiah was for a moment startled out of her train of thought and gave him a very puzzled look. But almost immediately another possibility occurred to her, and she laughed outright at the absurdity. Did he think she was a spring chicken? "I am not likely to have any accidents," she said. "Even if I had to worry I could handle that. I am not anxious for any more responsibilities either. I like children, mind you. But after all—And, you know, I'm not as young as I once was either." She couldn't help the coyness. Could he be so naïve? She felt again very young and carefree. She looked at him amorously, caressingly.

He could hardly look at her. It was as though he were seized up by something within himself, by a strong hand that gripped his insides tightly, then released them, gripped and released and gripped them again, each time more tightly, so that he seemed to rise and fall on a mounting wave of nausea, accompanied by a feeling of self-hatred that had grown on him from the moment, ages back, when he had left Ruth and the house.

"All my life," he burst out, "I have wanted only one thing: to grow, to discover, to build. Of all the voices that are given to a man I took the voice of praise; of all the paths I chose the path of creation, of life. I thought that merely in the choosing I had discarded all else. I thought that I could choose. One by one, with such ease, they were stripped from me. Wherever I look there is a shadow, a shadow that all my life I did not see, I tried to ignore. The shadow grows about me, filling in the corners of my emptiness, darkening my desire. You've waited for me, empty, all this time."

Laiah had listened patiently. She had heard, in an occasional word dropped around the kibitzarnia, that Abraham was not quite the same as he had been once, since his son had died. She could understand that. If he wandered off sometimes, as though trying to argue something out with himself, that was all right too. She could ignore it. But she was glad when his rambling took an understandable turn. "Yes, I've waited." He was right. What did the others really mean now? It was so simple. She gestured with her arms, empty and waiting.

"Why?" the question, momentous, was whispered from his throat.

Laiah didn't answer. Her eyes, large and moist, widened under his own. The game was deeply exciting to her now. Not since a very long time ago had she played it with such enjoyment, had it seemed so new, with whispered words and shadowy nuances. And he took it so seriously.

She didn't answer either. His impatience grew. "Why?" He was on his feet suddenly, leaning over her.

Startled at what was almost a shout, Laiah recoiled an instant. Then, looking up at him, conscious that her flimsy housecoat was open and that her nightgown was even flimsier, Laiah paused before she said defiantly, laughing a little, "Because." With a sudden gliding movement she pushed one hand through his beard, up his cheek and around to the back of his neck. At the same time she came to her feet and pressed herself up against him. "Because of this." She laughed deep, throaty laughter and moved against him. Abraham swayed against the table.

"Closer," Laiah murmured into his ear, "like one."

"Like one?" he repeated dazedly, feeling as though he really were sinking into the mass of her flesh. She was pressed up so close to him that it was almost as though she really were a part of him. "Why did you wait," he managed, "right from the beginning, watching me?"

She laughed again, brushing his beard with her lips.

"Because you knew?"

She laughed compliantly. "You ask so many questions. Haven't I told you? Of course I knew."

"Like one," he whispered. The other part of him—that was empty, unbelieving, the negation of life, the womb of death, the black shadow that yet was clothed in the warm, tantalizing flesh of life. Now she pressed herself closer to him, inward. She was bent slightly backward so that with one arm he was forced to support her, achingly, to keep her from falling. They swayed together, he back against the table and she falling now against him. His free hand reached behind him for support on the table. He felt a sharp pain in his palm as the blade of the bread knife bit into his hand. He moved his hand, which had suddenly become sticky, and brushed it feebly against his trousers before he braced it again on the table.

No matter what a man did, no matter how hard he tried, no matter how great his desire, was it all reduced to this, to a dream pantomime of life, a shadow of meaning? Did he come at last to accept the shadow, to embrace the emptiness, to acknowledge his oneness with the fruit without seed, with death, his other self?

Laughing, Laiah had reached up her other hand and was tangling her fingers in his beard. "Little father," she murmured in Ukrainian, "will you be good to me?" Her fingers gripped his beard, and she began to pull lightly. "Come into the bedroom," she whispered into his ear. Her fingers tightened. Her body undulating, she tried to pull him by its very movement after her.

"Don't!" he almost shouted. "Don't touch my beard."

"Shhhh." She giggled.

His beard, where she was tugging it, began to tingle in every hair root. His arm that was around her was painfully tensed, the pains shooting up and down raspingly from his shoulder. "Don't." He tightened his hold and pulled backward. Isaac had grasped his beard. The thought of Isaac made him pull his head back sharply and twist it frantically, trying to dislodge her hand.

"Does it hurt? Hurry, then." Laiah laughed. "You have to get home sometime, don't you? You don't want your Ruth to know you've been out all night. She'll be waiting for you," Laiah teased, "if you don't hurry. Listen, we can talk another time. I trust you. I'm not worried about you."

Her words brought back to him his scene with Ruth. His mind zigzagged back and forth from Ruth to the present moment, rebounding from the unreality of each. "I've hurt her," he mumbled.

Why did he hesitate? His hesitation caused a misgiving to stir inside of her. She didn't want any misgivings! She threw back her head and leaned against his arm, her hair flowing downward, her lips slightly parted, so that, she knew, he could see into the front of her housecoat. Then she raised herself slowly forward and, opening her eyes wide, looked into his. The nether part of her body moved all the while with practiced, lazy voluptuousness. "Do what you want with me," she urged. "I'm yours."

Abraham looked into the auburn eyes, the strange, indrawing, familiar auburn eyes. Again the sense, as of some past memory just beyond his grasp, nagged at his mind.

Still he did nothing. "Don't you love me?" she said, tugging his beard slightly to pull him out of his trancelike stillness. "Say you love me," she urged. "Come" Above everything else she wanted now that her moment should not become absurd. She stifled a resentment that was growing toward him for allowing it to begin to seem so.

He pulled his head back. Love—that word too played along his consciousness as though it belonged somewhere, and he could not quite place it.

"Come," she whispered. "I won't wait much longer." She gave a more violent pull that almost toppled them both over. He grabbed wildly back at the table again; bread crumbs glued themselves to his raw palm and stung. His hand grasped finally the smooth handle of the bread knife. He managed to keep his balance, but she moved a step backward, taking him with her.

"You want me," Laiah was whispering almost pleadingly, tightening the arm that was about his neck. "I can feel that you want me. I've known all along that you wanted me."

"All I have ever wanted," he protested distractedly, "is to build for my sons, to grow."

"Forget," she said impatiently, "forget all that. They're dead; we're alive."

Just like that she came out with it, just like that, as if it were something good, while her body heat glued her to him, stifling him, trying to stifle his memory. They were dead, and he was lost, and the present was as a dream in which he could find neither them nor himself but only this insidious excitement, urging him to forget.

"Avrom." There was an almost childish petulance in Laiah's voice that tried further to confuse him.

What are you? he wanted to ask her. Who sent you to mock me? Who? And the thought leaped, as though it had been waiting, electrifying, terrifying, to his mind. One he could seek who knew, who would speak if he asked, who would give if he offered—if he had the courage.

Suddenly Laiah sensed a change in him. She realized that she was no longer maintaining the embrace but that it was he who now strained her against him, holding her up. She felt a thrill of relief as his eyes moved with awareness over her. "Come into the bedroom," she murmured again. She let her eyes flutter closed under the ardency of his gaze.

Looking at her then, he was lifted out of time and place. Lifetimes swept by, and he stood dreaming on a platform, apart, gazing at her with fear growing in his heart, and somewhere his Master, waiting. As in a dream, the knife was in his hand, the prayer was on his lips. Praying over her, at some neutral point in time, he saw her as though for the first time, and yet as though he had always seen her thus, saw her as something holy as she lay back, a willing burden, to offer, to receive, as once another ... From inside him a tenderness swelled toward her, and for a moment he forgot his fear and felt as though he were almost on the point of some wonderful revelation.

"*... Eloheinu Meloch Hoaul'om ...* "

Laiah heard with amazement the Hebrew words. Even over this he has to make a blessing. Her lips twitched to a smile.

... She was laughing at him, still teasing him, his despair wreathed in smiles, the negation of his life. And yet there was something in him that ached to see how under her eyelids her eyebulbs were large and fine. Her forehead wrinkled and was somehow sad, like that of some time-forgotten creature that had crept out to seek the sun. Her hair flowed endlessly downward, falling gently over his arm. All this he could see, in the sacred place where he stood, and he could feel that it was trying to speak to him, to explain itself, for the moment was near.

Now, now was the time, in the stillness, as he stood once again, terrified, fascinated, on the brink of creation where life and death waver toward each other, reiterating his surrender; now was the time for the circle to close, to enclose him in its safety, in its peace. There must be a word, with them, in the room, hovering to descend. Almost it reached him there, beyond his mind, like the voice of a child, stuttering, excited, trying to break through the barrier of sound. He strained to hear.

"For God's sake!" In an excess of impatience Laiah's hand tugged sharply at his beard. "Hurry up!" Her voice jarred like a harsh command. "My back is—"

Even as his arm leaped, as though expressing its own exasperation, its own ambition, its own despair, the Word leaped too, illuminating her living face, caressing the wonder of the pulse in her throat, flinging itself against the point of the knife. Life! cried Isaac as the blood gushed from her throat and her frantic fingers gripped first, then relaxed and loosened finally their hold on his beard. Life! pleaded Jacob as Abraham stared, horrified, into her death-glazed eyes. Life! chanted Moses as he smelled, sickened, the hot blood that had spurted onto his beard. Life! rose the chorus as the knife clattered to the ground, and the word rebounded from the walls and the floors and the ceiling, beating against the sudden unnatural stillness of the room, thundering in accusation against him. Weightier in death, Laiah pulled him to the ground.

Kneeling, he cradled Laiah in his lap. "Please," he whispered. With one hand he propped her head, which sagged grotesquely, forward to try to close the gaping wound in her throat. "Please," he repeated hoarsely. With the index finger of his other hand he moved her slack eyelids gently up and down. "Live!" he begged her. He tried with his hand to cover up the wound, shuddering at the sticky wetness of her warm blood. "Live," he pleaded, shaking her a little, and had to grip her head more tightly to prevent it from lolling over. "Please!" Anguished, he tried to breathe on her still lips. "Live!"

He wept, his face against hers. "Live! ... Live ... "

Very early in the morning Jenny, agog to find out who the visitor was that Laiah had had so late last night—she had been awakened by the doorbell but had rushed to her door too late to see—knocked, as was her habit, on Laiah's door. Then she knocked more loudly and tried the doorknob. The door opened, and Jenny, after wondering briefly whether she should just walk right in—after all, her friend might not be alone—giggled inside herself and decided that that would be the shock of her life. It was.

FROM *THE EDIBLE WOMAN*
Margaret Atwood

"The surface on which you work (preferably marble), the tools, the ingredients and your fingers should be chilled throughout the operation ... " (Recipe for Puff Pastry in I.S. Rombauer and M.R. Becker, *The Joy of Cooking.*)

Marian had just got home and was struggling with her wrinkled dress, trying to get the zipper undone, when the phone rang. She knew who it would be.

"Hello?" she said.

Peter's voice was icy with anger. "Marian, where the hell have you been? I've been phoning everywhere." He sounded hung-over.

"Oh," she said with airy casualness, "I've been somewhere else. Sort of out."

He lost control. "Why the hell did you leave the party? You really disrupted the evening for me. I was looking for you to get in the group picture and you were gone, of course I couldn't make a big production of it with all those people there but after they'd gone home I looked all over for you, your friend Lucy and I got in the car and drove up and down the streets and we called your place half a dozen times, we were both so worried. Damn nice of her to take the trouble, it's nice to know there are *some* considerate women left around ... "

I'll bet it is, Marian thought with a momentary twinge of jealousy, remembering Lucy's silver eyelids; but out loud she said, "Peter, please don't get upset. I just stepped outside for a breath of fresh air and something else came up, that's all. There is absolutely nothing to get upset about. There have been no catastrophes."

"What do you mean, upset!" he said. "You shouldn't go wandering around the streets at night, you might get *raped,* if you're going to do these things and god knows it isn't the first time why the hell can't you think of other people once in a while? You could at least have told me where you were, your parents called me long-distance, they're frantic because you weren't on the bus and what was I supposed to tell them?"

Oh yes, she thought; she had forgotten about that. "Well, I'm perfectly all right," she said.

"But where were you? When we'd discovered you'd left and I started quietly asking people if they'd seen you I must say I got a pretty funny story from that prince-charming friend of yours, Trevor or whatever the hell his name is. Who's this guy he was telling me about anyway?"

"Please, Peter," she said, "I just hate talking about things like this over the phone." She had a sudden desire to tell him the whole story, but what good would that do since nothing had been proved or accomplished? Instead she said, "What time is it?"

"Two-thirty," he said, his voice surprised into neutrality by this appeal to simple fact.

"Well, why don't you come over a bit later? Maybe about five-thirty. For tea. And then we can talk it all over." She made her voice sweet, conciliatory. She was conscious of her own craftiness. Though she hadn't made any decisions she could feel she was about to make one and she needed time.

"Well, all right," he said peevishly, "but it better be good." They hung up together.

Marian went into the bedroom and took off her clothes; then she went downstairs and took a quick bath. The lower regions were silent; the lady down below was probably brooding in her dark den or praying for the swift destruction of Ainsley by heavenly thunderbolts. In a spirit approaching gay rebellion Marian neglected to erase her bath-tub ring.

What she needed was something that avoided words, she didn't want to get tangled up in a discussion. Some way she could know what was real: a test, simple and direct as litmus-paper. She finished dressing—a plain grey wool would be appropriate—and put on her coat, then located her everyday purse and counted the money. She went out to the kitchen and sat down at the table to make herself a list, but threw down the pencil after she had written several words. She knew what she needed to get.

In the supermarket she went methodically up and down the aisles, relentlessly outmanoeuvring the muskrat-furred ladies, edging the Saturday children to the curb, picking the things off the shelves. Her image was taking shape. Eggs. Flour. Lemons for the flavour. Sugar, icing-sugar, vanilla, salt, food-colouring. She wanted everything new, she didn't want to use anything that was already in the house. Chocolate—no, cocoa, that would be better. A glass tube full of round silver decorations. Three nesting plastic bowls, teaspoons, aluminium cake-decorator and a cake tin. Lucky, she thought, they sell almost everything in supermarkets these days. She started back towards the apartment, carrying her paper bag.

Sponge or angel-food? she wondered. She decided on sponge. It was more fitting.

She turned on the oven. That was one part of the kitchen that had not been overrun by the creeping skin-disease-covering of dirt, mostly because they hadn't been using it much recently. She tied on an apron and rinsed the new bowls and the other new utensils under the tap, but did not disturb any of the dirty dishes. Later for them. Right now she didn't have time. She dried the things and began to crack and separate the eggs, hardly thinking, concentrating all her attention on the movements of her hands, and then when she was beating and sifting and folding, on the relative times and the textures. Spongecake needed a light hand. She poured the batter into the tin and drew a fork sideways through it to break the large air-bubbles. As she slid the tin into the oven she almost hummed with pleasure. It was a long time since she had made a cake.

While the cake was in the oven baking she re-washed the bowls and mixed the icing. An ordinary butter icing, that would be the best. Then she divided the icing into three parts in the three bowls. The largest portion she left white, the next one she tinted a bright pink, almost red, with the red food-colouring she had bought, and the last one she made dark brown by stirring cocoa into it.

What am I going to put her on? she thought when she had finished. I'll have to wash a dish. She unearthed a long platter from the very bottom of the stack of plates in the sink and scoured it thoroughly under the tap. It took quite a lot of detergent to get the scum off.

She tested the cake; it was done. She took it out of the oven and turned it upside-down to cool.

She was glad Ainsley wasn't home: she didn't want any interference with what she was going to do. In fact it didn't look as though Ainsley had been home at all. There was no sign of her green dress. In her room a suitcase was lying open on the bed where she must have left it the night before. Some of the surface flotsam was eddying into it, as though drawn by a vortex. Marian wondered in passing how Ainsley was ever going to cram the random contents of the room into anything as limited and rectilineal as a set of suitcases.

While the cake was cooling she went into the bedroom and tidied her hair, pulling it back and pinning it to get rid of the remains of the hairdresser's convolutions. She felt lightheaded, almost dizzy: it must be the lack of sleep and the lack of food. She grinned into the mirror, showing her teeth.

The cake wasn't cooling quickly enough. She refused to put it into the refrigerator though. It would pick up the smells. She took it out of the tin and set it on the clean platter, opened the kitchen window, and stuck it out on the snowy sill. She knew what happened to cakes that were iced warm—everything melted.

She wondered what time it was. Her watch was still on the top of the dresser where she had left it the day before but it had run down. She didn't want to turn on Ainsley's transistor, that would be too distracting. She was getting jittery already. There used to be a number you could phone ... but anyway she would have to hurry.

She took the cake off the sill, felt it to see if it was cool enough, and put it on the kitchen table. Then she began to operate. With the two forks she pulled it in half through the middle. One half she placed flat side down on the platter. She scooped out part of it and made a head with the section she had taken out. Then she nipped in a waist at the sides. The other half she pulled into strips for the arms and legs. The spongy cake was pliable, easy to mould. She stuck all the separate members together with white icing, and used the rest of the icing to cover the shape she had constructed. It was bumpy in places and had too many crumbs in the skin, but it would do. She reinforced the feet and ankles with tooth-picks.

Now she had a blank white body. It looked slightly obscene, lying there soft and sugary and featureless on the platter. She set about clothing it, filling the cake-decorator with bright pink icing. First she gave it a bikini, but that was too sparse. She filled in the midriff. Now it had an ordinary bathing-suit, but that still wasn't exactly what she wanted. She kept extending, adding to top and bottom, until she had a dress of sorts. In a burst of exuberance she added a row of ruffles around the neckline, and more ruffles at the hem of the dress. She made a smiling lush-lipped pink mouth and pink shoes to match. Finally she put five pink fingernails on each of the amorphous hands.

The cake looked peculiar with only a mouth and no hair or eyes. She rinsed out the cake-decorator and filled it with chocolate icing. She drew a nose, and two large eyes, to which she appended many eyelashes and two eyebrows, one above each eye. For emphasis she made a line demarcating one leg from the other, and similar lines to separate the arms from the body. The hair took longer. It involved masses of intricate baroque scrolls and swirls, piled high on the head and spilling down over the shoulders.

The eyes were still blank. She decided on green—the only other possibilities were red and yellow, since they were the only other colours she had—and with a toothpick applied two irises of green food-colouring. Now there were only the globular silver decorations to add. One went in each eye, for a pupil. With the others she made a floral design on the pink dress, and stuck a few in the hair. Now the woman looked like an elegant antique china figurine. For an instant she wished she had bought some birthday candles; but where could they be put? There was really no room for them. The image was complete.

Her creation gazed up at her, its face doll-like and vacant except for the small silver glitter of intelligence in each green eye. While making it she had been almost gleeful, but now, contemplating it, she was pensive. All that work had gone into the lady and now what would happen to her?

"You look delicious," she told her. "Very appetizing. And that's what will happen to you; that's what you get for being food." At the thought of food her stomach contracted. She felt a certain pity for her creature but she was powerless now to do anything about it. Her fate had been decided. Already Peter's footsteps were coming up the stairs.

Marian had a swift vision of her own monumental silliness, of how infantile and undignified she would seem in the eyes of any rational observer. What kind of game did she think she was playing? But that wasn't the point, she told herself nervously, pushing back a strand of hair. Though if Peter found her silly she would believe it, she would accept his version of herself, he would laugh and they would sit down and have a quiet cup of tea.

She smiled gravely at Peter as he came up out of the stairwell. The expression on his face, a scowl combined with a jutting chin, meant he was still angry. He was wearing a costume suitable for being angry in: the suit stern, tailored, remote, but the tie a paisley with touches of sullen maroon.

"Now what's all this ... " he began.

"Peter, why don't you go into the living room and sit down? I have a surprise for you. Then we can have a talk if you like." She smiled at him again.

He was puzzled, and forgot to sustain his frown; he must have been expecting an awkward apology. But he did as she suggested. She remained in the doorway for a moment, looking almost tenderly at the back of his head resting against the chesterfield. Now that she had seen him again, the actual Peter, solid as ever, the fears of the evening before had dwindled to foolish hysteria and the flight to Duncan had become a stupidity, an evasion; she could hardly remember what he looked like. Peter was not the enemy after all, he was just a normal human being like most other people. She wanted to touch his neck, tell him that he shouldn't get upset, that everything was going to be all right. It was Duncan that was the mutation.

But there was something about his shoulders. He must have been sitting with his arms folded. The face on the other side of that head could have belonged to anyone. And they all wore clothes of real cloth and had real bodies: those in the newspapers, those still unknown, waiting for their chance to aim from the upstairs window; you passed them on the streets every day. It was easy to see him as normal and safe in the afternoon, but that didn't alter things. The price of this version of reality was testing the other one.

She went into the kitchen and returned, bearing the platter in front of her, carefully and with reverence, as though she was carrying something sacred in a procession, an icon or the crown on a cushion in a play. She knelt, setting the platter on the coffee-table in front of Peter.

"You've been trying to destroy me, haven't you," she said. "You've been trying to assimilate me. But I've made you a substitute, something you'll like much better. This is what you really wanted all along, isn't it? I'll get you a fork," she added somewhat prosaically.

Peter stared from the cake to her face and back again. She wasn't smiling.

His eyes widened in alarm. Apparently he didn't find her silly.

When he had gone—and he went quite rapidly, they didn't have much of a conversation after all, he seemed embarrassed and eager to leave and even refused a cup of tea—she stood looking down at the figure. So Peter hadn't devoured it after all. As a symbol it had definitely failed. It looked up at her with its silvery eyes, enigmatic, mocking, succulent.

Suddenly she was hungry. Extremely hungry. The cake after all was only a cake.

She picked up the platter, carried it to the kitchen table and located a fork. "I'll start with the feet," she decided.

She considered the first mouthful. It seemed odd but most pleasant to be actually tasting and chewing and swallowing again. Not bad, she thought critically; needs a touch more lemon though.

Already the part of her not occupied with eating was having a wave of nostalgia for Peter, as though for a style that had gone out of fashion and was beginning to turn up on the sad Salvation Army clothes racks. She could see him in her mind, posed jauntily in the foreground of an elegant salon with chandeliers and draperies, impeccably dressed, a glass of scotch in one hand; his foot was on the head of a stuffed lion and he had an eyepatch over one eye. Beneath one arm was strapped a revolver. Around the margin was an edging of gold scrollwork and slightly above Peter's left ear was a thumbtack. She licked her fork meditatively. He would definitely succeed.

She was halfway up the legs when she heard footsteps, two sets of them, coming up the stairs. Then Ainsley appeared in the kitchen doorway with Fischer Symthe's furry head behind her. She still had on her bluegreen dress, much the worse for wear. So was she: her face was haggard and in only the past twenty-four hours her belly seemed to have grown noticeably rounder.

"Hi," said Marian, waving her fork at them. She speared a chunk of pink thigh and carried it to her mouth.

Fischer had leaned against the wall and closed his eyes as soon as he reached the top of the stairs, but Ainsley focussed on her. "Marian, what have you got there?" She walked over to see. "It's a woman—a woman made of cake!" She gave Marian a strange look.

Marian chewed and swallowed. "Have some," she said, "it's really good. I made it this afternoon."

Ainsley's mouth opened and closed, fishlike, as though she was trying to gulp down the full implication of what she saw. "Marian!" she exclaimed at last, with horror. "You're rejecting your femininity!"

Marian stopped chewing and stared at Ainsley, who was regarding her through the hair that festooned itself over her eyes with wounded concern, almost with sternness. How did she manage it, that stricken attitude, that high seriousness? She was almost as morally earnest as the lady down below.

Marian looked back at her platter. The woman lay there, still smiling glassily, her legs gone. "Nonsense," she said. "It's only a cake." She plunged her fork into the carcass, neatly severing the body from the head.

I SPY MOTHER CUPBOARD

Maureen Harris

for baby Katharine

Here comes Mother Cupboard
arms spread wide to scoop us up
dispensing oceanic love
with the milk and honey
flowing from her breasts.

From the pockets of her flowered housecoat
she hands us chocolate, apples, raisins,
fresh bread and butter—
all we need of comfort.

With a snap of her fingers
raspberries leap whole and glowing
into the bowl of cream
and every spoonful whispers *love, love.*

She sings aloud in the kitchen
smelling of yeast and cinnamon.
It is always sunny.
The walls are yellow and smiling.
We smile, spirits rising with the dough.
Shaped by those strong floury hands
we grow happy, unafraid.

Her table groans with pleasure
under its burden of feasts.
We flutter round it
mouths gaping like birds,
creep closer into the circle of food
great arms, ample breasts, wide lap.

Mother Cupboard will feed us.
She loves us, gathering us into those great arms
folding us into her cupboard heart
where it is warm and dark and we can dream

dreams to fatten on flavoured with her.
We know. The real taste is her.

BONES AND BREAD
Su Croll

teeth I'm most afraid of clacking wooden teeth and the grinding
the grinding of that last huge mouth

you must manage to wrench enough flavour
from every morsel you must manage to keep
the sweet bubbles of fat breaking the moving
surface you might slip a lump of sugar
onto your tongue and suck the hot liquid
suck the hot liquid through it

eating and there she is eating me like religion eating me
eating me for breakfast spitting out the seeds pushing
back the plate and putting my bones on the window sill
to dry saved for wishing bones or crushed for home remedies

food (definition)
food is what is stuffed into you from the first moment
you were strapped on her mouth covering your mouth force
feeding all of what could not be fitted into her life
passing it by some anonymous grey feeding tube into your life
and you were not given time to swallow there is no time
to swallow and you want to choke but learn to breathe
through your nose to let a bubble of air inside your lungs
hold you up and you can tread water you can tread water, you know
and if you ever need to go under if treading water
becomes too difficult you can go under
you can go under and keep your eyes open and watch

trinity the dead may become meals for the living we carry our giants
we carry our giants with us what misery in that last huge mouth

eating (a quickening)
saved for wishbones crushed for home remedies

the bones are used   the dead are a meal
eaten by the living if they are lucky
the bones are used   how many ways must I say it
mother's milk: suck it through sugar   the bones are used
the bones are used   the bones are used

eating   (easter sunday)
I guess you can see my need   this is all supposed to add up
to redemption   not a mouth alternately stuffed with lilies
and dirty linen that's been allowed to flap for years
you've got to find some way to clasp your hands

you've got to locate some holy water   I guess you can see
my need   pulling and sucking at my hungry fingers   mother
hens all wanting to press me back together again   to press me
back into shape   stuffed and wired together like someone's idea
of a christmas turkey   like someone's idea of an easter lamb

even the bones are used I said even the bones are used

(notes)

pronouns ground along with the title
the addition of images
problem with gender, with *mother*
setting up fear that doesn't come through

GROUND READER DIRECTION THEY SAID
food imagery connecting with authorship they said
or 'she' or universal third section
reader looking for her place   looking for his place
place reader they said   ground reader they said

if these are stanzas   expectations are set up
where is the connection between the three stomachs
it is probably three poems   not one clear image
probably a trinity and even the bones are used

define character they said   I   you   she   and cut back
to propagate growth   propagate using disease

free plants   title to ground   and find more domestic
imagery to fill it out   to fill it up   or split it
or number it but make it more than a trinity

even the bones are used I said but even the bones are used

MARRIED WOMAN'S COMPLAINT

Marilyn Bowering

He is always greedy,
eating clams
and salal berries.
He has salmon bones
stuck in his hair.
He skinned the children
and brought them to me
to cook—
I have bad eyesight.

I am rock
from the hips down.
You might wake me up
by walking over me.
Though this rock
is strong,
he
can split it.

I go with him too easily,
My organs
flounder
in their fluid bath.
There is whistling all around
setting traps.
If you are called,
keep still.
These creatures
are always trying
to turn us around.

I was whistling once
at night,
now
here I am
with him.

SUMMER IN FULL BLOOM
Beverley Harris

On hands and knees into the kitchen
you came creeping up my skirt,
I was busy making salad for supper
my arms pumping up and down chopping onions
my eyes straight ahead unseeing
but you came creeping up my skirt
like an escaped prisoner, like
a bad boy you were eating a potato
you stole from the neighbour's garden
skin and all, earth on your mouth
your head between my legs, you had
the baby with you, she was laughing at you
your lips starchy, you were licking
your fingers, stroking my thighs
as the baby tickled the cat with a twig
from the apple tree, they were chasing
each other through my legs, the cat's fur
was warm from the sun, you were blowing bubbles
for the baby, rainbows bouncing on my skin,
your fingers slipping up, belly laughing,
when hot little flies came in from the garden
the baby reaching to catch one,
you took one in your mouth
your lips were buzzing, the fly
trying to get free, the baby imitated you
and then you couldn't stop laughing, shaking
my skirt, my tent of flowers, open,
my lovely tent of flowers.

CHOCOLATE: A LOVE POEM

Susan Glickman

Because he says it's his favourite thing after me
and the way he loves it
I'd be flattered to come second.
Because of the steadfast devotion with which he regards it.
Because of the purity of his greed;
his great happiness before, during, and after.

Because it is dark and mysterious
and native to this hemisphere.
Because the Aztecs cooked with it
and the Mexicans still make of it a sauce
which gives zest to the mild taste of poultry
and provides rich colour on the plate.

Because he is so easily made happy.
Because strawberries dipped in it are both decorative
and delicious.
Because the only doorprize I ever won
was a chocolate rabbit at the Montreal Children's Theatre
one Easter when I was twelve.
Because everyone eats the ears first.

Because it is best when partly bitter.
Because this is a natural metaphor.
Because seventeenth-century Jamaican sailors
named the northwest wind after it.
Because of the way he always thinks of buying some suddenly
while we are driving home
as if it is a novelty he has only just discovered.

Because if you serve it for dessert it doesn't matter
what happened to the main course.
Because the word "cookie" sounds silly
and nobody notices.
Because we all think everyone else
is a grownup.

Because I particularly relish its aroma.
Because it is the best possible beverage after skiing.
Because it is clearly a force to be reckoned with.
Because of his unwavering ardour and the purity
of his greed.

HIS KITCHEN
Annharte

My father was my mother. He took over
cooking and childcare when she left.
At first, our food came from a can.
He wouldn't let me near the kitchen.
I had to learn to cook at school.
He improved. I asked friends over.
He didn't mind. He heaped up potatoes
and gave us canned fruit for dessert.
Only for a short time, did we go out
almost every night to a restaurant.
Even now, I know I am in his kitchen.
A paint scraper sits with the utensils.
I want to put it back with the tools.
It is his egglifter so I know better.
Holiday dinners he cooks and I make gravy.
Hard to forget he's both mother and father.

MURIEL BETSINA, 46, YELLOWKNIFE, N.W.T.
– Interviewed by Laurie Sarkadi

Muriel Betsina has a husband, seven children and six grandchildren, but her tiny wooden house in Yellowknife's Dene Indian community has become home to a much larger brood. The boxy bungalow looks like every other on the dusty street on Latham Island, void of grass or landscaping, at the bottom of the hill leading into Rainbow Valley. "The Valley" got its name because the Dene were given brightly coloured paints to spruce up their ramshackle houses for a 1967 visit from Queen Elizabeth.

The steady stream of family and friends who come to Muriel's home enter by the side door leading into the kitchen, a brown, cluttered room with a large wood-burning stove, dominated by a homemade plywood table hemmed by 11 chairs. The far wall is devoted to a junior encyclopedia set, a bible, dictionary and other reference books. There's a sink without a faucet, a microwave, one of two fridges (the other is in the living room) and a portable cassette player which blasts out local native news and country music. Here Muriel, the diminutive woman with twinkling eyes and an infectious giggle, a self-professed "healer" of broken spirits, talks about herself and the room where she has spent most of her life.

Muriel Betsina

I was born in Fort Norman, near Willow Lake in the bush. We moved to Yellowknife in 1959. We lived in a big log house. There was no such thing as a living room or a kitchen, it was just one big area. There are nine or ten people living here (in Yellowknife). We have four bedrooms. Half of my kids, they sleep on the couch or the floor. I don't have no running water. In the wintertime I have two huge water barrels and the water delivery comes to fill my barrel twice a week. In the summertime I got water running outside. That's how come I got my automatic washer outside, but I don't got no running water in the house.

It seems like hard work but I'm so used to it. It's just daily, simple life, you know, that's what keeps me busy all the time and I like it. If I had everything automatic then I think I'd be bored, very bored.

Today the children make their own lunch. Everybody slept in. I've got fish chowder, if anybody wants some chowder. Care for a bowl? It's really nice. And a piece of bannock if you want? If we're out in the bush in the camp they (the children) cook bannock on a stick. And they cook little odd things over the fire. You put the dough on the tip and you have to turn your stick.

Everybody always eats in this house. This place is just like a restaurant. They can just eat, there's always extra food all the time. I'm very grateful. There's always something in the oven or something on top of the stove. I learned from my parents. My mom and dad, I remember ever since I was young, they always had extra food when they cooked. There was always people coming in and they were always feeding people. And as soon as a person came in, right away my mom said, 'Give him tea', and then right away she asked, 'Did you eat, are you hungry?'

Sometimes there was nothing on the stove and she encouraged us to cook something right away. That's what all Dene people are like. They come in and they just help themselves to tea and coffee, they don't ask.

I learned (cooking) from my mother. I never used recipes. I just put everything together, just throw anything together, it always turns out good. Country food (wild game and fish) is what I like best. It seems like every time you buy meat from the store you either have to spice it or it's too rich. But country food is good, you can make stew, you can fry it, cook it anyways, make soup out of the broth.

We have fish nets. Every time people see us lift the nets, then right away there's a bunch of people at my door asking for fish. Most of the time I feed the old people at the old folk's home and the hospital. I know how old people want their fish, some of them like boiled fish, maybe a little bit of salt flavour.

From December until April my boys go hunting. They go for caribou. We get a lot of caribou. We freeze our meat. They go for moose sometimes too, if they're lucky they'll kill one. We set rabbit snares all year round. Very, very seldom I have canned stuff.

At suppertime, we eat dinner about 7:00 and I cook one hot bannock each meal, so about 6:30 I start cooking one.

In the morning I get up at 6:00. Until 10:00 or 11:00 when I go to bed, all my time is here. I sew in here, everything from footwear right down to jackets, hats, mittens, everything. I always liked the kitchen. I don't know, it's like I can't get away from my kitchen, and I have a big table too, I just push everything away and do my cutting here. And it still is too small sometimes. My kids are grown up now and when they bring their families, their wives and children, we have to sit elbow to elbow. One Thanksgiving there was 18 squeezing in.

This kitchen means everything to me so far, you know. It gives me a really happy atmosphere. It's a meeting place, everything. It's just like a conference room. Everybody uses my kitchen door all the time. I teach my children how to cook, how to sew. A lot of the time people come here, especially young parents, they come here for counselling. They bring their little ones here and I just say let them be. There's nothing they can destroy in here.

Sometimes they've had spousal assault, sometimes drug and alcohol problems, sometimes they just need healing. Some of them are hurt, some of them don't know what to do with their lives. I think it gets to that point where a lot of them want to give up life. I'm always encouraging them to keep one step ahead of themselves and (telling them) that they're a special person. And I always tell them I care. There is someone that loves them, then it's me. Everything's confidential. People always come to me.

From '79 to '84 I was a drug and alcohol counsellor, but I got burned out, so when you feel like you're getting burned out, you always learn as a professional to step aside and let someone else take over. Also, my children are grown up now and I don't need the money as much as I did when I was younger.

You can see a lot of frying pans in my house. That's a life's savings. My mom gave me seven frying pans. My mom told me to give one to each child who is married. That's my dad's frying pan. He bought that for my mom many, many years ago and she used that for many years. My dad died in 1972 and so she said give something to the grandchildren.

That's an everlasting thing. That can go down to my great grandchildren. And this pot here, it's over 100 years old. This was given me by an old man. You know this old man has children alive yet and this old man told me this was his mother's pot when he first got married in 1920-something. MICHELLE SIK'YA. He was born in 1901. He said this was given to him by his mother when he got married. He was about 21. He told me he's got children alive yet, but he always comes here often and tells me a lot of stories. He said he favours me even though I'm not his relation. He favours me because he sees I keep things good. He said you'll probably keep this a long time, because I might die any day. He gave me this about five years ago. I cook a lot of beans in it and I cook fish egg bannock.

You ever had a fish egg bannock?

The radio is on all the time. Sometimes I have Nintendo, TV, radio, people laughing, kids laughing, people talking, you know. If a stranger comes to my home they think my house is noisy. And sometimes when the house is too quiet ... it's too quiet for me.

The day before yesterday I was all alone, the children were all playing outside. I had to open a door, I had to start washing clothes, do something, go outside. Then I started making dried meat. I had a couple of caribou thighs thawed out. The only silent time I really like is when we all go to sleep ...

We're moving from this location because we spent our life ... I got married in 1962. (Spent) all my life around here, I lived with my parents in this house too. Ever since I remember it's noise 24 hours. Sometimes people they're walking around at 3:00, 4:00 in the morning, 5:00 in the morning. Instead of passing on the road going over the hill to go to other places they walk right by here. There's two paths, one in the front or one in the back. And my bedroom's right here. In the wintertime it's the same thing with skidoo.

You know, it's never silent and this time I said if I ever build my house I'm going to get away from here. In a way I'll miss it because friends and everybody comes here all the time. If the band office is closed they come here. You know, they ask me to phone certain people for them or they come by and say hi, so if I move further, it may be too quiet. It'll take me a while I guess, or else maybe I'll never stay home.

I think I'm really going to miss my sticks right there over my stove where I used to just make dried meat instead of fresh caribou. You just cut it up and put it over a stick. I make dried meat in two days. It just dries in no time. That's the most thing I will miss, because I was brought up with dry meat. I like dry meat.

In the summertime I use the smokehouse. In the wintertime you cut the meat really thin, it might be really huge and you get a big towel. You hang it for maybe six hours and then you turn it around and hang it over the other side. After six hours you flatten it out, you can stand on it, walk on it, you have to put it between cardboard and it gets flat, it dries faster, then you hang it up again. And when all the blood drain out from when you start walking on it, it dries really fast.

The best way to teach them (children) is with a knife they get used to. I have an old knife I can make dried meat with. I have close to 50 knives, but I cannot go without my knife. That's the only knife I can use. That blade was a little bit wider eh, it was a bread knife. I keep filing it down and filing it down. I don't know how old it is, it must be 20 years old. I gotta have a handle. I still have one of my dad's homemade knives too. He made this knife. He used to make knives for my mom all the time.

CHILD THIS IS THE GOSPEL ON BAKES

Claire Harris

First strain sunlight through avocado leaves
then pour into a dim country kitchen through bare
windows on a wooden table freshly scrubbed
'I'm warning you a lazy person is a nasty
person' flurry of elbows
place a yellow oil cloth on this a bowl
a kneading board a dull knife spoons
then draw up an old chair with a cane seat on
the back of the chair have a grandfather carve flowers
birds the child likes to trace sweep of petals
curve of wings to tease a finger along
edges softened by age and numberless polishings
The initiate kneels on the seat
afterwards there will be a pattern of cane left
on her knees to trace
around her neck like a cape tie the huge blue apron
so that only her head and thin bare arms are visible
Place a five pound milk can painted green
with yellow trim and full of flour
a tall salt jar salt clumping together
fresh grated nutmeg sugar in a green can
butter in a clay cooler a red enamelled
cup brimming with cold water
Have someone say 'be careful now
don't make a mess'
The child takes one handful of flour makes a hill
outside a humming bird whirrs sun gleams
on her hill she adds another handful another and another
she makes a careful mountain then lightly walks

her fingers to the top   she flattens the crest   an old
voice in her ear   *'don't you go making yourself out*
special now'   she watches as flour sifts down
sides of her mountain   then scoops out a satisfactory
hollow   she can see humming birds at red
hibiscus   beyond a small boy   barefeet
on the plum tree his voice shrilling king
of the mountain threats   old voice eggs him on
Into the hollow   daughter   put a pinch of salt   a
a little sugar for each handful of flour
as much butter as can be held in a nutshell
'Ready' she calls   waits
Even if she looks straight ahead she still sees
from the corner of her eye   lamps their bowls full
gathering sunlight   the way girls should
waiting patiently for evening
Behind her there is always someone preparing pastry
on a grey marble-topped table
the rolling pin presses dough   thinner
and thinner towards the round edge
the maker pushing pastry
to transparency
ices the pin folds the pastry over butter
begins again   then finally the last stretching roll
till it seems skin must break into a ragged O
She is rigid with apprehension   this is something
to do with her
so she does not hear the voice over her shoulder say
'drizzle this baking powder all over'
handing her a spoon   until she is tapped lightly
starts to the chorus 'this child always dreaming yes
but what you going to do with her'
Her mother saying ever so carefully 'let her dream
while she can'   she begins to knead
butter into the flour   her mother sprinkles grated lemon
peel   and when she has crumbs she makes another hollow
adds water while someone clucks warnings
she begins to knead the whole together
not forgetting the recurring dream in which she climbs
through a forest of leaves she kneads   stepping

bravely from branch to branch   miles above ground
she kneads and kneads trying to make it smooth
she finds a bird that talks
and flies away just as she is beginning
to understand   she kneads   and finally someone says
'that's good enough' she kneads just a little more
she is watching the bird   which is flying
straight into the sun
where it lives bravely
a rum bottle full of water is thrust into her hands
which she must wash again   then flour the bottle
to roll out her dough which she has made into a ball
outside the high-pitched yelling of small boys at cricket
she is better at cricket than at bakes
she will never be as good at bakes as her mother is
or her aunt   or her great aunt   or her grandmother
or even the kitchen maid who is smiling openly
because the child's bakes are not round
her mother says gently 'I'll show you a trick'
she rolls the dough out for her again   takes a glass
cuts out perfect rounds of bakes
together they lay them out on a baking sheet
we'll decorate yours with a fork   dad will be proud
together they cover her bakes with wet cloth
when the oven is ready her mother will test the heat
sprinkling water on a tin sheet

MIXED MESSAGES
Jan Truss

" ... amamus, amatis, amant," we chanted together, my mother and I, she laughing and crying as she cut up onions, I from my cleared-off bit of the kitchen table trying to take her with me into this new world of Latin.

"Love!" she said, not ungenerously yet for her hair was still fair and her breasts flowed firm and free under her pretty green pinafore as she backed off from the onion tears. "What a place to start you off! Love, indeed!"

"Come on! Say it again, Mum," I insisted, leading her, "Amo, amas, amat—" It didn't matter that my little brother was turning the pages of my text, gloating over pictures of Roman soldiers conquering Britain, for I knew by heart the first verbs, and the first nouns; masculine, feminine, and neuter. I held my little sister's sticky hands in mine to keep them off my homework, clapping time to, "amamus, amatis, amant."

"You see, Mum, the person is included in the verb. We don't have to say the I, you; or the he, she or it; or the we, plural you, or they; masculine or feminine. The person is shown by the ending of the verb."

"Verb?" asked my brother.

"A doing word," I said promptly, busy 11-year-old girl, full of my new understandings. "The person is shown in the doing, in the action. The final word. At the very end of the sentence."

"Keep on learning like that," my mother said, bending into the black fireplace, pushing potato peelings and onion skins from an enameled tin bowl to pile up behind the smouldering coal to economize on the burning, "and you'll not end up serving YOUR sentence as a slave to the kitchen like your poor old uneducated mum."

"Oh, but you are the best cook in the world," I said, meaning every word of it. "Tu amo," I whispered with my chin in my sister's silky hair, experimenting, wondering if that was correct Latin. In school I was beginning Latin with the boys instead of domestic science with the girls. When the headmaster told my mother that was what suited me best, my mother was pleased. She felt complimented.

After that, for ever and ever when she was cooking she would say meaningfully, "Now, you get on with your homework, me girl."

However, I still had to do the shopping, my mother prefixing her every need with, "You just run up to—" It was to Tunnicliffe's the baker's at the top of the long railroad hill to get the yeast and the flour. "Two ounce of yeast. Make sure it's moist but not sloppy." To Ironside's the fishmonger's beyond the baker's. "Now don't let him pack you off with yesterday's herrings. If their eyes are dull, tell him to find you something fresh. Cod. Sole. Finny haddock. Remember fresh fish shouldn't smell fishy. Use the common sense God gave you. He knew about fish."

"That was Jesus, Mum, because of Simon called Peter, and Andrew his brother, and James the son of Zebedee and John HIS brother," I rattled off.

"That'll be enough cheek from you, Miss Know-it-all."

Early Saturday mornings were for standing on yellow sawdust lined up with the women vying for the best cheap cuts of red meat by long stalls in the old Victorian stone meatmarket. Women in drab coats shared hushed confidences, showing with measurements on their fingers how low their wombs had fallen, swallowing sighs for the sad but inevitable, gossiping with wise, veiled eyes about the latest 'poor thing' to die in a pool of blood getting rid of 'it' with a knitting needle, a corkscrew, a poker—while butchers with puns and repartee fitting for the land of Shakespeare flashed their knives against a background of desirable carcasses; cow, pig, sheep, lamb, all split down the middle, hanging on shiny butcher hooks, sawdust receiving their blood where it dripped.

A grandmotherly woman pushes me forward insisting roughly, "Hey, me lad, it's this little wench's turn. Here."

"So it is, me duck," he says, all smiles and beaming, and he makes me public to the lined-up women telling them, "This one's goin' to make a good wife for some lucky chap, you just watch 'er.

There's a grunt down the line and a bold voice yells, "Not if her's got any sense her won't!"

There's a chorused cackle of shrewd female laughter and the butcher with a fond smile wipes blood off his hands on his already gory apron saying, "Ah, you miserable old biddies, you know you can't resist our manly charms, when it comes to it." Then he turns his attention to me, giving me all his genial seriousness so that I feel I am the only customer in the market, and very important.

I've had my eye on a blade roast and a good lump of lean rolled brisket among the dozens of cuts that are set out on sheets of crisp butcher paper. I ask him the weight and the prices of both. He picks them up, one on each big hand, then with his eyes thoughtful and his lips pursed he ignores the scales and estimates the weights, quotes the costs, and I calculate which is likely to please my mother most. The blade has a bone. I choose the brisket, handing the butcher my mother's shopping basket. "And a big lump of fresh beef suet to grease the griddle," I tell him, "and bones for the dog." We don't have a dog but he'll give bones for the dog free whereas he charges for soup bones.

"Put it safe, me duck," he says, giving me my change wrapped up in a bit of paper. Not till I have it secure in my pocket does he hand over the shopping basket, full now, only a faint brush of blood showing on the paper, come off his thumb in the wrapping.

"The suet's fresh, is it?" my mother werrits. "Now you're sure? You saw him cut it off the carcass?"

Yes, I'm sure and I watch her fingers pull the firm cream-white fat apart, separating healthy flakes of it out of the silvery filaments of fine strong skin. "I shall make suet pudding today," she announces, radiant, sure of the joy her gift will give us. "Spotted dick, Mum, please," my brother and sister chorus, sustaining her happiness.

Although I have never made it, I could; I know the stages. The ritual is a film in my head; flour lifted high through the fingers, the inevitable drift of salt, suet scoured through the coarse grater, sultanas forked in like falling leaves just before pouring a little milk to congeal the mixture. "Firm but not sticky," my mother says.

After an hour's boiling in a cloth tied with string leaving enough room for the rising, it is brought before us on the pan lid to the meal table dangerously steaming. Dad cuts the string. Then he holds the lid under it while Mother gingerly peels back the hot cloth revealing the splendid sultana-spotted globe, its outside richly glutinous. Dad rolls it onto the serving dish saved from the big house. We admire it while Mum dashes to flop the tacky boiling cloth and the lid in the sink in the back kitchen. She returns and breaks the globe open, piling our plates. "That'll put hair on your chests," our dad says as we drizzle threads of Lyle's Golden Syrup making patterns on the fluffy insides of our mother's triumph.

She is wonderful, our mother, "Feeding us like kings, on a pauper's pittance," our Dad reminds us continually at his own expense, him being no provider, dragging us down. He takes the blame for we are all so innocent, still William Blake's children. History has yet to tell us we are living The Great Depression. We think our 'dark Satanic mills' are the cause and the shame of all our ills. At school in our uniformed choir, inspired and believing, I sing out with passion in soaring descant, " ... nor shall my sword sleep in my hand, till we have built Jerusalem in England's green and pleasant land."

My father sings operatic love songs to my mother when he is drying the dishes in the back kitchen, and she responds, tenor and soprano, clear as Nelson Eddy and Jeannette MacDonald. Sometimes, through the thin wall, the stooped next-door woman with broken teeth can be heard joining in with unquavering high power, although her husband only comes home late at night, and drunk.

In our little houses we do all our living in the kitchen and back kitchen, the bedrooms being too cold to escape to even in summer. We cannot avoid each other. On the other side of us, across a bit of clay garden, there is Mr. Hollings with his giant's body and coal-rimmed miner's eyes. "I never thought I'd bring children into the world to live like this," my mother wails, when Bill Hollings' acrid, stabbing voice perforates the good cooking scents of the air we breathe, his every second word a vile and violent Anglo-Saxon blasphemy.

"Don't listen. Don't listen," my mother pleads putting her hands over her ears. "He's to be pitied. He wouldn't need to curse if he had a bigger vocabulary."

My dad comes from behind and puts his arms around my soft and comely mother saying close to her neck, "He wouldn't need if he had a woman like you in his kitchen, feeding him right."

We believe our dad. Mrs. Hollings is a beaten-down little thing of a mouse who, gossip accuses, doesn't clean her toilet.

The lavatories in our houses are right next to the kitchens. Nothing is private. I have sat in our lavatory and heard Mrs. Hollings whimpering in her kitchen, and more than once, when I've been out in our bit of garden lying on my belly, hidden, reading under the rhubarb leaves, I have heard Bill Hollings as he was shaving at his kitchen sink by the window, thinking he was alone, singing *The Ashgrove* in the pure and fragile voice of a choirboy, "In yonder green valley, where streamlets meander, when twilight is falling I pensively rove, or at the bright noontide in solitude wander among the bright shades of the lonely ashgrove—"

"Mrs. Muck," he calls me if ever he sees me look his way when he's blaspheming.

Then he lets fly his vilest, most colourful crudities to describe me and my useless family. He says he's effing working to bloodywell keep all my bloody effing family on Relief. And he's bloody effingwell working to effingwell send me to that bloody useless effing school that'll bloodywell turn me out to be a bloody effing bitch, no bloody use to any good effing man."

On these occasions I retreat slowly, keeping my effing dignity with my nose held high. I walk the length of the cinder path under the washing on the clothesline and I turn slowly into the tiny brick porch with its three doors to coalhouse, lavatory, back kitchen. The back kitchen door is closed to keep out Hollings' and other street noises. Before I open the door I know how it will be on the other side. First, the sudden hot memory of the last meal, then gradually all the scents and fragrances of my mother's joyful thrift and success will wrap their messages around me; the oniony stockpot simmering with the handful of pearl barley; the yeasty bread rising in an earthen bowl under a white cloth in the warmest corner; a great crock of beetroot or dandelion wine fermenting; bunched herbs hanging.

There'll be no room on our laden table. "What about your homework?" my mother will ask.

I'll rescue my leather satchel from where I've stashed it behind the treadle of the sewing machine. I'll make room on the other battered armchair opposite my father's, tuck my legs up, spread my books around me. They're very old books, with generations of boys' names written in them, their notes and comments in the margins. These books have fragrances, scents of paper and storage, a mute and desirable mystery and mustiness: *Julius Caesar Conquers Britain. The Adventures of Odysseus. Jason and the Golden Fleece. The Idylls of the King. A Brief Illustrated History of England.*

My father smiles his love across at me, his admiration, his seriousness. My brother and sister snuggle close to travel whither I shall take them while my mother urges me to get on with my homework, to make something of myself. "If only I'd had your chance I wouldn't be here with dirty dishes," she grumbles, already pouring Lyle's syrup in a golden stream from its green tin to dirty yet another good aluminium pan. I know she's going to make toffee now. I've never made it but I could. The ritual and the recipes for clear or creamy, brittle or chewy, are indelible in my head.

"And never you forget," my mother is adding for good measure, throwing out her thoughts across us like salt across the flour, "never you forget, my girl, you come from the land of Boadicea and Queen Elizabeth, the great virgin queen."

She embarrasses me, but across the mess and muddle of dishes and pans I see the proud toss of her head and the angry flash of her eyes. I try to sit up straighter out of my curled-up legs to show her I'm worthy of her, to show her I understand what she is saying.

CRUSH
Bonnie Burnard

It's Thursday morning and it's hot, hot, hot. The girl is painting the kitchen cupboards. The paint stinks up the room, stinks up the whole house. Her summer blonde pony tail and her young brown shoulders are hidden in the cupboards and a stranger coming into the kitchen, seeing only the rounded buttocks in the terrycloth shorts and the long, well-formed legs, might think he was looking at part of a woman.

She's tired. She babysat last night. It's not the best job she can get; there are other kids, easier kids. She takes the job because of him, for the chance to ride alone with him in the dark on the way home. She thinks she's in love.

She remembers him at the beach, throwing his kids around in the water, teaching them not to be afraid. His back and thighs she will remember when she is 70 and has forgotten others. She does not try to imagine anything other than what she has seen. It is already more than enough.

Her mother stands over the ironing board just inside the dining room door. Thunk, hiss, thunk, hiss. The kitchen table separates them. It has been piled impossibly high with dishes and cans of soup and corn and tea towels and bags of sugar and flour and pickling salt. Spice jars have been pitched here and there, rest askew in the crevices of the pile. The cupboards are hot and empty. She has nearly finished painting them.

Neither the girl nor her mother has spoken for over an hour. It is too hot. She leans back out of the cupboards, unbuttons her blouse and takes it off, tossing it toward the table. It floats down over the dishes. She wants to take off her bra, but doesn't.

Her mother doesn't lift her head from the ironing. "You be careful Adam doesn't catch you in that state young lady. He'll be coming through that door with the bread any minute." Her sleeveless housedress is stained with sweat. It soaks down toward her thick waist.

Maybe I want him to, the girl thinks.

"Have you picked out the bathing suit you want?" Her mother glances up at her. The bathing suit is to be the reward for the painting. "It's time you started to think about modesty. It's beginning to matter."

"No." The girl watches the fresh blue paint obliterate the old pale green. She's lying. She has picked out her suit. It's the one on the dummy in the window downtown, the one the boys gather around. She knows she won't be allowed to have it. Mrs. Stewart in the ladies shop wouldn't even let her try it on, said it wasn't suitable for her. But it is. It's the one she wants.

She hears the scream of the ironing board as her mother folds it up and again her mother's voice.

"I'm going downtown for meat. You put that blouse on before I leave. Get it on. I'm as hot as you are and you don't see me throwing my clothes off."

Her mother stands checking the money in her billfold, waiting until the last button is secure before she moves toward the back door. "I'll bring you some cold pop." The screen door bangs.

The girl steps down from the paint-splattered chair. She goes to the sink and turns the water on full, letting it run to cold. She opens the freezer door, uses her thumbs to loosen the tray of ice cubes. She fills a peanut butter glass with ice and slows the tap, watches the water cover the snapping ice cubes. She sips slowly with her jaw locked, the cubes bump cold against her teeth as she drinks. She lifts a cube from the glass and holds it in her hand, feels it begin to soften against the heat of her palm. She raises her hand to her forehead and rubs the ice against her skin, back into her hair, down her cheek, down over her throat. The ice cube is small now, just a round lump. Her hand is cold and wet.

His hand was wet when he danced with her at the Fireman's dance. Not the same wet though, not the same at all. His buddies stood around and hollered things about him liking the young stuff and everyone laughed, even the wives. She laughed too, pretending she understood how funny it was, his touching her. But she can still feel the pressure of his hand on her back, anytime she wants this she can remember how it steadied her, how it moved her the way he wanted her to move. It should have been hard to move together, but it was easy, like dreaming.

She wonders how close he is to their house. She dries her hand on the tea towel hanging from the stove door. She undoes the top button of her blouse, then the next, and the next, and the next. It falls from her hand in a heap on the floor. She unfastens her bra, slips it down over her arms and lets it fall on top of the blouse.

She climbs back up on the chair and begins to paint again. Though the paint is thick and strong, she can't smell it anymore. She works slowly, deliberately, the chair solid under her feet. The stale green paint disappears beneath the blue.

She turns at his sudden, humming entrance, the bang of the screen door no warning at all. He stands on the mat with the tray of fresh baking slung round his neck, shifting his weight from one foot to the other, suddenly quiet. She comes down from the chair, steps over the heap of her clothes and stands in front of him, as still as the surface of a hot summer lake.

"Jesus," he says.

"I wanted to show you," she says.

He goes out the door quickly, doesn't leave Thursday's two loaves of white and one whole wheat.

Her mother's voice outside the back door sounds uneasy and unnaturally loud. The girl knows she will be punished in some new way. She bends down and picks up her bra.

He's in the truck and he's wishing he had farther to go than the next block. Lord, he thinks. What the hell was that?

He checks his rearview mirror. Her mother could come roaring out after him any minute. She could be forgiven for thinking there was something going on. He's a sitting duck in this damned truck. Deliver your bread, he thinks. And then, Shit. A drive. He'll go for a drive. Just to clear his head.

He goes out past the gas station, past the local In and Out store, out of the town onto a side road bordered by fence-high corn. He drives a few miles with the window down, letting the hot breeze pull the sweat from his face and arms. He eases the truck over to the side of the road.

He knows his only hope is that she tells her mother the truth, which could be unlikely. Shit. If her mother decides he was in on it, there'll be phone calls, there'll be hell to pay. His wife won't believe it. He doesn't believe it and he was there. Maybe the best thing would be to lie low and hope, pray, that her mother is embarrassed enough to keep her mouth shut. If it's going to come up, it'll come up soon and he'll just have to say it was a surprise, a real big surprise, and they can give him a lie detector on it.

The girl has never given him even one small clue that she was thinking in those terms, and he can see a clue coming. When he picks her up and drives her home she always hides herself behind a pile of schoolbooks hunched up tight against her sweater. She's a good sitter, the kids love her. He likes talking to her and always makes a point of being nice to her. And she helped him teach the kids to swim because his wife wouldn't and he didn't even look at her, can't even see her in a bathing suit.

So damned hot. He leans back in the seat, unbuttons his shirt and lights a Player's. The sight of her drifts back through the smoke that hangs around him in the air. It's been a long time since he saw fresh, smooth, hard breasts. Not centrefold stuff, not even as nice as his wife before the kids, but nice just the same, yeah, nice. He shifts around in his seat. Damn.

It's like she just discovered them. Or maybe she got tired being the only one who knew. Now he knows and what the hell's he supposed to do about it? Man, this is too complicated for a Thursday morning.

The picture drifts back again and this time he holds it for a while. He's sure they've never been touched. He thinks about dancing with her that once and how easy she was in his arms. Not sexy, just easy. Like she trusted him. He can't remember ever feeling that before. They sure didn't trust him when he was 17, had no business trusting him. And what he gets from his wife isn't trust, not exactly.

She could be crazy. She's the age to be crazy. But he remembers her eyes on him and whatever it was they were saying, it had sweet all to do with crazy.

Back the picture comes again and he closes his eyes and the breasts stay with him, secure behind the lids of his eyes. He can see a narrow waist, and squared shoulders. He hears words, just a few, although he doesn't know what they are, and he feels a gentleness come into his hands, he feels his cupped hands lift toward her skin and then he hears a racket near his feet and he opens his eyes to see a crow landing on the open floor of the truck beside the bread tray; it's already clawed its way through the waxed paper, it's already buried its beak. He sits up straight and waves his arms and yells the bird away and he throws the truck in gear and tells himself, you're crazy man, that's who's crazy.

The mother stands watching the girl do up the top button of her blouse. She holds the package of meat in one hand, the bottle of pop in the other. The pale brown paper around the meat is dark and soft where the blood has seeped through. She walks over to the fridge, puts the meat in the meat keeper and the pop beside the quarts of milk on the top shelf. She closes the fridge door with the same care she would use on the bedroom door of a sleeping child. When she turns, the girl has climbed up on the chair in front of the cupboards and is lifting the brush.

"Get down from that chair," she says.

The girl rests the brush across the top of the paint can and steps down.

"I could slap you," the mother says, calmly. This is not a conversation she has prepared herself for. This is not a conversation she ever expected to have. She cannot stop herself from looking at the girl's young body, cannot stop the memory of her own body and the sudden remorse she feels knowing it will never come back to her. She longs to feel the sting of a slap on her hand and to imagine it on the girl's cheek. But she puts the anger to the side, out of the way. She pulls a chair from the table, away from the mess of cupboard things piled there and sits down in the middle of the room, unprotected.

"Sit down," she says.

The girl sits where she is, on the floor, her brown legs tucked under her bum as they were tucked through all the years of fairy tales. But her mother can smell her fear.

"How much did you take off?"

The girl does not answer. She looks directly into her mother's eyes and she does not answer.

The mother begins the only way she knows how.

"I had a crush on your father. That's how it started with us, because I had a crush on him. He was only a little older than me but I think it's the same. I don't know why it should happen with you so young, but I'm sure it's the same. The difference is I didn't take my clothes off for him. And he wasn't married. Do you understand? It's wrong to feel that way about someone if he's married and it's wrong to take your clothes off."

The girl picks at a crusty scab on her ankle.

"The way you feel has nothing to do with the way things are. You've embarrassed him. I could tell at the gate that he was embarrassed. You won't be babysitting for them anymore. He'll tell his wife and they'll have a good laugh about it. You've made a fool of yourself." She wants only to pull the girl into her arms and carry her to bed.

"You will feel this way from now on. Off and on from now on. You have to learn to live with it. I wish it hadn't happened so soon. Now you just have to live with it longer. Do you understand?"

The girl shrugs her shoulders, lifts the scab from her skin.

"Women have this feeling so they will marry, so they will have children. It's like a plan. And you've got to learn to live within that plan. There will be a young man for you, it won't be long. Maybe five years. That's all. You've got to learn to control this thing, this feeling, until that young man is there for you."

The mother gets up from the chair and goes to the fridge. She takes out the pop and opens it, dividing it between two clean glasses from a tray on top of the fridge. She hands one to the girl.

"If you don't control it you will waste it, bit by bit, and there won't be a young man, not to marry. And they'll take it from you, any of them, because they can't stop themselves from taking it. It's your responsibility not to offer it. You just have to wait, wait for the one young man and you be careful who he is, you think about it good and hard and then you marry him and then you offer it."

The girl gets up from the floor and puts her glass, still half full, on the counter by the sink.

"I'd like to go now," she says.

The mother drains her glass. She feels barren. She is not a mother anymore, not in the same way. It is as if the girl's undressing has wiped them both off the face of the earth.

The girl has run away from the house, out past the gas station and the beer store onto a a grid road that divides the corn fields. She is sitting in a ditch, hidden, surrounded by long grass and thistles.

She knows she's ruined it, knows the babysitting days are over. Not because he was embarrassed. He wasn't embarrassed, he was afraid. It's the first time she's ever made anyone afraid. She will find a way to tell him she didn't mean to scare him.

She wishes her mother had slapped her. She hated hearing about how her mother had felt about her father, it was awful, and that stuff about getting married some day, she knows all that. That's what everybody does and it's likely what she'll do because there doesn't seem to be any way to do anything else.

Except maybe once in a while. If she learns not to get caught. And not to scare anyone.

She feels totally alone and she likes it. She thinks about his back and his dark thighs and about standing there in the kitchen facing him. It's the best feeling she's ever had. She won't give it up.

She crosses her arms in front of her, puts one hand over each small breast and she knows she isn't wrong about this feeling. It is something she will trust, from now on. She leans back into the grass, throws her arms up over her head and stares, for as long as she can, at the hot July sun.

KEEPING HER HOUSE

Kate Sutherland

The scar tugs at her breast as she reaches to take her apron from its hook on the kitchen wall. She ties it on, washes her hands and lines up the required utensils next to the mixing bowl. She deftly measures out a cup of flour and sifts it into the bowl leaving no dusting of white on the counter. With the same surgical precision, she adds the rest of the ingredients, each from a neatly labelled canister. She begins to stir. When the batter is smoothed by the 50 strokes dictated by the recipe, she spoons an even number of silver dollar circles onto the griddle. No stray spills mar the pattern. When the bubbles alert her that one side is done she flips each one over. She repeats this ritual until the bowl is empty and the plate boasts a towering stack of pancakes. She unplugs the griddle, absently wipes the clean counter, and checks the calendar for her next doctor's appointment before summoning her family.

RECIPE FOR A SIDEWALK

Kate Braid

Pouring concrete is just like baking a cake.
The main difference is
that first you build the pans. Call them forms.
Think grand.
Mix the batter with a few simple ingredients:
          one shovel of sand
               one shovel of gravel
                    a pinch of cement.

Add water until it looks right.
Depends how you like it.
Can be mixed by hand or with a beater called

a Readi-Mix truck.
Pour into forms and smooth off.
Adjust the heat so it's not too cold,
not too hot. Protect from rain.
Let cook until tomorrow.
Remove the forms and walk on it.

There is one big difference from cakes.
This one will never disappear.
For the rest of your life your kids
will run on the same sidewalk, singing
My mom baked this!

DREAMING DOMESTIC

Lorna Crozier

Baking is unpropitious for women.
To dream of an apron signifies
a zigzag course. For a school girl
to dream that her apron is loosened or torn,
implies bad lessons.

To dream of puddings
denotes small returns from large investments,
if only you would see it.
For a young woman to prepare a pudding
forecasts her lover will be sensual and worldly minded
and if she marries him
she will see her fortune vanish.

If a woman dreams of eating bread
she will be afflicted
                                        with children.
Of stubborn will.

To dream of noodles denotes an abnormal
appetite and desire.
There is little good in this dream.

A young woman dreaming of eating pickles
foretells an unambitious career.
If she dreams of basting meats
she will undermine her expectations
by folly and selfishness.

Beans are a bad dream.

To see or eat cooked beef
brings anguish surpassing human aid.

If beets are served in soiled or impure dishes
distressful awakenings will disturb you.

To dream of eating bananas
foretells an uninteresting and unloved companion.
To dream of eating an orange
is singularly bad. For a woman

to dream of making pies
implies she will flirt with men
for a pastime.

She should accept this warning.

*A found poem, the quotations from *10,000 Dreams Interpreted* or *What's In a Dream, A Scientific and Practical Exposition* by Gustavus Hindman Miller

THE UNQUIET BED
Dorothy Livesay

The woman I am
is not what you see
I'm not just bones
and crockery

the woman I am
knew love and hate
hating the chains
that parents make

longing that love
might set men free
yet hold them fast
in loyalty

the woman I am
is not what you see
move over love
make room for me

FROM *THE FIRE-DWELLERS*
Margaret Laurence

The X-ray results are negative. Stacey does not have tumor of the brain. She thanks Doctor Spender and puts down the phone. It is early afternoon, and Jen is asleep. Stacey moves around the house without knowing in advance what she is going to do. She goes upstairs to the bedroom and looks at herself in the full-length mirror. She is wearing a blue-and-pink-print dress, bought on sale last autumn. The pink is in the form of small clocks, all of whose hands indicate five minutes before noon or midnight. She removes the dress and her slip, and puts on a pair of tight-fitting green velvet slacks and a purple overblouse which has been hanging in the cupboard for some months, as yet unworn. She then rummages at the back of the cupboard, on the floor, and comes up with a pair of high-heeled gold-strapped sandals.

Okay, so of course I know you shouldn't wear high heels with sandals. But I love high heels. I just do. All right, Mac, I know these are vulgar, especially with slacks. But I like them, see? And I can do with the extra height.

She listens at Jen's door. No sound. Let sleeping kids lie. Stacey in golden high-heel sandals tiptoes downstairs to the kitchen, collects the gin bottle and two bottles of tonic, and goes down to the basement room, leaving the door between the kitchen and basement open in case Jen calls.

—This calls for some slight celebration. Reprieve. I'm not a goner yet. Did I really think I was? Well, it's in the middle of the night I start thinking about it, and then it seems pretty certain. Really, it's only what would happen to the kids. Yeh? It doesn't matter about you, Stacey? Well, it shouldn't matter. Why not? Because I'm thirty-nine and I can't complain. But they haven't begun yet. That's not how you feel about yourself, though. It matters. Okay, but so what? I think of Katie—maybe Ian, now, too—thinking of me like I'm prehistoric, and it bugs me. I'm sorry, but it does. I'm not a good mother. I'm not a good wife. I don't want to be. I'm Stacey Cameron and I still love to dance.

The floor is dark-red linoleum tiles. Stacey kicks aside the numdah scatter rugs with their rough embroidery of magic trees, trees of life flowering unexpectedly into azure birds, green unlikely leaves. She pours a gin and tonic, drinks half of it and tops it up. The records are kept in a mock wrought-iron stand. Stacey shuffles impatiently through them and finally finds what she is looking for. She changes the record player to seventy-eight and puts the old disc on. The needle skids a little, complaining at the scratches on the surface.

Tommy Dorsey Boogie. The clear beat announces itself. Stacey finishes her drink, fixes another one, drinks half of it quickly and sets the glass down on top of the TV. She looks at her gold sandals, her green-velvet thighs. She puts her arms out, stretching them in front of her, her fingers moving slightly, feeling the music as though it were tangibly there to be touched in the air. Slowly, she begins to dance. Then faster and faster.

> Stacey Cameron in her yellow dress with pleats all around the full skirt. Knowing by instinct how to move, loving the boy's closeness, whoever he was. Stacey twirling out onto the floor, flung by the hand that would catch her when she came jazzily flying back. *Tommy Dorsey Boogie.* Stacey spinning like light, whirling laughter across a polished floor. Every muscle knowing what to do by itself. Every bone knowing. Dance hope, girl, dance hurt. Dance the fucking you've never yet done.

—Once it seemed almost violent, this music. Now it seems incredibly gentle. Sentimental, self-indulgent? Yeh, probably. But I love it. It's *my* beat. I can still do it. I can still move without knowing where, beforehand. Yes. Yes. Yes. Like this. Like this. I can. My hips may not be so hot but my ankles are pretty good, and my legs. Damn good in fact. My feet still know what to do without being told. I love to dance. I love it. I love it. It can't be over. I can still do it. I don't do it badly. See? Like this. Like this.

—I love it. The hell with what the kids say. In fifteen years their music will be just as corny. Naturally they don't know that. I love this music. It's mine. Buzz off, you little buggers, you don't understand. No—I didn't mean that. I meant it. I was myself before any of you were born. (Don't listen in, God—this is none of your business.)

The music crests, subsides, crests again, blue-green sound, saltwater with the incoming tide the blues of the night freight trains across snow deserts, the green beckoning voices, the men still unheld and the children yet unborn, the voices cautioning no caution no caution only dance what happens to come along until

The record player switches off.

—Was I hearing what was there, or what? How many times have I played it? God it's 3:30 in the afternoon and I'm stoned. The kids will be home in one hour. Okay, pick up the pieces. Why did I do it? Yours not to reason why, Stacey baby, yours but to go and make nineteen cups of Nescafé before the kids get home. Quickly. Jen? Lord, she must've been awake for hours. Oh Stacey.

The black coffee washes around in her stomach like a tidal wave. She gets Jen up, murmuring carefully, and then goes to her own bedroom and Mac's and changes into her blue silk suit. She puts on a pair of medium-heel navy-blue shoes. She holds the gold sandals for a moment in her hands, then delves into the clothes cupboard and buries them under a pile of tennis shoes and snow boots. She brushes her hair, back-combing it slightly, then slicking it down into neatness and spraying it so it will hold. She applies lipstick and powder. She examines herself in the full-length mirror.

—Am I okay? No lurching hemlines, protruding slip straps, off-base lipstick or any other sign of disrepair? I think I'm okay, but how's my appraisal power? Shaken, no doubt. Remorse—overdose of same. I'm not fit to be in charge of kids, that's the plain truth. God, accept my apologies herewith. He won't. Would you, in His place? No. Come on, be practical. Dinner. Mac won't be here. Dinner downtown for him, the lucky bastard. When did I last have dinner downtown? Precious lot he cares. Goddam him, some night when he comes bowling in at ten o'clock expecting me to have kept dinner hot in the oven since six, I'm gonna say *Now listen here, sweetheart, want me to tell you something? There isn't any bloody dinner and if you want any, why don't you just go along and scramble yourself an ostrich egg? Why don't you just do that little thing?* Oh Stacey, this is madness. Get a grip on yourself. Yeh, well let's see now—pork chops, cauliflower with cheese sauce, mashed potatoes, and what for dessert? It'll have to be ice cream. Got half a carton in the freezer. Maybe I should make apple Betty. What a slut I am, not a cooked dessert for those kids. No, I can't I'm incapable of peeling an apple. Sometimes I want to say—*Listen, if all of you never had another dessert for the rest of your lives, would that kill you?* Answering chorus of *It sure would,* spoken with conviction. Come on, bitch. Another cup of coffee.

Stacey prepares dinner primly and with caution. When the children arrive home, she talks as little as possible. The meal is finally over and the noise begins to subside. The mist is beginning to clear. Stacey washes the dishes and then bathes Jen, reads two Little Golden Books to her, and puts her to bed. After some considerable time, Duncan and Ian are also in bed. Only Katie remains. Katie has finished her homework and is down in the TV room. Stacey goes down but does not go in. She stands near the doorway, looking, unnoticed.

Katie has put on one of her own records. Something with a strong and simple beat, slow, almost languid, and yet with an excitement underneath, the lyrics deliberately ambiguous.

Katie is dancing. In a green dress Katie MacAindra simple and intricate as grass is dancing by herself. Her auburn hair, long and straight, touches her shoulders and sways a little when she moves. She wears no make-up. Her bones and flesh are thin, plain-moving, unfrenetic, knowing their idiom.

Stacey MacAindra, thirty-nine, hips ass and face heavier than once, shamrock velvet pants, petunia-purple blouse, cheap gilt sandals highheeled, prancing squirming jiggling.

Stacey turns and goes very quietly up the basement steps and into the living room.

—You won't be dancing alone for long, Katie. It's all going for you. I'm glad. Don't you think I'm glad? Don't you think I know how beautiful you are? Oh Katie love. I'm glad. I swear it. Strike me dead, God, if I don't mean it.

At ten thirty, Katie is in bed at last. Stacey is now off duty. Mac is at a conference and will probably not be home until midnight. Stacey has a scalding bath, puts on a nightgown and housecoat, and goes downstairs again.

—What now? I should go to bed. Okay, Stacey, not more than one gin, eh? Well, all right, if it's going to be only one, let's make it good and strong. Too much has disappeared from this bottle. I'll go to the Liquor Commission tomorrow and get another bottle and pour half of it into this one. So Mac won't think it's odd. The other half strictly to be stashed away for emergencies. Yeh, I can see it all now. Every other minute is an emergency. Does he know? He must. Mac—listen. Just listen. I have something to tell you. No. It's not up to him. It's up to me. Any normal person can cope okay, calmly, soberly. And if you can't, kid, then there's something wrong with you. No there isn't. Everything is okay. Everything is *all right*, see? Only I'm tired tonight and a little tense. Why not try Ovaltine, then? Oh get lost, you.

Stacey takes her drink into the living room and sits on the chesterfield with the lights off, looking out the window at the city which is both close and far away.

Stacey, naked with Mac three quarters of a year before Katherine Elizabeth was born. The cottage at the lake where they'd gone for the one week holiday they couldn't afford. The pine and spruce harps in the black ground outside, in the dark wind from the lake that never penetrated the narrow-windowed cabin. Their skins slippery with sweat together, slithering as though with some fine and pleasurable oil. Stacey knowing his moment and her own as both separate and unseparable. Oh my love now

Going into the kitchen, Stacey swings the gin bottle out from the lower cupboard and fills a jug with water from the tap.

—No use wasting tonic water. Of course this will taste like essence of pine needles with a dash of kerosene, but then my mother always used to speak very scornful-like of ladies whose taste was all in their mouths. Couldn't say that about me. Nope. My taste isn't anywhere. Between my legs, maybe. Okay, doll, that's enough. So who wants to know?

Stacey returns to the living room and curls up on the chesterfield once more, her slippered feet underneath her. The big sliding door leads out into the hall and thence up the iron-banistered staircase to the bedrooms. Stacey leans around in the semidarkness to check. The door is closed. Should she put on the radio? She decides against it. If she uses her own voice, she can select the music.

There's a gold mine in the sky
Faraway
We will go there, you and I,
Some sweet day,
And we'll say hello to friends who said goodbye,
When we find that long lost gold mine in the sky.
Faraway, faraw-a-ay—

—Oh boy. Jen comes by her operatic tendencies naturally. Where did that song come from? Old man Invergordon used to sing it at local concerts in Manawaka when I was a little kid. Nobody knew how to tell him they'd rather he didn't. They weren't so bad, any of them, I now see. How I used to dislike them then, the Ladies' Aid and mother's bridge cronies and all of them, never seeing beyond their own spectacles and what will the neighbors think what will they say? But who here or anywhere, now, would put up with old Invergordon? *Drop dead,* that's what he'd get here and now. He stank all right but he had a lovely baritone. Only difference between Invergordon and Niall Cameron was that my dad was a private drunk and the old guy was a public one. It isn't the fact that there's no gold mine in the sky which bothers me. I mean who wants to say hello to people who are dead even if you happen to be dead yourself? It's the ones who say good-bye before they're dead who bug me. I start thinking—it's Mac. Then I think—hell, no, it's not Mac it's me and then I don't know.

Twelve thirty. Stacey takes the empty bottle into the kitchen and places it behind three bottles of wine and a bottle of vinegar. She takes the frying pan down from its hook and puts it on the stove. She takes the bacon out of the refrigerator and puts two slices in the pan. Cheese. Bread. The fried sandwich is made. She looks at it seriously, considering it. It does not look edible.

—Must eat something absorptive. Can't. Repulsive. Mac, talk to me. Mac? Katie? Ian? Duncan? Where are you or is it just me   I don't know what the hell I'm talking about well what you should be talking about kid is coffee

Stacey makes herself a cup of instant coffee. She looks again at the congealing sandwich in the frying pan and decides to heat it up. She switches on an element but does not put the frying pan on until the circular coil is red. She reaches for the frying pan, stumbles, puts out a hand to balance herself. The hand lands on the edge of the electrical scarlet circle.

—It hurts it hurts it hurts   what is it

She has without knowing it pulled her hand away. She regards it with curiosity. Two red crescent lines have appeared on the skin of her left palm.

—My brand of stigmata. My western brand. The Double Crescent. It hurts hurts.

She takes the frying pan and throws its sandwich into the garbage pail. She switches off the stove, reaches into the cupboard for baking soda, mixes some with water and applies it to her hand. She then applies a light gauze bandage, one which can be removed easily tomorrow morning without anyone noticing. She walks upstairs and gets into bed. Blackness scurries around her in the room but within her head the neon is white and cold like the stars in the prairie winters.

—How to explain this? Anybody can explain anything, if they put their mind to it. It's not difficult. I put the kettle on, and accidentally put my hand over the boiling spout. Mac—I'm scared. Help me. But it goes a long way back. Where to begin? What can I possibly say to you that you will take seriously? What would it need, with you, what possible cataclysm, for you to say anything of yourself to me? What should I do? I'm not sure I really want to go on living at all. I can't cope. I do cope. Not well, though. Not with anyone. Jesus I get tired sometimes. Self-pity. Yeh, I guess. But sometimes I want to abdicate, only that. Quit. Can't. What would it be like for one of the kids to come into the bedroom, say, one evening when Mac isn't home yet, any one of them, maybe waking up in the night and calling and me not answering, and coming in here and finding I'd gone away from them for good, overdose? Maybe they'd think it was their fault. I couldn't come back mysteriously and say *Listen, it wasn't anything to do with you, or not in the way you think, and I love you, see?* Even if I left one of those I'm-getting-off-the-world letters, saying I *care about you,* they wouldn't believe it. And they'd be right. Goddam you, God. I'm stuck with it. But I'm a mess and I'm scared. What if I had burned myself when one of the kids saw? Mac?

Stacey goes into half sleep, where the sounds of occasional cars and the light wind and the way-off ships can be heard but only in a way which needs no response.

DREAM KITCHEN

Jennifer Blend

"Win the kitchen of your dreams," trumpets the ad in my mailbox. How does one dream a kitchen, I wonder? How would it be? What would it look like, smell like, feel like? "Ah well, it's only a dream," I think, "surely a simple thing." I resolve to try. I will dream of kitchens.

Out of the cold white womb of my childhood I remember kitchens. Not the kitchens of someone else's Grandmother, suffused with cinnamon, sunshine and cheerful busyness. Not the kitchens of someone else's Mother—muffins and milk, friendly cups of once-hot coffee gone cold while a story is shared, a careless clutter of children and chatter. But a kitchen of ... blank, nothing. How is that possible, I think? Everyone had some sort of kitchen.

We did, of course, have a kitchen. But in my childhood home, only servants used it—"used" being the operative word. The kitchen seemed, to me, a sort of forbidden laboratory, where secret, mysterious machinations took place that occasionally erupted into food for us to eat. I remember the ambivalence I felt towards the fairytale heroine "Cinderella." Poor thing mopped and scrubbed all day, it's true, and had to deal with a dreadful stepmother besides. But, at least SHE was allowed into the kitchen. I have no memory of being allowed inside ours until I reached the age of 10.

What I do recall are my long afternoons spent in exile in my Grandmother's kitchen. I was allowed in there only under the supervision of Katie, the cook. Katie would carefully set a place for me at the small kitchen table, and then she would silently serve me. This tea-time "treat" was one of the few constants of my childhood. Grandmother must have heard somewhere that THIS was the one food craved by all young children, and so, to my misfortune, she took care that there was always plenty for me. Toasted Peanut Butter Sandwiches. Never a drop of jam, never a hint of honey. The only variation was from "crunchy" to "smooth." I preferred the smooth. It was easier to swallow. To this day, the memory of the mouth-clogging, throat-gagging dryness of those hopelessly awful, barely-edible, tea-time offerings instantly returns a small-child-scowl to my face.

I was in the kitchen so that I would be out of the way; that much was clear to me. I spent long, tedious, shadowy afternoons listening to the murmur of my Mother's, Grandmother's, and Aunt's voices as they slurred their way through another bottle of Four Roses blended whiskey. They were only interrupted, with faltering regularity, by Katie, who trundled in and out with a highly polished silver bowl of slightly melted ice cubes for their drinks. I don't think they noticed. I remember that the kitchen was a sort of ordinary faded green, the color of day-old grass clippings left out in the sun. It had that smell too, as though nothing fresh ever came out of the oven.

I remember the silence of that kitchen, though it must have seemed silent only in relation to the softly swelling sounds from the sitting room. Katie did her best to entertain me, and there were always books. If I needed something more to read, for there were never toys, I would go quietly into the sitting room and help myself to whatever appealed to me from the well-stocked shelves. It seemed as though the women's murmuring never changed, neither rose nor fell, as I passed through. Like the Hebrews murmuring in the desert, these three women had escaped the oppression of marital slavery, but, victims twice-over, they were now Outcasts, alone and adrift in the social desert of their kind. My Grandmother had divorced her alcoholic husband. My Aunt had never married. My Mother, unhappily married, was escaping into a bottle of Gilbey's gin.

I was not a child of the television age, and so was spared the unrealities of the "Brady Bunch." I knew, however, from my few friends, that other families had kitchens that were full of noisy life, and wonderful smells, and people laughing and talking together. I suppose that I accepted our difference from that norm. In my too serious, solitary sort of way, I secretly dreamed of a kitchen like theirs.

I married at 24. My first husband was a Welshman. I learned to bake for his afternoon tea. Scones, tea breads, doughnuts, and coffee cakes rolled out of my small ranch kitchen like warm, doughy affirmations of life in the Promised Land after the unleavened bread of the Exodus. Pregnancy, the fullness of my body and the smell of yeast sprinkled on warm creamy milk in a kitchen bursting with sunshine, became my focus in the dreamlike reality of my own first kitchen. I did not notice at first, that, even here, I was still alone.

Unlike the silent kitchens of my youth this home was full of sound: cows bellowing their bovine messages of maternal love, peacocks wailing in the late afternoon, calling to their mates across pastures patterned with patchwork shadows, and glorious Brahms on the record player. I learned to bake six dozen chocolate chip cookies in the span it took to sing my way through the 1st Symphony. I learned to knead dough with the same rocking motion with which I would later rock my child. I learned to measure time by the repeated risings of bowls of bread. I learned the cadence of the day by the hours of my wifely chores. I lived, in some ways, a monastic existence.

Into this happy isolation burst my first-born, red-headed magic child—my son. The dimensions of my dream kitchen were quickly altered by his small presence. The kitchen was now filled with his things: a baby chair, piles of not-quite-dry cloth diapers (cloth, not because they were the right ecological choice, but because Pampers had not yet been invented) and jars of poi, a revolting gelatinous mess made from the Hawaiian taro root he adored. The daily production of baked goods began to slow, though the act of baking remained for me a time of almost sacramental connection to warmth, food, and love.

We moved to a new place, and bought a new house, whose main attraction was the delightfully spacious kitchen/family room where I ruled my small kingdom of toddlers (by then there were two) and pots and pans. There was laughter. There was music. There were good-smelling roasts from the oven and cookies in the jar. I did beautiful needlepoint and nursed healthy, contented babies. My husband thrived. Then quietly, slowly, into the dream kitchen crept the 1970s Mother's Monster of Discontent. I had it all—at least all that any "reasonable" woman could want. I had erased the cold, white womb of my childhood and created a dream of a dream. The trouble was that the dream worked no better for me than it had for my Mother. But, unlike her, I had no intention of drinking my way out of this reality.

Perhaps I spent too many afternoons in my snug kitchen reading Simone De Beauvoir and Betty Friedan. Perhaps my women friends and I began to see our marriages as infantalizing extensions of our "Sleeping Beauty" childhoods. Perhaps I just began to be angry. In my sunfilled, middle-class, suburban kitchen I began to connect with what was wrong, what was missing. My friends and I shared our confusion and anger. Though few of us knew with any certainty how to proceed, we were sure that there had to be more to the dream than we were experiencing. One lovely June afternoon, tired of fairy-tales without happy endings, I packed up my babies and bags and simply walked out.

That was 17 years ago. My son is now 21 and has recently departed for a job in Australia. We talked the other night before he left. He is so much more aware of the importance of his dreams than I was at his age. He knows that this is the time for his "quest." He knows that he must begin it alone, and must himself meet and defeat the monsters guarding the particular secrets of his happiness. We share the same need for dreams, he and I. He also loves to cook.

These days, when my three children gather in our kitchen to share their "remember whens" with each other, the preferred locus of their remembering is the kitchen of our single-parent house of 10 years ago. They have a seemingly inexhaustible fund of favorite kitchen memories. That kitchen was a deep, vibrant, nearly visceral red, and did, at times seem almost to beat with the pulse of our growing family. We ate there. The children studied and did their homework there. Their friends, and my friends, and sometimes it seemed half the neighborhood, sat round the table and talked there. We planned trips there, escapes and journeys and "someday I'd like to's." My best friend and I planned a Montessori school there: dreamed it, organized it, and saw the dream completed. We also cried there, mourned together, and fought there. It was hardly ever silent. There was a wholeness about that kitchen. It was, for us, the perfection of all our imperfections, a circle of infinitely flexible proportions, expanding and contracting, stretching and concentrating, a round table of dreams dreamed, dreams shared, and dreams hoped for.

Now we have another kitchen. It is not so wonderful as the one we all love to remember. I have joined my last child as a student at the kitchen table, as a doer of homework, a debater of issues, a writer of essays. She and I sit at the table and dream dreams of both our futures. I dream of being an ordained Anglican priest. She dreams of quantum mechanics, and Outward Bound. Sometimes my husband and I risk sharing there.

All is not perfection in this kitchen. There are books everywhere, piles of them and papers half done, and yesterday's newspaper. My cooking is half-hearted, at best. I rarely bake. Sometimes now, when I am very tired, I wonder if the time for winning dreams is over. I miss my children, grown and gone, though I have only to sit at the table quietly, alone again, to recall them to me. Someday I will bake for their children. They will *all* be allowed into this Grandmother's kitchen!

My women friends and I still gather there, as women have gathered around the cooking fires since the beginnings of time. My teenage daughter and her friends eat lunch around the table almost every day. They are unaware of their part in this continuing women's ritual. In spite of, or perhaps because of the women's liberation movement, we have claimed the kitchen as our own once more. At first, many of us fought to escape it, and now we fight to validate our right to choose to come and go or to stay in it. It has become our place to be free, instead of confined as our mothers were. It is our place to argue, and laugh, and cry, and to share our struggles and fears instead of enduring the exile of estrangement and silence. It is our place to work, and play, and celebrate, or to sag, exhausted, against the countertops. Sometimes a man will join us, drawn, I think, to the essential warmth of our fire. But mostly the kitchen persists as the woman's domain.

When I dream of kitchens now, the kitchen abides as the most important place, the sun around which orbits my other spheres of work and living. It will continue to be, for me, the symbol of warmth and nourishment, of creativity and community. And it will always be, for me, a place of dreams.

PIETA '78

Mary di Michele

Between my mother and me the spaces are long and filled
with other things: TV, a companion, the moka, in its
jet rush, the pouring of espresso, the passing of sugar,
the clicking of spoons. Then she says something about the
weather, *fa brutto*, it's ugly, says the blue language of
the Mediterranean, all that dark oily slush that won't
come clean.

She is massing dough, she is baking for Christmas.
I am reading the *Memoirs of a Dutiful Daughter*
at the table, while the clock complains,
spitting out phrases, as if it's weary of telling time
when life doesn't change.
But this is a three-hour visit, after all, and not the house
in which I'm rooted. It is the only church I frequent,
the choir of household noises in attendance, the sermons
on money and the weather. It is the only temple I honour
because there are still some things I hold sacred:
the warmth of baking, its glow imminent in my mother's
brow as the light fans her hot face by the window, assaulted
by the dark breath of cocoa. I keep my feet up, sitting

in the kitchen, reading a good book. Part of my mind has
watched her work before, that part of my mind relaxes,
reassured by the routine learned off by heart, the simple
life.
While another woman stands trial in the pages of print I
try to understand,
my mother offers the bowl to lick up the batter.

Between my mother and me, the spaces fill with things other
than foreign words. In my chest revolves a spiral spring
that masterminds the blood. Mamma would like to knit her
own soft heart from a ball of white wool she tosses into my
lap.

NOTES ON CONTRIBUTORS

ANNHARTE (MARIE BAKER)

"His Kitchen" from *Being on the Moon*

Marie Annharte Baker is an Anishinabe poet, teacher and activist. Annharte's poetry combines the rich heritage of Native traditions with the harsh reality of life on the streets.

ATWOOD, MARGARET

from *The Edible Woman*

Margaret Atwood has published numerous books of poetry including *The Circle Game* (which won the Governor General's Award) and *Selected Poems*, several novels including *Life Before Man* and *The Handmaid's Tale* (which won the Governor General's Award), and collections of short stories including *Bluebeard's Egg* and *Wilderness Tips*. She has been shortlisted for the Booker Prize and has received countless literary and academic awards.

BAKER, BRENDA

"The Collection"

Brenda Baker is a songwriter with two albums to her credit. Her prose has appeared in several literary magazines and the anthology *Out of Place*. In 1989 she received a Saskatchewan Literary Award for short fiction.

BARFOOT, JOAN

from *Dancing in the Dark*

Joan Barfoot has worked as a journalist and editor. Her novel, *Abra*, won the *Books in Canada* First Novel Award. She has subsequently published several novels including *Duet for Three* and *Family News*.

BEEMAN, KATHERINE

"Eating Cajun"

Katherine Beeman is a poet, computer operator, active member of the Confederation of National Trade Unions and a socialist, feminist independentist. Her work has appeared in a number of North American publications including *Phoebus* and *Zymergy*.

BIRDSELL, SANDRA

"Spring Cleaning" from *Agassiz Stories*

Sandra Birdsell is a short story writer, novelist and playwright. She was runner-up in the Search for a New Novelist Contest and won the Gerald Lampert Award for *Night Travellers*.

BLEND, JENNIFER

"Dream Kitchen"

Jennifer Blend has interned as Assistant University Chaplain at the University of Saskatchewan. There she discovered that the spirited conversations around the office table resembled the best of times in "Dream Kitchen."

BOISIER, IRENE

"Kittens"

Irene Boisier was born in Chile, where she lived until 1975. She is an architect and community planner. Her writing expresses the still unresolved conflicts of a dual nationality. At present she is working on a collection of short stories about Latin American women.

BOWERING, MARILYN

"Married Woman's Complaint" from *The Killing Room*

Marilyn Bowering has recently returned to Canada after two years in Seville, Spain. She has published several books of poetry, and her most recent novel is *To All Appearances a Lady*. She is presently at work on a new novel.

BRAID, KATE

"Recipe for a Sidewalk"

Kate Braid is the author of *Covering Rough Ground*. She lives in Vancouver and works as a journey carpenter.

BRANT, BETH

"Hunger of Another Kind" from *Food and Spirits*

Beth Brant is editor of *A Gathering of Spirit*, the ground-breaking collection of writing and art by Native American women. Her books include *Mohawk Trail*, a collection of prose and poetry, and *Food and Spirits*, short fiction. She received the Michigan Council for the Arts Creative Artist grant in 1983 and 1986, and the Ontario Arts Council award in 1989. In 1991 she received a National Endowment for the Arts Literature Fellowship.

BURNARD, BONNIE

"Crush"

Bonnie Burnard's collection of stories, *Women of Influence*, received the Commonwealth Best First Book Award in 1989. Her recent publications are found in *Soho Square 111, Canadian Short Stories,* and *Best Canadian Stories 1992.*

BUTALA, SHARON

from *Luna*

Sharon Butala has published several collections of short stories, including *Queen of the Headaches*, and novels, including *Luna*. She has received the Saskatchewan Writers' Guild Long Fiction Award, and was short-listed for the *Books in Canada* First Novel Award and the Governor General's Award.

CAMPBELL, MARIA

from *Halfbreed*

Maria Campbell's acclaimed first book *Halfbreed* was followed by *Riel's People, People of the Buffalo,* and *Little Badger and the Fire Spirit.* She has travelled extensively throughout Canada and the United States, and has conducted innumerable writers' workshops in native communities.

CARR, EMILY

from *The Book of Small*

Emily Carr studied painting in California, Paris, and along the coast of British Columbia. Her first book, *Klee Wyck,* won the Governor General's Award. She wrote six more books before her death in 1943. Three of them were published posthumously.

CLARK, JOAN

"Italian Spaghetti" from *From A High Thin Wire*

Joan Clark is a novelist, short story writer and children's writer. She is winner of the Marion Engel Award. Joan Clark was co-founder and editor for six years of the literary magazine *Dandelion.* Her latest book is *The Victory of Geraldine Gull.*

CROLL, SU

"Bones and Bread" & "Unmixed Good"

Su Croll's first book, *Worlda Mirth,* is forthcoming. She was awarded first prize in *Grain*'s Short Story Contest, and her poetry has appeared in several literary magazines. She currently teaches Art and English as a Second Language.

CROZIER, LORNA

"Dreaming Domestic" & "Domestic Scene I" from *Angels of Silence, Angels of Flesh*

Lorna Crozier has published several books of poetry including *The Garden Going on Without Us* and *Angels of Silence, Angels of Flesh.* She writes, edits and teaches Creative Writing.

CULLETON, BEATRICE

from *In Search of April Raintree*

Beatrice (Culleton) Mosionier is originally from Winnipeg and now lives in Toronto. Her first play, *Night of the Trickster,* was recently produced by Native Earth Performing Arts. Previous works include *Walker,* a short film script for the National Film Board, and *Spirit of the White Bison.*

DHOLAKIA, JAGRUTI

"Sunanda"

Jagruti Dholakia holds a Ph.D. in Teacher Education. From 1971–83 she taught at the SNDT Women's University in India. She has also taught Multiculturalism at the University of Calgary and is presently a Coordinator at the Calgary Immigrant Aid Society.

DI MICHELE, MARY

"The Disgrace" & "Pieta '78" from *Bread and Chocolate Marry into the Family*

Mary di Michele has written numerous poetry books, including *Bread and Chocolate* and *Necessary Sugar.* She works as an editor and Creative Writing Instructor.

EMERSON, JULIE

"The Lady of the House"

Julie Emerson writes and paints. Her writing has appeared in several literary journals. She is interested in the psychological and social functions of narrative.

FORD, CATHY

"Teeth" (Parts 1, 2, 3) from *Desiring Heart*

Cathy Ford has worked as a writer, editor and teacher. She has written several books of poetry, including *Saffron, Rose & Flame* and *The Desiring Heart.*

GLICKMAN, SUSAN

"Chocolate: A Love Poem" & "Living Alone" from *The Power to Move*

Susan Glickman is a poet, critic and professor. She has been awarded the Harbourfront "Discovery" Prize. Her numerous books include *The Inner Ear* and *Missing Persons.*

GOM, LEONA

"Aprons" from *Private Properties,* "Mother with Child" & "Waiting" from *The Collected Poems*

Leona Gom was born and raised Alberta's Peace River country. She has published five books of poetry and three novels, of which *Housebroken* won the Ethel Wilson Fiction Award.

GUILFORD, IRENE

"How to Make Pasta" from *Carousel*

Irene Guilford is a one-time computer professional who prefers to spend her time reading and writing. She has published both short fiction and poetry.

GUNNARS, KRISTJANA

"in this kitchen"

Kristjana Gunnars has written five volumes of poetry, a collection of short stories, a novel and a creative autobiography, *Zero Hour,* which was nominated for the 1991 Governor General's Award. She has edited three anthologies and has translated the prose and poetry of Stephan G. Stephansson. Her novel, *The Substance of Forgetting,* is forthcoming. She presently teaches English and Creative Writing at the University of Alberta.

HARRIS, BEVERLEY

"Summer in Full Bloom" from *The Generic Journal*

Beverly Harris is a Calgary writer who directs an adult Native literacy project. Her short stories are published in *Three Times Five,* an anthology of short fiction.

HARRIS, CLAIRE

"Child this is the gospel on bakes"

Claire Harris has been poetry editor for *Dandelion* magazine and has published several volumes of poetry including *The Conception of Winter,* which won the Alberta Special Award for Poetry, and *Under Black Light.* She has won numerous prizes including the Stephan G. Stephansson Poetry Prize and the Alberta Culture Poetry Prize.

HARRIS, MAUREEN

"I Spy Mother Cupboard"

Maureen Harris earns her living as Coordinator of the Cataloguing in Publication Programme at the University of Toronto Library. A poetry manuscript is forthcoming, and she is currently writing a long essay-review of several books about the prairies.

IOANNOU, SUSAN

"Kitchen Territorial"

Susan Ioannou's latest collection of poetry is *Clarity Between Clouds: Poems of Midlife.* Her poetry, fiction and literary articles have appeared in magazines across Canada. Her children's book, *Polly's Punctuation Primer,* is forthcoming.

ISRAEL, INGE

"Mrs. A." & "Mrs. B." & "Mrs. P." & "Mrs. R." & "Mrs. S." & "Mrs. V."

Born in Germany of Russian/Polish parents, Inge Israel has been a Canadian since 1960. She has had five books of poetry published, including *Unmarked Doors.*

JASPER, PAT

"Mornings Like This" from *The Outlines of Our Warm Bodies*

Pat Jasper has had two books of poetry published and is currently at work on a third collection.

KOGAWA, JOY

from *Itsuka*

Joy Kogawa has written several collections of poetry including *Woman in the Woods,* and a novel, *Obasan,* which received the *Books in Canada* First Novel Award and the Canadian Authors' Association Book of the Year Award. Her most recent work is the novel *Itsuka.*

KOSTASH, MYRNA

from *All of Baba's Children*

Myrna Kostash writes short stories, scripts and articles. Her books include *All of Baba's Children* and *No Kidding.*

LANE, M. TRAVIS

"Mal de Cuisine"

M. Travis Lane has published seven books, one of which won the Pat Lowther prize. She is an Honorary Research Associate at the University of New Brunswick and has two more books forthcoming.

LAURENCE, MARGARET

from *The Fire-Dwellers*

Margaret Laurence's fictional town of Manawaka is the setting for several of her novels, including *The Stone Angel* and *The Diviners*, which won the Governor General's Award. She has written short stories, magazine articles and children's books.

LEE, ALICE

"hostage"

Alice lee's work has appeared in several anthologies and literary magazines. Her play, *Dance Me Born*, has been produced by Sweetgrass Players in Calgary, Alberta.

LIVESAY, DOROTHY

"The Unquiet Bed" and "The Taming" from *The Woman I Am*

Dorothy Livesay has worked as a journalist, social worker and professor. Her books include *Poems for People*, *A Winnipeg Childhood* (fictional memoirs) and *The Self-Completing Tree*. She was founder and editor of *CV/II*. She won the Governor General's Award in 1984 and continues to write and give reading tours.

LOWTHER, PAT

"Kitchen Murder" from *A Stone Diary*

Pat Lowther wrote four volumes of poetry including *The Age of the Bird* and *A Stone Diary*, which was published posthumously. She had been elected President of the League of Poets and was teaching Creative Writing before her untimely death.

MACEWEN, GWENDOLYN

"A Breakfast for Barbarians" from *A Breakfast for Barbarians*

Gwendolyn MacEwen was a poet, novelist, story writer and playwright. She is best known for her books of poetry, including two Governor General Award winners, *The Shadow Maker* and *Afterworlds*.

MARACLE, LEE

"Survival Work"

Lee Maracle is the author of the collection of stories, *Sojourner's Truth,* and of *Bobbi Lee: Indian Rebel.*

MARLATT, DAPHNE

"Listen" from *Net Work*

Daphne Marlatt is a poet, novelist and editor. She has published 13 volumes of poetry including *Steveston* and *Salvage,* two novels including *Ana Historic,* and edited the literary journal *Tessera.*

MARTINIUK, L.A.

"coffee on mary hill"

L.A. Martiniuk is currently working on an experimental fiction-narrative. Her work is primarily poetry and prose-poetry. She also works as a sculptor and printmaker, and as a technical writer.

McDOWELL, LYNN NEUMANN

"Cool Whip and Old Lace"

Lynn Neumann McDowell practices law and has published numerous profiles of individuals and groups. Her documentary film script on artist George Littlechild was produced and released by Great Plains Productions. Her book, *Long Man, Small Island,* was published in Australia.

McINNIS, NADINE

"Reliquary" from *The Litmus Body*

Nadine McInnis's first book, *Shaking the Dreamland Tree,* received widespread praise. Her poems have appeared in numerous literary magazines including *Arc, Event, Fiddlehead* and *Prairie Fire,* as well as numerous anthologies, including *Capital Poets* and *Up and Doing: Canadian Women and Peace.*

MILLER, ROSE

"A Saskatchewan Kitchen"

This is Rose Miller's first published writing. She works as a physician's aide in a group home for Mental Health clients.

MIODUCHOWSKA, ANNA

"I Wish You Had Flown"

Anna Mioduchowska's short stories, poems and essays have appeared in various Canadian literary journals. She is on the editorial board for *Other Voices*, a literary journal out of Edmonton. She is presently working on her first novel.

MOODIE, SUSANNA

from *Roughing It in the Bush*

Susanna Moodie moved to Canada from England in 1832. Her best-known book is the autobiographical *Roughing it in the Bush*. She wrote for most of her life, at times earning a living with her abundant articles and contributions to *The Literary Garland* in Montreal.

MORRISSEY, KIM

"Rising, Batoche" from *Batoche*

Kim Morrissey is a Saskatchewan playwright and poet. Her plays include an adaptation of Freud's *Dora: A Case of Hysteria* and *Building Jerusalem: A Medicare Cabaret. Batoche* was her first poetry book. It was shortlisted for The Lampert Memorial Award for Best First Book of Poetry.

MOURÉ, ERIN

"Polonaise" from *West South West*

Erin Mouré has published several books of poetry including the Governor General's Award-Winning *Furious* and her most recent publication *West South West*. She currently works at VIA Rail headquarters in Montréal.

MUNRO, ALICE

"How I Met My Husband" from *Something I've Been Meaning to Tell You*

Alice Munro has published numerous collections of short stories including *Dance of the Happy Shades*, which won the Governor General's Award for fiction, and *Lives of Girls and Women*, which won the Canadian Booksellers Award. She is also recipient of the Canada-Australia Literary Prize and was first recipient of the Marion Engel Award.

MURPHY, SARAH

from "XMas Baking: A Choose Your Own Morality Tale" from *Comic Book Heroine*

Sarah Murphy has been widely published in Canada and Australia. She has written a novel, *The Measure of Miranda*, and a collection of stories, *Comic Book Heroine*, and has a second collection, *The Deconstruction of Wesley Smithson*, forthcoming.

MUSGRAVE, SUSAN

"Conversation During the Omelette aux Fines Herbes" from *Cocktails at the Mausoleum* and "Love Wasn't Always"

Susan Musgrave has written numerous newspaper columns, pamphlets, broadsides and extensive magazine articles. Her books include *The Charcoal Burners* and *Selected Strawberries and Other Poems.*

NELSON, SHARON H.

"September" from *The Work of Our Hands* and "the woman's testimony"

For 25 years Sharon H. Nelson has published poems that explore the ways we construct realities. She probes personal, cultural and political relations in poems that push at the boundaries of textual and sexual constructions. Her most recent book is *The Work of Our Hands.*

PAGE, P.K.

"Brazilian House" from *Poems Selected and New*

P.K. Page has written poems, short stories and art criticism, and has published drawings in various magazines and anthologies. Her books include *The Sun and the Moon and Other Fictions, Poems–Selected and New,* and *Brazilian Journal.* She has won the Governor General's Award, the Canadian Authors' Association Literary Award and the National Magazines Award.

PHILIP, MARLENE NOURBESE

"Burn Sugar" from *Imaging Woman*

Marlene Nourbese Philip is a poet and fiction writer. Her publications include *Thorns, Harriet's Daughter,* and *She Tries Her Tongue; Her Silence Softly Breaks* (awarded the 1988 Casa de las Americas prize for poetry). She has been twice recipient of Canada Council Awards and was made a Guggenheim Fellow in poetry in 1990-91.

ROSTA, HELEN J.

"Ruth's Poem"

Helen J. Rosta's short stories have appeared in various anthologies, most recently in *Great Canadian Murder and Mystery Stories.* A collection of her stories, *In the Blood,* has been published by NeWest Press.

ROY, GABRIELLE

from *The Tin Flute*

Gabrielle Roy's *Bonheur d'Occasion*, awarded the Prix Fémina, was the first Canadian work to win a major French literary prize. The English version, translated as *The Tin Flute*, won the Governor General's Award. She wrote three Manitoba books, all linked stories, based on her past experiences.

RULE, JANE

from *Memory Board*

Jane Rule's novels include *Desert of the Heart, The Young in One Another's Arms* and *Memory Board*. She has been a teacher of English and Creative Writing, and has won several prizes and awards including The Fund for Human Dignity Award of Merit.

SAPERGIA, BARBARA

"Eating Avocados" from *South Hill Girls*

Barbara Sapergia writes fiction, as well as drama for stage, radio, television and film. She has written a novel, *Foreigners*, and has had eight radio plays produced. She has completed a feature film script, *Matty and Rose*, developed from one of the stories in her recent collection *South Hill Girls*.

SARKADI, LAURIE

"Interview with Joy Suluk" & "Interview with Muriel Betsina"

Laurie Sarkadi has worked as a journalist in Alberta and the Northwest Territories. In 1992 she earned a Canadian National Newspaper award and citation.

SERVISS, SHIRLEY A.

"Preservation"

Shirley A. Serviss is a freelance writer and editor. Her poetry has appeared in a variety of literary publications in Canada, Ireland and Britain. A collection of her work, *Model Families*, is forthcoming.

SHIELDS, CAROL

from *The Box Garden*

Carol Shields is a writer and professor. She received the Marion Engel Award and has been nominated for the Governor General's Award. Her novels include *Small Ceremonies, A Fairly Conventional Woman*, and *Swann*, which won the Arthur Ellis Mystery Award.

SIMMIE, LOIS

from *They Shouldn't Make You Promise That*

Lois Simmie has worked as a writer-in-residence and taught fiction at the Saskatchewan Summer School for the Arts. She has written several children's books including *Auntie's Knitting a Baby* and *An Armadillo is Not a Pillow,* as well as adult fiction and poetry.

SLIPPERJACK, RUBY

from *Honour the Sun*

Ruby Slipperjack is a widely respected Native Canadian writer. Her book, *Honour the Sun,* was published to much critical acclaim.

STUART, JUDITH

"Pastry Hook"

Judith Anderson Stuart writes poetry, fiction for children, and columns for newspapers. Her haiku chapbook, *seasoning,* is forthcoming. She is currently working on *the languages of family,* a poetry collection.

SULLIVAN, ROSEMARY

"The Table"

Rosemary Sullivan's biography, *By Heart: Elizabeth Smart/A Life,* was nominated for a Governor General's Award, and her collection of poetry, *The Space a Name Makes,* was winner of the Gerald Lampert prize. She has edited *Poetry by Canadian Women* and *Stories by Canadian Women.*

SUTHERLAND, KATE

"Keeping Her House"

Kate Sutherland is a lawyer. She writes poetry and fiction and has also published academic work in feminist legal theory.

SZUMIGALSKI, ANNE

from *Rapture of the Deep*

Anne Szumigalski is a writer of poetry, fiction and radio plays. She has received the Saskatchewan Poetry Prize and the Senior Arts Award as well as the Okanagan Short Story Award. Her books include *Doctrine of Signature* and *Instar,* both of which were nominated for the Governor General's Award.

THOMAS, AUDREY

"Mothering Sunday" from *Goodbye Harold, Good Luck*

Audrey Thomas has written six collections of short stories and seven novels, including *Goodbye Harold, Good Luck, The Wild Blue Yonder, Songs My Mother Taught Me* and *Latakia.* She is a recipient of the Marion Engel Award, and her novel, *Intertidal Life,* was nominated for the Governor General's Award for Fiction.

TREGEBOV, RHEA

"Chemistry"

Rhea Tregebov has written three collections of poetry, including *The Proving Grounds,* and is editor of *Sudden Miracles,* an anthology of eight women poets.

TRUSS, JAN

"Mixed Messages" from *Biographical Details*

Jan Truss won the First Alberta Search for a New Novelist for her book *Bird at the Window.* She won the Ruth Schwartz Award for her Young Adult novel, *Jasmin,* which was also runner-up for the Canada Council Award for Children's Literature.

TYNES, MAXINE

"Borrowed Beauty" from *Borrowed Beauty*

Maxine Tynes was awarded the Milton Acorn People's Poetry Award for *Borrowed Beauty.* Her work has been published in numerous literary works, including *Other Voices: An Anthology of Black Writing in Canada, Nearly an Island,* and *Fireworks.*

VAN HERK, ARITHA

from *The Tent Peg*

Aritha van Herk is a novelist, critic, short story writer and Creative Writing professor. Her first book, *Judith,* won the Seal First Novel Award and has been widely translated. Her third novel, *No Fixed Address,* was nominated for the Governor General's Award. Her latest publication is *In Visible Ink,* a collection of ficto-criticisms.

VOCAT, LAURA

"Kitchen Secrets"

Laura Vocat has recently completed a four-year Religious Studies Degree. She maintains an interest in journalism and continues to write poetry and fiction.

WADDINGTON, MIRIAM

"The House on Hazelton" from *Apartment Seven* & "Profile of an Unliberated Woman" *from Collected Poems*

Miriam Waddington holds a professional degree in Social Work, an M.A. in English and two honorary doctorates. She has published eleven books of poetry, including *Driving Home* and *Mister Never.* She has published dozens of critical articles, reviews and short stories.

WALLACE, BRONWEN

"Food" from *The Stubborn Particulars of Grace*

Bronwen Wallace was a poet and part-time teacher. She won the National Magazine Award for Poetry and the Pat Lowther Award. Her books include *Common Magic* and *The Stubborn Particulars of Grace.*

WELCH, LILIANE

"Calligraphy of a Maritime Kitchen" from *Syntax of Ferment*

Liliane Welch is a poet and professor of French Literature. Her books include *Syntax of Ferment* and *Word-House of a Grandchild.* She has won the honorary President's Prize.

WISEMAN, ADELE

from *The Sacrifice*

Adele Wiseman worked as a teacher and social worker to support herself as a writer. Her books include *Testimonial Dinner* and *The Sacrifice,* which won the Governor General's Award. She was director of the school of Creative Writing at the Banff School of Fine Arts.

WONG, RITA

"Have You Eaten Yet: Two Interviews"

Rita Wong's poems have appeared in a number of Canadian literary magazines. She is a former editor of *SansCrit,* a literary journal out of Calgary.